JEEP SHOW

A TROUPER AT THE BATTLE OF THE BULGE

A NOVEL

ROBERT B. O'CONNOR

OKPI Publishing

ALSO BY ROBERT B. O'CONNOR

Gumptionade
(Non-Fiction)

Jeep Show – A Trouper at the Battle of the Bulge

Copyright ©2024 by OKPI, Inc

All rights reserved.

Published in the United States by OKPI, Inc.

This is a work of fiction. Names, characters, place, and incidents either are the product of the author's imagination or are used fictitiously. Any resemblance to actual persons, living or dead, events or locales is entirely coincidental.

Jeep is a registered trademark of Stellantis. It is used in this novel in a historical and fictional context. This novel is not endorsed by or affiliated with Stellantis in any way.

Publisher's Cataloging-in-Publication data

O'Connor, Robert B, 1956-

Jeep Show – A Trouper at the Battle of the Bulge

LCCN 2024949707

ISBN 978-0-9908884-5-1

1. James Tanzer (Fictitious character—Fiction 2. World War II 3. Battle of the Bulge 4. The Home Front in WWII. I. Title.

www.JeepShowBook.com

1 2 3 4 5 6 7 8 9

Printed in the United States of America on acid-free paper

Cover by HighDesign. Interior design by Typeflow.

Dedicated to

James T. Hetzer, U.S. Army,
A. Clevland Harrison, U.S. Army,
Robert E. O'Connor, U.S. Army,
and George F. O'Connor, U.S. Navy

AUTHOR'S NOTE
September 29, 2024

Jeep Show – A Trouper at the Battle of the Bulge, has its origins in the Oxydol Circus. This and other Procter & Gamble legends were passed on to me and my fellow students by Gib Carey, at the company's Remedial Memo Writing School in the early 80's.

In 1967, promoter and impresario Jim Hetzer, the inspiration for the protagonist in *Jeep Show*, convinced the then Oxydol brand manager – Gib Carey – to sponsor a circus. The Oxydol Circus was the shambolic result.

In researching the topic for a non-fiction book, I discovered that Jim Hetzer enlisted in the Army in WWII at age twenty-nine, despite a draft deferment. He was assigned to Special Services (what I call the Morale Corps in *Jeep Show*). His Military Occupation Specialty (MOS) was 442: Entertainment Specialist.

A WWII U.S. Army Jeep show was three 442's and a driver in a Jeep. They went to forward areas too dangerous for the USO or the Red Cross. There they performed small variety shows for the American troops: jokes, songs, tricks, skits. One of the 442's would play the guitar or accordion. They would often pull a soldier out of the audience to perform for his buddies. Jeep show soldiers included Mickey Rooney, Red Skelton, and Sammy Davis, Jr. They performed as often as eleven times a day.

Private Jim Hetzer performed in hundreds of Jeep shows in the ETO (European Theatre of Operations). He often worked with Private Rooney. Jim also produced soldier shows, amateur theatre featuring regular soldiers, particularly after the war in Europe ended.

At some point, I learned that one of Jim Hetzer's daughters had published a collection of his letters home: *Mabel's Letters*. The book gave me so many ideas, I decided to write a novel. I also got ideas from the autobiographical *Unsung Valor – A GI's Story of World War II*, by A. Cleveland Harrison. I'm full of admiration for both men.

Jeep Show is inspired by many things, including historical events, the lives of real individuals, and elements from their letters and other writings. Nonetheless, it remains a work of fiction. The characters, events, and settings have been created or altered by me for the purpose of storytelling. Any similarities to real people, living or deceased, or actual events are purely coincidental and should not be construed as factual or biographical.

Jeep Show dialogue contains outmoded and offensive words to describe Black, Native, and Italian Americans. These words were common American parlance in the first half of the 20th century. The characters in *Jeep Show* are men and women of their time.

I am grateful to you for reading *Jeep Show* and will be interested in your comments. There is a Contact form at JeepShowBook.com. The website also has an extensive list of my sources. If you register there, I will contact you with behind-the-scenes information and special offers. Use the QR code below, if you like.

I will donate $1 per copy sold in 2024 and 2025 to Shields & Stripes, a non-profit rehabilitation program for our military veterans and first-responders.

Move out!

Robert B. O'Connor
www.JeepShowBook.com
Register for special offers.
No newsletter, no chickenshit!

Morale is to the material as three is to one.
Napoleon Bonaparte

Numerous reports have been received of "careless" handling of Billiard Tables. Future distribution of Billiard Tables will be made only to Hospitals, Posts, Camps, and Stations of a permanent nature.
**Addendum to Morale Corps Guide,
European Theatre of Operations, 1944**

1.

TRAINING CAMPS, FEBRUARY – AUGUST, 1944

> The social system doesn't exist that takes as good care of its civilians as does the United States Army of its soldiers. Food and clothing, medical and dental service, equipment, weapons, transportation are the best the world has yet seen. The soldier is stronger, healthier than he was. These things the Army has done.
>
> Morale Corps Guide, European
Theatre of Operations, 1944

> Check the men's insurance before action.
>
> Morale Corps Guide, European
Theatre of Operations, 1944

"Welcome to the Fort Thomas Induction Center," the sergeant says, parade loud. "You got a new mother now."

He stands ramrod straight in front of Jim Tanzer and the other thirty-nine recruits, all under orders, all still in their civvies. The sergeant's olive drab service uniform is perfectly pressed. His tan tie is tucked in between the second and third buttons of his shirt. His boots are deeply polished.

The recruits come forward to make a ragged line as the

sergeant calls their names off his list. "You'll be *saw-ree*" and other catcalls drift over from less-recent recruits in shiny green fatigues, who are picking up cigarette butts on the grounds nearby. They stop when the sergeant looks in their direction.

"Get yourself in formation here." The sergeant steps forward and tugs the recruits into straight lines. "Cover the front man, cover down. At ease," he says, ignoring the fact that they were never at attention. "You men are Roster Three. Don't forget that. Roster Three. You will be processed at this reception center for ten days, before you ship out for basic training. Keep your eyes and ears open while you're here, learn to do things the Army way, you'll get along. The command forward march, you step off with your left foot," he demonstrates. "The counts one and three, your *left* foot hits the ground. The counts two and four, you *right* foot hits the ground. Roster three, ten-hut. Right face."

He waits while the recruits come to agreement as to what right is. As a dance instructor, Jim Tanzer has no problem with a pivot turn.

"*FAW-WAH, HARCH!*" the sergeant shouts. "One two three four, one two three four."

THE SERGEANT PLACES two recruits at the foot of each of the twenty bunks, ten beds down one wall, ten back the other. "From now on—" he looks at the suitcase in Jim's right hand— "whatever you carry—suitcase, broom, shovel—you carry it in your *left* hand. Because you *will* salute officers with your *right* hand. Two fingers to your forehead above your right eye, good and snappy." He demonstrates. "You hold it there until the officer returns your salute. Do it now, three times."

There is some self-conscious chuckling as the recruits manage three attempts.

"I will not return your salute. Sergeants are not officers.

Practice in the mirror tonight," He points over his shoulder to the latrine. "You smokers—" that's most of the recruits in front of him—"you can *walk* while in uniform. You can *smoke* while in uniform. You may not walk *and* smoke while in uniform. Keep your cigarette in that left hand. Officers do not want a smoking salute." The sergeant does not smile. "You'll see a movie about military courtesy after chow." He ignores a whispered "chickenshit" from the end of the room. Plenty of time to iron out a wiseacre.

"Barracks Three is your home now," the sergeant says. "You are responsible for your home. You walk on your floor, you mop it. You sleep in your bed, you make it." The sergeant proceeds to make Jim's bed the Army way, then tears it apart. "Now *you* do it. Everyone. Ten minutes. I'll inspect, you'll re-do your bed, then you'll draw your uniforms, get those injections you've been looking forward to, final physical, dental exam, chow, a lecture, the movie, then clean-up and lights out. We start tomorrow at zero four twenty hours." He pauses two beats to register you're-in-the-army-now. "Make that zero four hundred, so we have time to discuss what someone thinks is chickenshit."

Jim blinks; that's 4:00 a.m.

"You'll take the General Classification Test tomorrow," the sergeant continues. "Get some sleep tonight, if you don't want infantry."

"Next man." Jim Tanzer hops up three steps to the entrance of the plywood and tarpaper building and proceeds through the door under a sign that says "Interview." There are six check-in clerks in six small cubicles. A corporal in the closest one is standing. He says "you," and beckons to Jim.

"Don't salute. Just give me that." The corporal points to the large manila envelope Jim is holding. "I'm going to ask you some questions about your background." He pulls a folder out of the envelope. "Relax."

"Thank you," Jim says.

"Thirty years old, married, one child. Enlisted. What are you doing in the Army, Tanzer?"

"To protect our freedom, protect our home."

"You could have *stayed* home."

"I want to do my part."

"Before you enlisted, you were a…" The corporal looks down at the folder. "Song and dance man." He looks up to briefly re-examine Jim's large head and jug-handle ears. "Most recently a dance instructor and theatrical agent. How was business?"

"Good. People have money now, all the defense work." It isn't necessary for Jim to add that teaching dance bores him and that he is no businessman. "My mother-in-law makes sixty-five dollars a week at Alabama Dry Dock." Jim recalls the photograph of four-foot-eleven Edna Polk in a welding hood on the deck of a Liberty Ship.

"Are you trying to find a better home in the Army than the one you got? Running from something?"

"Nothing like that."

"Just good old-fashioned patriotism."

"Maybe us older men can set an example for the young ones. In combat."

"That's what sergeants are for, Tanzer. But now that you mention it, you can help your fellow recruits here at the reception center. The colonel wants a soldier show on Saturday night. Amateur-hour type of thing. For morale. I'm going to pass on your name."

"Sure. I can get Stella—my wife—to sing. She's not an amateur, but the men will like her."

"Your wife is here?"

"She just finished a week at Castle Farm in Cincinnati. Stella Sterling is her stage name."

"Free housing, free clothes, free chow from Uncle Sam, and the comforts of a wife off-base. You're in Shangri-La, Tanzer. Too bad she can't follow you overseas."

"I know she can't."

"Say, Tanzer." The corporal pushes a form across the desk. "You haven't signed up for GI life insurance. Pays your wife ten thousand dollars if you get killed. You don't sign up, the government only pays for your funeral. Six hundred. Now…" He smiles at Jim. "Which soldiers you think they send into battle first?"

"Sure." Jim signs and returns the form.

"Okay, Tanzer." The corporal hands Jim the envelope. "Take this back to your sergeant."

"I will, sir. Thank you."

"That was a fine salute. Save it for an officer."

"You look like a real soldier in your dress uniform," Stella Polk Tanzer says to her husband. Jim's wife is a pretty brunette of twenty-three, big brown eyes, a dancer's physical poise. They married in 1940. Before that, she was briefly a student at The Tanzer Academy of Dance, then his partner in *Tanzer and Sterling, Rhythmic Steppers*. An agent might say she resembles Judy Garland with more conventionally attractive features and a performer's smile. She's not smiling now.

It is after the soldier show. Stella is still wearing her red stage dress. "Comin' In on a Wing and a Prayer" is coming out of the jukebox at the Fort Thomas PX. Stella and Jim talk over the Song Spinner's 1943 hit. "Two Cokes," Jim says to the counterman. "Bag of salted nuts."

"Please," Stella says.

Jim pulls several paper napkins from the dispenser. "It's called a service uniform."

"Can I have a napkin? And a straw, please?" Stella says. *Are you going to look after your wife, mister?* she thinks. Then, "And they just give it to you?"

"Sure. And we got a fatigue uniform, what we wear every day during detail."

"Detail?"

"Work. Like policing the…uh, picking up cigarette butts from the Company area. Cigarettes grow on trees in this man's Army. Or warehouse detail, or KP. That's kitchen patrol."

"After the war, maybe we can share kitchen patrol at home."

"I'll make the beds."

Sure you will, she thinks. "What else have you learned?"

"We spent two hours this morning on close order drill." The Coke bottles arrive.

"Thanks."

"Close order drill?"

"Marching as a unit. They gave us two pairs of boots because they said we'll wear out a pair before we get out of basic." Jim pours a few salted peanuts into his Coke, takes a long swallow, and wraps a paper napkin around the bottle. "Nice and cold."

"Two pairs?"

"And five pair of socks. There's a boy in my roster, looks about fifteen, says these are the first pair of shoes he doesn't have to share with his brothers. I'm pretty sure it's also the first time in his life he's had three meals in a day."

"Just like those boys you met at Camp Roosevelt," Stella says. Jim has many stories about his time in the Civilian Conservation Corps.

"Gained twenty pounds the first month, most of them. Probably in the service now, like me."

"Do they have dance teachers in the Army?" Stella says. She has not touched her Coke.

"No. I put in for paratrooper. There's extra pay."

"Why would you…?" She shakes her soft curls. "Can you

do something else? Can you put on shows like we did tonight? Isn't that an Army job?"

"That's USO. Civilians."

"Oh." She puts a straw in her Coke bottle but doesn't drink. "You signed up for the insurance, right, Jimmy?"

"Sure," he says. "You get ten thousand simoleons if I'm killed. Enough for you to buy the farm, like the boys say."

Stella stamps her bottle lightly on the counter and colors up. "I don't want a farm. I want my husband, and Betty Jo wants her father. I want to work, raise our daughter and grow old with you, Jimmy."

He leans back. "Sure. We'll do all that after the war."

"Okay. But you don't need to jump out of airplanes to make a difference."

"I got my dog tags yesterday." He pulls them from around his neck. "Look."

"Hmm." She turns the embossed metal tags over in her hands. "They're like little license plates. What's the 'P' for?"

"Protestant."

"They gave you a fine silver chain for two little tin tags."

"I bought the chain myself. Isn't it nice?"

"It sure is. Nice." *You haven't bought me a piece of jewelry since my wedding ring*, she thinks.

Jim drains his Coke, chews the peanuts, and stifles a burp. "Got two cavities filled yesterday. The Army takes care of us soldiers. I'm going to buy war bonds with part of my pay each month."

"Is that the best thing to do?" Managing money isn't her husband's strong suit. "When does the monthly allotment for dependents start?"

Jim grimaces slightly. Just this morning a sergeant pulled him and two other recruits out of formation to say he was missing their allotment requests and he was sure—busy as they were, what with chow, and playing cards, and drinking beer at the PX—they want to act like the responsible men he knew them to be and complete the allotment form before they ship out to basic. The other two men were 19 and 20, unmarried. Their allotment goes to their parents.

"I just filled out the form," Jim says. "I give twenty-two dollars each month and the government adds forty to it, because of Betty Jo. You know they only pay me fifty a month."

"Doesn't the Army give you everything you need?"

"Let's get you to your motel. I have to be back in camp by midnight."

Fun and games again tonight, Stella thinks, rolling her eyes. "What did Frank Woolston say about my audition?" she says.

"Shoot. I'll write him tomorrow. Been so busy here I forgot."

"Awwright, ladies, today you are going to learn to *far* this mighty *way-pon*." A red-faced sergeant stands in front of Jim and the rest of the training squad on the heavy weapons range at Fort Benning Infantry School. Their dungaree fatigues are stained with red clay. Slouch hats have been replaced by steel helmets. Jim shifts his feet to ease the ache in his lower back from a heavy landing that morning on the obstacle course.

"*Siddown*, ladies," the sergeant continues. "By now you love your best friend, your M1 *raffle*." Jim looks down at his swollen thumb. He does not love his M1 rifle. "Now you *needa* know the M-9 rocket launcher. Here at Fort Benning, we call it a bazooka." A beat. "Those of you thinking, 'Forget the *way-pons*, I'm gonna be a rear echelon *sojer*.' Well, in a *wah*, like you in now, one fine day you drinkin' *gub-mint* coffee and typing a requisition form, mashing *taters*, rollin' up maps, the next day you a-runnin' and a-shootin'. You don't know when some G-3— that's your operations officer, ladies—thinks you *needa* be up at the front line. Or the enemy pushes the front line behind you, you *needa* fight your way back."

An explosion from the grenade range far to their right is followed by a faint whoop. The sergeant does not look over. He goes on to cover the basics of the bazooka. Two-man weapon, D-cell battery-powered electrical firing system, no safety, ten-foot back-blast ("watch out, loader!"). He emphasizes the bazooka's ability to blow up a machine gun nest or kill a tank from two hundred yards. He goes so far as to call the bazooka the safest way to win a Silver Star ("After the wah, you never hafta buy you own drink agin"). He ignores the ambulance speeding by.

Two members of the training platoon end up qualifying as experts on the bazooka, the my-first-pair-of-shoes private (like the bazooka, turns out squirrel guns have open sights), and Jim Tanzer (beginner's luck).

THE CAPTAIN RETURNS Jim's salute without getting up from behind his desk and says, cigarette smoke trailing out of his nose and mouth, "At ease, Private. Sit down."

"Yes, sir."

"Private Tanzer, what are you doing in infantry school?"

"I'm too tall for a paratrooper...sir."

The captain glances at Jim's file on his desk. "You're thirty years old, a family man, and you want infantry."

"Yes, sir. I'm going to try for a heavy weapons platoon. I qualified expert in bazooka."

"You've been assigned to Camp Sibert. Chemical Weapons and Morale Corps."

"I don't want Chemical Weapons."

"That's good, because you're getting Morale Corps. No choice in the matter, Tanzer, you or me. I have orders to produce two candidates. Your classification score and your show business background make you an easy choice."

"What about my bazooka rating?"

"You'll be entertaining combat soldiers in places where the USO can't go. It makes a difference. I saw that with ENSA, those British enlisted entertainers in North Africa. True, they used to call them 'Every Night Something Awful,' but the Tommies were glad to see them."

"What if I—"

The captain waves his hand, silencing Jim. "Pack your gear, Private Tanzer, and report back here in one hour for your travel vouchers." He stubs out his cigarette with his left hand, holds out Jim's file with his right. "Dismissed." Three beats. "It is customary to salute an officer at this point, Private."

MICKEY ROONEY PUTS a forkful of mashed potatoes in his mouth. "Delicious!" he says to Jim and smiles. "When I get back to Hollywood, I'm going to tell Leon at The Brown Derby—" Rooney puts on an aristocratic British inflection—"please make sure my mashed *po-tah-toes* are slightly grey and room temperature. Jolly good! Oh, and Leon, old chap, I'll have Spam instead of the filet with Béarnaise sauce, rice pudding instead of your Baked Alaska. And from now on, I'll take my coffee weak as Andy Hardy's mustache."

Jim laughs. It's funny. And it's Mickey Rooney.

"That's between us," Rooney says. "Louis Mayer told me it wouldn't be good for my image if the press hears me bellyache about Army life."

"There's plenty of complaining in the barracks," Jim says. "No one says *Army* without putting *goddamn* in front of it." He waits for Mickey's reaction.

Rooney apprises him coolly. "Good one," he says. "Thought

you were a dancer. Maybe we can do something with that line." Rooney should know what goes over; he was America's biggest box office attraction from 1938 through 1940. Age twenty-four, he's in the Army now. As the number of Americans under arms snowballed in 1943, Rooney felt public pressure to join the fight. Like Jim, he enlisted in March of 1944, three months before D-Day. *National Velvet* with Elizabeth Taylor was in the can. His third jockey role, but not his last.

Rooney can sing as well as Bing Crosby. He dances like a third Nicholas Brother. He does brilliant slapstick and stand-up comedy. He writes songs. He plays piano and drums. He once learned the banjo in a day. Laurence Olivier considers Rooney "the best there has ever been." There's nothing in show business Mickey Rooney can't do, except grow an inch over 5'2". Or control himself. He has bees in his bonnet. He still thinks his monstrous talent is a studio pass on life. He is not yet aware that he has no friends. He is not yet aware that he can chew the scenery but he cannot eat the world.

Private Rooney could have stayed home, joined the First Motion Picture Unit at Fort Hal Roach Studios, eight miles west of his Hollywood home. But like many boys who enlisted, Rooney wanted the whole shebang. To be away. To be under threat from enemy fire. To be safe from his own ruinous behavior. To have one last chance to grow up.

"On the other hand," Mickey says, "I met Miss Alabama at that war bond rally last Saturday, Betty Jane Rase. We've had two dates, and I'm gonna ask her to marry me. She's no Ava Gardner; that gal put hot coals in my pants." He remembers his stunning first wife and their brief marriage, over now not even a year. "But she's a nice girl. A soldier needs a wife back home to write to him, don't he?"

"Sure," Jim says.

"I *could* write to Louis Mayer at MGM," Mickey says. *That goddamn bully*, he thinks. "He isn't as keen on me as he used to be. I'm too old for Andy Hardy, too short for a leading man, too tall for a producer."

"That's a good line, Mickey."

"I'll see if Miss Alabama has a friend for you, Jimmy. Maybe Miss ArmsAroundYa." Rooney makes a ridiculous smacking noise.

Jim laughs, then, "I'm married."

"Well, if you're gonna be snooty about it, Tanzer." Rooney laughs. "Any news since I've been gone? Give out. Where's the show stand, and do I still have the most lines?"

"It's called *Hip Hooray* now, not *Yanks a Poppin'*. We're up to fifty-three men, including Jimmy James and the orchestra. It's gonna be variety, different acts, singing, dancing. Saroyan and Loesser wrote it. Scripts tomorrow. Clurman is directing." Jim smiles. "Our wrestling skit is *in*."

Mickey starred in the 1943 film *The Human Comedy*, based on William Saroyan's novel. He had a few belts and sang with lyricist Frank Loesser at Sardi's the same year. He took Harold Clurman to dinner the only time the director was in Hollywood. He notices how pleased Jim is with himself. It's nice. "You reel off those names like an insider, Jimmy. You've found a home in the Army."

"I'll say. We'll do the show here and Camp Rucker, take it to New York or San Francisco, then overseas. If it's New York, that'll be my first time on Broadway."

"You've worked in New York?"

"In '39 and '40. Closest I came to Broadway was The Nut Club."

"In Greenwich Village. I know it!" Mickey is delighted. "The Yule Family performed there in 1930. I hear it's gimmicky now, full of tourists."

"If roach racing is a gimmick, it's gimmicky."

"*Hip Hooray* is going to New York, Jimmy," Rooney says. "That's where the radio networks and the weeklies are. The

Army wants the American people to know that Mickey Rooney is going to war. Walter Winchell called my publicist about the first interview when we get there."

"That's swell. My wife is back in New York now."

"Swell for you, maybe." Mickey sees *something* in Jim, not sure what. "Say, my agent is coming down tomorrow. You should meet him. He could help you after the war."

"I'm more of a dancer than an actor," Jim says.

Mickey can see that he is thrilled. "I'm too short for ballroom and you're too tall. We average out perfect! He'll know what your act should be." *Probably some kind of backwoods character, Bob Burns plus dancing*, Mickey thinks.

"I'm starting to think production," Jim says.

"Who wants to be in an office when you can be onstage?"

THE MORALE CORPS brass takes advantage of Camp Sibert's chemical weapons facilities to prepare their men to survive poison gas and build unit solidarity through shared suffering. Like every soldier in the chamber, Jim reaches up and touches his gas mask with both hands. Like every soldier in the chamber, he looks to the door, sees the sergeant watching though the small round window, handkerchief held in front of his nose and mouth.

The only sound Jim hears is hissing gas and his own breathing. Sweat trickles down his spine. He starts to get up. Mickey puts a hand on his forearm and says a muffled, "He'll just make us do it again."

THE TIP TOP VAUDEVILLE AND MOVING PICTURE REVUE
May 21, 1927

"Well, Charlie, say hello to the good people of Huntington."

The spotlights pick out a handsome young man sitting on a cane chair, a few feet in front of the red velvet stage curtain. He faces stage left and cheats out towards the audience. The wooden dummy on his lap is wearing black tie.

The dummy swivels his head towards the audience while shielding his eyes with his gloved right hand. "They sure dress funny in Huntington," he says.

"That's not how you talk to people, Charlie," the young man says. "Apologize."

"I'm sorry they dress funny."

"Never mind, Charlie. This performance is a big step for you. You're on the same bill as Rae Samuels, the Blue Streak of Vaudeville."

"She asked me out."

"Rae Samuels asked you out?"

"I was in her dressing room at the time."

Eleven-year-old Jimmy Tanzer laughs along with the rest of the audience, although that one went right over his head.

"That's enough, Charlie," the young man says. "I got a letter this morning from Mr. Ramshackle, the truant officer in Huntington."

"Uh-oh."

"He has no record of your enrollment in any school."

"Is that so?"

"And he says he called you twice. Is that true?"

"That's a lie. He called three times." Laughter.

"Charlie, you don't mean to tell me you've been skipping school?"

"I didn't mean to tell you, Mr. Bergen." More laughter.

"Oh, Charlie, I fear what life will be like for you when you grow up."

"I'm never going to grow up."

"What will become of you when I get old?"

"I'll run away to the enchanted forest, where I can stay pop-lar." Less laughter.

The dialogue moves on to other topics including grouse hunting ("If it moves, I shoot, if it shoots, I move"), baseball ("…then it hit me"), bill collectors ("I told him, you can *expect* payment anytime you want"), Prohibition ("better than no liquor at all"), and ends with robots ("It's not me who should be worried, Mr. Bergen"). The act goes over.

While the audience applauds, Jimmy waves his right hand back and forth in his lap and thinks, *hello, folks, thank you, thank you. I'm brave. I'm Prince Valiant in Camelot. No, I'm Charles Lindbergh, winning the prize.* Jimmy has for the moment forgotten the sobering fact that he is deceiving his formidable mother. Lavinia Tanzer does not countenance low entertainments. She thinks he's at the Huntington Library on this Saturday afternoon.

One of the patrons in the colored section looks his way and smiles at the happy white boy. The audience has already seen the two-painters-one-ladder dumb act, followed by cross-talk from an unknown duo, Burns and Allen ("You mean, a little girl like you can eat four lamb chops alone?" "Not alone. But with potatoes I could"). Baby Rose Marie, the little girl with the big girl voice, has belted out big-girl songs. Vaudeville's greatest minstrel pair, Sam and Ham (Bartolomeo Ciarlo and Benjamin Aschkenasy), did a bit about Charles Lindbergh's attempt to fly across the Atlantic (in *de Spirit ub Louie Armstrong*). They also covered Mae West's ten-day jail sentence for corrupting public morals (*Ooo Wee!*), Prohibition and the flood of medicinal whiskey (got me a *resription*), the Scopes' monkey trial (*De evalootin' kestion*), the revival of the Ku Klux

Klan in the Midwest (*I'se regusted!*), and the national manias over the Ford Model A, crossword puzzles, Mah Jong, and Florida real estate.

Then Jimmy Tanzer and the rest of the audience witness the first and last performance of *Plantation Prince*, Sam and Ham's anti-Jim Crow burlesque of Hamlet's famous speech on suicide. "*To is or not to is, dat be de kestion.*"

All this before intermission.

Vaudeville.

"Jimmy, I told you to come home with a book under your arm." Norma Tanzer says as her younger brother enters their small backyard on Railroad Street. She scatters breadcrumbs for the five chickens and palsied rooster at her feet.

Jim's sister is a tall, flat-chested, seventeen-year-old redhead. Almost pretty, but her large front teeth give her long face a slight horsiness her bob hairstyle cannot overcome. Her below-the-knee dress hem doesn't hide her wizened right leg. Polio. An auto-didact, Norma has worn Bakelite circular-framed glasses since reading Little Blue Book #360, *The Wasteland and Other Poems of T.S. Eliot*. Although she is finishing Huntington High School as a straight-A student, there is no expectation of college. Her father Bill left school to work in the mines the day he turned nine years old. Her mother Lavinia's schooling ended with her emigration from Germany at age fourteen. Money is tight. The boy is the hope of the family. It hasn't been said, but Norma is sure that if she doesn't marry, she'll never leave her parents' house.

"The show was swell, Sis."

"Mutti will blame Poppa if she finds out you skipped the library. She is *heute nicht gut drauf*," Norma says in an uncanny imitation of their mother's native German.

"Huh?"

"In a bad mood. Aunt Sally asked her how the new chicks

were doing and wasn't it a shame we don't have space for a milk cow."

"So?"

"Mutti doesn't care to discuss Poppa's chickens, least not with a woman who buys eggs at the store." Norma smiles at the image of her Bunyanesque mother cracking an egg on Aunt Sally's head.

"I'm going to be in show business when I grow up. A ventroquist."

"Ven*tri*loquist, you mean. And nobody wants to watch you digging in your nose, Prince Valiant. Use your handkerchief."

2.

THE QUEEN MARY, SEPTEMBER, 1944

Soldiers and Airmen—You will never be bored on your troopship if you know how to examine the ocean world around you. This book will acquaint you with the scientific understanding of wind, waves, weather, the stars in the heavens, seabirds and other oceanic phenomena that most servicemen have never before considered. Prepare to be astonished.

What To Do with Your Time on A Troopship, a Morale Corps Publication

If the Curtiss P-40 Warhawk was circling the face of a clock instead of the sixty square miles of ocean in front of New York Harbor, the *Queen Mary* would be docked at the numeral six. To the plane's pilot, the gangplank looks like a thin harpoon in the side of the ship, the troops boarding like a trailing green rope. The largest and fastest ship afloat, the *Queen*'s red, white, and black paint is gone for the duration of the war. She is battleship grey from bow to stern, including her three giant funnels.

Private Jim Tanzer is well over his glad-to-be-finally-moving feeling. Up at zero four hundred hours for barracks maintenance and breakfast. Back to barracks for inspection. Marched in formation to the Camp Shanks train depot, car number chalked on his helmet. Jammed onto the train. Gear, including musical instruments, filling the overhead racks and blocking the aisles.

He sits for an hour, itchy in his wool service uniform, before the train pulls out of Camp Shanks. Another two hours' wait at the Hudson River Terminal 9 before being ordered off the train. Jim puts in the time reading back issues of *Variety* and *Billboard* Norma sent him, and eating a pressed fruit bar from the K-ration all the departing soldiers were given.

At around sixteen hundred hours, the sixty cast and crew members of *Hip Hooray* and the other six hundred enlisted men of Morale Corps Battalion 6817 shouldered seventy-pound duffel bags and were herded the half mile to Pier 90. Each GI also carried his rifle, a pack with bed roll, musette bag, entrenching tool, canteen, flashlight, gas mask, haversack, and Red Cross ditty bag filled with toiletries and cigarettes.

Looking down eighty feet from B deck, one of the Cunard Line crew says to his shipmate, "What raddles me is not how far the Yanks will go to fight. It's how much cargo they bring with 'em."

"And we'll be scraping their *foo-king* gum off everywhere but Captain Bisset's bald knob," his shipmate says. They both laugh.

"Won't be bringing them all back when it's over, neither. It's a bloody show in France."

"They're the saving of us, the Yanks."

Jim is engulfed by shadow as he marches out of the long shed covering most of the pier. He seems to be moving towards a towering black wall. Soldiers ahead of him shuffle single file up the long narrow gangplank, bowed over by the gear they carry.

Jim pulls out his dog tags and gives his last name to a Transportation Corps private checking off a list. A corporal steadies

Jim with a hand on his arm, tucks a printed letter from President Roosevelt in his musette bag. He pins a silver-dollar-sized red celluloid button to the lapel of Jim's field jacket like a flat boutonniere, and says, "This is the section of the ship you'll have access to. Up you go, soldier."

Jim and the rest of Battalion 6817 are led through a maze of hatches and companionways and down five flights of stairs to the Lower Orlop deck. They arrive at what had been second-class cabins for two passengers before the war. Each cabin now holds eighteen two-by-six-foot stretched canvas racks deployed in three columns of six. There is twenty-four inches of vertical space between racks. The pipes on the ceiling are twelve inches above the face of the man on the uppermost rack.

"Toto, we're not in Club Sibert anymore," Mickey Rooney says to Jim. "You're gonna have to turn on your side to get a hard-on."

The aisle between the columns of racks is just wide enough to walk on, if you can move around the duffel bags and other gear. The Lower Orlop deck is below the waterline. The cabins have no portholes. Ventilation is adequate to maintain consciousness.

Morale Corps Battalion 6817 will be followed onboard by ten thousand Golden Lions of the 106th Infantry Division, as well as six battalions of replacements. The latter will be distributed piecemeal to infantry divisions already in the fight, to replace dead, wounded, and missing soldiers.

"This is the most important cabin on the ship," Mickey declares.

"What's so important about it?" Jim says, playing straight man.

"I'm in it." He gets a laugh.

"Stow your gear on your assigned rack," a Transportation Corps private announces. "Keep your valuables in your pockets. These are hot racks. You have yours for twelve hours each day. Another soldier has it for twelve. Stow your bedroll under the lowest rack when you leave."

Jim looks at the size of his rack and sighs.

"We won't be underway until tomorrow," the private continues. There are groans. "Fifteen thousand men and cargo to load. Blackout begins at dusk and ends dawn plus forty. No smoking on deck during blackout. There's a $250,000 prize offered by Hitler for the U-boat that sinks the ship that's keeping you dry."

"Feels like jail," Mickey says, "with the added chance of drowning." Another laugh.

"The *Queen* zigs or zags sharply every few minutes, as a precaution. Do not go near railings on open decks. We don't stop for man overboard. And stay off open decks completely in a storm."

"And I didn't pack my swim trunks," Mickey says. "Hey, don't look so worried, Jim. The *Queen* is too fast for U-boats."

The Transportation private has to deliver his monologue another fifty times today. He begins to talk faster. "You'll have general quarters and abandon ship drills. Your sergeant will show you how to get to your station. You hear the klaxon, you drop everything and go there on the double."

"I *soytently* will," Mickey says in perfect Groucho Marx.

"Your sergeant will let you know what's expected of you during your twelve hours away from your quarters. And where you can and cannot go onboard this ship." Mickey looks at Jim and winks. "You get two meals a day. Your battalion eats breakfast at…" The private looks down at his clipboard. "Zero seven fifteen, dinner at fifteen forty-five. Write your times on your meal card. You won't be fed if you miss your slot. There are trays. Don't bring your mess kit."

"They removed the good china?" It's Mickey again.

The Transportation private can't help himself and gives a short laugh. Said by another man, the lines aren't funny. It's the posture, the gestures, the facial expressions, the intonation, the timing. It's Mickey Rooney. The Transportation private catches his breath and plows ahead. "No meal until breakfast tomorrow." Groans. "We're loading all night. Eat the K-rations you were issued this morning."

"When will the wine steward be coming by?" Mickey says. It goes over.

The private pinches himself on the wrist. "You will now stack arms by platoon. Your rifles will be stored until you disembark. Write the serial number on your troop assignment card."

"Tha-tha, tha-tha, tha-that's all, folks!" Mickey says.

RAIN ON THE third day. Mickey falls in holding an umbrella as if it were a rifle. After calisthenics and drill, Jim's battalion is permitted salt water showers. Fresh water is too precious. Jim is the last man. He notices a distinct coconut smell in the empty, dank shower room. It's the soap. Regular soap doesn't lather in seawater. Hershey's Cocoa Butter Soap will, if applied briskly. The wrapper, long gone from this bar, suggests rapid rinsing.

Jim washes and shaves. After much rubbing of the soap bar on his head, he works up a rich lather. Wait, was that an explosion? He's not sure, water was streaming in his ears. Then the ship shudders. It *was* an explosion! *Below the water line* flashes in his mind. The shower stops. The General Quarters klaxon sounds, terrifying. The clanging of hatches closing makes his heart drop.

Towel around his waist, Jim runs out of the shower room and back towards his cabin. The hatch to that corridor has locked. He can't get to his uniform or helmet. In his bare feet, he pads up the five sets of stairs, jostling with other frightened but fully clothed soldiers, down the corridors and across the weather deck. He runs to his station next to the Port #20 lifeboat and stands at attention, soap still in his hand. The *Queen* has not yet begun to list. It's cold on the weather deck.

Mickey breaks out a big smile. "Jesus Christ, Tanzer! You've got big balls."

The crew member assigned to Lifeboat #20 takes it in calmly. "Them Yanks don't half take the piss," he will tell his shipmates when recounting the scene. "Bloody *bangin'* tha' was."

The sergeant comes to a stop in front of Jim. "Private Tanzer, what the hell you think you're doing? Where is your life jacket?" He sniffs. "What the fuck is on your head?"

Jim is already shivering. "Su-su-soap, sergeant."

Mickey digs for the pencil in in his pocket. This bit is going into the movie he plans to make after the war.

A lookout thought he had sighted the wake of a torpedo passing a few hundred feet astern the *Queen*. The explosion Jim had heard was a depth charge. The ship's company remains at battle stations. Eventually, a bright sun breaks through the clouds and beams down on the deck and on Jim's head. He is grateful for the warmth. He feels his scalp tighten. Twenty minutes later, the lather is cemented in place.

"Station, *attention!*" A bantamweight captain from the 106th Division comes around the stern, accompanied by a clerk. Jim is upstaging Mickey Rooney and everyone else. "Name and rank, soldier," the captain asks.

"Tanzer, sir. Private. James Tanzer. Entertainment Specialist."

"Are you aware of military courtesy, Private?" The captain then returns Jim's hurried salute, scowling at the bar of soap in Jim's right hand. "Have you been drinking?"

"No, sir."

"Private Tanzer, you are on deck without your life jacket." The punishment for this offense is to forfeit shoes for a day. The captain looks down. "Where are your shoes, Private?"

"In my quarters, sir. I was in the—"

"And what in blazes is on your head? Is that scalp treatment?" He takes a step back. "Have you got lice?"

"Sir, I—"

"What's that smell?"

"Soap, sir, coconut so—"

The *Queen* zigs hard. Jim staggers into the captain, knocks him down. The towel drops to the deck. Mickey cannot believe his luck; the scene is writing itself. "Sorry, sir," Jim says, stepping back into line without picking up the towel.

The captain gets to his feet. "Take this man's name."

"Request permission to speak, sir," Mickey says.

"Permission granted, Private." Of course. It's Mickey Rooney.

"Sir, Private Tanzer is in the Morale Corps. He's an eccentric dancer, a comic, who volunteered to serve his country even though, as you can see, he's too old to be drafted. He puts on shows for morale purposes. Some planned, some improvised." Rooney continues in this vein. The captain tries hard not appear starstruck, but Jim is off the hook.

After the all-clear announcement, the sergeant barks, "Resume duties, men. Get dressed, Private Tanzer, and get that crap off your head."

"Jesus, Jimmy," Mickey says afterwards. "You're a natural. You and I are doing a movie after the war, like Hope and Crosby. Working title is *The Road to Berlin*. This scene is *in!*"

Dear Norma,

Well Sis, I'm sitting on the top deck—no deckchairs on this cruise, Hey!—of the famous ███████. It's called the weather deck, guess why! We left ███████ in a convoy, █ days ago, destroyers on either side, blimp overhead, planes circling. By nightfall we were in the open ocean by ourselves. Safer that way, they told us, because ███████ does ███ "knots"—more than ████ miles per hour, which is faster than the escorts and most important, faster than German U-boats! She makes a sharp zig or zag every █ minutes, knocked me off balance the first couple of days. We feel engine vibrations and the ship creaks when she turns. I'm used to it now.

The line for chow is an hour long. Enlisted men are fed in what was the first-class dining hall before the war. They feed one thousand of us at a time, it's elbow to elbow. We sit on benches at long tables, like at Camp Roosevelt in the Civilian Conservation Corps. All the style of gassing up a Jeep at the motor pool, plus belching and a lot of mouth-open chewing. We get mostly Bully Beef, that's British Spam, and hard-boiled eggs, potatoes, green peas, and hot tea. Forget about coffee.

The ██████ grand staircase is still here, but the carpet's been pulled up and the wood paneling is covered with burlap. It's like an oriental bazaar, soldiers selling everything from liquor to deck passes. You have to step carefully not to put a foot in a poker game. I haven't seen an officer since we left ███████.

Sis, I'm dealing with some bad news. Stella and I are on the rocks. I got no letters from her the last three weeks I was at Camp Sibert, the phone in her apartment just rang and rang. After our battalion arrived at Camp Shanks, I rushed to see her in New York, hoping to create some good memories.

She wouldn't let me in. She said she wanted nothing to do with someone who would drop his family responsibilities for some kind of Army Shangri-La. That she and Betty Jo would be better off on their own—already were! This to a man going overseas to serve his country! She asked me to leave, but I sat in front of the door in the hallway. A neighbor called the police, so I left. What do you think, Sis?

Enough about my troubles. We played six *Hip Hooray* shows at Camp Shanks. The New York critics came—to see Private Jimmy James and Private Mickey Rooney, not just Jim Tanzer. Hey! Everyone said it was the best Army show they had ever seen. Better than *This is the Army* in '42, and that was Irving Berlin! After the last show, Mickey took a bunch of us to The Stork Club.

I got those last two fillings put in at Camp Shanks. Uncle Sam has finished fixing my teeth and my feet. I'm fit as a fiddle.

We hold auditions tonight for the soldiers' amateur hour show. Something other than craps to entertain the men.

Don't send me any more clothes. The Army has me loaded up. You can still send candy and the newspaper and *Billboard*.

There isn't much else to mention, my meal time is coming up. It helps to get in line early, so I will stop now and go get some British chow.

Your brother the soldier,
Jimmy.

THE FINALE OF the *Queen Mary* soldier show is the barn dance routine lifted from *Hip Hooray*, in this case put on by long-john-clad amateurs. The dance goes haywire during the fourth show of the evening. On "swing your partner," the by-now inebriated dancers toss each other into the audience. Fights break out between dancers and audience members, quickly stifled by fire extinguishers and loud threats of permanent KP. Medics treat two concussions and evacuate a broken arm. Many of those present will remember this performance as a highlight of their service overseas, and for some as one of the last good moments before things turned bad.

By day five, the stagnant air of the Lower Orlop deck has taken on a palpable rankness from wet wool, mildew, intestinal gas, and the funk of hundreds of male bodies. Once again, Jim is unable to sleep on a too-small rack with soldiers snoring above and around him. He decides to try the weather deck. It's nighttime and the ship is in blackout. He uses his flashlight to make his way through the corridors and up the stairs to the blackout curtains that open onto the deck. Approaching the curtains, he pins his bedroll against his hip with his left hand and uses the flashlight in his right hand to push through.

"Stow tha' *fookin'* torch!" explodes in his ears just as the ship zigs sharply. Jim bangs his hand on the side of the hatch and drops the flashlight, which rolls on the slanting deck. A sentry traps it under his right boot. He sits down on the flashlight and then turns to Jim and shouts, "*Nay leets* on deck, Yank. Blackout orders."

"Sorry, I forgot." Jim flushes hot and red in the cold and dark.

The sentry switches off the flashlight, stands up, hands it to Jim. "Yull want it when yuz get ta *Loondin*."

An easterly wind is pushing the exhaust from the *Queen*'s giant funnels out in front of the ship. The air on the aft weather deck is bracing. Jim breathes deeply, feels a pleasant tang of salt in his nostrils. This is swell. Then he looks back. A phosphorescent green wake trails for miles behind the ship.

"Don't fret, mate. We're too quick for a U-boat to follow

that!" the sentry shouts over the wind. He turns away and continues, too faintly to be heard, "We'd best be. Fifteen thousand onboard, lifeboats for three thousand."

Jim makes out the prone shapes of sleeping men when he gets to the area behind the bulkhead. One man is on his knees, hands clasped in front of his chest. Jim hears, "Where can I flee from your presence?" and makes the man for a zealot. They can be chatty. He moves a good bit away, unrolls his bedding, gets in with his boots on, puts his life jacket under his head and falls into a deep, beautiful sleep.

"ALL ENLISTED MEN BELOW DECKS." It's the loudspeaker.

⌃

VETERANS OF FOREIGN wars will tell you that being on a troopship in a bad storm is worse than combat. You're basically loose cargo. You're not only terrified; you're also nauseated. The nausea blocks out the terror, then things reverse. You want to run away, but there's no escape, and anyways, you're too sick to move. If you make it to the latrine, half a foot of bilgewater and vomit shifts fore and aft over your feet with the movement of the ship.

Like several other GIs, Jim sits on the deck in front of his rack, unable or unwilling to get up and empty the puke out of his helmet. He can hear the wind howling against the side of the *Queen*. Worse is the roaring whine as her propellers thrash air when she crests each North Atlantic roller, followed by a sickening drop, then a frightful shudder as her bow smacks the trough.

Some GIs are riding it out on their racks, holding the frames with outstretched arms and feet. They look crucified and pale. Every few minutes one is thrown onto the deck, his fall broken by men, duffel bags, bedding, and other gear. The storm has conjured up a temporary religious revival. Bibles are produced and sacred rites are invoked in English, Italian, Polish, and Yiddish.

Mickey is among the few GIs who are not seasick, only frightened. They chew gum, read, smoke, whistle, play cards as best they can. "I'm starting to think the Army isn't going to be all beer and skittles," he says to Jim. "I should've joined the Motion Picture Unit, like Louie Mayer told me to."

Jim manages a "yeah." Wouldn't have bothered to answer anyone else. It's dawning on him that enlisting may have been a mistake. You can lose your wife and drown before you even get to the war.

The sergeant enters the cabin and grabs onto the top rack of a bunk. "Don't worry," he says. "The *Queen Mary* was made with North Atlantic storms in mind." He dry heaves into his handkerchief.

"In that case, you'd think there'd be more toilets," says Mickey as Clark Gable.

"The battalion won't muster today," the sergeant continues. "Meal service is suspended until sixteen hundred hours. You can make your way to the mess hall at any time and get a K-rat." He dry heaves again.

"Permission to chain myself to the mast," Mickey says as the ship begins another almost vertical climb. The joke doesn't go over.

THE TANZER HOME
May 21, 1927

"Who did you zee at zah library, James?" Lavinia Tanzer asks her son, seated on her right at the dinner table. Jim puts a forkful of cabbage in his mouth to buy time. His mother is six feet tall, with large feet and hands, and a shelf-like bust. Considered unmarriable in Germany due to the effect of childhood measles on her looks, not to mention her personality, she was exported in 1898 to her older brother Adolf in America.

"Jenny next door told me Lindbergh was sighted over France, Mutti," Norma says.

Bill Tanzer turns to his wife. "We'll give the radio a go after supper, Mother? See who knows what?" He speaks with the Elizabethan cadence heard in West Virginia coal mines, an artifact of 18th-century British immigrants, isolated from the rest of America by the Appalachian Mountains and sheer cussedness. He is a man of medium height, not an ounce of fat on him. As Bill Boyd, he went to work as a slate picker in the mines at the age of nine. Graduated to the coal face at thirteen. Fled for his life during the West Virginia mine wars. Made his way to Huntington, found employment in Adolf Tanzer's brewery, married Adolf's sister, and swapped his Boyd surname for Tanzer, to avoid reprisals for his union activities.

"*Showgeschäft.*" Lavinia says. Show business.

"There's a $25,000 prize, Mutti," Norma says. Her father made $900 in 1926, and considered himself lucky.

"I'm going to join the Air Corps," Jim says, "and fly like Eddie Rickenbacker."

"*Dummheit,*" Lavinia says. Nonsense. "Doctor Professor Tanzer, you will be."

"No digging coal, no hundred-weight flour sacks for a man what has the learning." Prohibition turned Adolf Tanzer's brewery into a bread factory in 1920. "It's college for thee. Mother says so."

"Won't we be proud to know him then," Norma says, applying a light elbow to her brother's ribs.

"Thee will be more than me, Jimmy Tanzer," Bill says.

"What will I be, Poppa?" Norma says.

"What ye are, sweetie, the most precious girl in creation."

"I could be more than that," she says, getting up and going into the kitchen.

"Poppa, can we fetch the battery so we can hear the radio after supper?" Jim asks.

"I done it. Heard the Cincinnati game whilst ye were at the liberry. Hendricks' men give them Phillies a proper skutching."

"Do they play again tomorrow?" Jim's young voice rises with hope.

"They do. Course, baseball on the Sabbath is a scandal." Bill smiles, glances at his wife, then turns back to Jim. "How be thy dance steps, son?" he adds.

Precious dollars have gone to ballroom dancing lessons, to prepare Jim for Lavinia's vision of life in Huntington society. The teacher recently added tap to the curriculum. Instruction in clogging comes for free during visits to his Boyd cousins.

"Good, Poppa. I learned the shuffle ball change. Watch." Jim stands up and does the step.

Norma calls from the kitchen, "Shuffle in here, Little Nemo. Your icebox-pan-empty-itself magic spell isn't working tonight. There's water on the floor."

3.

GREAT BRITAIN, OCTOBER, 1944

> The puer aeternus—the eternal boy—dances along the border between boyhood and adult male life, both attracted to and repelled by the suffocating mother image. He may undertake fruitless quests for utopian worlds where he can avoid the imperfections of adult life, with its laborious adaptations and manifold disappointments.
>
> **THE PSYCHOLOGY OF CARL JUNG, BLUE BOOK #126**

JIM'S SECTION CANNOT see the aircraft during morning calisthenics, but they hear the engine drone. After scrambling off the deck, they assemble at the foot of the aft stairs. A crewman in the corridor puts down his mop and cocks his ear. "We're 'ome safe an' dry, lads. That's a Spitfire, on far end o' his North Channel patrol. You'll see Ireland today, leavin' out 'eavy fog." He pauses, touches the lucky George V sixpence in his pocket. "Outran the devil again, thanks be to God."

Too big for the dock at Gourock, the *Queen Mary* anchors in the Firth of Clyde. The troops will move to the pier on tenders. It's misting down cold. Jim has both his wool sweaters on under his field jacket and raincoat. The air smells of salt water, fuel oil, and peat smoke from the stone chimneys of the red-roofed cottages scattered around checkerboard farm fields. But for the bombed and burned structures around the port, Scotland looks a green and pleasant land.

"Snowdrops coming up the gangplank. Somebody's in trouble," Mickey says. Nobody gets off the ship. Three minutes later the two miliary policeman head down the gangplank holding either elbow of a GI in a straitjacket.

"That's the fella who was praying on deck during the storm." Jim says.

"Can't be shellshock, that's for sure," Mickey says to Jim. "Though this be madness, yet there is method in it."

"Shakespeare," Jim says.

"I was going to play Prince Hamlet—the pinnacle of acting, Jimmy—for Evans and Webster in '39. My agent wanted me out of Hollywood and away from Andy Hardy. Louie Mayer said no, made me do *Babes in Arms*. He knows his onions. I'd have won Best Actor, but everyone was rooting for England during the Blitz, so they handed it to that *Goodbye Mr. Chips* guy, what the hell was his name?"

A dozen middle-aged Scottish Home Guards pipe Morale Corps Battalion 6817 off their tender with a wheezy "Highland Laddie." They pass a group of airmen waiting to board. These men have survived thirty-five combat missions, daylight bombing through concentrated German anti-aircraft fire. For the rest of the war they'll be in the States, training thousands of new pilots. Even the religious among them can't quite fathom their luck.

"Turn around. Before it's too late!" one shouts. He's feigning terror, but he has plenty left over. There is also, "You'll be *saw-ree!*" "What's your wife's phone number?" and "Hey Mickey! Mickey Rooney! Where's Betsy Booth?"

Mickey yells back, "In St. Louis. Don't you read the papers?"

"Glenn Miller with you?"

"Throw me a football to take home to my boy!"

On their way to the railroad depot, the battalion passes by rows of men on stretchers. Jim notices missing limbs, bandages covering faces. He sees his first German soldiers, prisoners of war still wearing grey field coats and caps, waiting to carry the American wounded onboard the tenders.

"They must be closing the high schools," one pilot says as infantry companies come off the tenders.

"Replacements," his navigator says, looking away.

"Jesus, Jimmy, you're sweating like a pig," Mickey says as they wait to board the train.

Jim unbuttons his raincoat. "What if we stayed onboard the *Queen*, to entertain the soldiers on the way back home?"

"You're a stitch, Tanzer. Even if we weren't court-martialed for desertion, the press would never let me live it down. 'Rooney Hightails It Back to New York, Leaves the Final Push to Others.'"

"No, I was just…there'll be wounded onboard. We could visit—"

"I can hear Louella Parsons already. 'Mickey Rooney, the human yo-yo.' No. It's root hog or die for us now, Jimmy."

"Sure, but—"

"I need to catch up with this war before everything's over."

A walking wounded soldier on the platform, empty right sleeve pinned to his chest, hears the exchange, says, "Don't worry, boys. Plenty of Krauts left to fight." He can't be heard over the bagpipes.

△

IN ITS FIFTH year as a target for German attacks, London has the barren feel of a school during summer vacation, if several classrooms had been bombed out. The fizzy threat of invasion—*We shall fight on the beaches; we shall fight on the landing fields; we shall never surrender*—is long gone. The inland American sea, a million and a half soldiers and all that cargo, has drained across the channel since D-Day. Britain is a red-rimmed vigil now, waiting for Jerry to throw in the towel, with some murmuring about *then what?*

Mickey is being wined and dined at the American Embassy that night, where he'll make a well-received but ultimately fruitless pass at the Duchess of Marlborough, Sarah Churchill. Mickey and Jim's wrestling skit partner, Private Wenceslaus "Wes" Novak, a professional accordion player from Shiner, Texas, has a date with a nurse from Albuquerque. Jim has set out alone from the Red Cross Milestone Club to see *Hamlet* at the Haymarket Theatre. John Gielgud is directing and playing the Prince of Denmark. Peggy Ashcroft is Ophelia. Jim believes this will be useful for a play he's writing, *Spamlet*, a combination Shakespeare burlesque and exposé of the Army.

He walks around the shadow that a barrage balloon over Kensington Palace casts on the path. A statue stops him in Kensington Gardens. It's a boy blowing a pan flute, perched on an intricate plinth depicting fairies, rabbits, mice, and squirrels. A beautiful fairy in a clingy shift—she reminds Jim of Stella on their wedding night—has climbed up high enough to touch the boy's legs, but he pays her no attention. Jim reads the sign at the base of the statue:

> *Peter Pan, the boy who would not grow up*
> *Sculptor: Sir George Frampton*
> *R.A. 1860–1928*

"Nice for '*im*.'" Jim jumps at the thin voice behind him. He turns to see a gnarled little man with a trim white beard. The man is clothed in a navy-blue double-breasted frock coat and a shako of the same color with the letters *RH* embroidered on it. Bent almost double over his cane, he tilts his head up to look at Jim. There are three rows of service ribbons and medal bars on his coat. "Was 'ee a *real* boy," the old man continues, "His Majesty would 'ave him in uniform and marched over to France by now. Then who would the loovelay fairies chase after?"

"Were you a soldier?" Jim asks.

"I were, aye. Pensioned off now."

"Where did you serve?"

The old soldier points a trembling index finger at a service ribbon, pale blue with yellow edges. "I were a drummer in the Sutherland Highlanders. Lord Campbell's 93rd Foot. God bless my dear old comrades at Balaclava."

"Balaclava?"

"Crimean War."

"When was that?"

"1854."

"You must be..."

"One hundred and one. Were just a wee laddie, eleven my guess, when I took the Queen's shilling. 'Twere ten guineas, sure, but I had to buy my drum and uniform."

"You enlisted?"

"'Twas that or starve. Parish child I were. Father transported before I were born. Mother dead of the cholera in '52. I found a home in the Highlanders. Victoria's boys, we were."

"How was it?"

"Plenty of hard graft, many good blokes. Awful things now and again." He points to the Peter Pan statue. "You may grow old in the army, but you don't have to grow up. I were pensioned out before the second Boer War."

Jim steps up to the old man and salutes. "Private Jim Tanzer, Morale Corps Battalion 6187, United States Army."

"Thomas H. Lloyd," the old man says, returning the salute

with a shaking, blue-veined hand. "Chelsea pensioner. Last of the thin red line."

"How did you get through all that combat, Mr. Lloyd?"

"Tommy. Terrified at first, 'course, but the Sergeant Major stands you up, don't he? Gets you busy with your job. Drum calls give orders in battle, settle the men. Gives 'em a sense of what's regular in all that hurly-burly, the noise and smoke. My drum says somebody sees; somebody knows what needs to be done. We had twenty different calls. I had to attend to my drumming, not the battle. Kept my head as low as were decent, of course, but there's an awful beauty in men advancing under fire. You want to see it."

The old soldier taps his cane on the ground twice. "You'll find, Yank, you fight for your mates more than some idea, more than for your country." He looks away, then back at Jim. "Ave ye touched every fairy on the plinth? It's the good luck. 'Tain't enough to be careful in war; ye must be lucky. Go ahead now, soldier." He puts a hand in his coat pocket.

Jim walks around the statue. He locates and touches all nine fairies. When he finally looks up to give his count, he sees only a thin red line of chalk where the old soldier had been. "That's a swell bit, Tommy!" Jim shouts, but the old soldier is out of sight.

After a few minutes' walk, Jim approaches a large roundabout at the junction of several streets. In the middle is a large octagonal island. The curbs are checkered black and white, as are the bases of the four lamp posts at the octagon's four outer points. For visibility during blackout. Piccadilly Circus. A four-story-high billboard just across Shaftsbury Avenue shows "4:40 War Time," and proclaims "Guinness Gives You Strength."

Jim crosses onto the island. About a dozen women sit on the benches, talking amongst themselves and smoking. "*Coom see me after dark,*" one says to Jim and smiles. She's missing a couple of teeth. He looks away. Like every GI in London, he knows Piccadilly Circus is the center of gravity for retail prostitution. Much less active since D-Day, but still the hub.

A bobby, hands clasped behind his back, walks by Jim and says, "Keep moving along, there's a good chap!" in a friendly tone. "The tarts don't clock in 'til dark anyways, Yank," he says under his breath.

Jim has a twilight doubleheader in mind, a play and a lay. Two government-issue condoms and a pro kit in his jacket pocket keep company with his wedding ring. If he's going to get a Dear John'd by Stella, he might as well have some fun.

Hamlet starts at six. During the Blitz it was thought prudent to give post-show audiences time to thin out on the ground before German night bombing commenced. The practice has been maintained despite the fact that buzz bombs now arrive at all hours of the day.

"Too early, mate." It's an usher, smoking outside the theatre. "Why not pop across the way for a pint and a natter at the Queens Head?"

Jim passes two MPs on the way to the pub. "What's the rush, sojer?" one says to him, making him stop. "What brings you out in Piccadilly Circus tonight? Show your pass."

Jim presents it to the MP, who looks it over and hands it back. "AWOL soldiers moving around London these days. Seen any fellows we should talk to?"

"No, sergeant. Just got here."

"Morale Corps, huh? Congratulations on finding a fine way to fight a war."

Walking around London with a white pot on your head is pretty good duty too, you snowdrop son of a bitch, Jim thinks. "I'm going to the theatre," he says. "*Hamlet.*"

"If you say so, private," the MP says in a not-unfriendly voice. "In case your plans change, there's a pro station through the doorway under the Guinness billboard. Open all night. No pecker checker, just sinks and the chemicals. Get there within an hour after you disengage."

∧

The windows at The Queen's Head have been boarded up since 1940. Jim steps through the blackout curtain into a fog of mold, stale beer, cooked cabbage, tobacco smoke, and, when the barmaid puts her hand on his forearm, Evening in Paris toilet water. "What can I bring you, Yank?" she says with generous dip of cleavage.

"I'll have a…Guinness," Jim says. The barmaid nods, walks over to the taps, then looks back over her shoulder at Jim and smiles while she pulls his pint.

"Piccadilly Ranger," says a sailor in a navy-blue crackerjack tunic, a diamond-shaped Construction Battalion patch on the sleeve. "Before D-Day, you couldn't walk there at night without being tackled by a hooker. Full blackout—you heard them before you saw them. They'd wait to see your rank before they gave you a price. Ten shillings for enlisted men, a pound for officers."

"Ten shillings, huh," Jim says, thinking, *I have that coin*.

"It was mass-production sex," the sailor says. "Forget about hotel rooms or the back seat of a car. It was doorway and wall jobs, or on a bench. Bobbies and Snowdrops patrolling, but you couldn't see twenty feet in the dark."

The barmaid returns and sets an enameled tin mug in front of Jim. "Sorry, love." She gestures towards a dartboard mounted on the tail section of a Dornier Do 17 bomber. "Jerry broke our pint glasses." She puts her palm on his chest. "But not our hearts of oak. Right, then, big man, one and six." Jim stiffly offers her several coins. She takes two shillings. "Spare a fag?"

"I don't smoke," Jim says, taking his first sip of stout and silently gagging.

The barmaid leans in between Jim and the sailor. "Will *yas* go down to the cellar with me after closing time, gents?"

"I'm going to the theater," Jim says.

"I'm engaged to a nurse, meeting me here in a few minutes," the sailor adds. "I'll have another, Miss. And here's that cigarette you wanted."

"Cheers, Yank." She picks up his empty glass with one hand, puts the cigarette behind her ear with the other.

"Give me a light, would you, bud?" The sailor pushes a small box of wooden matches towards Jim and holds up his left arm, in a cast from elbow to fingertip.

"Sure." Jim lights the sailor's cigarette and slides the box back. "I'm Jim Tanzer, Morale Corps."

"Chester Ruggles. Demolition. Call me Chesty."

Jim points to the cast. "Million-dollar wound?"

"I wish. Waiting on orders. Ike's gonna need the Navy to get across the Rhine."

The barmaid brings Chesty the fresh pint. "Cheers, love."

Jim points to the cast. "What happened to your arm?"

"Easy Red zone happened, Omaha Beach."

Jim pulls back a couple of inches. "D-Day?"

"We were on the *Princess Maude*, the front of the front edge of the invasion fleet. I went ashore in the dark, H-hour minus 100. Low tide. I was the second man to step in France on D-Day, right behind Lieutenant Bertelsmann. Clear and mark gaps through seaward beach obstacles."

"Beach obstacles?"

"Underwater gates, mines on log posts, anti-tank Hedgehogs. Then blow up bobwire when we got to the dunes, flag the paths for advancing armor. Never got that far."

"What do you remember?"

"I looked back after dawn—incredible sight—ships from one end of the horizon to the other. So many. I could have walked back to England without getting my feet wet. I wanted to. Then I saw infantry come off landing craft under fire, move forward onto the beach." The sailor rubs his eyes with the thumb and forefinger of his right hand. "Most of them were hit. I did my job for three hours before *I* was hit. Felt like three days... This isn't good for morale, is it, soldier?"

⌃

"G-G-GHOST!" A DRUNK GI yells out at the appearance of King Hamlet. The same GI yells "Sez you!" during King Claudius's opening speech, and "Hello Blondie!" when Ophelia comes onstage. Gielgud has had to remind his cast that these young philistines are the saving of England. And that they buy lots of tickets.

After Hamlet says, "And still your fingers on your lips, pray," Jim hears a distinct buzz pulsing overhead. Marcellus looks up at the ceiling. Someone yells "Buzz bomb!" Audience members begin to crawl under their seats. Several start to move towards the exits.

"Let's hope it gets here before the second act!" Gielgud ad libs, and waits for the laughter and clapping to settle before getting back on script. "Nay, come, let's go together." An unfunny explosion is heard in the far distance, and the play continues.

Jim gets up to stretch during the intermission, goes to the Gents in the basement. Washing his hands, he reads a "Conserve Water" sign above the sink. A slender middle-aged man in a tuxedo limps up to the sink next to him. The man turns the tap and looks at Jim in the mirror, then down at Jim's left hand, then gestures at the sign and says in a plummy British accent, "His Majesty's government advises 'The Eighth Army crossed the desert on a pint a day. Three inches in the tub is enough.' I want at least six inches if I'm going to remove my clothing!" He chuckles.

Jim notices the Maltese Cross hanging from a scarlet ribbon pinned just below the left lapel of the man's dinner jacket. "We have showers at the barracks."

"Six inches will do in the shower as well, although more is always welcome, don't you think?" the man says, smiling.

"I guess so." Jim shakes the water off his hands. "Well, back to my seat." *Fairies can be war heroes in England*, Jim thinks as he pivots and steps away. *That's something.*

⌃

THE CLOUDS PART and the indifferent moon casts a blueish light as Jim walks back towards Piccadilly Circus. He's astonished by what he's seen: the play, the story, the performances. He comes around after a few blocks when he notices toys in a shadowy shop window. He wants to send a doll to Betty Jo for Christmas. He steps into the recessed entryway for a closer look.

A blonde woman wearing only a trench coat slips soundlessly in behind him. "Ten bob," she says and opens her coat. Jim cries out and whips around in one violent motion, hitting his right thumb hard on the window frame. He stands with his back up against the glass. "Do the business right here, love. Got a Johnny for yez." She holds out a small tan envelope. "Or use your own." Her skin is gray in the dim light, her bush a shocking black.

Jim manages "Hey!" while he pulls his eyes back up to her face and shakes the pain out of his thumb. He smells Evening in Paris. "I'm married, ma'am," he finally says, and chuckles nervously. "Looking for a doll for my daughter."

"What is it with you Yanks and *ma'am*? We're the same age, by the looks of yez. But I'm happy to meet a bloke what respects the institution of marriage. My Tom did."

"Yes," is all Jim can manage.

"I'll knock off early tonight." She turns away and ties her coat closed with the belt. "Not much traffic." She turns back. "Where you from, love? I've got an aunt in Syracuse. I'm Nell. What's your name?"

"Jim. West Virginia. I've got to get back."

"Wait, Jim," Nell says. She steps out of the entry and looks to the sky. "Listen." It's that pulsing buzz. "It's over the docks. We won't make the tube station if it's coming 'ere." She pushes Jim farther into the entryway and pulls him down to the ground on his back. The buzz is louder. She lies down on top of him, whispers in his ear, "Five bob for a fumble, Jim. I'll just take a pack of Camels, tonight."

"I don't smoke." The buzz is close.

"Cover!" Nell pulls his arms over his eyes and ears.

The buzz stops abruptly and Jim tries to roll out from under the woman. "What happened to the—"

"It's 'ere!" she shouts, covering her ears and pressing her head to Jim's chest.

Three beats, then a brilliant flash lights up the entryway, followed by a monstrous *crack*. Jim feels the ground shudder as the pressure wave hits them. He doesn't hear the shattering glass, nor the thumps of things landing on the pavement. He snorts at the sharp smell of cordite as a curtain of dust and powdered mortar rolls in.

Nell pushes up on her knees, coughing. She is coated in grey, flecked with bits of red brick. She stands up, staggers a step, then beats some of the dust off her arms, looks down at Jim. "That devil Hitler." She spits. "You hang him and all his bloody Nazis after the war. You do that, Yank." Jim sits up, but cannot answer. He doesn't know who she is. He doesn't know where he is. He does know he wants to get out of there.

He starts to stand, wavers, Nell steadies him. "Catch a breath," she says, "then we'll see what's what." As Jim regains his senses, his head begins to throb. She takes his hand and steps towards the fires. The heat is palpable in the cool night.

The Queen's Head is destroyed. There's a section of a first-floor wall left, and a blackened stove where the kitchen was. The buildings on either side have been cut in half vertically.

There's a white bulldog lying still in the middle of the street, as though it was sleeping.

A gargled "Oh, oh, 'elp, 'elp me!" scream comes from the half-collapsed house to the right of the flattened pub. A siren can be heard approaching. "The civils are coming," Nell says, then sniffs loudly. "Gas! That lass can't wait." She starts towards the wreckage. Jim hesitates, then follows.

He sees the light grey head and torso of a now unconscious woman stretched out in the wreckage. She's coated with dust. But for the crimson shock of blood spreading under her nose, the woman could be an Elgin marble from the British Museum. She comes to as Nell and Jim pull hunks of plaster, broken wood, and bricks off her legs. "I went downstairs to get Dad his cuppa," she says, in a voice Jim recognizes. "'e must be in there!" It's the barmaid. She turns her head and cries in a rising falsetto, "Dad! Where are yuz? Dad!" No answer.

The barmaid's legs are bleeding but not broken. They help her to her feet. She's going into shock. "We'll walk to the next corner, dearie," Nell says, putting an arm around her shoulder. "Away from 'ere." When they get there, Nell sits her down on the curb. "Your coat, Jim. I'd give 'er mine, but that would distract the civils, wouldn't it?" She smiles. In spite of the adrenaline and the headache, Jim manages to smile back as he takes off his raincoat.

The Civil Defense trucks and ambulances arrive. The barmaid is put on a stretcher and taken away. Police are on the scene.

"Goodnight, Yankee Jim," Nell says. "Yer faithful brave. Keep your five bob, the bumble is on me tonight. I hope you find that doll for your daughter. Don't wait to send it. London is a dangerous place while Germany goes tits up."

Two days later, Jim is heading back to London in the back of a Bedford QL 4x4 truck with several British performers. He'd been sent to observe a small ENSA show at a defense plant in Surrey. *Hip Hooray* has been closed Army-style, i.e., without explanation. Scuttlebutt is the brass felt there was already too much entertainment for GIs on leave in Paris, and that everyone was scrambling to keep up, now that the Army was moving so far, so fast.

Morale Corps Battalion 6817 is under orders to put together three-man shows that can be delivered by Jeep to combat troops near the front lines. Mickey requested to work with his wrestling skit partners, Jim and Wes. He claims Jim is likely to be shot first, due to his height.

The ENSA comedian, a man of about fifty, is sitting on the bench across from Jim in the back of the truck. "No work for me nigh on three years before the war," he says to Jim, loud enough to be heard over the engine noise. "Unless end-of-Skegness-Pier Punch and Judy is what's show business." One of the other ENSA performers smiles at this. "Brought 'ardship to the British people," the comedian continues, "this war. But for me, well, it's the best of times, ain't it? Five pound a week, been all over the empire with ENSA."

He points to Jim's shoulder flash. "Done my turn in The Great War. Royal Warwicks. Came through the Somme and Wipers without a titch, me mates fell left and right. All me mates. I couldn't get a grip after the war, joined a circus."

Jim starts to say that that he too joined a circus, but the words are swallowed by a jarring bang as the truck hits a pothole.

"T'was just a Lucky Dip show tonight," the comedian says. "Marionettes, juggling unicycle—that were Boy Foy—a girl singer, me. And there's always an accordion, there's always 'Roll Out the Barrel.' It's become a joke."

Jim rubs his temples and leans forward. "The marionettes

were—" Another pothole smash. *One aspirin left in my first aid kit*, he thinks.

"Be sure you see the big ENSA show in London before you're off the France, Jim," the comedian says. "*Stars in Battledress*—that's our USO mob. Vera Lynn, Tommy Trinder, Sandy Powell and Chico, smashing ventriloquist. Wilson, Keppel and Betty's sand dance, and Gracie Fields sings 'The Lord's Prayer' at the end."

"Sings a prayer? In a show?" Jim says, surprised and interested.

"It's a blinder. You wait."

"Where did you go, overseas?" Jim asks.

"I were in France in 1940, entertaining BEF units. British Expeditionary Force. The lads what were lifted off the beach at Dunkirk. The signal for ENSA to evacuate France was the word 'amlet, during the BBC news on the wireless. To be or not to be, I'll tell you, mate!"

"I saw *Hamlet* at the Haymarket."

"Ain't you posh, Yank! I did a seven-month tour of Africa in '42. Now, you saw me tonight. I'm naught but a poor man's George Formby." The comedian answers Jim's blank look with, "The music hall and film star?" Jim shakes his head. "But imagine you're a 19-year-old Tommy from Lancashire," the comedian continues. "Never been farther than Blackpool for a donkey ride. Him and his mates are guarding an oil field in Libya. A thousand miles from 'ome. Mail and rations delivered once a week, 120 degrees at noon, sand fleas, bath once a month, can't even get Lord Haw-Haw on the wireless. Well, you're chuffed to see anyone from England, aren't you? *Scoot-lyn* will do. Even *Oy-err-lyn*," he says in a passable Irish brogue.

"You're good with impressions," Jim says, to be agreeable.

"Not a bit," the comedian says. "My act is half pie. I'm no name and never will be. Don't have the gifts. But the thing is, mate, morale is the showing up, the being there. The performance, sure, but also the natter over tea and a biscuit. Letting the lads know they're not forgotten. Like letters from 'ome. That I can do."

"Being there. Huh."

"Don't know what I'll do after the war, I'm sure. They won't need me to perform. You going to have an act, Yank? When you get home?"

"I don't know what I'm going to be when I get home."

THE BILLY SUNDAY OLD TIME RELIGION REVIVAL
November 16, 1929

"What has gotten into you, Jimmy?" Norma turns towards her brother, who is quietly weeping. They are seated by themselves in the back of a patched canvas circus tent, attending the last night of the Billy Sunday Old Time Religion Revival in Huntington. Despite being a budding agnostic after reading *What Is Religion?* by Bertrand Russell (Little Blue Book #70), Norma had wanted to see the most prominent evangelist of the first two decades of the 20th century, a time when evangelists were as famous as presidents.

"You'll see history in the flesh," she had told Jim, and read to him from the Huntington Library copy of *Billy Sunday, The Great American Evangelist*. "His father died in the Civil War. Billy Sunday was three when Lincoln was assassinated. Fourteen when Crazy Horse licked Custer at Little Bighorn. Fifty when the first Model T came off Mr. Ford's assembly line. Billy Sunday saw the cowboy go from a mounted farmhand to movie star. He saw immigration and secularism push Protestant Christianity from the center of American life. He saw faith in science and technology grow at the expense of scripture. He regretted the rise of the consumer culture, particularly the transformation of American life brought by radio and the automobile."

Jim was unmoved, but his sister's offer to buy him popcorn *and* a Coke—never allowed in Lavinia's house—had tipped the scales. Jim imagined a big crowd, and that he'd run around with his friends, maybe talk to a girl. He sorely regrets his decision, and not because the audience is small, none of his friends are here, and he's missing *Amos 'n' Andy* on the NBC radio network. Billy Sunday is scaring him.

"What is it?" Norma says.

"I didn't *mean* to oppose God." He wipes his eyes on his sleeve. He recently traded a yo-yo for a well-thumbed copy of *Wedding Night Confessions* magazine, and has been at himself.

Billy Sunday moves through the hellfire-and-damnation-for-the-unrepentant part of his sermon. "It's not death you need to be afraid of, folks!" he shouts. "It's what happens *after* you die. They tell you Wrigley's Spearmint Gum lasts a long time, but heaven and hell are…" He slams his fist into his palm. "FOREVER!"

"Oh!" Jim gasps, puts a hand to his mouth. Billy Sunday may be a visitor from that foreign country called the past, but he's all too present for the boy.

Norma puts a handkerchief in Jim's hand. "Blow your nose."

Revival meetings are to church as burlesque is to Vaudeville; same formula, lots more *oomph*. For twelve weeks in New York in 1917, forty thousand people a day came to hear Billy Sunday preach in a wooden tabernacle purpose-built for him by John D. Rockefeller and Franklin Woolworth, men more interested in saving capitalism than souls. In Huntsville tonight, the Great Evangelist has a secondhand circus tent. He's preaching to less than a hundred. Like Vaudeville, revival meetings have all but died out.

"Am I God-hating, Sis?"

"What are you talking about?"

Prohibition robbed Billy Sunday of the demon alcohol, his indispensable antagonist. He never got his whiskey grip on Darwinism, jazz, socialism, church dances, racy movies, smutty magazines, installment plans, and what he called the United States of Advertising.

Norma puts a hand on Jim's shaking knee. "It's all right."

The meteoric rise of radio in the 1920s brought flamboyant preaching into people's homes. On cloudy nights, listeners in West Virginia heard Aimee Temple McPherson in Los Angeles, preaching in her Church of the Foursquare Gospel. They could hear Father Coughlin, the radio priest, all the way from Detroit.

"I don't want to go to Hell, Sis. It scares me."

"He doesn't mean you, Jimmy."

Billy Sunday is still out on the road. At five foot eight, 145 pounds, tough as a boiled rooster, he bounces on the balls of his feet, as he did in his playing days with the pre-modern Chicago White Sox. He paces across the stage like a caged lion. At sixty-seven he no longer stands on the lectern, but he can still scare the fool out of the unsophisticated.

"What's going to become of me, Sis?"

"You'll be fine, Jimmy. Fine." She realizes her brother is too young for fire and brimstone, and considers walking him out of the tent.

Billy Sunday is winding things up. "I want you folks to join me in a pledge that you will never rest—" a beat—"until this sin-soaked, Sabbath-breaking, blaspheming, infidel, bootlegging old world—" he raises his right hand up to ear level—"is bound to the cross of *Jesus Christ*—" and then throws an invisible fastball at the audience—"by the golden chains of love. Raise your hands if you want to be saved, if you want a personal relationship with Jesus Christ your savior."

"For goodness' sake, Jimmy, put your hand down."

"Nail your hopes to the cross. Give your life to Jesus. Hit

the sawdust trail and let me shake your hand." Ma Sunday, the Great Evangelist's wife and manager, begins to play "Onward Christian Soldiers" on the road-weary upright piano.

"I'm going up," Jim says. Norma sits back to wait it out, hoping that her frightened sibling doesn't confess his sins to Mutti when they get home.

Jimmy rips up *Wedding Night Confessions* that night and decides to run away with the Billy Sunday Revival to save his soul. He regrets his haste the next day.

4.

PARIS, FRANCE, NOVEMBER 10, 1944

> Anyhow, so far as your military duties permit, see as much of the City of Light as you can. You've got a great chance to do now what would cost you a lot of your own money after the war. Take advantage of it.
>
> SERVICEMAN'S POCKET GUIDE TO PARIS,
MORALE CORPS, NOVEMBER 1944

"Paris sure is the berries," Wes says, leaning back from his chocolate mousse. "Billeted in a classy hotel. Real beds, clean linens. Hot 'n' cold runnin' maids."

"Like sleeping on butter after those straw mattresses in England," Jim says, taking a large spoonful of poached pear and vanilla ice cream. "And the hotel doesn't zig or zag every few minutes."

"I don't miss the *Queen Mary*," Wes says. "Those racks. Got our own bathroom and tub now, clean towels, wool rug on the floor."

"Mess in a swanky cafe on the Champs-Elysees. French waitresses. Army rations, though. The best French food is going to the black market. Then to restaurants like this. We're gonna have a big bill, Wes."

Wes picks up his wine glass. "No one can call *us* chairborne rangers. Those evac hospitals and the replacement camps in Normandy? Must've been a hundred shows. We're doing our part."

"Makes you wonder why the Army needs so many replacements," Jim says. "With things going so well."

"We'd better settle up and get going if we're gonna catch the show," Wes says. Mickey Rooney has invited his Jeep show buddies to join him at the La Cigogne. "Headliner is Gypsy Markoff."

"Gypsy Markoff the virtuoso. The *accordion* virtuoso, Wes. You better be on your toes."

"Ya know, she almost died in that USO plane crash last year in Portugal. The one that killed Tamara."

"And that war correspondent, what was his name? And a bunch more folks. She was on Broadway when Stella I were working—or not working—in New York in '39. Cole Porter show, *Leave It to Me!*"

"Gypsy Markoff was on Broadway?"

"No, no, Wes. Tamara Drasin."

"How was the show?"

"I read it was good. Couldn't afford Broadway."

"It's amazing Markoff can play at all, let alone be a headliner."

"You might learn something from her, Wes."

"The only thing I could learn is her phone number. She's a coupla levels up from me. Hey Jimmy, you know who opens for her?"

Jim knows. He's got some butterflies about the opening act.

"That blonde bombshell you introduced me to in London," Wes says.

Jim thinks about Kitty Carlson's hair, her blue eyes, her white teeth and full lips, her form-fitting red sweater. "Kitty's a friend. She and Stella were production singers at WNBC before the war."

Jim doesn't mention that instead of writing his wife while he was in London—he fears "Return to Sender"—he wrote Kitty a half-dozen increasingly feverish love letters and dropped the last of these off at her hotel on a night he drank too much. Jim has also initiated flirty correspondence with three other women back in the States, including his high school English teacher, a forty-year-old maiden lady who corresponds with a dozen soldiers, airmen, and sailors she taught at Huntington High. She ignores Jim's inappropriate subtext—several ex-students have discovered feelings for her after being shipped overseas—and responds with best wishes and news about the boys he knows.

"This one's on me," Wes says, pulling ten packs of Camels out of his musette bag. "A nickel per pack at the Champs-Elysée Post Exchange, two bucks on the street. Or here at Foo-*ketts*."

"Fou-*kays*, Wes. I have some invasion money we could use."

"Only cigarettes and greenbacks accepted here." Wes puts two fingers to his lips to pantomime smoking a cigarette.

"French national salute," Jim says. They both smile.

"Paris is Shangri-La for GIs," Wes continues. "The food, the wine, the beds. The women."

"If it wasn't freezing cold," Jim says. "Krauts stole all the coal before they scrammed."

"Glenn Miller playing every night at the GI club at the Grand Hotel."

"Can't get a taxi. Just bicycles in Paris."

"Best of all, Jimmy, Paris is two hundred miles from Metz." Both men know the price German defenders are extracting from units of Patton's Third Army in the months-long battle over that medieval fortress city. "Even farther from the Siegfried Line. I hope they lose our orders."

"We enlisted to be in the fight."

"*You* enlisted," Wes says and sings, slurring a few words:

Your best destination is the
Zone Communication.
Service of supply will get you by,
Stay with SHAEF and you'll be safe,
Type, file, or meet the train,
Just avoid the ground campaign.

"Stick with the accordion."

"I've found a home in the Army, Jimmy."

"As long as we're in Paris, you mean. Which we won't be tomorrow night."

"We'll be doing shows in Berlin by Christmas," Wes says, draining his eighth glass of Château Latour-Martillac. "The Krauts need to hold out for a while. We finish up here too fast, we'll be sent to the Pacific."

"Unless we get bad wounded or killed first," Jim adds dryly.

"I'm glad we're taking Jeep shows to the combatmen," Wes says. "No, really. About time they got some entertainment."

"You calling an accordion *entertainment*, Novak?"

"Nuts to you, Panzer," Wes says, smiling broadly. "And we aren't going to be rear echelon no more. K-rations, hemorrhoids, frozen feet, snipers, bed rolls not bread rolls."

"You just make that line up?" Jim says, thinking of his *Spamlet* script. "*Merci*," he says to the elderly waiter pouring strong, fragrant coffee from a heavy silverplate pot.

"Nah, Mickey said it. But I could kill some Germans, they attack our show."

"Wes, the only thing you're gonna kill is 'Lady of Spain.'"

"Ha! I'll make them dance to 'Beer Barrel Polka.' Anyways, they'll be shooting at you, Jimmy, tall as you are." Wes doesn't go on to mention Jim's ears, because he and Jim are buddies.

"This is real coffee," Wes says.

"Almost forgot what it tastes like."

"Where was our Hollywood star today?" Wes wonders. Then,

"*Le* sugar for *le* coffee, *s'il vous plait*," to the waiter sweeping crumbs off the tablecloth.

"Armed Forces Radio. Lunch with Ernest Hemingway, that writer, and his wife. She's a war correspondent for *Collier's*."

"Mickey still married to that doll from Alabama?"

"He says so. Hell, it's only been a couple of months."

"You still think that wife of yours is gonna Dear John ya? Where is she, anyways?"

"Stella's still in New York." Jim has this intelligence via Norma. "I don't—"

The waiter places a bottle and three snifters on the table. A black-haired man in his mid-twenties strolls over from the bar. "Coffee wid-out cognac is like flowers wid-out the nice smell, gentlemen," he says in Chicago English. He wears a pinstripe suit of fine navy-blue wool serge and leather brogues polished a rich black. Striped silk tie. Diamond ring on his pinky. "Drinks on my cuff. Join ya?"

Jim hesitates. "Be our guest," Wes says. "Thanks."

"It's the least I can do for quartermaster soldiers," the man says, pointing to the embroidered Army Service Forces patch on Jim's sleeve at the shoulder. While Jim corrects him, the man extends a gold cigarette case towards them. "Take a couple. Gauloises. French. Better than Luckies and a lot harder to find!" He laughs, pulls out a gold Zippo and lights Wes's cigarette. "To a Frenchman, one of these is worth two Lucky Strikes. Ten Fleetwoods. They're all patriots now that the Germans are gone. I'm Johnny Lester." Jim and Wes introduce themselves.

"Morale Corps, huh? The Army says morale is to the physical as three is to one. But I don't know. You can *sell* the physical." He laughs, Wes laughs. Jim does not. Lester reminds Jim of the wise guys he served when he was a singing waiter at Butlers in New York. Especially that oily booking agent who conned him into emceeing a "show" in New Haven that could have gotten

Jim arrested for violating the Mann Act. Lester slaps Wes on the back, looks right at Jim.

"What paper are you with?" Jim asks, although the man is too well-dressed to be a reporter.

"I'm not a warco. I'm a businessman."

"Were you doing business here before the war?"

"I must look older than I am. War'll do that to you. I got to Paris in September, just after the liberation. There was still a few Krauts shootin' at us when I came in."

"The brass let a businessman into a combat zone?"

"I came in with the 28th Division. Krauts call us Bloody Bucket soldiers, 'cause of our division insignia."

"That red keystone," Jim says. "You're a soldier?"

"Sure. Survived the hedgerow fighting, then our own bombs at Saint-Lô. Marched down the Champs Elysees, the Victory Parade."

"That must have felt great," Wes says.

"The feeling passed quick. We kept goin'. I heard the sound of guns again, decided to march myself back to Paris," he says. Jim would later discover that Johnny Lester actually stole a truck, drove it back to Paris, then sold it and its cargo, jerry cans of gasoline, on the black market for five thousand dollars. The two morale soldiers watch Lester swirl the three fingers of cognac in his glass a few times, then toss it back in one gulp. "Hines XO," he says. "Booze like this has been hid since 1940." Pours himself another glass. "Drink and be merry, boys."

Wes drains his glass and—"Whoo!"—exhales sharply. "You gone over the hill?"

"I'm separated from my unit. Tryin' to find my way back, someday. But my ma's a widow, and my older brother got killed in Italy last year. I need to make sure she's got a son to care for her in her old age."

"What unit was he in?" Jim asks, leaning back a bit. "Your brother?"

"First Army VII corps is all I am allowed to tell ya."

"First Army is in Holland and Belgium," Jim says. "Fifth Army in Italy."

"Nix the cross-exam, soldier." There's an edge to Lester's voice. "First, Fifth, they're all sausage factories and we're the pigs." There is silence at the table. "In the meantime, I'm not drawing my Army pay, so I gotta work if I wanna eat. Prices in Paris."

"Why don't you just go to a replacement depot?" Jim asks. "Tell 'em you got kidnapped."

"They'd just put me right back in combat. That don't agree with me. I'll find my unit when the shootin' stops."

"The 28th is in the Ardennes, just across the border from Germany, rest and refit," Wes says as Jim winces. "We're gonna do Jeep shows for them. It's a tourist area."

"No, no, Wes. Italy," Jim ad-libs, "but they won't tell us yet where in the forward area we are going."

Lester points at Jim. "Don't sweat it, soldier. I ain't in Paris to spy for Hitler. And if my division is on the German border, he already knows."

"Nobody tells us anything," Jim says.

"You'll be entertaining a lot of replacements," Lester says. "Speaking of replacements, General Cota, he runs the 28th, good old Dutch's order of battle is one-third in the field, one-third in the hospital, and one-third in the cemetery. You wanna get in on that?"

"Holy moly," Wes says.

"I'll get back in uniform after the new year. My girlfriend says Paris is beautiful at Christmas time. Couple of her friends over there." He points to two young women sitting at a table near the wall. "You could meet 'em tonight if you want. Clean as a whistle."

Sure, Jim thinks, *like every prostitute in Paris.* "We're going to a party for Jeep show teams," he says.

"What's a Jeep show?"

"New thing. Three entertainment GIs and a driver," Wes says.

"You get a Jeep from the motor pool?"

"Sure. Could be gone a week, up near the front."

"You must have requisition forms for gasoline. From any oil depot."

"Any that's got it," Wes says. Jim nudges his foot under the table.

"I'll give ya five hundred bucks in greenbacks right now, ya slide me a dozen of those forms. And a night wid those girls." He gestures towards the two young women. "They'll screw you so hard, you'll be cross-eyed by morning".

Wes looks over at the women, turns back to Jim and nods.

"We don't have them on us," Jim says. "And anyway—"

"Give you another thousand you lose your Jeep somewhere I can find it." Jim is pushing back from the table, but Lester puts a hand on his forearm. "You get a deuce-and-a-half, I'll give you three thousand to have it hijacked by French bandits. Don't have to be a deuce. I could even use a donut truck. You guys work with the Red Cross, right?"

Jim slides his arm away, looks at Wes. "We don't requisition trucks."

"You know any drivers who might be okay to get hijacked? You can split the three grand with them."

"Truck drivers are from Transport Corp," Jim says. "Coloreds. We don't know them."

"So, what can you put your hands on, other than gas and oil?"

"Theatre kits for soldier shows," Wes says, oblivious to Jim kicking his shoe. "Wigs, costumes, stage money, makeup, PA system, scripts, microphones, generator." Jim coughs loudly at Wes.

"Generator? What kind of generator?"

"PE-95. Gas," Wes says. Jim kicks his foot hard. Message received, finally.

"Now you're talkin'," Lester says. "I can move gas generators if I have fuel requisition forms. I'll give ya two grand for the theatre kit. You keep the wigs. No wait, I'll take the whole package. Some of my girls got shaved heads for sleepin' with Germans. There's a market for wigs."

"We gotta go now," Jim says, hoping to put this crook off and never see him again.

"What can you guys get me *tonight?*" Lester says, holding up a wad of hundred-dollar bills.

"Mickey Rooney's autograph on a yo-yo," Jim pulls it out of his pocket. "I'll trade it for a nice doll to send to my little girl for Christmas. Can't find a single one in Paris."

"One of my French buddies likes Mickey Rooney," Lester says, taking the yo-yo. "I'll make a call. Pick your doll up at Le Sphinx after midnight. Francois the bartender will have it. He'll mail your letters for a cigarette. No censor."

"Okay," Jim says, content to trade a yo-yo for never-see-this-crook-again.

"So, you two are square Joes. Guess that's easy in Morale Corps. Nobody's shooting at you. But hey, you change your mind, want to make some dough, have more fun, come and see me at Le Sphinx." He gets up and walks towards the two women, then stops, comes back, and without a word takes the cognac.

△

JIM AND WES enter La Cigogne just as nine high-breasted Gallic beauties are finishing "La Folie du Jour." Their height is accentuated by headdresses of feathers a combatman might say resembles a small white phosphorus explosion. The club is packed. "Provincials and Amis," a Parisian says to his wife. "Only the Follies Bergères is worse."

Wes points to a table in front of the stage. "There's Mickey. Let's go."

"Let me introduce Olga Markoff, Gypsy to her public,"

Mickey says, gesturing towards a petit raven-haired beauty in a spangled off-the-shoulder crimson dress, beaded bracelets on her wrists, and red camelia above her right ear. "Olga, say hello to my buddies Jim Tanzer and Wes Novak. Jim here is a dancer with a big future in Hollywood after the war. Wes is the most talented accordionist in this man's Army."

Gypsy Markoff gives them a hundred-watt smile that's only improved by her slight overbite. "Charmed, darlinks," she says, extending her hand to be kissed. Born in Milwaukee to immigrant parents, she speaks with a strong Eastern European accent.

Wes isn't a hand-kisser. Jim gives it a shot; his lips feel the scars on the back of her hand. "You are too tall for ballroom," she says, pulling the hand into her lap.

"And I'm too short," Mickey says. His tragic face becomes a mischievous smile as he says to Jim, "I believe you know Kitty Carlson. She tells me you two are friends." Kitty is extra blonde and shiny tonight. She is wearing her stage costume, a tight, royal blue satin dress slit halfway up one side of the skirt, with a sweetheart neckline that accentuates her all-American figure. Her smile up at Jim is served with a side of raised eyebrow.

Gypsy Markoff is a different creature altogether. Her brown eyes are magnetic, her neck long, her shoulders thin and square, her bare arms strong and shapely. Sex appeal radiates from her sensuous little body. Never mind his buddies, never mind the show; Jim wants to take her to bed right now, a fact that Kitty intuits.

Mickey steps into the void, turning to Wes. "Olga isn't just the most beautiful accordion player in the world; she's the best." A waiter approaches the table. "Champagne, *s'il vous plait*," Micky says with a flourish. "Now, Gypsy, my buddy Wes here is an ace accordion player." Wes looks down at his hands, says nothing.

Gypsy Markoff looks at Wes, nods, and says, "As we American girls say, oh goody! Let us play for each other." She beckons over to the bar. A man in a gypsy costume brings over an accordion. "Now, American GI, Mr. Wes Novak, vanquisher of the Bosche, liberator of Paris, darlink boy, come over here in such numbers and so healthy, let us see how I conquer you with your own instrument." Jim sees Mickey leaning in, a wide smile on his face. "Play me your best," she says. "Perhaps I will top eet." She nods and offers the accordion to Wes, who takes it and turns it over in his hands. Talking has ceased in the club.

Mickey stands and signals to the emcee that there's an unexpected performance coming. The emcee holds the next act, directs a spotlight over to their table. "Oh Wes, you're in trouble," Mickey says. He looks at Gypsy Markoff. "No red-blooded Texan is going to go down without a fight. Remember the Alamo!"

"I've never played a Scandalli," Wes says to the table. He goes up and down the scales a couple of times. Mickey puts his hands flat on the seat of his chair and sits on them. Wes starts into "San Antonio Rose." He can play this song backwards in his sleep. He can certainly play it drunk. He improvises a gypsy vibe, plays in G minor, bends notes. Markoff loudly claps her hands in front of her face, laughs with genuine delight.

Mickey sings in on the third verse. Although they've never done this number, Wes was expecting it. Mickey can do anything except leave the spotlight to someone else. But Wes finishes alone; Mickey knows to grant a musician a solo finish. The whole club applauds.

"Darlink cowboy," Markoff says, holding her hands out for the accordion. "I play for you now." She starts "Tico Tico." The notes and the tempo quickly mesmerize. Her arms are beautiful as they shift and flex, only two fingers and a thumb on the keyboard.

Jim shakes his head back and forth a little, wondering how she does it. Kitty notices, turns and puts a hand on his shoulder, and whispers in his ear, "She *has* to play the way she does.

It's genius." Jim nods, wants Kitty to leave her hand there. She does not.

Gypsy Markoff shifts abruptly into "Besame Mucho." She throws back her head in laughter and finishes with an impossible progression of notes. While the club is erupting in applause, she reaches out her left hand and pulls Wes across the table by his tie and kisses him smack on the lips. Mickey does the same.

Kitty Carlson turns back to Jim, flashes her fine smile and says, "Any news from Stella?"

"We're on the rocks," Jim says.

"Well, get off them." Smile gone, she pulls Jim's letter out of her purse and hands it to him. "From now on all I want to hear from you is news about the weather and your shows. Grow up, Jim Tanzer!"

She turns away towards Wes, who is pretending he didn't see that. Mickey is singing the first verse of *Amor, Amor, Amor* to Gypsy. Bottles of champagne begin arriving at the table.

⌃

"Here comes the train. There's Mickey," Wes says to Jim. They're standing on the #2 platform at the Gare du Nord. "That's timing. Christ, there must be fifty cars."

A PR officer and a Signal Corps photographer are with Mickey. "Hello boys!" Mickey calls out. "Another day in this man's Army." Then, "Charge!" as he jumps up on the train as it hisses to a stop. Jim and Wes follow.

There are no seats in the car. It's all wounded, heads to boots on stretchers on the floor, six across, about a foot clearance on each side. Several have a plasma bottle suspended above their right shoulders. A few have their eyes open. It's quiet except for snoring and the occasional groan. There is no nurse or medic in the car. "This isn't our car," the PR officer says.

Mickey kneels next to a stretcher. "How you doing, soldier?"

"Mickey Rooney," the soldier says softly. "I'll be goddamned."

"In the flesh. You prefer Betty Grable, I know, but I'll have to do. How'd you get this light duty?"

"Shoe mine. Hurtgen Forest. Every man in this car is 28th Division." He raises his head.

"It's going to be a month of ice cream and beautiful nurses for you," Mickey says. "We got to go to our car now. Here." Mickey puts an autographed yo-yo in the soldier's hand. "Something to do while you get better."

As his squad is leaving the car, Mickey turns back to the wounded men and shouts in a conductor's voice, "All aboard the Big Rock Candy Mountain Express, destination Garches and the American First General Hospital! Three hots a day, ice cream, fresh linens, and sponge baths from topless nurses. And *miles* out of .88 range!"

Smiles appear on a few faces of the dozen or so conscious men on the floor. The rest are in sedative comas, simply unconscious, too weak to react, or in the case of Sergeant Joseph Emmerbach of Waterloo, Iowa, twenty-five, recently deceased.

"No shots of wounded on the train," the PR officer says to the Signal Corps photographer. "You'll get better angles in the wards at the hospital. The men won't look so damaged."

Dodge WC-54 ambulances, German POWs, and several hundred men on litters are waiting on the platform at the Garches depot. "Headed to Cherbourg, evacuation to England," the PR officer tells Jim. "On to the US for the men who won't recover in six months."

Mickey begins to sing an ad hoc version of "Chattanooga Choo-Choo." This is new. Wes accompanies on the accordion; Jim harmonizes as best he can. The three walk among the stretchers, repeating the song. Mickey and Jim shake every hand offered up from the platform.

*Leave the German border 'bout
a quarter past four
It's your lucky day because you're outta the war
When your wounds are minor
Nothing could be finer
Then to have your Spam an' eggs in Carolina.
You're the lucky bastard;
could you ask any more?
Halleluiah, pal, because you're outta the war,
Good old Zone Interior,
Sit on your posterior,
Bye bye, bazooka, there-a you are.*

The photographer moves in to shoot Mickey among all the stretchers. The PR officer puts an arm on his shoulder. "Better at the hospital, corporal."

⚐

"WE HAVE TWO thousand beds," the hospital commanding officer tells them as he greets the Jeep show squad in front of the sprawling compound. "That's about two hundred patients on each floor, divided into three wards. Casualties are exceeding plan. Some patients are on litters in corridors until we find a bed for them." The PR officer looks at the photographer and shakes his head slightly. "We're taking in about three hundred wounded a day," the C.O. continues, "and trying to ship out just as many; some to England, some back to duty. Most of the soldiers just want to get back to their units."

"Brave men," Mickey says.

"Yes. We've got six hundred Army personnel assigned here, including attached units, and about the same number of French civilians. And about fifty German POWs."

"This place is the hospital version of River Rouge," Mickey

says, referring to the massive Dearborn auto plant, now turning out a B-24 bomber every hour, 24 hours a day, seven days a week.

"Ford assembles bombers. We *re*-assemble men," the C.O. says.

"Save that one for *Spamlet*," Mickey says to Jim. He looks over at the highway just east of the hospital. "Lotta trucks on that road."

"You've heard about the Red Ball Express," the PR officer says, "carrying cargo from Cherbourg. Ammo, rations, gasoline. The front line is way beyond where the Army thought they'd be in 1944."

"I sure as hell wouldn't want to be hot-rodding a deuce and a half full of gasoline right up to the German border," Mickey says.

"Transport Corps," the PR officer says. "Colored boys."

The wards are long, fifty beds on either side of an aisle. Mickey, Jim, and Wes stop in the middle of each ward, do their new Jeep show act as well as they can. Mickey adds a dead-on impression of the C.O. he just met.

They see an orderly putting a lit cigarette to the mouth of a GI who has no arms below the elbow. Mickey goes over. "How you doing, soldier?"

"Mickey Rooney, whaddayaknow," the soldier smiles. "I'm pretty blown up."

"How'd you get hurt?"

"Round hit our gun while I was holding a charge. Killed the rest of the crew. You can see what it did to me. I'd be outta here by now, but I've got septa…I've got blood poisoning. Needs to be fixed before I go home and get me a pair a robot hands, so I can hold my son. And bowl."

"Man, you got gumption," Mickey says. "Call my agent when you get back. I'll put you in a movie about GIs returning to America after the war."

After the routine in another ward, Jim goes over to a weeping soldier. The man sitting in the next bed, foot in a fresh cast, says, "Kid's just eighteen. First day in combat. Metz. His whole platoon killed in five minutes. Lieutenant, sergeants, everyone. Except him. That wound won't even get him to England. His cast is coming off tomorrow and he'll be back in combat by Thanksgiving, a replacement, all his buddies dead."

"That's rough," Jim says.

"It's rough Uncle Sam don't rotate infantry out, like the Brits do," the soldier says. "Like we do for air crews, you know, thirty-five missions and back to the States to train new pilots. Infantry may get pulled back for a refit, forty-eight-hour pass, but then it's back to the front line. For the duration."

"I didn't know that," Jim says.

"I'm 1st Division. Been fighting since Tunisia. Sicily, Omaha Beach, Aachen. We're not going home until Hitler gets a slug in the brain. Not even then; they'll send us to the Pacific to fight the Japs."

"Something should be done about—"

"Meanwhile, the rear-echelon cowboys…" Jim retreats a step. "Eating ice cream while we're eating mud. Hogging the good gear and the good smokes. Giving each other medals, the officers." Jim nods. "I swear, a combatman has more in common with the German soldiers than with those rear-echelon sons of bitches. I mean the regular Krauts, not those SS bastards."

"That's something," Jim says, a bit tentatively. "I've got to catch up with—"

"I'll tell ya what's so funny. They march you into the meat grinder with no regard for your life. But if you get wounded, they treat you like the son of a senator. Top-notch medical care. Hospital chow is great, and there's plenty of it. Clean sheets. Nurses from home. All of a sudden, your life counts for something. All of a sudden, you're not cannon fodder. Does that make sense to you?"

"No sense," Jim says.

"Makes plenty of sense. They think you may survive long enough to vote in the next election."

⟁

November 22, 1944

    Dearest Family:

    I got a packet of letters and the package from you yesterday. I'd about given up on the idea of letters from home. Hey!

    Thank you for the peanut brittle and the *Billboards* and *Variety*. Glad the hens are finally laying, Poppa. We dream about fresh eggs in the Army!

    I still haven't heard from Stella. It's hard being over here and not knowing if I'll have a wife to come home to, when this is over.

    Yesterday Mickey and Wes and I were at a Repo Depot. It's a big camp full of replacement GIs waiting to join units at the front. You can tell the replacements by their shiny uniforms and the quartermaster tags on their rifles! We saw a lot of ASTPs. That's college boys from the Army Specialized Training Program that was supposed to teach them engineering, foreign languages, medicine, all that technical stuff. But it got closed down because more infantry is needed. They told us they never thought they'd be going into combat as privates.

    I'm working up a burlesque of "To be or not to be." From Hamlet. Norma, you know that "soliloquy." I'm re-doing it to cover the subject of Army chow. Everybody jokes about it, and it's funnier than thinking out loud about suicide, which is what Prince Hamlet was doing. There's a bookstore here called Shakespeare and Company. Just the place for a bookworm, Norma. Hey!

    We have worked out our Jeep show. Just a K-ration version of a Vaudeville show, Mickey says, portable and barely good enough! We rehearsed in a shower stall yesterday. Drew a big crowd. Mickey said the acoustics were better than Carnegie Hall.

Tomorrow, we head east. Don't let that worry you, we won't be working in artillery range, and the Luftwaffe has become the Luft*waffle*. I just thought that one up. Got a million of 'em!

The Brits have begun daylight bombing. I feel sorry for the innocent Germans—there's lots of them, I'm sure—just wanting to survive until all this ends.

I am not going to see Mickey Rooney again until we move out. He's got Armed Forces Radio and some press thing and dinner at the Hotel George the V with Marlene Dietrich and General Jesus-Christ-Himself, John C.H. Lee, the Boss of Supply for the whole European Theatre of Operations (ETO). I'm glad Mickey will get to know him! Our Jeep will hold a case of Cokes nicely.

Speaking of stuff, I tried to buy a French doll to send to Betty Jo but my connection let me down. I'll keep trying. I do miss my little girl, and all my family. Give her a kiss for me.

Don't worry about me, I'm in swell shape. My teeth are good, my feet are good, the Army's Jim Tanzer improvement plan is working!

God bless you all.

Your loving son and brother,

Private James Tanzer

P.S. I'm giving this to someone to mail for me, so it won't get censored. Please don't share it with anyone at home. Wax lips sink ships. Hey!

MARSHALL COLLEGE
HUNTINGTON, WEST VIRGINIA
September 13, 1933

"Hey, froshie!"

Jim Tanzer keeps walking.

"I know you hear me, froshie. Take your medicine now." The students on the path ahead of Jim stop to look.

Jim turns on his pursuer. "Say, what's the matter?"

"Three violations," the boy says. "Not wearing your beanie, you're on the Long Walk unaccompanied by an upperclassman, and your tie isn't green. Do you think it's been Homecoming already?"

Jim's accuser is a freshly-minted Bucket and Dipper Society member, a boy of medium height and build, like Jim wearing serviceable but not fashionable clothing. The weakest of the ruling class are the most enthusiastic about punishments.

"No, sir. I left my beanie in my room. I didn't know about the Long Walk rule." He doesn't add that this brown and yellow paisley job is the only tie he owns, nor that his room is in his parents' house on the other side of the B&O train tracks.

"No one tells you the rules, froshie. You have to ask; you have to watch." The Dipper boy holds up a scarred wooden paddle. "Three smacks with the Ruler. Bend over now, hands on your knees."

A knot of students has gathered to watch, including several wearing tiny green and white circus tents on their heads, the freshman beanie.

"If you won't bend over then I..." the Dipper boy says, face turning an angry red.

Jim turns to walk away. He can't be late for his Youth Administration job. "Got to get to the—"

Thwack! The blow lands on Jim's lower back. The spectators gasp. He pitches forward and down on the gravel path.

Three textbooks, several sharpened pencils, and a wax paper-wrapped sandwich spill on the ground in front of him. Jim remains on his hands and knees for a few seconds trying to decide what just happened. His back throbs. His hands sting. His face is burning. Tears have come.

"10…9…8…!" the Dipper boy says. A few male students chuckle to cover their discomfort at the unexpected violence. "Get up, froshie. Take the rest of your licks." The boy's voice runs too high. "Or you'll get 'em on the ground."

"That's not varsity," says a man, stepping in between Jim and his attacker. He wears a white sweater with a green felt M on the chest. He's the football captain. Married man. Campus god. "You done your business. Leave him be."

"But the rules," the Dipper boy starts. "We have to—"

"And lookit the size of him." The letterman points to Jim. "He could get up and break that paddle over your head." This hasn't occurred to Jim, but he takes the cue to stand. "Who's to stop him?"

The Dipper boy backs a step. "But—"

"Save your carrying on for the Maypole scrap," the letterman says, and looks around at the crowd. "Okay, Buffaloes, time to go get some learning in our heads."

"Let's go," from other upperclassmen present.

5.

HOSINGEN, LUXEMBOURG, DECEMBER 15, 1944

15 December 1944
For Brig. General Balmer
s/A.E. Baker
Lt. Col., AGD
Asst. Adj Gen.
Jeep Shows number one to six were attached to VIII Corps Morale Corps Officer on 5 December 1944. Every effort was made to book the teams with the combat troops, close to the front. The benefit to morale projected by the hard work of these performers in putting on as many as eleven shows in one day, in places formerly thought unapproachable with entertainment, has made their outstanding performance of duty exceptionally valuable to this command. This office urgently requests additional Jeep Shows.

THE HEADLIGHTS OF the Willys MB Jeep light up the slate barn in front of sixty GIs sitting on raincoats or cardboard. A handful of sergeants and officers are on their feet in the back.

A squad just returning from patrol looks around for cover. All but one of these men and boys will be killed or captured in the next three days.

"Ladies and gentle*men*," Private Jim Tanzer says into a T-30 microphone connected to the Jeep's battery. Empty B-ration cans protrude from the headlight sockets. Exhaust streams thick and white in the cold Ardennes night.

"Company K," Jim continues, "3rd Battalion, 110th Regiment, 28th Division, 13th Corps, 15th Army, 12th Army Group…" He pauses for a beat. "Is proud to present the main event of the evening." Two beats. "A wrestling match, for the catchweight championship of the European Theatre of Operations."

Private Tanzer wears a khaki-colored sweatshirt adorned with a hand-drawn bow-tie, olive drab wool trousers and brown service boots. He looks ridiculous. The desired effect.

"In this corner!" Jim unfolds his right arm palm up towards stage right. "Man Mountain McGillicuddy! A-weighing two tons, four ounces." He turns his eyes right. Wes bounds in from stage left and hits his mark, elbows up, chest out. He wears OD wool three-button long johns and socks. He is shirtless, despite the cold. A few chuckles float out of the audience.

"Introducing the title holder!" Jim continues. "The Mosquito Menace! A-weighing four ounces, two tons." Jim unfolds his left arm, palm up, towards stage left. He turns his eyes left. The short man struts in from stage right.

There is an intake of breath in the audience, a widening of eyes, and involuntary smiles of recognition. It's Private Mickey Rooney of Hollywood, California. Mickey's costume is a sleeveless OD undershirt and boxer shorts cinched at the waist by a khaki pistol belt. His auburn hair is piled three inches above the top of his round head. He mugs furiously, balling and unballing his fists. There is whistling, cheering and laughter.

"All right, boys, I want no fair wrestling in this match," Jim says. Mickey and Wes pivot to face each other. "Biting, gouging, everything goes. And may the worst man win."

Jim claps them both on the back. They crash heads and stagger back three steps. Mickey does a half turn, revealing a large wrench tucked in his pistol belt. Wes pulls it out, places it on the ground stage left. This move allows Mickey to yank a crowbar out of Wes's long johns and chuck it stage right.

"All right, boys, go to your corners and come out farting." Jim backs away, pulling the mic stand with him. Mickey moves downstage and performs a series of rapid-fire knee bends, feet in second position.

The pantomime goes into slow motion. Every move is exaggerated. As the wrestlers lock fingers, Mickey's face becomes a mask of agony. He escapes, pulls Wes down to the ground, and wraps his legs around Wes's chest from behind, cheating out. Wes grimaces in theatrical pain. A few seconds later, Mickey pounds the ground in distress as Wes gnaws on his left shin. Jim pulls Wes away. From his knees, Mickey silently begs for mercy. Wes pulls him down and slowly pantomimes pounding his head on the ground. A kneeling Jim as referee follows the action with approving nods.

The wresting burlesque—lifted from *Boys Town*, Mickey's 1938 hit with Spencer Tracy—plays out for another minute and a half. Finally, Jim steps in just as Wes launches a slow-motion roundhouse right intended for Mickey. He hits Jim instead, who slowly crumples to the ground, unconscious. Mickey then drops Wes with a haymaker. While bowing to the audience, Mickey is struck by an errant foot as Wes collapses on top of Jim. Mickey reels and collapses on the pile.

Three beats. The performers jump up, acknowledging applause and cheers. They exit stage right.

On the same day as this performance in Hosingen, Luxembourg, Private Jim Tanzer was featured in Leeland Adair's local interest column in the *Huntington Herald Advertiser*. Adair assured readers that Jimmy still had that old spark and Tabasco, reporting that he and his fellow performers in uniform—including former Hollywood movie star Mickey Rooney—were now travelling up and down the front line in Jeeps, entertaining GI audiences of all sizes.

Adair added that the Jeep show soldiers carry out their morale mission despite occasional German snipers and shelling. Embellishment, perhaps, but accurate about the risk of working so close to the front line. He closed by reporting that Jimmy's wife Stella, Stella Sterling onstage, had just finished a month at the famous Stage Door Canteen in New York, and their four-year-old daughter Betty Jo is with Jimmy's parents, Mr. and Mrs. W.T. Tanzer, of 14 Railroad Street.

⌃

Mickey is back, wearing OD wool trousers, garrison cap, *Ike jacket*, trench knife in his pistol belt. *He* lowers the mic. "Hey kids, let's put on a show!" Cheers and applause. "I want to thank you, K Company, for the welcome you gave us when we pulled into Hosingen. You were down on your knees. What a reception. What a tribute. What a crap game!" Laughter.

He continues: "Jeep shows are about as much like those rear-echelon USO shows—" boos—"as K-rations are to dinner at The Brown Derby. Not as hot, not as fancy, but much more portable!" Laughter. "And what does the USO got that we don't, except beautiful girls! Another example of combat-men getting the short end of the stick." More boos.

Mickey turns to Wes, who has strapped on his accordion. "Hey, McGillicuddy. Is we is, or is we ain't, gonna play 'GI Jive' tonight?"

"We is, Mickey!" Wes says, then squints a little as Mickey says "3/4 foxtrot" to him. They've always done it in 4/4-time, F major.

"We is g'wan do it jump blues style tonight," Mickey says. "De *Billboard*'s number one jukebox record las' summa. A l'il race music." Some applause.

Wes begins to play. Mickey proceeds to sing "GI Jive" Louis Jordan-style. R&B. Mickey has done it swing-style, the way Johnny Mercer wrote it, in every show until now. Now Mickey sings behind the beat, growls and scats. Wes has played the song several hundred times. He gets there.

The audience nods and smiles. A couple of GIs begin to sway. Behind Mickey, Jim begins an eccentric dance step. The top half of his body is immobile while his legs impel him around the stage: *1-2-3-4 kick, jump across and 2-2-3, 1 kick back-tap. 1-2-3 tap, start over 1-2-3-4…*

Mickey steps back from the mic. He mirrors Jim with steps more antic yet more precise. He returns to the mic and, with a wink at Wes, switches to 4/4-time for the last verse. Wes pretends to drop his accordion. Mickey ends with a few bars of "My Funny Valentine" in Judy Garland's voice. What Mickey Rooney has can't be called talent. He has something else entirely. Or it has him.

He steps back up to the mic. "Thank you. *Dankeschoen*. Gonna be some show in Germany in 1945, won't it, boys?" he says, then grimaces slightly. The combatmen in the audience don't clap. They've seen that show. "For now, though, your Jeep show buddies are glad to be here with K Company." Mickey sweeps an arm towards Jim. "Jimmy Tanzer. He's from so far up in the holler, Eleanor Roosevelt asked the WPA to pipe in daylight." Laughter and a little applause. Mickey gestures towards Wes. "Wes Novak. McGillicuddy himself, our accordionist extraordinaire, a Spoetzl Bohemian boy from Shiner, Texas. Czech and double Czech." A little applause but no laughter. "Give that one a minute, fellas," Mickey says. "Wes was a regular on WOAI radio before Uncle Sam offered him this European tour. Jimmy and Wes and I…and let me not forget the guy behind the wheel." He points to the Jeep. "Private Pettigrew."

A few audience members turn towards George Washington Pettigrew, MOS 345 (truck driver, light). On loan to Morale Corps from the 514th Quartermaster Truck Regiment (Colored). He is back behind the Jeep's headlights; they can't see him clearly.

"We've been doing shows up and down your lines yesterday and today," Mickey says, "and I can tell you that the 110th Regiment looks in pretty good shape…" A beat. "For the shape you're in." Ragged cheers. "But I'm not looking so good. Before the Army, I was six feet two." Laughter. "I'm five feet three now. But it's all gristle!" Laughter. "Think of me as Van Johnson at half-mast." Laughter.

"By the way, we had a rough sail over from New York. Besides the 106th Infantry Division and all their gear, we had a cargo of yo-yos." A beat. "The ship sank 167 times before we got to Scotland." Laughter. On cue, Jim and Wes each toss a yo-yo into the audience. The combatmen flinch.

"We were in Clervaux this morning. Nice town. Spas. Pretty girls. Cold beer. So, tell me, why would they pick Clervaux for Regiment Command and stick K Company in Hosingen?" Smiles and boos. "Colonel Franklin sends his regards, by the way. He wanted to be with you tonight, but he had to stay in Clervaux and shine his medal." Laughter, applause. "I don't know how you boys feel about it, but I'm a little impatient these days. 'You'll be home for Christmas,' they told me in September. At the speed this Army is moving now, they musta meant Christmas 1949!"

"This soldier here—" Mickey gestures towards Jim—"says he's found a home in the Army." Loud boos. "I guess that's the slick move, Jimmy. We're never gonna live anyplace else!" Jim keeps the smile on his face.

"My buddy Clark Gable sent a telegram to President

Roosevelt saying..." Mickey switches on his perfect Gable impression. "'I want a bigger role in the war effort than bond rallies.' Roosevelt cables back—" Mickey now owns the President's voice—"'We need you to stay where you *ahh* and do what you're already *do*-ing. So *I* send the President the same telegram. The next day he cables me, '*Get o-va they-a!*'" Mickey staggers back three steps. Laughter.

"Now, you boys know I'd rather fight than tell jokes," Mickey says. "I'm the only soldier who can look Tojo in the eye." Laughter. "I was gonna be a paratrooper. Glory and five dollars more a month. First jump, red light by the door switches on. I'm too scared to move. Jumpmaster says to me, 'Jump, or I'll put my boot up your keister.'"

Jim, from the wings: "Did you jump?"

Mickey shrugs. "Just a little." Heavy laughter. "Thank you, thank you. Now it's time for one of your own Company K boys to entertain *us*."

A thin, dark-haired young man in a shiny uniform steps up next to Mickey. Rooney takes the young man's M1 rifle, quartermaster's tag still attached to the trigger guard. "Let me hold this while you sing." He turns back to the crowd. "Your Private Levy, Jacob Levy, was a cantor in Newark before the war." Mickey examines the rifle's receiver. "Manufactured by Underwood. And his rifle was a typewriter!" Laughter. "We heard him sing at the Repo Depot a few weeks back. Give him a warm welcome." Applause and calls of encouragement. Levy is a replacement. Most of Company K have never heard his name.

Levy sings "Am I American?" in heavily accented English. He heard the song at the American Common pavilion at the 1939 New York World's Fair, and then sang it in the PS 34 Glee Club. The song is part of the Federal Theatre Project's *Ballad for Americans*, a cantata promoting the *e pluribus unum* dream of a nation composed of different regions, ethnicities, and religions. Wes plays in on the second verse.

Born in Ansbach, Germany, son of a kosher butcher, Private Levy emigrated to the United States in 1936 at age twelve. He is nervous in front of his fellow GIs. But now they know his name. His chances of surviving the war have increased. He responds to the applause with a truncated "Lili Marlene." Wes can play this one in his sleep.

⚹

Obergfreiter Sepp Ackerman puts down his field glasses. His assault rifle is slung across his back. "They will be leaving soon," he says in German to Grenadier Willi Hoch. The two artillery spotters are prone on the ground behind a tree at the edge of a patch of woods, almost two hundred yards east of the barn. Hoch is watching the Jeep show through the telescopic sight of his Mauser.

"Bloody Bucket insignia," Hoch says. "As expected, these are of the 28th Division."

"They were at the Hürtgenwald battle," Ackerman says. "State of Pennsylvania guards. I spoke with one we overtook during a counter-attack. He was from Pittsburgh. A bus driver. Died before the stretcher bearers could treat his wounds. His last words were Arlington Heights, Smithfield, East Carson, Yosephine."

"What a show, comrade," Hoch says. "Mickey Rooney! A wrestling pantomime. Dancing. Singing. The only thing missing is cowboys and Indians!"

"You are a child, Willi Hoch."

"I'd like an autograph."

"We are not here for souvenirs, grenadier." He raises his field glasses up to his eyes.

"We'll go to Hollywood after the peace, Sepp. There will be many movies made about this war. They will need actors who speak German."

"Your Milwaukee accent will be a problem."

"The studios won't notice. And I will play an American soldier if they need me to."

"You'll need Yiddish, Willi. Jews run Hollywood."

"The California Jews speak English, Sepp."

"Fucking Amis! It's not enough they come so far to fight us, bring so many machines and so much gasoline. But to drop Mickey Mouse—"

"Mickey Rooney, Sepp."

"On the border of Moselland as easy as kiss my hand, it's really too much."

"Perhaps now would be a good time to surrender."

"Willi!"

"We are surrounded, after all."

"I'll be denouncing you the first chance I get," Sepp says. Then he thinks, *how am I going to keep this boy alive?* He hands Willi a thick slice of dark red blutwurst. "Bread, please. Willi. We'll take a meal now before the tank chocolate makes us too brave to eat." Their *Panzerschokolade* is laced with methamphetamine.

"Schnapps?"

"Self-sacrifice, Willi! Mission before drinking!"

"I'm more of an entertainer than a soldier, Sepp. Have I told you about my family's trapeze act?"

"Many times, Willi. So many times."

"In 1934, we were in Florida. The Depression. No work. Then we secured a European tour with The Von Duke Circus. There was plenty of work in Germany, with the Back to the Reich movement. We stayed and—"

"I know, Willi. I know. We'll wait an hour after the farmyard clears," Sepp says. "Then find the railroad tracks and be far west of this unlucky garrison before General von Manteuffel turns on the lights. Perhaps one drink apiece, now. We'll finish the bottle after Clervaux falls."

"I'm going to smoke."

"I'll have to stab you, grenadier," Sepp chuckles. "Shooting you would give away our position."

"Ecksteins are half cabbage now, anyways."

"Eat, Willi. We have a hard day ahead." In combat since 1939, Sepp considers himself already dead. His wife, his three children, and his dog were consumed by the Hamburg firestorm in the summer of 1943. He *does* want Willi to live.

Crump!

"Holy haystack! A mortar round!"

"American," Sepp says.

⌃

THE JEEP HEADLIGHTS go dark. Mickey runs into the doorframe as he, Jim, and Wes scramble back into the barn. The replacements in the audience look around for cover. The combatmen know what an American .81mm sounds like and just listen for next thing. A second round lands, no closer.

Captain John Quinn, K Company's commanding officer, silently counts off twenty and calls out, "As you were, Task Force Rooney." This will be the captain's favorite order of the war.

A combatman informs Levy in a stage whisper, "Practice rounds, range-finding. Against Division orders."

Things will be said in a citizen army, Quinn thinks, giving no outward indication of having heard this. "You know something that far away is harmless," he says. The Jeep's headlights come back on.

Mickey steps to the mic, rubs his forehead, and says, "That's swell, Captain, but some harmless things'll scare you so much, you hurt yourself." He looks back towards the barn. "Trouble's over, Private Tanzer. Wha'cha waiting for?"

Jim walks up and leans down to the mic. "You told me not to come onstage until you got a laugh." That gets a laugh, then applause.

"I'm glad you think Jim is funny," Mickey says, palms open. "Adjusting to Army life hasn't been easy for him. Before he got drafted, he had a great job in a ladies' panties factory. He was pulling down fifty a week." *Ba-dum-chingggg*. Wes pulls a reedy sting out of his accordion.

Jim leans in to the mic. "I've never been so insulted in all my life."

Groucho Marx Rooney: "Well, it's early yet."

Back and forth they go, ending the double act when Mickey says, "Time to move on with the show. Sing page fourteen."

"There is no page fourteen," Jim says.

"Sing page seven twice."

Ba-dum-chingggg.

As Jim backs away stage right, Mickey does his Jimmy Cagney impression: "You dirty rat. Come back and take it, or I'll give it to you through the door." Then he tap dances while singing "I'm a Yankee Doodle Dogface," adding a verse about riding Ava Gardner. New material, but by now Jim doesn't think *where the hell did that come from?* It comes from Mickey Rooney, whatever that is.

Jim re-enters, holding his mess kit against his chest. "Ladies and gentlemen," Mickey says. "Reason not the need, but lend your ears to Jeep Shakespeare, Private Jimmy Tanzer with a soliloquy from *Spamlet*, his soon-to-flop stage show."

Jim steps to the mic:

> *KP or not KP, that is the question*
> *Whether 'tis nobler in the mind to taste*
> *The powdered eggs of field kitchen breakfast,*
> *Or to take knife against a can of Spam,*
> *And with canned cow, eat it.*

The audience leans in, catching the Army chow slang, but not sure what the story is. Jim continues his *Hamlet* burlesque.

> *The heart-burn, and the thousand farts*
> *That Flesh is heir to? …*
> *But that the dread of marching after lunch,*
> *The mid-afternoon runs, from*
> *whose burn no briefs return,*
> *Puzzles the will, and makes us*
> *rather bear the chow we have,*
> *Than eat the others we know not of.*

Captain Quinn, two lieutenants, and one corporal have placed this in the Shakespeare canon and are quietly amused. Mickey is pulling his earlobe, the "pick it up" signal.

Jim skips ahead and winds it up in under a minute, not as quickly as most of his audience would have liked. Novak is ready—Jim has tried this Shakespeare burlesque twice before—and begins "SNAFU Jump." The bouncy Glenn Miller hit references the enlisted men's motto "Situation Normal, All Fucked Up," which Miller bowdlerized to "All Fouled Up" for public consumption.

Now Mickey re-appears on stage, sitting on a wooden milking stool and playing a jerry can like it was a snare drum. He plays rhythm and then solos. Then Mickey and Jim sing "I'll Be Seeing You." There is a long silence after the song ends. Then quiet applause.

Jim steps up to the mic. "Thank you, Company K. That's our show. Mickey will sign autographs. Then we're gonna get some chow and high-tail it back to Bastogne."

―――― ▲ ――――

THEY WEAR THEIR overcoats as they fall to their meal in the dining room of the Hotel Schmitz, K Company headquarters. The enemy took Hosingen's coal with them when they retreated across the German border in August. For this famous GI and his squad, the field kitchen has produced pork chops, scrambled eggs, mashed potatoes, carrots and peas, brown gravy, fresh bread and butter, vanilla cake with butterscotch frosting, and hot coffee. Captain Quinn sits at the table with them, drinking coffee and smoking his pipe.

George Washington Pettigrew eats his dinner sitting at the steel counter next to the dishwashing sink in the hotel kitchen. "It's easier for me this way. Easier for everyone," he told Mickey, who was concerned. "You don't risk Southern officers. And I can keep an eye on our Jeep in back, see that the spare tire stays put." He has the distributor in the left-hand pocket of his field jacket. He would be happy to drive this show around for the rest of this war. With Mickey, he gets everything the white soldiers get, including this fine meal. He tips gravy off the slab of cake onto his potatoes. He recalls his wife's biscuits and gravy, then her figure, then consciously pulls his thoughts to tonight's drive back to Bastogne. Blackout headlights, the slight risk of German commandos, the greater risk of being fired upon by an American sentry.

The Army makes a habit of ordering *start right damn now for somewhere else*, so Pettigrew sticks a pork chop between two slices of buttered field kitchen bread, wraps his handkerchief around the sandwich, and tucks it in the right-hand pocket of his field jacket, next to his toothbrush and a hand grenade.

Mickey turns to Captain Quinn. "If my agent knew where I was, he'd be scouting for a new leading man. If he ain't already." He smiles. "I've been meaning to ask all day, what's the 110th Regiment doing here? We can't be more than a fifty-cent cab ride from Germany."

"I can only speak for K Company," Quinn says. "After our deployment in the Hurtgen Forest campaign—" *shit show*, he doesn't say—"28th Division was transferred to Eighth Corps, General Middleton. Sent to rest and refit here in the Ardennes. About three weeks ago." Smoke trails out of his mouth. "The 110th covers the German border here in Luxembourg. We have company-size strong points in the towns along the main north-south road."

"Skyline Drive," Jim says. "We did shows for all of them, last two days."

Because this Jeep show squad might take a wrong turn tonight and be captured, Captain Quinn doesn't add that K Company can't pinch the gaps between the cavalry platoon screen to the north and B Company in Weiler, the next strong point south of Hosingen.

Mickey smiles. "What's keeping the Krauts from capturing the world's best-looking movie star? I got a kid on the way!"

"Been a quiet sector. It's four miles uphill from the Our River at the German border. Pasture, ravines, wooded draws. We patrol down to the river, maybe a little farther. So do the Germans. The men aren't trading Lucky Strikes for schnapps, but we don't run into them and they don't run into us."

"It'll probably stay quiet," Mickey says.

"Of course, if the Germans ever *did* counterattack in strength," Quinn says, "K Company is parked in front of the road to the bridges over Clerf River." *And the Germans have only rolled through the Ardennes twice before in the last thirty years*, he doesn't say. Nor does he mention the motor noise the mics are picking up from beyond the river, and all the activity a local girl told them she saw on the German side. "You'd really see something, if they came this way," Quinn does volunteer. "Hosingen is just an hour-twenty quick time from the German border."

"What kind of something, sir?" Jim says, tilting his mess kit to slide gravy off his cake.

Quinn pauses to recall the fighting at Vossenack. "You'd be shelled until you're half deaf, the whole town would be lit up by fires, then German artillery stops and you'd hear those bone saws." Jim's hand moves of its own accord over his groin. "42s. German machine guns. Then you see the first wave of those grey men advancing, proper spacing, fire discipline, and behind them black smoke and motor noise, loud clanking. As the ground starts to shake, you'd see the first Panzer top the crest." *Hair-raising*, he doesn't add.

Jim licks his spoon and puts it in his pocket, leaving the cake on his mess kit, then looks around for the door.

Quinn also doesn't add that there are no American tanks in Hosingen. "Now, a field spotter, if he's still alive, will call in fire from Division artillery." Quinn omits that, per Division, no final protection fire line is established in Hosingen. "We'd get it danger close. But the Krauts have probably pushed through the gaps." He clicks his tongue. "And artillery is already pulling back." The entertainers stare at Captain Quinn but say nothing. "K Company will stand and fight. Krauts will probably just pin us down, go around, and have reserves mop us up later. That's what I'd do. Oh, and you'd see horses pulling German guns."

"Horses?" Mickey says, surprised. "Sounds like one of my jockey movies."

"Pack horses. The Germans have generals, but they don't have General Motors or General Electric," Quinn says, happy to get off battle plans. "They eat 'em, too, the horses. The last fellow we captured said he had been nineteen months in Russia, survived on horsemeat plenty of times."

"Sounds like the MGM cafeteria," Micky says, pulling the face of a disgusted child.

"He thought Army bread was cake." Quinn says. "Thought we were trying to fool him."

"What do *they* eat for bread?" Mickey asks.

"*Schwarzbrot*," Jim says. "Black bread. My mother—"

"Private Jimmy Tanzer, German spy," Mickey says with a smile.

"Sure," Quinn says, also smiling. "Been quiet so far. We mostly fit in replacements these days. Haven't been Pennsylvania National Guard since Hurtgen Forest."

We lost so many men, he doesn't say. And once again, Quinn sees First Sergeant Heinie Behr sitting up against a dripping pine tree, staring through Salvator D'Angelo. Sal the medic dabs sulfa powder on the grey skin and pink bone that frame a silver dollar-sized section of Behr's blue-grey brain.

"But the Germans are licked," Mickey says, "mostly fending off the Reds in the east. They can't mount an offensive here."

"Let's hope they don't," Quinn says. He doesn't add that if they did, it would take a battalion to defend Hosingen per Division plan, even if he had enough fire. "It's too cloudy for air support these days."

"But it's quiet here?" Mickey says.

"It's good duty so far." Quinn nods. "The men take turns sleeping inside, water to wash with, hot chow." He restrains himself from saying they're not exhausted, cold, and scared to death now that they're out of the forest.

Stepping out into the darkness in front of the hotel, they hear the Jeep motor before they see it—Pettigrew is behind the wheel, looking straight ahead. "Well, Captain Quinn," Mickey salutes, "it's been like a two-week vacation with pay to spend the evening in Ho—"

They all turn towards the medic running up. Sal salutes the captain. "Sir, Culley. Private Culley fractured, compound, left leg." Quinn waits for the rest. "Moving a tube, sir. Fell down steps." Jim recalls struggling with 81mm mortar tubes at Fort Benning. "On him. I need to evacuate Culley, sir, tonight."

The medic's shadow appears, pointing west. Jim looks down and sees his own. A pale grey light has overtaken Hosingen from the east. Dawn already?

"The Germans bounce searchlights off low clouds," Quinn says, "to rattle us or condition us to it." Turning to Sal, he says, "Bring Culley. Fast. With this light, German snipers may move up from the river."

Concerned the Germans are preparing a spoiling attack, Captain Quinn doesn't release a vehicle, but orders the Jeep show squad to evacuate Culley. Mickey has to be back in Bastogne for an Armed Forces Radio interview the next morning. Jim loses the coin flip with Wes and will catch a ride with the first delivery truck in the morning.

On the road since five a.m., Jim lies down in his clothes and boots on a long horsehair sofa in the cold lobby of the Schmitz. *You fend for yourself in the goddamned Army,* he thinks. *Unless you're Mickey Rooney.*

△

AN EXPLOSION JARS Jim awake. No. It was a door slamming. After few minutes, he gets up and moves into the radio room, where there's a coffee pot and a typewriter. He will work on *Spamlet.*

Around midnight, Sergeant Gregory Azadian enters the radio room. The top third of his steel helmet has that blue sheen Jim never sees in the rear echelon. Combatmen use their helmets to heat water for coffee or, occasionally, for shaving. "The north OP hears engine noises," he says to Jim. "Observation post. In the water tower. They think the Krauts are playing records again. Course they can't see twenty yards, now the searchlights are off."

"Guess not," Jim says.

"Gonna go listen," Azadian says. "Come with. Carry these." He points to a walkie talkie battery and a full water bag on the floor. "You're goin' to the front of the front line, Private. Million men and machines stacked up behind you. A story to tell the wife after the war." Jim brushes his hand on the left breast pocket of his field jacket, where his wedding ring lives.

Jim and Azadian walk with shaded flashlights northeast, past empty foxholes covered with white bedsheets, to the eastern edge of the town. "Follow directly behind me now, Private. Flare mines just to our right. See the phone wire? Don't kick it."

Jim feels the looming water tower before he can see it. A three-story hexagon, one hundred feet in circumference, bricks around a steel skeleton. The OP is the cupola circling the top of the water tank.

Azadian shakes his head upon finding the metal door open. He and Jim climb the circular metal staircase bolted to the inside of the structure. "Airish up here," says Jim as they step onto the cupola. Two soldiers are there. "Cold," he adds, putting down the water bag.

Azadian points to the soldiers. "Private Corrigan and Corporal Bromberg. Bromberg is mortar squad. Corrigan is a telephone operator. They were at your show last night." He turns to the two soldiers. "Private Tanzer here is visiting the front line."

Patting the wall, Bromberg says, "Good place for it. Brick shithouse."

Then silence as Azadian listens out into the darkness. "Motorcycle. With these hills, can't tell just where," he says. "I'm gonna bring the lieutenant up. Keep lookin' for lights." He turns to Jim and says, "Wait here," then moves down the stairs before Jim can ask to go with him.

After a period of silence, Jim says, "We're a long way from home, aren't we?"

"Yes, sir," Corrigan says.

"I got drafted," Bromberg says without putting down his binoculars. "In the Division since Louisiana maneuvers, '42. I know Azadian since he was a private. He's a good man. This one—" he gestures towards Corrigan—"green as grass, a replacement. Enlisted. You could be his uncle. What swell idea put you in this cold and dark place, Private Tanzer?"

When Jim hesitates, Corrigan says, "Getting here was a cinch for me. The papers, the radio, my friends, everybody in Waterbury felt the same way about the war: gung-ho, 'Remember Pearl Harbor,' fighting back, the big adventure. It was like a grand parade passing down my street. I just stepped off my porch, fell in, signed my name. Been in K Company two weeks."

"Turned himself into a grown-up," Bromberg says. "Just like that." He points to Jim. "But you were already grown-up."

Jim begins his practiced explanation. "The world has become a dangerous place for free peoples. I've got a daughter. I wanted to do my—"

"Jesus, Joseph and Mary!" Bromberg says. He puts down the field glasses, picks up the field phone receiver. "HQ, this is first platoon O-P. There are pinpoints of light all along the German side. Either they're shootin' off fireworks or we're about to be shelled."

"First Platoon OP, repeat message."

"We see pinpoints of light," Corporal Bromberg says, "all along the—DOWN!" A freight train noise rumbles up the musical scale towards them, horribly loud. The train flies over the water tower and back down the scale. There's a shocking crack. The water jumps inside the massive steel tank. Jim hears whizzing and clanks as shrapnel hits the tower. The encore rains down on the roof, a shower of dirt clods, stones, broken wood, blasted masonry, half a cat, and a steering wheel. Then the faint tinkling of broken glass. Then more freight trains coming down the tracks. With all his heart, Jim wants to be flat and small.

"Blessed be the Lord my shepherd." It's Corrigan. "My goodness, my fortress, my high tower, my deliverer." Bromberg looks at his watch, whispers "fuck-fuck-fuck" in quarter notes, and holds a whole note, *fuuuck*, after each explosion.

German artillery walks like a giant up and down Hosingen, each step a frightful blast. There is relief for Jim when it moves away, choking dread and fist-clenching resentment when it returns. *They're trying to kill me!* he thinks. *They don't even know me! My daughter—*

"The name of the Lord is a strong tower," Corrigan continues.

"I lift up my eyes to it, my righteous runneth into it, my rock and salvation."

Jim can't hear that, can't hear anything, but does feel the basso vibrations of the water tank after every blast. A warmth spreads over his abdomen. His heart sinks. *Betty Jo, darling girl, Mutti. Stella. This is a terrible mistake.* He reaches down to touch the wound.

THE PARTHENON
The Voice of Marshall College Since 1898
Volume 19, Issue 11 / November 3, 1933

New Student Union Funding
The majority of the student body has voted to approve a fifty-cent increase in the enrollment fee in order to help pay for the erection of the new Student Union building.

Moo-Moos to Stage Robot Hamlet, Original Play
On November 11 at 7 p.m., the Moo-Moo Chapter of Fi Bater Capper will present their annual stage show at the Hatfield Auditorium. This year it is a play they have written. *Robot Hamlet* is based on Shakespeare's *Hamlet*, the Drama Society's recent triumph, and *Rossum's Universal Robots*, by Czech writer Karel Čapek.

This newspaper has learned that *Robot Hamlet* will dramatize the inevitable conflict between labor and capital in 20th Century industrial America. The all-male cast features freshman James Tanzer of Huntington as Hamlet 11-2, and senior Albert Jenkins of Weirton as The Stage Manager. The director is junior Nathanial Norris of New Berlin, Pennsylvania.

Dean Shawkey Warns Against On-Campus Drinking
Dean of Students Nathaniel Shawkey has reiterated the prohibition of alcohol on campus. He advised that any Buffaloes or Lady Buffaloes found in violation of this edict shall be subject to stringent disciplinary measures. This paper has previously reported on the flood of moonshine in Cabell County caused by ten-cent corn.

6.

HOSINGEN, LUXEMBOURG, DECEMBER 16, 1944

> Every commanding officer knows that boredom can be more dangerous than the Germans. Homesickness, boredom, AWOL, venereal disease, they're birds of a feather, they go together.
>
> MORALE CORPS GUIDE, EUROPEAN
THEATRE OF OPERATIONS, 1944

JIM'S JACKET IS wet but not torn, no entry site, no pain. What happened? Then the urine begins to turn cold against his belly.

A thick cloud of smoke and cordite drifts in. Jim's nose is running and a tear has made its way down his face. His mouth tastes like an ashtray. New horrors fly overhead with a frightful *hee-woo-hee*. "Screaming Meemies," Bromberg says. "Rockets. Welcome to combat, Tanzer. You hear a lot more than you see."

"MOVE DOWN FROM HERE!" Azadian has returned to the OP. He jerks his thumb towards the heavy wooden door to the stairs, now blown open. "They could drop one on the roof. We'll take turns up here observing. Me first."

Jim is on his feet and moving. Guided by the beam of Bromberg's flashlight behind him, he circles down the narrow metal stairs. He cannot move as fast as he wants to.

Only his grip on the metal railing keeps him from falling when the stairs jump against his boots as a shell lands. The water tank turns white as light shoots through the barred windows. *Flash bulbs*, Jim thinks. *Like standing next to Mickey in front of the press pool.* His heart pounds in his ears, but he can hear, "Mother Bromberg don't want her boy in this, no she don't."

Jim's field jacket lights up yellow-orange. He stops at the window. Flames illuminate grey-black smoke boiling out of several buildings. A wall folds in on itself. "Something gonna fly through that window, cleave your skull" comes from behind. Then a hard push forces Jim to jump the last three steps. He drops onto the concrete floor and crawls under the steel staircase. Bromberg wedges in, then Corrigan. Tires explode in the distance, cartoon pops. "Some show!" Jim hears. He reaches down and touches the scabbard of his bayonet. *I can't stab a man*, he thinks. Then, *where is my rifle?*

"This town ain't healthy no more," Bromberg says. Water leaking through small holes in the tank is covering the floor. The fronts of their uniforms are soaked.

"Gum?" Bromberg holds a pack of Wrigley's Spearmint six inches in front of Jim's nose. "Gets the taste out of your mouth. Take a coupla sticks." After the next shell lands, Jim pushes the gum in his mouth and thank-you's the pack back to Bromberg, who passes it to Corrigan.

By 0700 hours, no shell has landed for ten minutes. They sit out of the water on the lower steps. "Might as well be dancing, Showbiz, you're shaking so much," Bromberg says.

"Wet and cold," Jim says, stuffing his hands in the pockets of his jacket.

"First time is the worst," Bromberg says. "Always lousy to be shelled, but the first time is the worst."

Sergeant Azadian appears above them on the stairs. "Gonna check on the mortar squads." He points towards the staircase. "Bromberg, go up. Full light in an hour. Call in targets as soon as you make them. Channel 50 for now. We'll run new phone lines."

"Yes, Sergeant."

"Hold this position until further orders," Azadian says. "No firing unless you hear Krauts below you."

"They'll be the ones speaking German," Bromberg says to Jim. He recognizes a punchline, but is unable to smile.

"Drop grenades down the stairs before they can shoot up through the floor," Azadian says. He offers a hand grenade to Jim. "You probably didn't bring one with you." It feels heavy in Jim's hand. He eyeballs the pin and spoon, then gingerly puts the grenade into his field jacket pocket.

"You're ready now, Showbiz," Bromberg says, looking at Jim and smiling. "He'll kill 'em with his bare hands, Sarge, comes to that."

Jim looks down at his boots, but looks up when Azadian says, "I'll take Private Tanzer with me. Give him your mess kits and canteens, and he'll bring back hot chow and coffee." Jim's shoulders drop.

Bromberg notices. "You're better off here than standing next to an officer when the shooting starts. I—" He stops at a hard look from Sergeant Azadian.

⌃

"Take the watch a minute, Jim," Corrigan says. He hands Jim the binoculars and crouches below the wall to light a cigarette. Jim edges out of the faint yellow match light.

To look like he knows what he's doing, Jim scans the one hundred eighty degrees in front of the water tower. Over and back. It's coming on full light. Over and back. The ground fog is lifting. On the sixth over, he stops on a handful of vibrating squiggles. They become a half a dozen small white ghosts. He must be dreaming. More ghosts appear behind them. "What's that yonder, fellas?"

"POPPA 10, THIS IS MIKE 3!" Bromberg shouts into the walkie-talkie. He gets an answer, lowers his voice. "Company-size formation, cresting the hill, moving west through the beet field half left of OP Water Tower. Range estimate five hundred yards. Adjust fire from Whiskey Poppa. Map 22 Whiskey Poppa Bear. Grid 15342367. Over." He turns to Jim and Corrigan, "One round. HE…high explosive, Jim. Look for fall of shot."

Jim crouches down as low as possible while still being able to see out, his sweaty left hand on the top of the wall, his sweaty right hand on the pineapple body of the grenade in his pocket. He doesn't think he can move an inch, let alone pull the pin and drop it down the stairs. He notices the Germans' winter white uniforms as they begin to move at quick time, silently becoming the size of flies on a ceiling, three groups, each twenty wide, five deep.

A ripping sound starts up in the distance. The Germans bend forward noticeably. "Kraut machine guns. Firing over their heads," Bromberg says. "At our boys. We got a box seat to an infantry assault without armor, thank you Jesus, against a defended position. Krauts must think we were killed by their artillery or we ran."

Over his heartbeats, Jim hears a *ponnkk*. Half a minute later a brown and white geyser erupts in front of the middle German formation, followed by a *pang*. Two Germans drop like abandoned marionettes. A third falls to his knees. The soldiers behind step around them, continue forward.

"This is crazy," Jim says. "What are they doing?"

Bromberg calls in again, then says, "Rifles still at high port. They keep advancing towards our defensive line, ordered not to fire until they can pick out a target. That's discipline." He turns to Jim. "Take some deep breaths, Showbiz. You'll feel better."

Jim hears firecracker pops and a rhythmic chugging. One of the Germans is yanked back, as if by a rope. "Those wavy white lines," Jim says.

"You seen tracer bullets in basic, Showbiz," Bromberg says. "That's our machine guns."

Jim hears more *ponnkks*. "Look how those bastards keep their square," Bromberg says. "Radio City Rockettes couldn't be tighter. Our fire is well sighted, now we—*ooh*." A geyser erupts within the left German formation. Jim hears a faint scream.

"Those guys are getting butchered," Corrigan says.

Butchered. Jim thinks back to Uncle Clete's huge pink and grey pig, big brown eyes focused on corn cobs on the ground. *WHOPP!* The axe poll smashes into its skull. The scream and upwards jerk, snot and blood shotgunned onto his uncle's pants. The red mist in the air, the iron tang. Twelve-year-old Jimmy Tanzer dropping the blood bucket and running for his aunt's kitchen.

"Waste of good infantry, what that is," Bromberg says. Turning to Jim, he continues, "But we don't want them shooting at us through the floor. Do we, Showbiz?" Jim just shakes his head.

He jumps at a voice behind him. Sergeant Azadian is back. "They won't reach a hundred yards from our first defense gun." Jim takes his first deep breath in ten minutes.

"Sarge." Bromberg hands Azadian the binoculars. "Long column north of town. Armor, vehicles, horses, infantry. Fucking bicycles!"

Azadian scans north for thirty seconds, picks up the walkie-talkie. "This is water tower OP. Repeat, tower OP." A pause. "Enemy armor and infantry bypassing Hosingen to the north. Estimate range three thousand yards. Marching pace. ...No sir. ...Yes sir." He turns and says, "Out of mortar range. Captain Quinn will call in artillery. Let's hope our guns are still in place."

Jim looks back east to see one German stop, push his helmet down on his head, raise his rifle, and begin to fire while stepping backwards. The whole formation follows suit. The little men work their bolt actions six times before turning and trotting back down the hill, leaving several white and red heaps on the ground. One heap is trying to crawl.

"We whipped them!" Jim says, wide-eyed, shivering with relief and cold.

"They'll be back," Azadian replies. Bromberg nods to Jim. "Entertainment soldier gonna earn a combat infantry badge before this day is done."

※

"Smells like gasoline and toast," Jim says. He and Sergeant Azadian are moving from the water tower to the company headquarters, skirting around smoldering piles of rubble. There's a haystack-size bonfire in the middle of the road.

"Better to burn our Christmas packages than let the enemy get them."

"Should we leave the fruitcake as a trap?"

Azadian looks square at Jim and smiles. "That's a good one, Private. I see why you do shows."

"When will we leave?" Jim says. "And why…" He looks further down the road, sees two deuce-and-a-half trucks, a tractor, a road grader, and a Jeep facing each other in a circle. Inside the circle are barbed wire coils, shovels, tools, a typewriter, stretchers, rolls of bandages and gauze, two field ovens, several dozen C-ration cans, three one-hundred-pound sacks of flour, and a dozen or so Jerry cans. Anti-tank mines are strung under the vehicles and around the pile. "We're gonna blow up all that?" Jim says, shaking his head.

"Supplies and equipment we can't evacuate have to be destroyed, to prevent their capture by the Germans," Azadian answers. "Plenty more where that came from."

Jim and Azadian enter the Hotel Schmitz. Captain Quinn

is standing in the lobby with Private Levy, the cantor. Levy's uniform is covered with light grey powder. His right hand is wrapped in gauze. After a couple of seconds Jim remembers to salute. Quinn returns the salute and says, "Private Tanzer, your orders are to escort Private Levy running a message to Battalion headquarters in Clervaux, Colonel Franklin. I want him—" Quinn points to Levy—"out of here. Gestapo will be right behind German infantry if we get overrun. We can't spare two riflemen. And you give the Germans someone else to aim at." He smiles.

Missing the joke, Jim says, "I'm an entertainment specialist."

Quinn ignores that. "If one of you is hit, the other render what aid you can, but then proceed to Clervaux alone with the message. You will do what needs to be done to carry out the mission. Understood?"

Levy nods. "Yah, sir." Jim simply stares at Quinn.

"We're surrounded. You're safer on foot. You should cover the nine miles in about three hours, but take to the woods if you need to." Quinn turns to Jim. "Sergeant Azadian tells me you were an actor in civilian life."

"More of a song and dance man, really."

Captain Quinn has already turned to an orderly approaching with a black wool cassock. "Here's a priest costume. Pull the hood over your helmet. The disguise may buy you time to use your weapon."

"Song and dance man."

"Levy, you wear this," Quinn says, and gives him a grey wool monk's cowl and a rope belt.

"Jesuit," Levy says. "My father must never know." He smiles, as does Quinn. Levy has become his favorite replacement.

"Enemy troops are converging on the bridges over the Clerf river—it's here," Quinn says, holding a map up to his chest, indicating with a finger. At the top of the map, above a maroon smear of blood, is the word *Ardennenkarte*.

"Sergeant Azadian took this off a wounded German officer." Jim hears shouts in the distance and a burst of small arms fire. Quinn and Levy seem not to notice. "There are Krauts in American uniforms behind us messing with street signs, so use the map. I don't want to see you back here, unless you arrive in front of a column of Shermans."

"No, sir," Levy says. Jim manages a nod.

Quinn gives directions, tracking the journey on the map with his finger. Jim can't remember anything from map training. He can't focus, hears only fragments: "324…Kreuzgasse…An Der Triecht…Weschbichsbaach stream…Neidhausen." He sees that Levy is getting it. "…then 226 to 18 into Clervaux." Quinn finishes and hands the map to Levy. "The map is the message, private. Get it to Colonel Franklin. Stay away from civilians on the roads."

"Yah, sir," Levy says. Jim rubs his eyes.

"Call out to the sentries when you approach Clervaux. You want to be challenged, not shot. Yell 'Snap Crackle Pop,' or 'Quick, Henry! The Flit!' The Germans know Dixie and the Pledge of Allegiance."

"Yah, sir," Levy replies. "Pop Snapple Crap."

Quinn squints at Levy, then turns to Jim. "You do the talking. Sentries hear Levy's accent, they'll shoot you both for German spies."

"Sir, what if the Germans are already in Clervaux when we get there?" Jim asks.

"Bounce north and head for the Bastogne Road at Antoniushaff. It's on the map." He pauses, looks at Levy, and says, "Circumcised?"

There's a beat while Levy catches on. "Yah, sir."

"Me too," Jim says, not wanting to be left out of any calculations.

Quinn extends his right hand to Levy, palm up. "Your dog tags, Private." Levy hesitates, then pulls off his tags, drops them in the captain's hand. Quinn brings the tags up to his eyes. "Thought so. Great big H for Hebrew. Private Levy, you might look like some Nazi's idea of a Jew." *No question about that,* Jim thinks. "Don't want your tags to confirm it." He puts them in his pocket and turns to Jim. "Give him your tags, Private Tanzer. Take them back in Clervaux." Quinn turns back to Levy. "When you get new tags, tell 'em you're a Quaker. Your father need never know."

"Yah, sir."

Jim wants to mention his silver chain, decides it can wait.

"Memorize who you are now," Quinn says. "If you both are captured, you—" he points to Levy—"are Private Tanzer." He points to Jim. "You are somebody else. You lost your tags at a bathhouse. You're an actor. Make up a character to be." There's an explosion in the middle distance. "Wait in the lobby for dark. An engineer will walk you through our mines."

⌃

"Last year I played George Gibbs in *Our Town*, my high school play," Levy says to Jim. "My accent didn't go over too vell then either." Levy's German accent reminds Jim of his mother. He and Levy are alone in the lobby, ersatz priest and phony monk facing each other from either end of the horsehair sofa Jim slept on the night before. They can hear sporadic small arms fire in the distance.

"I thought, during your show last night," Levy says, "did you perform in zah Catskills? I vorked at Zah Concorde in zah summer of 1943."

"My...wife and I danced there a couple of times when we were working at Stiers. We weren't married then."

"How did you end up there?"

"We auditioned for a big talent booker in New York, Sam Gold. You know him?"

"No," Levy says. "I'm a *kosher metser*—a butcher." He gives a small laugh. "I don't know every Jew in New York."

"He got us jobs at Stiers. Social staff. We ate with the guests. I know about kosher," Jim continues.

"There was a joke at zah Concord," Levy says. "An iceman makes a delivery to one of zah gentile resorts. He sees his father, an Orthodox rabbi, by zah pool, necking with a beautiful blonde shiksa. 'Papa,' he cries out, 'you, of all people?' Zah old man looks up and says, 'Yes, my son, but I don't eat here!'"

"Hey! You can sing *and* tell jokes, Levy. We could use you in Morale Corps."

"Thank you. What did you do at Stiers, you and your vife?"

"Social staff. We did a Baby Astaires act. Stella also sang and I ended up producing the nightly shows. We had name talent for the Saturday night show."

"Saturday was Able Fur Night at zah Concord," Levy says, referring to the famous rent-a-fur establishment in New York's Garment District.

"I heard that line. We had Fanny Brice: 'I'm a bad woman, but I'm demm good company.' Hey! She closed the show with 'My Yiddishe Mama.' Had half the audience weeping."

Small arms fire erupts again, then quiets. "What we got this morning lays over anything I saw in live fire training," Jim says. "I wanted to crawl up in my helmet."

"My first combat," Levy says, "I was just off watch, sleeping in zah cellar. Zah house was hit. I thought I might suffocate. Took us half an hour to dig out, get to our positions."

"I about pissed myself, I was so scared."

Levy looks up at the ceiling in silence, then says, "Our sergeant told me he did zat zah first time he heard an .88 in Normandy. After zah war, he's going to shoot zah gemeyn mamzer who invented that gun."

"Were you afraid? When the fighting began this morning?"

"Shaking in my boots. Until I got busy. Sarge knew what we needed to do."

"You kill any Germans?"

"I don't know," Levy says. "I could barely see them. I fired a lot of clips." He lifts up his cowl and pulls a K-ration can of Spam out of the hip pocket of his field jacket. "Trade?"

Two crackers and a thumb-sized can opener spill on to the floor when Jim stands as Captain Quinn re-enters the lobby. Quinn returns Levy's salute. "Turns out the German officer we took the map off of is going to live. Levy, I need to keep you here to help me interrogate him. I have to send you alone, Tanzer. Sorry." The last thing a soldier in a combat zone wants to be is alone. "Here." Quinn hands Jim the map. "Good luck. And here's my letter to Private Skoda's parents. I may not be able to mail it." By now Quinn knows he will not be able to mail this letter of condolence. "And one for me, please, since you're getting out of Dodge." A letter to his wife.

Quinn has already reported the details of the map by radio to battalion, and has been told that similar maps have been captured. He suspects that his copy will be superfluous, but his orders are to get it to Colonel Franklin.

"Yes, sir."

"We found a bicycle," Quinn says. "Save you a couple of hours. Walk it up hills and around blind curves, so you don't ride into an ambush."

"Yes, sir," Jim says, unaware his head is shaking slightly, side to side.

"First get the map to Colonel Franklin in Clervaux. Then take my letters to the Regiment post office. If the clerks are already in the fight, mail them at your next stop."

△

"Okay, Private Tanzer you say," from a GI two hours later, holding the map in one hand and pointing a rifle at Jim with the other. The GI is Johnny Kucharski, before the draft a soda jerk at the West Philadelphia Rexall's, now mess cook in the 110th Regimental Headquarters Company. Kucharski is deeply unhappy to be on sentry duty east of Clervaux during what rumor and his own ears tell him is an escalating emergency. He is also slightly drunk. "Who don't know the code word, don't have no dog tags, don't know Danny Litwiler plays for the Phillies, nor 'wiz' means 'wiz onions.'"

"I know Rip Sewell and Paul Waner," Jim says.

"Nobody cares about them Pirates."

"Leo Durocher, Cookie—"

"Bums! *Hände hoch*! Keep your hands high," Kucharski says. "Has this German map, dressed like the pope, face covered in blood, shaking like a leaf, no cigarettes. Tell us your story again and better this time, so we don't turn you and your map over to the MPs. Them miserable pricks," he says under his breath.

"I'm just cold," Jim says, untruthfully.

"Krauts don't chew gum, so I'll give you another chance. Here, this'll help the shakes." He hands Jim his canteen. Jim spits his played-out gum onto the ground, takes a pull. Warm coffee and brandy. Delicious.

"Okay Holy Father, save some a dat for Christmas. Now start singing."

"What I said. I'm Private James Tanzer, Morale Corps battalion 6187. I'm from Huntington, West Virginia. I'm married to Stella Tanzer…uh, Sterling."

"Make up your mind. Tanzer or Sterling?"

"I've been doing Jeep shows here. Me and two other fellers, Mickey Rooney and—"

"That goldbrick came through last night. Why don't I just call him and check on you."

"Take it easy, Danny," the other sentry says. "This guy's no Kraut."

"We did Jeep shows on Thursday and Friday, here," Jim says. "Hosingen, Weilum, Munshausen. Other places I can't remember." He can hear artillery rounds landing not far to the east.

"Let us know when you do remember, Father."

"I was stuck in Hosingen yesterday. Germans opened up on us before dawn. Captain Quinn ordered me to evacuate with Levy—the runner—and take the German map to Regiment."

"Where is this Levy?" Kucharski points to the map. "Is this his blood? Did you murder Levy, you Nazi bastard?"

"Danny," the other sentry says, lowering his rifle.

"Levy was called back. He has fluent German. My orders are to take the map to Colonel Franklin in Clervaux. You take it. That's better."

"Christ, Danny. Let up," the other sentry says. He looks at Jim. "We're all jumpy. Looks like the whole division is falling back. What's going on up there? They don't tell us nothin'."

⚐

"How were you wounded?" The medic shakes sulpha powder on the cut on Jim's cheek and tapes on a dressing. Jim's eyes are twelve inches from the purple stump where the medic's right ear used to be. "Courtesy of a German sniper at Mortain," the medic says, brushing the stump lightly. "Won't get me sent home, but now I can pretend I don't hear chickenshit orders."

Remember that one, Jim thinks. He is sitting up in an armchair in the lobby of the Hotel Claravallis, Regimental HQ. Colonel Franklin and a G-2 have the German map spread out on the front desk. Officers and soldiers are carrying papers out the back.

"I went off the road in the dark, hit a tree just before the turn up to Clervaux," Jim says. "Wrecked my bicycle. I was on a bicycle." He met only civilians moving west on the roads. An owl's hoot had spooked him into pedaling too fast.

"You are combat wounded, Private. Purple Heart. If things calm down here, talk to the G-1 about putting you in," the medic says, pointing to a personnel officer moving briskly through the lobby.

"I will."

"Okay, Private. Good as new. Get that dressing changed when it gets wet."

⟁

"I didn't expect to be danger close," Willie says to Sepp. "I'm covered in plaster dust." Shells are falling close enough to shake the house, even though Sepp hasn't called in the coordinates for what is obviously an American command post in the hotel down the street. Just after 4 a.m. that morning, the two Volksgrenadiers pried open the back door of the recently abandoned Rodesch Pharmacie Clervaux, by chance installing themselves with a direct line of sight to the 110th Regimental Headquarters.

Sepp takes a crouching look out the window by the front door. "The Amis are sniping from the ramparts of the castle," he says. "It reminds me of the Smolensk battle, but without Ivans, thank God. And they are evacuating casualties to the railroad station. A priest just went in to the headquarters. Must be to give last rites to a dying man."

Willie goes to the top floor family apartment. He finds some clothing and a jar of pear preserves. He silently puts the trousers and a sweater on under his uniform. He may need to pass for a civilian. He knows Sepp won't do this, nor want to be told that he has.

Willi scoops half the preserves into his mouth with his fingers. The rest is for Sepp. "To sweeten your day, comrade," Willi says, coming down the stairs with the best smile he can manage. Sepp grunts in appreciation, puts the jar in a pocket of his field blouse, and bends down to turn on their FuG 5 radio. He doesn't miss Willi's newly padded silhouette, but makes no comment. The boy is only eighteen. He must survive.

"Be quick," Willi says, unnecessarily, for Sepp knows from his Russian service that radio operators can be triangulated and destroyed. "Ask why we are still exposed. The 77th was supposed to be here eight hours ago."

Sepp reaches their artillery battery. "Give me fall of shot, won't you?" the fire control officer says from somewhere east of Clervaux. They both know the problems with Russian guns and German charges.

"If only we could, Hauptmann," Sepp answers. "The Amis are moving house to house. We have to stay ahead of them."

"Give me what you can now!" the officer shouts.

Sepp answers, "Team leader #2, target azimuth" as Willi stamps his hobnail boots loudly. "We must…" Sepp turns the radio to another frequency, and then off. "Right, sure. That would be calling down fire on our own heads. Our mission as forward spotters is more important than shelling American officers."

Willi nods. "As you say, comrade."

"I'll call in this position after we fall back," Sepp says. "No need to target the railroad station aid center. The Amis' resistance will only be weakened by caring for so many wounded." He recalls the most shocking thing he has witnessed in combat. "When the Ivans stopped for wounded comrades, their commissars shot them in the back."

Willi nods. Sepp has recalled this many times. "We might be wounded here ourselves and will appreciate an American aid station," Willi says. "Although I'd prefer to be captured in one piece."

"Remind me to denounce you when we get back to Paris."

Colonel Franklin walks over to Jim. "It's just what Captain Quinn said, Private." He points to the map, which confirms what he's already been told. "The Germans think they're going all the way to the Meuse."

"I'm Morale Corps, sir, not Infantry."

"They'll never pull it off," Franklin says. "But they'll be hard on us before they're stopped. Runner job done, Private. I'll keep the map. You are now attached to this Headquarters Company. Someone will get you hot chow and take you to the aid station. You'll report in there."

Jim notices the now familiar and still dreadful sound of shelling has increased in volume.

THE FEDERAL THEATRE TROUPE
Camp Roosevelt, Virginia
April 3, 1935

Jim Tanzer stands with the rest of the Civilian Conservation Corps boys as the Blue-Sky Buckaroos play the national anthem. Then the Buckaroos, Muncie, Indiana's answer to the Light Crust Doughboys, play "Cowboy Polka" and "Tiger Rag." The lead singer does a few lasso tricks. He's no Gene Autry, but the campers don't mind. They're starved for entertainment.

The Federal Theatre Troupe's next act is twenty-eight-year-old Pearl Olson, the Teenage Swedish Sweetheart. She will sing "Dear Old Stockholm" and "Farmers Waltz." The name on her Lithuanian birth certificate is Gertroda Lipšicas. Gertroda is twenty-eight. Her jet-black ringlets are hidden under a braided blonde wig. Her breasts push urgently against the bodice of her blue gingham frock, pulling attention from her Slavic features. Gertroda sings on the beat, keeping an eye on the notes, but Jim can tell she's pushing her voice and is a little sharp.

He manages to pull his eyes off the Swedish Sweetheart and look around to see how the audience is reacting. They are transfixed, smiling, almost in pain. Gertroda could be singing the Brooklyn phonebook, Jim realizes; they wouldn't care. Plentiful food, fresh air, hard work, and testosterone have them primed for her act. Jim recalls Gracie Allen. Pretty girl singers go over.

Next come the Deflation, Cotton Patch, and Soil Conservation scenes from *Triple-A Plowed Under*, the Living Newspaper show. Earlier this same day, Senator Robert Reynolds of North Carolina accused the Federal Theatre Project of spreading the cardinal keystone of Communism—free love and racial equality—at the expense of God-fearing, home-loving American taxpayers.

After the Living Newspaper come a two-man balance act, then an Irish tenor who finishes with "Danny Boy." Jim sees the campers, most of them younger than him, rubbing their eyes. Sentimental goes over.

Next is a Vaudevillian, Owen O'Dowd. He has a declamation act. This Federal Theatre show is the first non-janitorial work O'Dowd has had since 1930. It's been hungry times for him, professionally and literally. Earlier in the evening, the old man had astonished Jim and several other campers with the quantity of supper he ate and the speed with which he ate it, all the while regaling the table with fabulous yarns from Vaudeville's golden age. It was O'Dowd's best performance of the night.

The Vaudevillian disguises several burps during "The Charge of the Light Brigade:" "Into the jaws of Death, Into the mouth of Hell!" He continues with "Mother o' Mine" and "Gunga Din," then finishes with a mélange of Shakespeare soliloquies. There is a too-long silence, then respectful applause. The old man receives it with a bow and times his exit perfectly. Vaudeville is a back number, Jim thinks.

Another venerable act is next, a one-man baseball pantomime by Casimir Modjeska, stage name Eephus Jones. Every CCC boy knows baseball, plays baseball, loves baseball. Baseball routines go over, Jim notes.

The Swedish Sweetheart returns as an Indian squaw. Buckskin vest, no blouse, fringed skirt hemmed a foot and a half above the top of her cowboy boots. The CCC boys sit up stiffly. She wants to be a cowboy's sweetheart, she sings; she wants to learn to rope and ride. The Irish tenor, in a cowboy hat and chaps, joins her. *Whoo-ooh-ooh-doo-di-di*, they yodel through "Cattle Call." The National Barn Dance has come to the Civilian Conservation Corps, courtesy of the Works Projects Administration. The boys remain seated and clap for a solid minute.

The cast finishes with "Happy Days Are Here Again," sung hand in hand, a nod to their President, Franklin Roosevelt, who has conjured up, from airy nothing, paying work for the entertainers *and* the CCC boys.

The campers are in their bunks by evening colors. Jim ignores the rustling sheets and snoring after lights out. The main idea has hit him. Never mind medicine. Never mind heading back to college with help from his family and the CCC wages he's saving. He's going to be in show business. He's *got* to be in show business.

7.

CLERVAUX, LUXEMBOURG, DECEMBER 17, 1944

> The Chaplain carries out his historic mission. The importance of that mission is known to every officer and enlisted man, personally. There are no atheists before going into battle. Nor after.
>
> — Morale Corps Guide, European Theatre of Operations, 1944

"You a chaplain?" the corporal asks Jim, as they walk several feet apart down Clervaux's Rue de la Gare.

"The cassock is a disguise. I'm Morale Corps," Jim says. "A 4-4-2, entertainment specialist." He pats the yo-yo in his left breast pocket. "We do Jeep shows up front and produce soldier shows in the rear."

"You like it in the rear?" the corporal asks, chuckling.

"It's not why I enlisted."

"Good." They walk on.

"Hey, private," the corporal says. "Keep six feet from me. Clervaux is a combat zone now. We both get hit, there's no one to drag us to the aid station."

"Sure," Jim says and stops while the corporal limps three paces ahead.

"You enlisted?" the corporal says. "Grown-up like you?"

"Sure."

"Rob a bank, sumpthin' like that? On the lamb, hiding out in the Morale Corps?"

"No." Jim looks down at his ring finger. "I didn't choose Morale."

"Nobody here's bored now; Krauts are providing the entertainment. But morale *is* a little shaky. The weather don't help… What happened to your face?"

"Tree branch. What happened to your leg?"

"Shrapnel." The corporal doesn't say that the soldier standing next to him caught it in the neck and almost bled to death. "Not good enough to get me evacuated, but good enough to be on light duty. My leg don't keep me from firing this," he jerks a thumb at the rifle slung on his back. "If I have to."

The corporal is short and slight. Purple-grey bags under his eyes, three-day growth of beard. He could be twenty, he could be forty. In his too-large overcoat, he evokes a photograph of immigrants arriving at Ellis Island. Instead of a black-clad wife and amazed children in tow, he has Private Jim Tanzer.

"You know Bob Hope?" the corporal asks as he stops and looks through the front window of a barber shop.

"That's USO. Civilian."

"Did you say Sicilian? Maybe I could get on the USO."

"Hey! Not bad. I could use you in a show."

"I'm already in one. I call it the Germans-pull-some-crazy-fucking-stunt-nine-days-before-Christmas show."

"That's a good line too," Jim says.

They walk another deserted block.

"I saw Bob Hope in England with Martha Raye and Gypsy Markoff," the corporal says.

"I met Gypsy Markoff at a nightclub in Paris. She's a doll… and a goddamn genius with that accordion."

Jim hears small arms fire as they make another half a block.

"I couldn't get within fifty yards of either of 'em," the corporal says. "They was surrounded by officers."

"Bad for morale," Jim says,

"Improve my morale to be sitting on the deck of the *Queen Mary*," the corporal says, "sailing to New York. Hey, keep your six feet from me."

The two soldiers walk on through the night. Shelling is close enough that they bend a little at the waist when rounds land, but not so close they throw themselves on the ground. Pops of small arms fire are closer. The corporal pulls Jim into a doorway before two MPs in a Jeep overtake them. "No time to explain ourselves to the Monkey Patrol," he says.

The mess is inside the Café du Château. The café is warm and smells of yeast, hot grease, and coffee. Jim notices German graffiti on one wall: *The Führer commands, we follow*. Written below it in English is *Back to hell*. Drawn above this exchange is that cartoon face with a phallic nose, peeking over a fence, and the words *Kilroy was here*.

"Chow and hot coffee. Just the ticket to boost morale," the corporal says as they walk back to the kitchen. Jim realizes he is famished. A mess private is there, a kid, tapping a ladle on a #10 can of beef stew perched next to a three-gallon coffee pot on a field stove. On the counter are ten loaves of Army bread, open cans of butter, Army spread, evaporated milk, a #2 can of sugar, and two canvas buckets of water.

The private quickly looks Jim up and down. "I'm glad to see a chaplain, sir."

"He's a morale soldier, Cookie," the corporal says. "Entertainment. Give him some chow."

The mess private wipes his hands on his apron. "Sure. No plates, though. Krauts broke 'em."

Jim pats his right hip pocket. "I only have my spoon." His mess kit is on the side of the road just outside of Hosingen.

"Use your pot," the corporal says.

"Uh, sure." Jim takes off his helmet.

"Leave your helmet liner on your head," the corporal says, "so's you don't get hairs in your stew. Or stew in your hairs." He chuckles at his turn of phrase. "Welcome to the infantry," he adds.

"Last hot chow for a while, I guess," the mess private says as he ladles a quart of gravy, potatoes, beef, and green peas into Jim's helmet.

"You here by yourself now, kid?" the corporal asks.

The mess private purses his lips. "The rest of the detail got their rifles, went off to the castle."

"That's the Alamo," the corporal says. "Don't follow them."

The mess private points to several wooden crates. "Take some K-rations. Engineers'll blow up what's left, so's the Krauts don't capture our food." He pauses. "'cept the battery acid. The Krauts can drink that." He smiles weakly.

I like the lemonade powder, Jim thinks, and puts a K-ration box in each hip pocket of his field jacket. He holds his helmet in the crook of an arm—it's hot—and butters eight pieces of bread, pairs them into four sandwiches, and puts them in the pockets of his jacket, next to the K-rations.

"*Mangia ora*," the small corporal says. "'Cause them Krauts will take it if you get captured or something."

Jim fills his canteen with coffee. The small corporal pulls something wrapped in a clean handkerchief out of his field jacket pocket. A porcelain teacup, eggshell white with a royal blue band around the top and a gold rim. "Bone," the small corporal says. "Found it on top of a busted house in Metz." The teacup glows palest yellow as it translates light from the ceiling. "*Amuleto*. Good luck. Get me home in one piece." He fills the teacup half with milk and sugar and half with coffee, stirs it with a finger, drinks it off, and repeats the process twice. He then fills the teacup to the top with sugar, re-wraps it, and carefully puts it back in his pocket.

Going out the back door, Jim and his guide have to step over torn-open K-ration packs. The corporal points down at the jumble of little cans and packets spilling across the alley. "They just took the smokes. Cigarettes are money now."

"I don't smoke," Jim says.

"You some kinda health nut? Anyways, keep 'em for buying things you need. Gum is for making change." The small corporal reaches down to gather a few packs of toilet paper. "*'Chi non butta via niente, non gli manca niente.*" He looks at Jim. "Waste not want not. My mudda taught me."

Jim kneels, puts some toilet paper packs and a can of peaches in his field jacket pocket. They proceed down the alley and through an open back door into a house. "Safer than outside," the corporal says, "long as there's no Germans had the same idea." They sit on the living room sofa while he smokes and Jim eats his stew and butter sandwiches.

Fifteen minutes later they approach a burgundy steam engine slumped on the single track in front of the train station. "Looks like a roast pig on six dinner plates," the corporal says. "Wheels knocked horizontal by German sappers. Fussy bastards. We woulda just blown the whole thing to bits."

Jim hears a generator, smells the exhaust. Sandbags are piled in front of the station windows. "This a train station?" he asks. Jim having eaten, his fatigue now makes him stupid.

"Was. No trains now. We bombed most of the tracks. Krauts did the fine work before they pulled back last summer. Turns out dey're good at retreating."

The strong smell of iodine, iron, urine, and coal smoke hits the two as they push through the thick wood and cut-glass doors into the waiting room. About forty men are lying on cots, cocooned in white sheets and olive drab blankets. Another dozen patients are on the black and white terrazzo tile floor. Walking wounded sit against the walls. IV lines snake out of upside-down quart bottles of pale-yellow plasma. The outlines of a few patients lack a leg. One lacks both legs. Many have gauze wrapped around their foreheads, a few around their eyes. One man with a wounded foot is handcuffed to his cot.

Twelve bodies are laid out on the floor in the back of the room, blankets covering heads and torsos. The bodies are different lengths, but their boots are lined up. A sergeant is kneeling there, holding the hand of a dead man. The sergeant's head bobs up and down. He's saying something Jim can't hear. The dead man's upper sleeve shows the red keystone insignia of the 28th Infantry Division, the Bloody Bucket. There's a single gold bar on the dead man's shoulder. He was a second lieutenant. The sergeant gets up and leaves without looking around.

Jim points to a corpse exactly parallel to the formation, but ten feet away. "Colored soldier," the corporal says.

"Oh." *Too short to be Pettigrew*, Jim thinks with relief. He becomes aware of groans, rattling breathing, snoring, coughing, and muttered encouragement by a medic.

A captain wearing a Medical Corps pin on his lapel walks towards them. The small corporal salutes. "Sir, this is Private Tanzer. He's a 4-4-2—"

"Chaplain's assistant?"

"Morale soldier," the small corporal says while Jim pulls off the cassock. The aid station is warm. "Colonel Franklin posted him to you."

"Salute the rank, Private," the doctor says. He returns Jim's salute and looks at his shoulder flash. "Unit?"

"Morale Corps, Battalion 6817. Entertainment specialist."

"You do impressions?"

"A few, sir. I'm more of a song and dance man."

"Wash your hands, then do your impression of a pretty nurse. Empty bed pans. Give a sponge bath and a shave to the men who want it, or if they're unconscious. Good for morale. Mine at least." He points to a twenty-gallon pot steaming on top of a field stove in the far corner. "Hot water and washcloths. Don't disturb their dressings." He looks closely at Jim's face. "Or yours."

"Yes, sir," Jim says. "I won't."

The captain looks down at the bulging pockets of Jim's field jacket. "Do you have any morphine?" He turns to the corporal. "Either of you?"

"Got no Murphies, sir," the small corporal says as Jim reaches in his field coat pocket and pulls out his hand grenade, then two morphine syrettes.

The doctor takes one and says, "Be careful. Two boys arrived today with morphine poisoning. One of them is over there." He nods towards the line of corpses, then walks away.

"I have to report back at HQ," the corporal says. "Good luck, Private." He claps Jim on the back. "Don't smoke your last cigarette."

⋀

"Hello, soldier. How are ya?" Jim says. The grime on this man's face and neck has rubbed a grey halo on his pillow. Two squashed morphine syrettes are pinned to his collar like wrinkled E.R. Squibb and Sons medals.

"You a medic?"

"4-4-2. Entertainment specialist."

"For God sakes, no 'Danny Boy,'" the soldier says. "This place is depressing enough already."

"That's funny, soldier. I need to put you in a show."

"The only show here is the not-die-of-wounds-and-get-sent-home show."

He has timing, too, Jim thinks. "How you feeling?"

"Besides the bullets in my calves, and my thumb—" there's a ball of gauze the size of a cantaloupe at the end of his left arm—"what throbs amazing, even though it ain't there anymore."

"That's shit luck," Jim says.

"Could be worse. My balls are still attached."

"You got a Purple Heart and a ticket home." Jim has played many hospital bedsides by now. He has his patter. "You'll be back in the States months before the rest of us. Women will be buying *you* drinks. And you probably bowl with your right hand," Jim improvises, deciding on the fly on "bowl," not "jerk off," as Mickey sometimes says.

"Only if we—" the soldier sweeps his arm to indicate all the wounded men—"don't end up in a prison camp."

"The Army won't—"

"My million-dollar wounds won't be worth a plug nickel in Germany. And I don't want no sponge bath from a fella."

Jim lowers the washcloth. "There are ambulances—"

"Every two ambulances that pull out of here, only one comes back," the soldier says. "They'll get low on gas, they'll have to go looking for it, they'll need a tire, they'll need more plasma, they'll need anything but to turn around and get back here. Rear-echelon troops. I don't blame them."

Jim takes a deep breath, smiles, and says, "Adjusting to Army life hasn't been easy for me either. Before I got drafted, I had a great job working in a ladies' panties factory. I was pulling down fifty a week." The soldier looks at him blankly, then laughs.

After an hour, Jim has worked his way to a soldier who looks about sixteen. Still in his boots. They look new. Two large M's are written on his forehead in dried blood. He got morphine in the field. Except for his eyes, the boy is still as Jim approaches. "Hi, kid," Jim says, raising the basin.

The boy moves his head and inch up and down twice. "Yes, please." Jim can barely hear him. With each shallow exhale, a half-inch crimson bubble advances out of a rubber tube protruding from the gauze wrapped around the boy's chest.

A light purple vein behind the boy's right temple emerges as Jim sponges his face and neck. He leaves the M's, wiping red dots off the boy's blue-grey lips and the straw-colored down above them. "Where you from, soldier?"

The boys neck muscles move and his head raises a fraction of an inch. "Laverne," he says in a strained whisper. "Minnesota."

"Your shit luck is behind you now, kid. You got a Purple Heart and a ticket home. You'll be back in the States way before the rest of us. Girls will be buying *you* ice cream sodas."

The boy pushes his head back into the pillow. His lips turn down. "I never had a girlfriend." Jim leans in to hear him better. "I lied about it with my squad, lied about Bonnie Anderson. She's a nice girl."

"How old are you, soldier?"

"What's it like? You know, with a woman?"

"What's it like?" Jim pauses to collect that line of Mickey's. "It's the most fun you can have without laughing." He smiles, then frowns slightly. *You never know if she's satisfied,* Jim thinks as he squeezes the washcloth out, *if you're letting her down, or you won't be able to support a family with your grab-ass dancing school. Or if she'll have to do club owners to get work, if she'll want to, since I'm over here and we're getting divorced.* "You'll find out soon enough," he says to the boy.

"I'd like to. Thank you, sir."

"Where were you wounded?"

"In the chest."

Jim points to the door. "I meant, where around here?"

"Weiler. Only got there a week ago. That's why the fellas stay clear of me, 'cause I'm…" The boy takes a shallow breath. "A replacement."

He's not in pain, Jim thinks. *He's never going to do anything except lie still while his life floats away.* "You think you're uncomfortable?" Jim begins. "Adjusting to Army life hasn't been easy for me either. Before I got drafted, I had a great—" But then he realizes the boy can't hear him now.

Thirty minutes later, Jim hellos a soldier whose eyes are

covered by bandages. The soldier tilts his head and reaches up. Jim takes his hand. "Bless me, Father," the soldier says, "for I have sinned. I can't remember my last confession. I'm sorry I offended you and I detest my sins. With your grace I will sin no more. Your mercy goes in peace. Thank you, Father. Hail Mary, the fruit of your womb. Pray for me at the hour of our death."

Thanks to *Angels with Dirty Faces*, Jim recognizes a Catholic confession. He decides to go with the chaplain role and sings "The Old Rugged Cross," working his best Irish accent into the chorus: "Oy will cling to the oold roo-ged cross…"

The soldier smiles. "Never heard that one, Father. You got a smoke?"

Jim lights one of his cigarettes and puts it to the soldier's mouth. "Here you go, soldier."

"Chesterfield?"

"How can you tell?"

"That's what my wife smokes. Nothing to 'em. Better than Fleetwoods, though."

"I wouldn't give one of those to a wounded man."

The soldier reaches a hand up and gingerly touches his bandages. "You got any morphine, Father? My damn eyes burn like coals." Then without waiting for an answer, "Will you sing me that rugged song one more time?"

The soldier loses consciousness before Jim finishes the first verse. As he cleans and shaves the soldier's face, Jim hums the song.

⚔

December 17, 1944

Dear Jimmy:

I just heard today that there is some kind of new German attack going on. I guess Hitler is not going to quit by Christmas. You wrote that you don't do any shows near the fighting. That sounds good. I hope it's true.

We received your last letter on Monday. Of course, Mutti and Poppa are burning to know where you wrote from. "France" is a big place. We were glad to hear you got turkey with all the trimmings between shows.

Mutti had flu last week, she's better now. Pappa and I didn't. We did finally get our chicks in the mail. Since Mrs. Roosevelt put chickens in the Victory Garden at the White House, every Tom, Dick and Harriet wants chicks. We'll have fresh eggs again by the time you get here! I asked about getting a hog, so Mutti would say *das ist keine Bauernhof*! She almost smiled! *Bauernhof* is farm, Jimmy, if you've forgotten that German word.

Speaking of farms, we used our gas ration for a drive to Uncle Clete and Aunt Minnie. They wanted to hear all about you. Logan is a humming town now. The miners are working double time. The bosses are pulling new men and boys into the mines as fast as they can. Uncle Clete says they are up to $8.00 a day with the overtime. Though it was fifteen killed at the Eccles mine, by the way. Methane.

Aunt Minnie and Cousin Sally put a fine meal "on the board," as they say. Sally is to get all her teeth pulled and dentures fitted. Said it will be the first time in her life she's been to a dentist! I love Poppa's people, but life is different up in the Holler. It's wonderful the Army fixed all your teeth, Jimmy!

I make as much as a miner. Somebody has to count the company's money! It's all coffins now, we haven't made a stick of furniture in a year and a half. They say we'll need an extra shift for the invasion of Japan. Please don't be part of that, Jimmy.

We are desperate for help in the factory. There's talk of bringing German soldiers over from the POW camp in Ashford. I'm the only person in the office who has any German, so *Es wird interessant sein*—it will be interesting!

Jimmy—the Miller boy was killed. At the Leyte Gulf. His ship was hit by a "kamikaze" plane. He was only nineteen. The Millers put the gold star flag in the window and pulled their shades down. They don't answer the door or pick up the phone. It's awful. Please be careful!

Lowell Thomas is still on the radio drumming for war bonds, but no more of those for me. I'm going to buy shares of General Motors stock. Uncle Sam is buying every machine they can make. They have big profits for the first time in years. Hasn't been a new car made since 1941, so they'll sell a lot after the war. People have money now. I have a book from the library about investing by two fellows, Graham and Dodd. Slow going.

Poppa fears there won't be enough work again when all you soldiers come home from the war. Mutti is sure of it. I don't think we'll go back to Depression days. President Roosevelt says we'll have prosperity, which gets no traction with Mutti. She thinks he's a dictator.

I got a letter from Stella. She wrote more about how things are between you two. It sounds bad. Stop the big freeze and write to her, Jimmy. She'll write you back, I'm sure. Stella says she has lots of holiday shows. She will visit down here in January, then take Betty Jo back to New York with her. I'll miss my niece, she's a little charmer. But children need to be with their parents and parents need to be with their children. Perhaps your daughter will grow up in New York. After the war, perhaps you will too. HA!

Last thing: your packages have not reached here. Don't worry, we have a Christmas doll and a pretty frock for Betty Jo already wrapped and under the tree.

I'll write again soon.

Love, Norma

At zero five hundred hours, two three-quarter-ton Dodge ambulances pull in quickly in front of the station. A driver gets out and runs in. "Eleven!" he shouts from the doorway, waiting a fraction of a second too long before adding "Sir," and saluting the captain. "Six in the first car, five in the second. We picked up a casualty along the way."

The captain says nothing, walking out to the driver side window of the closest ambulance, looking at a soldier in the passenger seat. "You," the captain says. "Out and inside. I'll patch up your arm after we evac the badly wounded." He turns to the driver, who followed him out. "You'll take fourteen criticals from here, Private," he says. "Your buddy is lightly wounded — I'll pull the shrapnel out of his arm in ten minutes. He can walk back from here or get in the fight."

The driver follows the captain back into the station, saying, "Nossir, nossir. That's not how it's gonna be. I—"

The captain turns and puts his right hand on his sidearm. "That's an order, Private." The ambulance driver looks at the pistol, then the doctor, then at Jim, then around the room. One of the patients sitting against the wall is wide awake and cradling a carbine.

The ambulance driver is almost choking with anger. "There are German tanks on the heights above town. Third ambulance was hit, driver burned black! Still sitting in the car. You can smell him from here."

"I can't help that man," the doctor says. "Two ambulances, fourteen criticals, two sitters. I'll show you which."

Jim helps load patients on the ambulances. At one point the driver looks at Jim and says, "Goddamn Jew sawbones. Goddamn Army. Goddamn Krauts gonna be here any minute now. I'm not gonna leave Ronnie behind. He'll go on my fucking lap, never mind the size of him. I'ma write my goddamn congressman."

Several patients moan in pain as they're rolled onto

stretchers. One curses bitterly. The boy from Laverne has died, is moved to the floor. Newly wounded come in on litters and on foot, leaning against other soldiers. Jim and the medic settle them into the still-warm cots.

After the ambulances leave, the doctor turns to the room. "That may be the last ride out. If you can walk, you can start west on 332. You'll see the sign. You'll get to Bastogne in eight hours. Let me look at you before you go. Drink as much water as you can hold now and fill your canteen. Salvage warm clothing off these men here." He points to the dead. "Wear your blankets. Don't stop to sleep. You'll die of exposure."

About a dozen soldiers stand up slowly. One soldier uses a cot to pull himself up from the floor and stands up carefully. "If I have walkin' pneumonia, I guess I can walk outta here." He coughs and grimaces with pain.

"See you at Grossinger's, Doc," another soldier says as he pulls on an overcoat. "Sir. I'll be the fat guy smoking a big cigar and holding my wife's hand to make sure I don't float away."

"Private Tanzer, give that man your cassock. You'll stay with me," the doctor says, ignoring Jim's slumping shoulders, "until we get orders to fall back." *If we get orders to fall back*, Jim thinks. "But take a pair of shoepacs—" the doctor points to the dead men—"if you can find any that'll fit."

Through the front windows, Jim sees an American tank, unevenly whitewashed, pass the aid station heading east up the road towards the castle. The commander is standing in the hatch, facing forward.

After being relieved mid-morning, Jim sits in a corner, pulls a butter sandwich out of his pocket, opens a can of K-ration cheese and begins to eat. The food has a tang. There is blood on the bread, blood on the cheese, blood on his hands. It's not his blood. Jim is too tired to care. He eats. He pulls out the can of peaches, then decides to keep it for later.

Jim sleeps on the floor, despite the groans and sobs of the

remaining patients, despite the explosions and small arms fire in the distance, despite more casualties being carried into the station, despite the pockets of his field jacket being rifled by a walking wounded soldier who liberates a cigarette, then examines and puts back the wedding ring that has lived in Jim's left breast pocket since he shipped out.

"Sojer, wake up. Sojer, *wake up*! Colonel Franklin has orders." The Sicilian corporal from Regiment is pushing Jim's shoulder with one hand and offering his canteen with the other. "Coffee," he adds as Jim opens his eyes. Jim holds out his canteen cup. The corporal fills it with coffee, then reaches into his pocket and adds a fat pinch of sugar. Jim stirs with his finger and drinks it down.

"What about…" Jim waves his cup to indicate the men lying in cots and on the floor.

"Not enough fire to hold out here, or fit sojers to defend it. Who *can* get out *needs* to get out. Now. The rest will surrender. You report to Colonel Franklin." The corporal picks up a white bedsheet, turns to the captain, salutes, and says, "Permission to hang this sheet out a window, for surrender, in case the Krauts get this far."

"Yes," the doctor says, returning the salute and turning back to his patients.

Fires ahead spread a flickering orange light as Jim and the corporal exit the train station. From their left come pops of small arms fire, the clanking of tank treads, shouts in German, and the sharp notes of breaking glass. "Kraut infantry is high as a kite," the corporal says. "If they weren't looting the market street, we'd be overrun already. As it is, we only hold the castle and streets around the HQ."

After two blocks, they come upon the whitewashed tank, billowing smoke. One tread is on the ground ahead of it, like an outstretched forearm. The commander is lifeless, draped over the right side of the turret, a curtain of blood on the side of the tank below him. Jim stops to try to make sense of it.

"Brave man," the corporal says. "Keep walking, sojer."

"What about the crew?" Jim finally says.

"Lookit the smoke," the corporal says. "Ammo inside cooked off. Those tankers are gone or dead."

Another block and the noise of fighting has died down. They approach a pharmacy. Inside the pharmacy, Willi has come up from the cellar. He holds several large turnips against his chest with one hand. He winces when the trap door to the cellar slips from his other hand and closes with a bang.

On the street outside, the corporal whispers "Get down," drops to a knee and raises his rifle. Jim throws himself down flat on the street, scraping his hands.

Back inside the house, Willi comes into the front room. "Turnips," he announces. "Not a treat, but better than—"

"Quiet!" Sepp hisses. "We must displace. We'll—"

Willi sees the front window explode, hears a sharp crack. He drops the turnips. They've been hit by lightning. No, they are under fire. Sepp pulls his rifle around from his back and drops to the floor. A hand grenade comes through the window frame and bounces nearby.

Willi turns to run, steps on a turnip and falls hard. He's facing the wrong way to witness Sepp pull himself onto the grenade. Willi does see a bright flash then hears a deafening bang, as do Jim and the small corporal outside. No one sees Sepp rise a foot in the air or hears him fall back to the floor.

Outside, the corporal jerks Jim up off the ground. "Run! Prob'ly more Krauts in there."

Inside, Willi turns and sees his comrade's body, crooked and streaming smoke. Willi crawls away on his elbows. There could be more fire to come from the street.

Jim and the corporal run into the Hotel Claravallis. The Regiment headquarters is a bear-slapped beehive. Staff officers and clerks buzz around with maps and other papers, while soldiers load their rifles with full clips. A machine gun has been lifted onto the front desk, barrel pointing towards the front doors.

The corporal steps in front of a captain and salutes. "This is Private Tanzer," he says, "the runner." The captain nods, takes Jim by the arm, and walks him to the switchboard where Colonel Franklin is scowling into a telephone receiver.

"Repeat. Company strong points are overrun or surrounded," Franklin says. "Our armor is destroyed or displaced. Request permission to withdraw remaining troops. Clervaux is lost. I repeat, Clervaux is lost." He looks Jim up and down as he listens to the answer. A window shatters. Franklin says, "I'm out of time, Colonel," and hangs up, turning to the switchboard operator and saying, "Get me Second Battalion. I'll be back."

He steps away and grabs Jim's arm. "Follow me," he says, pulling him up the main staircase to the third floor, then over to a window facing out the back of the hotel. Several soldiers follow behind them. "Fire escape," Franklin says.

An explosion downstairs sends them staggering across the room. Franklin pulls Jim in closer. "Your orders." He gives Jim the map. "Proceed to Bastogne with the message. And mail this for me when you get there." He gives Jim a letter, then gestures out the window at the steep wooded hill immediately to the rear of the hotel. "Across, over and down through the woods. Head north and west, you'll hit the Bastogne Road at Antoniuschaff. It's on the map."

At the window, Jim looks down through oily smoke to the alley three stories below. Men are feeding papers into a blazing trashcan. The flames illuminate the fire escape, a narrow steel ladder now spanning the fifteen-foot gap from the window to a cement pad on the steep hill opposite. If the ladder was three feet off the ground, he'd just walk over on the rungs.

Jim is unaware his head is shaking *no*. Franklin is, and makes eye contact with a sergeant behind Jim. The man steps forward, says, "Follow me," reaches out the window to a rung of the ladder, and moves feet-behind-hands over to the cliff. "Now, Private," Franklin says to Jim. "Get going before I put my boot up your keester. Look ahead, not down."

Jim's first thought is that officers aren't allowed to kick soldiers. He hears gunshots in the street below, screams, cursing. He leans out the window and grasps the fourth rung of the steel ladder. He feels the cold through his gloves. He gets his knees up on the windowsill, takes a deep breath, leans forward, and pulls his right foot around and onto the closest rung. He moves away from the window, looks down and freezes. After a few seconds, the colonel puts a hand on the back of Jim's right boot. "Bridge walking, Private, just like the obstacle course in basic." Jim starts to hum a couple of bars from "GI Jive," he doesn't know why. "That's it," the colonel says. "Cool as a cucumber." Jim moves his right foot forward. "One hand, one rung," the colonel says. "One foot, one rung." Jim moves forward.

As Jim's hand reaches out for the last rung, the sergeant pulls him by the collar over to the cement pad. "Atta boy," he says. "You made it. Get going now." The sergeant turns and walks back across the ladder, arms outstretched for balance.

Jim stands there, thinking of the tightrope walker he knew in the Von Duke Oriental and European Circus. That was 1937, a lifetime ago. *Maybe I could put that sergeant in a…nah.* Then he turns and begins to scramble up the steep path, humming again. Topping the hill a few minutes later, legs burning, he looks down. The hotel is on fire. He sees muzzle flashes in the alley. The shapes around the flaming trash barrel lengthen as the bangs reach Jim's ears. "Get outta Dodge," he says to himself out loud.

As soon as he starts down the back of the hill, Jim loses the light from the hotel fire. He can make out the trees just in front of him, but not a path. They are so close together he can hand himself from one to the next. He slips and skids, falling several times, before reaching the forest floor and then the road. Jim moves slowly away from the clamor behind him. He thinks about the Sicilian corporal, Colonel Franklin and the others. *Were they able to fall back?*

After a couple of hours of walking, Jim is hungry. He pulls a K-ration out of his pocket. It's a B box. He has an early breakfast on the side of the road. He burns the wax-coated box, warms his hands, puts the cigarettes, toilet paper, and empty cans in his pocket—*leave no clues for any krauts coming up behind me,* he thinks. *Use an empty can for heating water, keep your helmet on your head.* He pats the map and letters in his pocket. On he goes, humming softly.

⟨⟩

JIM HEARS A metallic click up ahead.

"Hands up! *Hände hoch!* Password!"

"I'm American!" Jim shouts.

"That's not the fucking password, Fritz. On the ground!"

THE VAUDEVILLIAN'S FUNERAL
CAMP ROOSEVELT, VIRGINIA
APRIL 4, 1935

THERE'S A COMMOTION the next morning around the male performers' tent. Owen O'Dowd was a replacement. They didn't know him, thought he meant to sleep through breakfast. When Eephus Jones went to wake him for move-out, he saw that the Vaudevillian was dead. His heart, they thought.

The Federal Theatre Troupe improvises a memorial service before they leave for Camp Jefferson, their next show. Jones reads the 23rd Psalm. The Irish tenor sings "Ave Maria." Pearl Olson says the Kaddish.

The sheriff and the county coroner get there around noon.

Looking for information on next of kin, they open O'Dowd's trunk. Inside is a skull with "Yorick" written in pencil on the top. There's also a bayonet inscribed "2nd Calvary Brigade Kettle Hill July 1, 1898—Brother in Victory!" and four faded letters from Ireland that the Vaudevillian's mother had dictated to a scrivener. Owen O'Dowd's given name was Eoghan McGlinchey.

A couple of the boys fashion a simple pine casket for the Vaudevillian. A priest arrives. A firing party wearing pieces of their old uniforms comes up from the men's camp. Camp Roosevelt holds a proper funeral for the Vaudevillian outside before sunset. Jim helps carry the casket to the bed of a supply truck. He watches the Vaudevillian make his exit stage right, next engagement in Arlington, Virginia. *The man died so far from his home,* Jim thinks, *so far from his people.*

8.

ANTONIUSCHAFF, LUXEMBOURG, DECEMBER 18, 1944

> Here's the German. His helmet is easy to spot. Notice the strong lip on the side. Like the Jap, he's tough—if anything, better trained. When you meet up with him in the field, you think of him more as a cog in a big machine than as an individual.
>
> KNOW YOUR ENEMY. A MORALE CORPS PUBLICATION

"WELCOME TO THE most im-paah-tant foxhole in the wah," the young soldier from Boston says. He covers the lens of his GI flashlight with his hand and turns it on to get a better look at who the sergeant has brought.

"What's so important about it?" Jim says, crouching next to him, below the rim of the foxhole.

"I'm in it."

"Hey!" *Heard that line before,* Jim thinks.

"I'm Henry Allison. Allie."

"Jim Tanzer."

Allie points to the dressing on Jim's face. "How's you get hit?"

"Ran a message right into a tree." Jim likes that line, now that he's said it. "In the dark."

"Risky to be a runner." Allie points his covered flashlight at Jim's feet. "Nice shoepacs, Private Tanzah. Where can I get a pair? My feet are soaked."

"I got mine at the aid station in Clervaux."

"I'll pass on Clervaux for now."

"Fighting there."

"I know. Here next, maybe. We're gonna have to dig deeper, though—" Allie points at the bottom of the foxhole—"you being so tall. Here." He unfolds his entrenching tool and gives it to Jim. "Dig for ten minutes, then we'll switch off."

Jim unslings his rifle. "Where are we?"

"The intersection of West Jesus Street and Holy Mother Avenue. Called Antoniuschaff. When the sun comes up, you'll see it's not a real place, it's just where the road from Clervaux meets the road to Bastogne. Where the German tanks start to stretch their legs, if they have any legs left. Low crest of plain, flat farming country. Tank hunting country for our Mustangs. When the weather clears."

"I'm going to Bastogne," Jim says.

"A few German divisions going there too. It's a road hub. Tanks need roads in the Ardennes."

"What are you, Allie?"

"CIC, counter-intelligence clerk. I decode messages."

"You here doing counter-intelligence?"

"Not by a long shot. Colonel Gilbreth combed support staff out of Combat Command, sent us to fight. Decided he could read his own messages. Now I'm here with you in cold and dark somewhere, waiting to see who comes our way, what they bring with them. I don't care fah it."

"What are the Germans up to?"

"Nobody knows."

"What outfit is this?" Jim can't recall what the sergeant told him as they walked to this foxhole, after Jim's identity was cleared up.

"This isn't an outfit, it's Task Force Rose. From 9th Armored Combat Command reserve."

"Rose the flower?"

"Rose the captain. You like a Jewish officer in combat. They don't waste men."

"How would we be wasted?"

Allie points to the Morale Corps insignia on Jim's sleeve. "That flash—not 28th Division. Seen them falling back."

"I'm Morale Corps. Battalion 6817. A 4-4-2, entertainment specialist."

"Hell's bells, Jim, what are you doing at the front?"

"Trying to get to the Comm Zone, to my—"

"Everybody wants to get to the rear. Especially now."

"We have shows booked. Down in Lorraine. Third Army."

"You'll have to get through this show first. Hold your hand over my flashlight." Allie picks up Jim's rifle and brushes dirt off the stock. "Let's check your action. We're both gonna want this thing to shoot."

"Thanks."

"Safety's on, good start," Allie says, pulling back the bolt, which locks with a metallic clink. "Chamber's empty. 'Course, what you think is the rear gonna depend on where you find yourself. If the sergeant picks us out for a patrol, this foxhole—three hundred yards in front of our tanks—this foxhole is the cozy home we want to get back to." Allie pulls the ammo clip from the magazine and turns it over in the muted flashlight beam. "All eight rounds are here. How many clips did you bring with you?"

Jim pats his field jacket pocket. "Two more."

Allie lifts the receiver and barrel assembly away from the stock. "I'll give you some of mine if things heat up. Get a couple of bandoliers when you can. Combatmen say to carry twelve clips at all times at the front."

"I'm not a combatman."

"But while we're in this foxhole—" Allie points over his

shoulder—"back there is the place we want to be. If we're back there, though, Platoon Command Post is the safest place in the world."

"I need to get to—"

"If we were at Platoon, we'd be thinking about how to get back to Company HQ. At Company, we'd look for an excuse to visit Battalion." He takes the flashlight and shines it down the rifle barrel. "Nice and clean, Jim. 'Course, at Battalion we'd begrudge Regiment; at Regiment we'd curse the bastards in Division. Division wants to be at Corps, Corps at Army, Army at Base Section, and, believe it or not, Ripley, Base Section has a low opinion of soldiers back in the States."

This needs to go in Spamlet, Jim thinks. He takes off a glove and reaches down into his jacket pocket for his pencil. It's frozen to the edge of the last butter sandwich. His thumb hurts when he tries to pull the pencil loose. He settles for making a mental note.

Allie re-assembles the rifle, then puts the clip back in with the ham of his hand. "Learned not to leave my thumb in the way," he says as the bolt closes with a distinct snap.

"Sure," Jim says. He has a black thumbnail as a reminder.

Allie gives back the rifle. "You are ready to discourage the enemy from advancing."

Jim snaps his head towards engine noise behind them. "*Whahh?*"

"Just one of the Shermans re-positioning. Smoke?"

"No thanks."

Allie pulls a pack of cigarettes out of his breast pocket. "Never smoked before the Army. Parents were against it. Got a carton of Lucky Strikes while I was boarding the troopship. Took it up out of boredom, mostly."

"They're money."

"Don't worry, this isn't my last cigarette. I plan to survive this war."

It's quiet as Allie squats further down in the foxhole, lights up, and takes a long drag. Jim wonders if the task force has pulled back without them. It's too dark to see. He wants to ask Allie, but doesn't want to appear as frightened as he feels. "I need to catch up with my squad," he says instead. "Probably south of Bastogne by now."

"Before you get wherever on God's frozen earth you're going," Allie says in a plume of smoke and frozen breath, "you just may be the first show business soldier to earn a Combat Infantry Badge. It's the only medal that counts."

"Why?"

"Because officers can't give it to each other."

⌃

"You dig any deeper, we'll be charged with desertion," Allie says. "I need to be able to see out. You can bend your knees a little."

"Okay," Jim says, folding the shovel and giving it back to Allie.

Ten minutes pass. "You're about the oldest private I've met," Allie says. "No deferment?"

"I enlisted."

"Huh? Why?"

"It's…I wanted to do my part. To protect our freedom. The dictators have to be stopped here or we'll be fighting them in America. They want to make slaves out of everyone."

"Sure, we don't want the Germans to enslave us," Allie says. "But you Southerners drive your negroes pretty hard, don't you?"

"I'm not from the South. I'm from West Virginia."

"No Jim Crow there?"

"Not like in the South."

"Were you out of work?"

"Plenty of work since the war started. People have money for lessons. I'm a dance instructor."

"Bored?"

"I had things going on."

"Okay. You're a patriot. That's not so bad."

"I have a daughter."

"No kidding?"

"My wife, she's a singer, Stella Sterling. We run…we ran Tanzer School of Dance in Huntington."

"My parents are still in Bah-ston. So is my fiancée. Ruth. Ruth Pah-kah."

"I know some Parkers in Huntington. I also had a theatrical agency. Have you seen Mr. Chang and his Swing Band?"

"No tickee, no laundry?"

In the dark, Allie can't see Jim frown at this oft-repeated quip. "He's an act I book. Booked. In West Virginia and Ohio. I closed my business for the duration." He thinks briefly of his creditors. "My wife is singing in nightclubs around New York. She sounds a lot like Martha Tilton."

"Your daughter sing?"

"Betty Jo is three. Staying with my parents while Stella—that's my wife's name, she's Stella Sterling onstage—looks for steady work in the city. We were there in 1940."

"Does she *look* like Martha Tilton?" he says.

"I think we're headed for divorce."

"She Dear John'd you?"

"Not yet."

"She take up with an officer while you're over here?"

"It wasn't like that. She got mad that I joined up, wouldn't act like a wife to me after a while, you know—"

"No smooching."

"She didn't even want to *see* me."

"That's a tough break."

"I'll say." Jim's head has started to ache. "How did you get here, Allie?"

"Congress lowered the draft age to eighteen, that's how. My

'Greetings from the President' letter arrived during my freshman year at Boston College. I passed the Army-Navy exam, chose the Army Specialized Training Program. ASTP."

"Why not the Navy?"

"Being on a ship is like being in jail. Plus the chance of drowning."

"I've heard that one," Jim says.

"Borrowed it from Samuel Johnson. Just to prove the point, Uncle Sam sent me over here on a Liberty Ship. Took two weeks for our convoy to cross the Atlantic. Thought our ship would come apart at the rivets. Good preparation for combat, but I can't face the trip back."

"My battalion came over on the *Queen Mary*."

"You don't know how lucky you were."

"We had a cargo of yo-yos. The ship sank 167 times before we got to Scotland."

"I've heard that one."

"Everyone's using it now."

"Goddamn Army sent me to Ol' Miss," Allie says. "Never mind the four ASTPs in Boston."

"That's the Army for you."

"Great duty, though. Tucked away studying math and physics, drinking Cokes, dating co-eds. Just friend dates, since I'm engaged."

"College on Uncle Sam's dime. While there's a war on."

"It was the War Department's plan for manufacturing engineers," Allie says. "Turned out we couldn't bomb Germany out of the war, and the brass underestimated how many soldiers would get chewed up in the ground fighting. They killed the ASTP and made us infantry replacements. Classrooms to foxholes. I'm just lucky my dad had me take typing in high school."

"I went to college for a year myself," Jim says.

"What do you remember about it?"

"I was a cheerleader for a month."

"Let's hear one, Jim. Not too loud."

Jim starts to move his arms in front of his chest and over his head: *"Boogercat, Boogercat, sis boom bah. Give out hope for West Vah-gin-ya! Flim flam, green ham, who the hell are we? Marshall, Marshall, Uni-ver-sa-tee."*

"Entertainment soldier." Jim can sense Allie smiling from the tone of his voice. "Why only a month?"

"I got a Youth Administration job," Jim says. *Had enough of being on the bottom of the pyramid*, he thinks.

"You meet all kinds of folks in this man's Army."

"I was in a play at Marshall."

"What play?"

"*Robot Hamlet.*"

"Never heard of *Robot Hamlet*. Tell me about it. Don't leave anything out. It's a long night in this hole."

"It went over big," Jim says after retelling as much as he could, including how moonshine-drunk the Moo Moos got before the performance. And how they drenched themselves in Bay Rum aftershave and chewed Sen-Sen breath mints to survive the interview with Dean Shawkey the next day.

"Quite a show," Allie says, well pleased with the tale.

"I'm working on a sequel, *Spamlet*. An expose of the Army. Robots instead of soldiers."

There's more clatter behind them. "Wish I was in that tank right about now," Jim says.

"You're better off in this hole than in a can. Panzers have longer range, more armor, bigger shells. If their tanks fight here, half our Shermans will shoot and scoot in the first five minutes, or get lit up." Allie bends down and lights another cigarette. "No cover for them, except back down the road."

"Back down the road?"

Ally takes a long drag. "But in a tank is better than being a lieutenant. They have to run around in plain view giving orders and acting calm while the captain stays back and thinks up dangerous things for us to do. Sargeant Kowalski was in Normandy, told me he saw more lieutenants on the ground bleeding than standing up." He picks a tobacco shred off his lower lip. Jim shakes his head.

"You and I are only responsible for ourselves," Allie continues. "Those poor lieutenants, they're responsible for themselves *and* us. Some of them don't even shave every day." Allie rubs his cheek. "Neither do I for Chrissake." So ended Jim's thoughts about what Stella would think if he got a field commission.

Allie closes his eyes and smokes. After a couple of minutes, he adds, "You know who else I feel sorry for? Those German bastards. Not the SS gangsters. But the draftees, those Volksgrenadiers, some of them are older than you." Jim grimaces slightly. "Or boys. Out here in this weather. Being sacrificed to buy Hitler, what, another month or two? Their people back home getting hit night and day."

Tank motors start up again behind them. *Too far behind us,* Jim thinks. "What's gonna happen now?" he asks.

"Artillery has to keep the Krauts out of range until the cavalry arrives."

"Artillery?"

"73rd Field Artillery Battery west of us. Howitzers. They have a forward observer back near our Shermans." Jim looks back but can't see the tanks in the darkness. "They need to drop enough fire to hold back the German column long enough that we get reinforced."

"Who will reinforce us?"

"Don't know. Patton's army is in France, a hundred miles south of here. Maybe Airborne will drop here. Don't spill that, if you get captured."

"Captured?" Jim says, beginning to piece together "I surrender" in German. *Ich mich* something.

"If that artillery battery displaces, we're gonna get clobbered," Allie says.

"What about air support?"

"Ceiling's too low. You'll see when the sun rises. We're on our own until the weather clears. Captain Rose's fondest hope has to be that we look bigger than we are, bounce the Krauts north a couple of miles, and we reach our fallback positions before they do."

"Fallback positions?"

"Longvilly." Allie grinds his cigarette out on the side of the foxhole. "Bastogne, if Longvilly doesn't hold."

"If they don't bounce north?"

"We take a bite out of their column before they kick our teeth in."

"Can we fall back now?"

"We were put here to buy time, Jim. Only way we do that is to stand and fight. If the Germans come up this road."

"I hope they don't."

"You and me both." Allie says. "You and me both." He field strips the cigarette butt and sprinkles the shreds on the bottom of the foxhole.

"Can we fall back now?" Jim knows they can't, but has to say it again. "I need to get back to my squad."

"You'd have to get past the sergeants."

"In the dark?"

"There are MPs down the road."

Jim shivers. "I hope it warms up some."

"I'm afraid it's gonna."

"What? Oh."

"There are woods five hundred yards up the road in front of us. Kraut infantry forms up there, if they're coming at us." Allie points to Jim's rifle. "How did you rate?"

"Marksman."

"Oh well, they have to get close to throw grenades at us."

"I qualified Expert in bazooka."

"Keep that to yourself."

"One of your lieutenants asked me."

"Shit."

"Allison?" from several yards behind them.

"He'll find us anyways," Allie says to Jim. He covers his flashlight and turns it on. "Here, sir."

A second lieutenant goes down on one knee next to their foxhole. "Okay," he says, returning Jim's salute. "I brought up a bazooka and a satchel of rockets. Private here is rated Expert. You load, he'll shoot."

"I need to be back with my squad," Jim says.

The lieutenant continues, "You two are in defilade. The next soldier on your right is Omar Bradley at 12th Army in Luxembourg City. Do not allow the enemy to flank you."

He doesn't understand, Jim thinks. *I shouldn't be here.*

Allie doesn't bother to challenge the idea that two riflemen with a bazooka are going to stop a Panzer company from executing a flanking maneuver. Allie does register the sword and key insignia on the young officer's collar. Quartermaster Corps. Jewish Calvary. Christ almighty. "Sergeant Kowalski coming up, sir?" Allie says.

"He's up here," the lieutenant says, an edge in his voice. Even quartermaster officers know that in combat, GIs want their orders from their sergeant. "Checking the other men. Listen to me," he says, and repeats what he's been told. "No air recon today. The Germans will send scouts first, like we would. Look for little grey men at the edge of the woods up ahead around first light. They'll try to draw fire, see what we have stacked up here."

Jim raises a hand. "My unit is on the way to—"

"Your unit is Task Force Rose, Private," the lieutenant says, then turns to Allie. "Don't fire at their scouts unless they're close enough to toss a grenade at you. Don't leave your hole without an order."

"Got it, sir," Allie says.

"Don't shoot our patrol coming back," the lieutenant says, looking at Jim. "What's the password?"

"Ophelia," Allie says.

"Good. Now, if the Krauts try to advance through our position—what they came here for—they're gonna walk infantry behind tanks. Our machine gunners will knock down the infantry. Then bazooka teams—you guys—hit their tanks." Allie barely nods. Jim looks down. He can just about see his own feet. "Don't shoot at a tank rolling towards you. Let it roll past you, even right over your hole. You did that drill in basic."

Jim recalls how shitty that tank-rolling-over-your-foxhole drill was—the noise, the exhaust, the trapped feeling. "I'm a—"

"Then you fire the rocket into the back of the tank," the lieutenant says to Jim. "The ventilation screen. If you miss, you miss low. You don't hit us behind you."

"What a—" Allie bites his lip and looks away.

The lieutenant ignores the interruption. "Duck down in your hole after your shot. What's left of Kraut infantry is gonna look for the bazooka that stopped their tank. Count to ten, throw grenades out in front, both of you, cook them two seconds—no more—so they can't come back. Don't stand up and throw; you'll get shot. Throw from inside the hole." He mimes a shot-put. "Pop up right after the explosions and empty a clip at any Krauts still standing."

Allison puts his hands in his pockets. He's not buying this John Wayne crap, but what can he say? Jim continues to stare at his feet.

"Take out any Kraut infantry carrying Panzerfausts. We can't have them near our Shermans." Jim has heard about those single-use anti-tank weapons. He doesn't want to see one.

"Sir," Allie says, "what if the Panzers just stay back, hit our tanks from three thousand yards?"

The lieutenant stares at Allie for a few seconds. "You have your orders, Private. Safety off for the watcher, fix bayonets." Even Jim knows you don't fix bayonets in a foxhole. The lieutenant continues, "Krauts could infiltrate these front positions in this dark. Keep your helmet strapped. It's not gonna pull your head off in a blast. That's hooey."

Jim has started to shake. "You're gonna be too busy killing tanks to be scared, soldier," the lieutenant says to him.

"I'm not scared," Jim says. "I'm cold."

"I'm scared *and* cold," Allie says.

"Hold on. It'll be warmer after sun-up," the lieutenant says.

"I'm a 4-4-2, entertainment GI. I need to be back—"

"You're gonna put on a show here," the lieutenant answers. "Questions?"

"You think this war will be over by Christmas?" Allie says with a smile.

"No. But the Krauts are giving you more chances to win that Silver Star and be a hero." The lieutenant stands up and walks away.

"That's not a plan," Allie says to Jim. "That's a fucking fairy tale." He gives a deep sigh. "The lieutenant ought to be the entertainment specialist."

"Does he know I'm—"

"Silver Star. What bullcrap. Not only would we have to survive doing something crazy, an officer would have to see us do it, and *he* has to survive long enough to make a report. And his CO has to care enough to get the paperwork done. We get our decoration on the fourth of July—graveside ceremony."

After a few minutes of looking east, Jim says, "Still don't see anything."

"This dark, German scouts more likely to fall into our foxhole than to shoot us."

Jim touches the scabbard on his belt. "Use my bayonet as a knife?"

"Your shovel will be better, if it comes to that," Allie says.

"Don't have one." It's next to his mess kit by the side of the road, near Hosingen.

"We don't know those guys in the other holes," Allie says. "They don't know us. First combat for most of us. Never mind about tanks rolling over our foxhole. If artillery doesn't keep Kraut armor a half mile away, we fire and fall back. Not gonna hang around shooting spitballs at a Tiger tank."

"Then what?"

"By then, something's gonna be on fire behind us." Allie has listened to combatmen talking. "We run back straight, we're silhouetted, Krauts will pick us off. You and I are going south through the field for a quarter mile, then come up *behind* our tanks, get back in the scrap."

"Let's go."

"We have to fight before we fall back," Allie says.

"What?"

"I didn't leave my mom and dad and my fiancée in Bahston and do all that lousy training at Fort Benning and Ol' Miss and Camp McCain, and puke on a troopship for two weeks, and march around England for two months in the rain and sit in France for three months and polish my boots and wear a tie, so I could run away before Fritz even shows his face. What would I tell my folks? What would I tell Ruth?"

"I'm supposed to be in Lorraine by now," Jim says, stamping his feet to try to warm them.

"I'm supposed to be halfway to an accounting degree by now. The sooner we whip the Germans, the sooner we get back to our lives." They leave off talking.

"Hear that?" Jim says, his voice rising to countertenor.

"Birds. Dawn is coming."

"Too cold to sleep, anyways."

"Too dangerous, anyways," Allie answers. "I'm not even gonna try. We can make a fire now, have coffee." He pulls a Luger out of his field jacket pocket. "Time to say goodbye to this beauty. Won it in a poker game." He stands up and flings it end over end into the field to the right of them. "Say we're captured, I don't want some SS murderer finding that souvenir on me."

The black darkness is shading to grey. Water has come to a boil in Jim's helmet on Allie's Coleman stove. Jim leans down to add the Nescafe packets. "Jesus *Christ*," Allie says. "I see them!"

Jim stands straight up. Allie pulls him down below ground level and points over his shoulder. "Patch of woods at two o'clock. Those little pine trees are *men*. Put your helmet on. Take a look but stay low. May be snipers up in the trees."

His eyes at ground level, Jim sees flashes in the tree line. Then comes cracks of rifle fire and that machine gun rip. He hears buzzing overhead, looks up and sees elongated red flashes above their hole. "Tracer bullets," Allie says. "German."

Jim hears a steady *bink! bink! bink!* as the American tanks are hit. He sees white tracers knuckleball towards the woods as Task Force Rose returns fire. His head is hot. Liquid seeps down his face. He's about to ask Allie if he is bleeding through the dressing when some of the liquid reaches his mouth. It's coffee.

Allie and Jim alternate watching to the front for Germans, and to the back for signals from Sergeant Kowalski. "Remember, they don't advance, we don't fire," Allie says. The firing ebbs and flows for a few minutes. Jim winces when three grey and white geysers erupt two hundred yards in front of the foxhole—*fu-wamp, fu-wamp, fu-wamp*—followed by a rush of air on his face. He ducks down.

"Artillery letting the Krauts know they have this road sited," Allie says, a bit breathless.

"What do we do?" Jim says, a bit squeaky.

"We wait." Allie pulls the bazooka tube into the foxhole, shakes his head. "Not gonna use that on German scouts. They aren't coming any closer. They just want to get an idea of what we got here. Hope we look scary."

The Germans withdraw by sunrise, zero nine hundred hours in

the Ardennes in December. Jim and Allie eat breakfast, K-rations Kowalski brings up from the roadblock. Jim makes coffee again, adding malted milk tablets and D-ration bar shavings. "Good to the last drop," he says, relaxed now. He has convinced himself that the Germans aren't coming back this way.

They drink their coffee, hands wrapped around their canteen cups to use the heat. Sergeant Kowalski returns with a precious can of white gas for the Coleman stove, more clips and hand grenades, but no change in orders. Allie sleeps during Jim's watch.

Around 1200 hours, Jim hears a faint whistle, then a *fu-wamp*. Allie wakes. Shells begin to land out of sight in front of them, one every two minutes. Other than occasional motor noise behind them, nothing else happens. Jim calms his nerves by talking—somewhat rapidly—about Charlie McCarthy and Edgar Bergen, the Civilian Conservation Corps, his short stint as a circus clown, working in the Catskills and at the New York World's Fair of 1939, the crazy show he produced in New Haven, and teaming up with Private Mickey Rooney.

The shelling stops a little after 1300 hours. After ten minutes, Allie says, "This isn't good for us."

Twenty minutes later, thick white smoke begins to flow out of the woods in front of them. "Look at that fog," Jim says.

"Willy Pete," Allie says.

"What?"

"White phosphorus."

"Why?"

"For cover. They're gonna move up."

"What should we do?"

"Be ready to shoot. They can't see us either now."

The ripping sound returns after several minutes, then the *pang!* of mortar rounds landing. The task force returns fire into the smoke. Jim begins to hear clanking and motor noise, loud behind them but also up ahead, fainter.

He startles and cries out when Sergeant Kowalski dives next to the foxhole. "You come with me," he says to Jim. "Allie, I'll be back."

Allie looks at the sergeant and shakes his head a bit, turns towards Jim and smiles. "Good luck, Jim. See that you make it back to your wife and daughter."

Jim nods, says, "Luck."

Jim and the sergeant weave their way back to the roadblock, crouching as low as they can and still run. Jim's thighs burn, he's not cold anymore. It seems a mile back to the Shermans. They straighten up as they run past the tanks. Jim heads towards a Jeep pointed away from the fight. He sees an MP in the driver's seat and two passengers—one collapsed against the back seat, bloody bandage over one side of his face, the other in the front passenger seat, an officer, bent double. It's the quartermaster lieutenant. A medic is crouched next to him.

Kowalski catches Jim by the sleeve. "Stay with me!" They run to a tree. A radioman and a captain are there. Captain Rose. The sergeant lets Jim loose, shouts, "Private Tanzer!" then turns and runs back the way he came.

"Your orders, Private," Captain Rose says, handing him back the map. "Take the message to Colonel Galbreath in Longvilly." Rose holds up an envelope. "And mail this letter for me." Then he points to the idling Jeep. "Go with them. Hold the wounded men so they don't fall out."

⌃

Task Force Rose loses support from Field Artillery Battery C at 1400 hours. Shortly thereafter, German tanks initiate concentrated fire. It appears to Captain Rose to be at least one battalion.

He loses a third of his tanks within the first ten minutes, but destroys or immobilizes several German tanks and assault guns. Bazooka fire from infantry deployed forward of the task force's gun positions delays the enemy advance, but German armor and infantry numbers are far superior, and the enemy begins to prevail around the thirtieth minute.

Reached by radio, Colonel Gilbreath communicates General Middleton's order to block the road for as long as possible, rather than pull back to Longvilly in good order. The task force stops being a coherent combat unit shortly thereafter. Captain Rose later forwards notices of conspicuous bravery by several soldiers, including Sergeant Stanislaus Kowalski and Private Henry Allison, who were observed directing timely and accurate bazooka fire on advancing German armor. Both are rated as missing in action.

⟁

THE QUARTERMASTER CORPS lieutenant is grey and still by the time the Jeep approaches the sentries in front of Longvilly. *I'm the only person in the world who knows he's dead*, Jim thinks, continuing to hold the lieutenant by the collar. *He's still alive to his family.*

The Jeep is subject to long stares from the sentries. Battle sounds have been filtering back from the roadblock. A sentry asks, "How's it going up there?" but not for a password. The MP replies, "It's a fight." The wounded GI and the dead lieutenant are dropped off at the field hospital, now preparing to fall back. The MP pulls the Jeep up to a stone farmhouse.

The 9th Armored Combat Command headquarters in Longvilly is its own version of yesterday's scene at Regiment in Clervaux; preparing to hold their ground, but waiting for the order to fall back. A colonel is next to a map table in the front room, holding a telephone receiver to his ear. Two captains are bent over a map. Four junior officers and two clerks are also in the room, including an operator looking at his switchboard, but listening intently to what the colonel is saying.

A clerk in the corner is typing loudly, hoping to show that form SF-44 requires him to stay at his desk and out of combat. A layer of cigarette smoke fogs the ceiling. On a table by the wall is a pile of thick Spam and cheese sandwiches and a steaming white enamel coffee pot. Jim reaches down to his pocket and touches the can of peaches.

The colonel talks into the receiver. "Sir, Task Force Rose is cut to pieces. Task Force Harper is under bombardment. German force reported as SS tank battalions, infantry, and assault guns."

One of the captains looks up at Jim and the MP, points to the door, and follows them out. The MP salutes. "Escorting runner with a message from Task Force Rose to Colonel Galbraith, sir," he says. "Turning over to you. Request permission to return to Task Force Rose."

"At ease, Sergeant. Follow your orders. Bring back Captain Rose, wounded or not." The captain turns to Jim. "Give me the message, Private." Jim hands him the map. The captain is aware that this printed representation of Hitler's delusions has been corroborated by several other captured documents, and that events on the ground are already rendering it obsolete. This runner's life has been risked in order to deliver what is likely just a terrific souvenir. He shakes his head and unfolds the map.

"It needs to get to General Middleton," Jim says, then adds, "I'm an entertainment specialist."

The captain looks it over. "You got it this far; deliver it to the general yourself. In the meantime, take your orders from Sergeant Rizzo." The captain points to a short, stocky man waiting in the doorway.

"Not for non-coms in *this* Army," Rizzo says in response to Jim's salute. "Come with me. Your new squad is gonna plant some anti-tank mines. You're with combat engineers now. Nothing better in the Army."

The firing has stopped up the road. "It's so quiet here, Sergeant," Jim says as they step away from the farmhouse.

"You ever had to wait while your mother picked a switch to beat you with?" Rizzo says.

THE HUMAN CANNONBALL
Ironton, Ohio
July 16, 1937

"*Aahhh*" from the crowd as a spotlight up in the fly rigging cuts through the smoke and hits the cannon. The spotlight above the cannon hits the net at the other end. "*Oooh.*" Jim Tanzer, JoJo, and the two other clowns are ostentatiously cycling their heads back and forth between the cannon and the net, shaking with fear. It's funny.

Jim did not return to Marshall after the Civilian Conservation Corps, but took a job at his uncle's bread factory instead. This allowed him to help his family—the economy had reversed course after several years climbing out of the Great Depression, and Norma's work hours were cut back—and to professionalize his ballroom dancing with lessons. The colored janitor at the factory gave him advanced tap instruction, showed him how to dance with a mop for a partner. After a few months, Jim began doing a solo routine for tips on Tuesday nights at Froggy's Lounge. He didn't tell his mother he was done with college, but did delight her by dating Vicky Snodgrass, a chubby society girl he met at Marshall.

After fourteen months of this life, however, he impulsively began his full-time show business career by hiring on with the Prince Von Duke European and Oriental Circus, a coal circuit outfit. Jim's novel dancing clown ideas were rapidly subsumed by the traditional slapstick.

A third spotlight hits the ringmaster, Lou Prince, in the middle of the floor. "Ladies and gentlemen, boys and girls!" he shouts into his megaphone. "I must ask you to remain calm and in your seats—" he holds for two beats—"as Mario Zaccardi attempts a new world record human cannonball shot."

The spot picks up Mario, lithe as a matador in his tight red and white leather jumpsuit, and his fat cousin Zeppo. To gain experience, the two have been farmed out to Lou Prince for the 1937 season. Human cannonball is the Zaccardi family business.

The act slots for eight minutes. Shooting-flying-landing takes four seconds. There will be much stage business before Mario is fired out of the gun. The orchestra, led for this season by the German refugee Walter Szell, plays "Mars, the Giver of War." The audience recognizes it as the leitmotif of Mingo the Merciless in the radio serial *Flash Gordon*. Just under the "Mars" score, the orchestra has "Stars and Stripes Forever" at the ready for an accident or, much worse, a fire.

After much tinkering with the cannon, Zeppo and Mario exchange Mussolini-style Roman salutes, arms outstretched, then a grave see-you-in-the-next-world-if-no-longer-in-this-one embrace. As usual, Zeppo's breath is garlicky horrible. Mario steps away and crosses himself three times, then dons his helmet. He climbs a stepladder and eases into the gun barrel up to his waist. Jim and the other clowns stop their shenanigans. Mario's life hangs in the balance. They are not to break the spell.

The audience is bought-in. You could hear a pin drop. Mario waves farewell, turns, and pretends to say something important to Zeppo, who solemnly nods. Mario disappears into the gun barrel.

The house lights come up. A sharp drum roll begins. The Ringmaster commences the countdown. At "five" the prop man drops a cherry bomb into the bang barrel. The cannon works on compressed air, not gunpowder. Light and barrel smoke are supplied by the flash pot positioned just under the cannon, concealed by a knee-high cloud from the fog machine. The human cannonball must be past the flash pot when it pops, or get another burn on his face.

"Three, two, one…" The lions reflexively crouch at the *bang!* but keep their eyes on the net. They've seen this act before. A pink blur exits the barrel. Mario. He thrusts his arms wide, arches his back, and jackknifes his legs as he reaches the peak of his trajectory. *Long!* he thinks as he rotates to land on his back.

Jim winces as Mario skids off the back of the net and breaks his right wrist on one of the hay bales. Why would anyone want to make their living risking injury and death every day and twice on Saturday? Jim isn't yet aware of how well it pays.

The spot follows Mario as he walks back across the tent floor to the cannon, slight wobble at first, then measured and steady, waving his good arm and gauging his pace by how long he judges the applause will last. Seeing that Mario is going to make the distance unaided, Jim and the other clowns retreat to Clown Alley. The Ringmaster announces the new world record. Here come Hailey's Parrots. The show continues.

9.

LONGVILLY, BELGIUM, DECEMBER 19, 1944

> The German 88mm gun, also known as the "eighty-eight," is a high muzzle velocity anti-aircraft gun the Germans sometimes deploy for anti-tank operations. It fires HE (High Explosive) and AP (Armor-Penetrating) rounds. It has a rapid rate of fire and the ability to engage targets at long distances. Effective reconnaissance and accurate counter-battery fire will suppress or eliminate the threat posed by the 88mm gun.
>
> Know Your Enemy, a Morale Corps Publication

Sleeping on the farmhouse floor in all his clothes and his boots, Jim is oblivious to the muffled shout of "Romeo" from outside the back door. The subsequent rapping on the door wakes him. A dripping Sergeant Rizzo walks out of the dark into the kitchen. "Douse that," he says, pointing at the iron stove. "Come dawn, fog lifts, Krauts will see the smoke."

The nine GIs in the house gather around their sergeant. "Combat Command is falling back to Bastogne," he begins. "The task forces east and north of us are moving in the same direction. Things are all balled up. We buy them time to get to Bastogne, then we displace, regroup with 9th Armored there."

"Who is 'we,' Sarge?" from a wiry soldier. Unshaven, dirty, with dark circles under his eyes, this man appears to Jim to have seen plenty of combat in the last few days. Jim doesn't realize that he looks the same, with the addition of a wound dressing on his face.

Rizzo takes off his helmet. "Us here, plus a Tank section, two .81 mortar squads."

"How far behind us are they?" The wiry combatman asks.

"Three hundred yards."

"Mortars sighted?"

"No."

"Spotters?"

"Us."

"Mines?"

"We spread anti-tank mines last night," Rizzo says. Jim remembers. Hair-raising. "Around the elbow on the road. Ground's not frozen; German tanks have to stay on the road. Where they hit the mines, we're in defilade. We hold them there for an hour, Combat Command makes it to Bastogne."

"An hour is a long time," the wiry combatman says.

Rizzo nods. "This farmhouse is cover. From here we kill or discourage the engineers they send to clear mines. You know not to waste fire on tanks unless you have a target standing in the turret."

"Anything else, Sarge?"

"We have a tube and a couple cartons of rockets," the sergeant says. "Anyone here qualified on bazooka?" The men look off into the middle distance. Jim looks down at his shoe-pacs. "Sure," the sergeant continues. "I'll shoot, choose a loader when the time comes."

"Sarge, what if the Krauts get on us before dawn?" the wiry combatman says.

"That'll be a patrol. Snap them up. They sound like a drawer full of spoons when they walk."

A soldier holds out a pitchfork. "Won't have to shoot them bastards, give away our position."

"Jesus H. Christ, Smiley!" the wiry combatman says. "You're a cold-blooded son of a bitch."

"*Gesù Cristo*," Rizzo says. "Use your rifle. This ain't *Frankenstein*."

"Um," Jim speaks up. "Like I said, Sergeant, I'm a runner." He touches the dressing on his face. "I have a captured German map. Important that it get to General Middleton in Bastogne."

Rizzo has had enough. "It can't be too important, they let you keep it," he says, and points to Jim's rifle. "What you got there, Private Tanzer?"

The combatman smiles. He's heard this routine before.

"My rifle, Sarge."

"Correct. Are you a man or a woman, Tanzer?"

"Yes, Sarge, a man," Jim says.

"You're a man with a rifle," Rizzo continues, smiling. "You're a fucking *rifleman*, Private. And these men—" he extends his arm—"are your fucking buddies. And *you* are *their* fucking buddy. And you don't run down the road, leave your buddies in a tight spot. *Capisci?*"

"Yes, sir. I don't."

"That's right, Private," Rizzo says. "We're lucky you joined us." There's silence around the room.

"What unit were you?" the wiry combatman asks Jim. Everybody listens.

"Morale Corps."

"Bring us a movie?"

"That's an 0-6-0. I'm 4-4-2. Jeep shows, soldier shows."

"Put on a good show here, Private," Rizzo says, "then we *all* go to Bastogne, have drinks with General Middleton." There is a long silence.

"We know how much is coming?" the wiry combatman finally asks Rizzo.

"This weather, no recon. But enough to roll over three roadblocks," he says.

Jim closes his eyes and thinks of Allie, hopes he's okay.

Sergeant Rizzo addresses a young GI holding a Springfield rifle with a sniper scope. "Up to the attic at first light, Bobby. Be ready when the fog lifts. Third tank in, that's the commander. Blow his brains out, or button him up at least. Then discourage their engineers digging up our mines."

"Sarge," the boy says, nodding.

"It's pretty still outside. Your windage will be close to zero."

"I'll check it," the boy says.

"Good." Rizzo looks around. "You guys see a Jeep coming from that direction, not under fire, it's Krauts. Kill the driver, let it wreck, then kill any passengers that move. Kill any horses pulling guns. Get the cows out of the barn and in front of us at first light. Cover. Krauts'll hesitate to destroy rations on the hoof."

"After that?" the combatman asks.

"We hold as long as we can. On my order, or yours—" he points to the wiry combatman—"if I'm…" He takes a breath. "We displace, re-form south of the town, see what we can do from there. Then we're back down the N-4 to Bastogne. Through the woods if we have to." He looks at Jim. "You're still attached to the 9th Armored when we get there, don't forget." Jim just nods. "I'll be back," Rizzo says, puts his helmet on his head and steps out the door into the dark. Jim pats the can of peaches in his field jacket pocket.

"I can't shoot a horse," Smiley says.

"But you'll shoot a man!" the wiry combatman says.

"No horse is trying to kill me."

"You might as well shoot Colonel Galbraith if you're going after people trying to get you killed," the wiry combatman says, then turns to Jim. "How'd you get into a Morale unit?

"I volunteered."

"For Morale?"

"For infantry. Army put me in Morale Corps."

"How'd you do on rifle marksmanship?"

"Marksman."

"Don't be the first to shoot. You'll irritate the hell out of us if you draw fire."

Jim passes the next hour and a half alternatively crouching by the east-facing window or pacing around the dark house. He pulls his can of peaches out of his pocket three times, and three times puts it back. A weak light creeps into the farmhouse kitchen around zero nine hundred hours. Fog has visibility at forty feet.

That freight-train noise. Jim's heart sinks as shelling begins. He winces at each *fu-wamp!* as they land. He wants to ask who was firing what, but doesn't want to sound like a rube and, really, what does it matter? He takes a drink from his canteen, almost chokes at the first moan from German rockets overhead. The wiry combatman glances in Jim's direction. "That mail isn't addressed to us. Nebelfuckers do make a noise, though, don't they? Screaming meemies. They're just for show. The .88s are the danger. The round is on you or past you before you hear it."

Jim hooks his canteen back on his belt. "Got any smokes you can spare your buddies?" the combatman asks.

Jim hands around three K-ration cigarette packs, comes off as a square Joe. Then he says, "I need to fall back. The map…" He pulls it out of his jacket pocket.

"Only a crumbum falls back without his buddies," Smiley says.

"He knows that, Smiley," the wiry combatman says, looking squarely at Jim. "He'll do okay. Wasn't trained for combat."

"Goddamn Army trains every soldier for combat," Smiley says. "Emilio here's a fucking baker. He's not crying to run and cook biscuits for Ike. Lemme see that." He grabs the map out of Jim's hand. "Whoa! Now *that's* a souvenir." He passes it around.

"I have to get it to General Middleton," Jim finally says, taking it back.

"Bad to get captured with souvenirs," the combatman says, holding up an ornamental SS dagger. "Got it from a German officer. In front of Saint-Lô. He was on the ground, shot through a lung. He traded this fancy knife for a round in the head." He sees Jim startle. "You don't take SS prisoners, Tanzer. You know they wear a different uniform from the German regulars, right?"

Jim can only manage a nod.

"I don't want you caught with a bloody German map," the combatman says. "I'll push it in the manure pile out back along with the knife. Retrieve it all when this is over."

"Sure," Jim says, thinks he'll tell General Middleton where to find it when he gets to Bastogne.

"Fog has lifted," a soldier at the window says. "Shit, there's a—"

A bright flash knocks Jim to the floor. He doesn't hear the deafening *whanng-crack*. He floats in silence until a low roar slowly manifests itself. He settles back down on his back, not able to breathe. Finally, he gasps a breath. Then another. He remembers where he is. The only thing he can see through the smoke and dust is daylight streaming through a manhole-sized breach in the kitchen wall.

Jim hears "Who's hit?" above the roar, but can't answer. His mouth and nose are clogged with plaster dust and paint chips. He rolls over and up on his knees, then spits three times on the map on the floor directly below his face. Crimson drops of drops are landing around Bastogne. He sees the SS dagger sticking out of his hip. He cries out, "Mutti! Medic!" but makes no sound.

The roar in his ears subsides. Jim recognizes his own heartbeat. His hand brushes against a rifle butt. He remembers that German soldiers are approaching. How close? He picks up the rifle and unlocks the safety. "Which way?" he calls out, a high-pitched "*wha-wah?*"

"Don't shoot!" It's the wiry combatman, crouching nearby. Other figures rise in the smoke and dust. Covered in plaster dust, they look like ghosts.

"My hip!" Jim gets it out this time. The wiry combatman kneels next to him, puts a hand on the hilt of the dagger and yanks it out. A scraping sound. Jim feels no pain. Water gurgles onto Jim's leg.

"Your canteen's caught it, Tanzer." The wiry combatman puts his finger over the gash and lifts the canteen from Jim's web belt. "Rinse your mouth."

Jim rinses, spits, hears gasping to his right. The wiry combatman is crouched over a grey figure lying still, right arm under his back in an impossible angle. Smiley. "No one else down?" the wiry combatman asks. "Okay. Take your positions, wait for targets." The other GIs nod, pick up their rifles, and move to the windows. The machine gunner and his assistant walk to their position. Jim slowly gets to his feet. He steadies himself on the kitchen table as the room zigs and zags.

"Stuff this up your nose." The wiry combatman hands Jim a pack of K-ration toilet paper.

"What? Oh."

"That was an .88. Armor-penetrating round, thank Christ. In the back wall, out the front. If it was an HE round, we'd be burning like torches. Krauts must want this house intact, don't know if anyone's home."

Jim's head begins to throb. He puts a hand to his temple. The dressing on his face is gone, but the wound has scabbed up. "That's your eighty-*ache*," the combatman says. "Concussion headache. We all have it. Goes away in a day. Or two."

"This map. I've got to get…"

There's a bang in the middle distance. "Krauts finally hit a mine," the combatman says with a thumbs-up, then points to Smiley. "Take him to the aid station."

"What?"

"Take him to the aid station. Just off the road, about three hundred yards back. Then come back, you hear us still firing."

"He's too big for me to carry," Jim says.

"Can't spare a man, this fight." Smiley moans as the wiry combatman pulls him up to sitting. "Drag him by the collar." With a dainty motion of thumb and forefinger he pinches the wounded man's right sleeve. Smiley screams as his unmoored arm is pulled around and placed on his stomach. Blood from his ear spreads down his powdered neck.

"His war is over, but he's gonna be bowling leftie from now on," the combatman says to Jim. *Might be worth it, if he lives*, Jim thinks. The combatman reaches into his jacket pocket and pulls out a small aluminum tube with a long plastic tip covering a needle. Morphine syrette, Jim registers, and pats the one in his pocket. The combatman pulls up Smiley's field jacket, sweaters, and shirts, stabs him in the belly at a shallow angle. He squeezes the tube flat, pulls it out and pokes the needle through the collar of Smiley's jacket.

Jim nods his head and silently offers his syrette. The combatman looks at it, pauses, then shakes his head. "Let's be careful with him," he says. "The doc can give him more at the aid station." He points to Jim's rifle. "Leave us your spare clips. We'll give them back when you return."

Smiley opens his eyes. "Got your million-dollar wound," the combatman says to him. "Hold your broke arm so it don't flop, Smiley. You're gonna be all right."

There are bangs from the attic. The boy sniper has targets. The Germans know the farmhouse is defended. The combatman looks Jim in the eyes. "Go." Jim begins to pull the wounded man across the kitchen floor. Smiley screams again and passes out.

Jim is willing to drag Smiley to Bastogne, but Sargeant

Rizzo runs up and helps him pull the wounded man into what remains of the aid station. Then he turns Jim around to go back. They walk behind a Sherman moving up the road towards the farmhouse. The smoke from a smoldering heap of papers makes Jim's eyes tear up. Then a piercing *whinnngg* and a jarring *crack*. Rizzo and Jim are knocked on their backs. The Sherman rocks violently back and forth, begins to spout grey and orange. It's still rocking when Rizzo climbs up the back and reaches for the hatch.

Another *whinnngg* and *crack*. Jim doesn't see Sergeant Rizzo blown up in the air, but he does hear the *thud* when Rizzo lands, sees him lying on his stomach, head back on his shoulder blades like the hood of a raincoat. For a few seconds Jim can't understand what's happened. Then he mashes his helmet down on his head and undoes the chin strap.

The tank is brewing up, enveloped in smoke and flames. Jim feels the heat, hears muffled bangs as ammo cooks off inside the hull. The roar in his ears is back, but even so, Jim hears that awful ripping sound of German machine guns. He gets to his knees, sees a soldier come out of the farmhouse, run for a few steps, bend over as though to pick a flower, then fall. *The rest of the fellas will come out the back of that farmhouse any second now*, Jim thinks. *No sense in running through machine gun fire to get back. I'll explain it to Sarge later.* Then he remembers about Rizzo. *People die so fast, in a war.*

Looking ahead, Jim sees a column of German tanks stopped at the elbow of the road up beyond the farmhouse. Their guns are turned ninety degrees, pointing at him. He recalls the model train setup in the Lazarus window at Christmas he loved as a child. Then he sees little grey figures spilling off the road and down the hill towards the farmhouse. He pulls his rifle off his back and fires his clip at them from a kneeling position, just like on the range at Camp Sibert.

He turns to the west, still on a knee, and sees two soldiers carrying a man on a stretcher towards a half-track facing towards him, about a hundred yards down the road. He stands up. The dead Sherman is good cover. He yells, waves, then runs towards the half-track. Halfway there, a corporal carrying a radio on his back and a coffee pot in his hands steps out of a tent in front of Jim. The corporal sets down the coffee pot, fishes something out of his jacket pocket, pulls at it and throws it in the tent. *Grenade!* Jim thinks and dives to the ground. After a few seconds, smoke begins to billow out of the tent. *Thermite grenade*, Jim realizes. *Melt metal, burn things up.*

The corporal picks up the coffee pot and runs towards the half-track. Jim pulls himself back up too fast. He staggers backwards two steps, falls on his backside, gets up slowly, sets his feet and begins to run. He raises an arm to push his helmet down on his head. It's not there. Nor his rifle, he realizes. He looks back. They are on the ground where he fell.

Jim isn't gonna get docked for lost property. He runs back, kneels down, jams his helmet on his head, feels a fresh stab of pain in his temples, grabs his rifle, turns and runs towards the half-track. He has to be careful not to trip on helmets, rifles, blankets, and other Army property scattered all across the road. *Not gonna get docked!* he thinks. *Stupid, stupid, stupid!* He keeps running. With all his heart he wants to be small, to fit entirely under his helmet. And to be in that halftrack, which is backing down the road, away from him.

He yells, "Hey! Hey!" and waves an arm. Backing the half-track off the road to turn and face west, the driver sees Jim out the hole in his side window armor. Half-tracks being the target of choice after tanks, the driver finishes his turn and zig-zags slowly down the road. Jim gets there, grabs the back gate, is pulled in, and ends up on the floor, next to the unconscious Smiley.

The half-track accelerates quickly, rolling Jim against the wounded man until the other soldiers pull Jim onto the bench.

A tall GI standing behind a .50 cal machine gun mounted on the roof of the cab wheels it around and opens up, shooting over Jim's head, back at Longvilly. "Don't hit the farmhouse!" Jim yells. "Men up there. Be heading this way." Bent at the waist, Jim sees one of his boots is untied. His hands are shaking, so he settles for pushing the laces into his boot tops. He checks if he has pissed himself. *No.*

"Testing Ma Deuce for a jam," the gunner says. He points back east. "You talking about that pile of stones?"

Jim stays bent over. "They fell back through the woods."

After two hundred yards they follow a sharp curve in the road and the half-track is out of direct fire. Jim sits up and starts to take deep breaths. He thinks about his buddies in the farmhouse.

"That shoulder flash?" the radio corporal says, pointing to the patch on Jim's sleeve. "What are you?"

"Morale Corps. 4-4-2. Entertainment soldier."

"Some kinda entertainment you put on," the corporal says. "Let's call intermission, skip the second half." Good timing, Jim thought. I'll put him in a soldier show in Bastogne.

The half-track hasn't gone half a mile before it hits heavy fog, slows to a crawl, stops. "Traffic jam," the gunner says. "All I can see up ahead is a towed anti-tank gun and a deuce-and-half trailing a field stove." Trees close to both sides of the road prevent the column from dispersing laterally. "Just red tail lights beyond the deuce-and-a-half," the gunner says, moving the machine gun barrel up and down for emphasis. "Like to get that anti-tank gun between us and the Krauts coming down the road from Longvilly. This could be the George Washington Bridge at rush hour, but with more shooting." *Remember that one,* Jim thinks.

"'Get the hell out of Longvilly' has got stuck behind 'get the hell out of somewhere else,'" the radio corporal says. "We're tail-end Charlie. Those Krauts behind us are gonna start asking questions. We need to take to the woods."

Jim hears *PINK! PINK! PINK!* as the half-track is hit. The gunner fires bursts of .50 cal back east while Jim and the other soldiers slide lower on the bench. Jim notices that *PINK! PINK! PINK!* is coming from the front of the half-track as well as the back.

"Some Panzer column has got so far, we're retreating right into it," the radio corporal says, "Not safe here."

This is a big mistake, Jim thinks. *Enough! No! Leave me alone!* "Let's go!" the corporal shouts, pulling him to his feet. Jim follows him over the back gate of the halftrack. He sees bright orange and yellow shapes through the fog, but can't tell what's burning. Soldiers are on the road, some running, some crawling, one lying still, his clothes on fire. Jim looks back to see who else is coming out of the half-track, hears *smack-smack-smack*, sees red and black bits explode out the back of the gunner's jacket. The man drops straight down out of sight. A red mist hangs in the air where he was standing. Jim turns away.

He follows the radio corporal over a ditch and towards a shallow cave carved out of the side of a steep hill. He stops in front of a long-haired man standing behind a stone table inside. On a shelf behind the man are four rows of guttering candles. *It's Jesus*, Jim realizes. *I've been killed.*

"Statue!" the radio corporal yells, six inches from Jim's ear. "Nothing to do here," he continues, "but—" *Whinnngg-crack.* Screaming. Jim recognizes the sound of an .88. Then another *whinnngg-crack.* "Turkey shoot," the corporal says. "Stay here, we're captured by the Krauts coming from Longvilly. If they don't kill us. Follow me." The corporal trots towards the path next to the grotto. He returns and pulls Jim with him. "C'mon! We have to take *ourselves* to Bastogne."

They run up the switchback trail on the hill behind the grotto. Where there's tree cover, they walk, Jim is exhausted, nauseous, his head pounding. He stops caring about getting away from the danger; he just wants to stop and rest, close his eyes for a minute or two. The radio corporal keeps him moving up. They pass more statues along the way. Disciples. They meet a seven-foot-tall Jesus at the top. Jim turns to look down at the boiling mess below. "Keep moving," the corporal says, pointing to where the index finger has been shot off on Jesus's raised right hand. "German snipers have this hill sited."

They jog down the winding path through the trees on the other side of the hill, cross a road and make their way south through fields and groves of trees. The noise behind them is fainter as they progress, then stops altogether, but for an occasional artillery round landing in the far distance. Jim and the radio soldier pick up the Bastogne Road around fifteen hundred hours. They feel able to talk. The radio soldier mentions that his older brother, a Marine fighter pilot in the Pacific, spent a year in the Civilian Conservation Corps in 1937. Jim unspools several stories from his hitch at Camp Roosevelt. They walk and talk, talk and walk.

It's dark when they approach combat engineers felling trees across the road on the outskirts of Bastogne. The engineers aren't surprised to see them. Hundreds of soldiers are streaming by foot or vehicle into Bastogne. No sentries, no passwords. MPs are on the other side of Bastogne, stopping soldiers from continuing west. They will have to turn and fight.

As Jim and the radio corporal gain the center of Bastogne, they pass a tank battalion heading out. A platoon of paratroop infantry follows behind. Disheveled in appearance, they resemble an armed mob. They don't march; they walk with purpose. It's clear they're a unit. The paratroopers ask for ammo as they pass. Jim gives one of them his grenade.

There's a field kitchen truck in the central square, handing out thick slices of ham on Army bread. He and the radio corporal each eat some, put some in their pockets. "Not bad," the corporal says. "Course, all the mustard is in the officers' mess."

He laughs. Could be a great alternate title for *Spamlet*, Jim thinks. Hey! The food has relieved his headache.

The corporal says goodbye and good luck, goes off to find the 9th Armored command post. Jim gets directions to General Middleton's headquarters. Mission first. An orderly there tells him Middleton and staff have withdrawn to Neufchâteau. The orderly can't tell him who's in command or where they're located, won't take the map, but can direct Jim to the Heintz Barracks for a billet.

Jim walks slowly through the streets. It's air raid dark. The cold is deepening. Heintz Barracks is a huge compound of brick buildings. An MP at the front gate directs Jim to one building. An orderly at the door takes him to a room in the cellar, brick walls and brick floor. Coal stove. It's wonderfully warm. Couple dozen soldiers are asleep on the floor. Two soldiers sit and smoke, two quietly play cards, one reads a book by flashlight. Jim lies on the floor with his boots on, overcoat under his head. He falls asleep immediately.

Three hours later, some bastard sticks his head in the room and yells, "Get up, sojers! Up, men! Time to get in the fight!"

IRONTON, OHIO
July 17, 1937

"Here's a buck, Jimmy." Lou Prince holds out four quarters. "Buy the headache powders for Mother, get yourself a soda, get our poster in the window at the drugstore—" he points down Center Street—"while I make my sales call." They're standing in front of Kessler's Jewelry: Diamonds—Watches—Opticians.

Jim doesn't ponder the meaning of the rattling sound coming from Mr. Prince's cardboard briefcase. His mind is working on the problem of buying a rubber. Jo-Jo the clown told him it earns a fifty-cent discount on jelly roll from the coochie tent girls. A virgin at age twenty-two, Jim thinks he might be ready to buy himself some of that, one of these days. Mother, aka Mrs. Lou Prince, aka Lola the Lion Tamer, must never know.

Jim does manage, "Why do you only sell program ads to jewelry stores, Mr. Prince? Shouldn't we try the barber shop or the hardware store?"

"I don't have time to go up and down hick town Main Street. Jewelers have ready cash."

"Good morning, young man. What brings you to Ironton?" An older man wearing a white pharmacist's coat addresses Jim from behind a marble soda fountain counter. Because Jim's clothes aren't wrinkled or filthy, and his hair is combed, the pharmacist doesn't make him for a young drifter looking for work, a handout, or to steal. Plenty of vagabonds move through Ironton as the Great Depression slides towards its eighth year.

The pharmacist smiles at Jim. Customers are scarce. Of the people who can still afford to visit a doctor, many can't afford Coca-Cola, ice cream sodas, or candy, let alone what the doctor prescribes. The repeal of Prohibition ended the sale of medicinal alcohol in 1934. If it wasn't for tobacco and aspirin, the pharmacist would already be bankrupt.

"I'm with the Von Duke Oriental and European Circus," Jim says. The pharmacist's smile disappears. "I'd like an ice cream soda, please. And a box of your BC powders."

"Your soda's ten cents, young man. Eleven cents for strawberry."

Jim holds up the coins. "There's a show tonight, and a matinee Sunday. We hope leading citizens of…here will attend. May I put a poster in your window?" Jim puts the poster and two passes on the counter.

"I don't countenance entertainment on the Sabbath," the pharmacist says. Jim gives up on the rubber and adds a quarter to the poster and the passes.

"Well, Jimmy, we made another big sale." A smiling Mr. Prince hands him the empty briefcase. "Onward to the bank! Let's turn this—" he holds up the light green paper check— "into cash money, buy a present for Mother, and get back to our people."

It turns out Lou Prince was taking risks that made Mario the human cannonball's job look like a Sunday school. Lou was abducted and murdered three days later by the gangsters for whom he was fencing stolen jewelry. This long-running caper kept the circus solvent. JoJo explained it all to Jim, said Mrs. Prince was devastated but not shocked. Within the week, she sold the fixtures and the animals to Orloff Brothers and took her grief back to Sarasota. Jim returned to Huntington, got his job back at Uncle Adolf's bread factory. For a long time, he regretted leaving the circus.

10.

BASTOGNE, BELGIUM, DECEMBER 20, 1944

> This act must be as big a "hit" as any on the bill. It is next to intermission and the audience must have something really worthwhile to talk over. And so we select one of the best acts on the bill to crown the first half of the show.
>
> Writing for Vaudeville by Brett Page,
The Home Correspondence School,
Springfield, Mass, 1915

The song, the song, the song. Jim and Stella are dancing to "Moonlight Serenade." Her hair floats up in his eyes. He can't seem to push it away. The stage floor is soft and his feet are heavy. He's having a hard time keeping up with her. She's singing, "*Soldier, soldier…*"

"Soldier. Soldier. Showbiz soldier. *Tustanuggee*." Private Osceola Jones is holding Jim's web belt from behind. He has recognized Jim from the December 15th Jeep show for Company C in Munshausen.

"Wha?"

"You're inna beet field. Road turned north; you kept on east like you're gonna march to Germany."

"I fell asleep." Jim looks at his Timex. Zero two hundred hours. He looks around for a place to lie down.

A sergeant arrives. "Stow the gab, you two, and get back," he orders. "We're in a forward zone." They are part of Team SNAFU, a hastily-organized unit composed mainly of 28th Division survivors, dismounted tankers and artillerymen, and rear-echelon soldiers stuck in Bastogne. "Situation Normal, All Fucked Up, for sure," the sergeant says to a corporal as he rejoins the formation. "Summa these numbskulls can't even know how to march. How they gonna fight?"

Ten minutes later, the SNAFU column is stopped by an ordnance captain waving a flashlight. There's a deuce-and-a-half idling just off the road. Rectangular green ammo cans and wooden crates are stacked on the ground behind it, like a spring-cleaning soap display at the A&P. Empty cans and crates are scattered nearby. "Hump as much as they can, Sergeant," the captain says, "for yourselves and for the airborne men up ahead."

"Every man bring a can of .30 cal!" the sergeant shouts, tugging men into a line. "We're gonna want a lot of machine gun fire." In the dark, he sees the illuminated hands and face of a soldier lighting a cigarette. "No smoking, goddammit! Ammo dump!" He turns away and says, "SNAFU screwballs gonna get us all killed" to no one in particular.

The Sunday night buffet at Stiers, Jim thinks. *All you can get on a plate, something for everybody.* Like the other soldiers, he loops bandoliers of 03-06 M1 clips over his shoulder and puts grenades in his gas mask holder. He picks up a can of .30 cal. He can tell the thin metal handle is going to hurt his fingers.

"You still got a gas mask?" one soldier says to the man next to him. "Chuck it and put ammo in the holder."

"Haven't fired a rifle since I left Camp Shelby," the other says. "I'm a barber."

The ordnance captain shines his flashlight on several wide and stubby wooden boxes marked *Rockets—Caution*. "Any bazooka men here?" There are not. "Team SNAFU needs bazooka training," he says to the sergeant. "Plenty of Kraut tanks heading this way."

"D bars in those cartons," the captain says, pointing to a neat pile of cardboard boxes. It's the emergency chocolate ration, not tasty and hard as a rock. Nobody likes them.

"Every man take three," the sergeant says. "We may be gone a while."

⟨⟩

"Les enfants, cheeldren. Civeels. Ne tire pas. Don' shoo.'" The SNAFU column moves past a swayback horse pulling a cart containing an old man and three children heading to Bastogne. Jim thinks of Betty Jo, holds out a pack of gum. The old man accepts the handoff with a "*Merci*, tank you." Then he raises his voice as the SNAFU column moves past in the dark. "*Dieu vous protègez.* God you protect." The children are asleep or mute.

It has been raining for a while. Jim notices waterlogged overcoats on the side of the road. A rumble grows behind him. The dripping pine branches begin to vibrate.

"Divide ranks," the sergeant calls out. A column of M8 Greyhound armored cars and Jeeps comes through, a nod or two, but mostly looking straight ahead.

"Reconnaissance platoon," Private Jones says to Jim. "Don't want that job."

Within a minute, a Tank Destroyer company pushes loudly through. Jim is reminded of the Von Duke's Circus's show-opening spectacle, but it's Hellcats instead of elephants, Jeeps instead of clown cars, half-tracks instead of floats, anti-tank guns with muzzle covers instead of horses wearing plumes.

As the guns roll by, Private Jones says to Jim, "Stay clear of them. They draw attention."

The final float in the parade is four machine guns mounted together on an M20 trailer. "What's that?" Jim asks.

"Quad .50 machine gun," Jones says. "Anti-ground attack aircraft gun. Krautmower. Turn a platoon into hamburger and helmets in thirty seconds, catch them in the open. Wicked."

"Glad all that's going in front of us," Jim says.

"Don't you worry, Showbiz. Combined arms. They gonna leave plenty of room for us to come up in between."

The Tank Destroyer column accordions, halts, starts again, halts, and then moves out of sight in the dark.

▲

"Sam Doodle, American GI." An amplified voice pulls Jim out of his foxhole doze. It's still pitch dark. "You fought bravely yesterday; you lost many friends. Ve haff many bodies of GIs, including John O'Malley and Louis Rodriguez. Do you know these dead boys? Ve haff many prisoners, including Carl Anderson and Kenneth Fontaine."

"Kraut psyops," Private Jones says to Jim. "You'll get a kick out of this."

"Ve are treating vounded GIs in our varm und dry field hospitals," the voice continues. "Your friends here are eat breakfast—pen-cakes, fried heggs, baconspeck, hot coffee und Camel zigarette. Hot showers, they take. You are surrounded. It is honorable zarrendha."

"This is rich," Jones says.

"Ve keep you safe in Chermany until end of the vahr, zoon, then ticket you home to your girl und your farm. Or come with us to Paris for the zig zag and the shows." The sound of machine gun fire is audible in the distance. "Do you know? Germany und Russia have made peace und the whole German Army und Tiger tanks are coming this way to crush the British imperialists und their Jewish bankers. Vhy give up your life for zem?"

"Fritz must think we're morons," Jones says. Jim can only

nod in agreement. He's recalling the parade of German tanks he barely outran in Longvilly.

"Leave zis fight to your officers und the warmongah Roosevelt. I remind me, zhey are happy to have you zuffer und die while Jews back home love up your girl mit silk stockings."

"He's laying an egg," Jim is finally able to say.

"Nazi chickenshit," Jones says, pulling a pancake out of his jacket pocket and screaming, "WE'VE GOT PANCAKES, FRITZ! SO MANY PANCAKES, WE CAN'T EAT THEM ALL! HERE, HAVE ONE!" He throws it out of sight in the dark in front of the foxhole. Then he slaps the ground in front of the foxhole three times, climbs out and moons the German lines. He pulls up his pants, jumps back in the foxhole, and yells, "I'LL SMOKE FLEETWOODS BEFORE I SMOKE YOUR FUCKING *ZIGARETTES*! VOTE FOR DEWEY, YOU BASTARDS!" There are hoots from other foxholes.

"What the hell was that?" Jim says.

"War deed. Taunting," Jones says between breaths. "Seminole psywar."

"Pipe down!" It's the sergeant. "That's an order."

"Sun's coming up," Jones says to Jim. "Here we fucking go."

△

"I HEAR TANKS," Jones says. "Can't see twenty yards in front—hey!" A coal scuttle helmet on top of a grey coat stumbles out of the fog. Jim freezes. Shocking *bangs* as the German and Private Jones fire at the same time. The German throws up his arms and disappears. Jones falls at Jim's feet.

"Get your head up and start shooting!" Jones says, holding his right shoulder, "so some Kraut don't throw a grenade in our hole." Jim gets his rifle over the lip of the foxhole and fires a clip towards the ripping sound ahead in the dark. "Gimme a dressing from my first aid kit, Showbiz. In my pocket."

After five minutes, the firing stops. "He just winged me, but I'm bleeding," Jones pants, pointing to the dressing, now crimson. "I got to find the medic."

Jim pushes him up and out of the foxhole. "*Man*, it stings," Jones says as Jim helps him to his feet. They move back about fifty yards. "I'm okay to walk, Showbiz. Stay with the other fellas. I'll get patched up and come back."

Not until he gets back to the lip of his foxhole does Jim see it contains a German soldier. The man is small and slight, bare-headed, his overcoat unbelted. He holds Jim's rifle up over his head with one hand, butt end towards Jim, extends a piece of orange paper with the other hand. "I surrender," Willi says in Midwestern-accented English. Jim stares at him. "My safe conduct from General Eisenhower." He waves the orange paper. "I am your prisoner. I am declared out of the war and protected by the Geneva Convention. My name is William Hoch. From Milwaukee. 14 Elm Street." He hands Jim the rifle. "I put the safety on."

Jim is able to point the rifle at Willi, but unable to speak.

"Please escort me out of the danger zone at your first opportunity. Now is good. My unit has pulled back to regroup." Willi sees that Jim may be confused. "I will keep my arms over my head. You point your rifle at my back and we will walk towards the rear. Maybe take me yourself to an intelligence officer so I can be questioned promptly."

As he and hands-up Willi walk back, Jim can't recall the day's password, instead yelling, "Preacher Roe, Jean Harlow, the Shadow knows, cornbread, check and double check."

"Not quite so loud, comrade," Willi says. "You'll draw fire."

A disembodied voice says, "No sentries up here, but bring me back a cuppa Joe, will ya, buddy? Two sugars."

The sergeant's voice is next: "Pipe down!"

They make their way past an anti-tank gun and crew of three. "Just shoot him," one of the gunners says.

"I'm not SS, Mac," Willi barks. By the time the gunner thinks of an appropriately profane response, there's the oncoming freight train sound of artillery rounds. He and the rest of his crew jump into slit trenches.

"Those are coming here," Willi says and breaks into a trot, hands still over his head. Jim follows.

⋀

"Lookie here," the dismounted tanker says in a southern Alabama accent. "General Middleton done combed up some Buffalo soldiers!"

Having escorted Willi and two other POWs back to Bastogne and turned them over to MPs, Jim now sits on the hallway floor outside the temporary mess in the basement of Heintz Barracks, Building A. His headache has calmed to a low hum. He's been focused on the sliced Spam, scrambled eggs, and pancakes in his scavenged mess kit. Three black privates are thirty feet further down the hall, eating by themselves.

"Those are truck drivers, service and supply. Quartermaster corps," Jim says. "I don't belong here either. I'm Morale Corps."

"Goddamned Jewish Cavalry sends them boys," the tanker says loudly. "Not to cook, oh no, but to sit and eat with us, lahk they was white." He winces. The ceiling light bulb is reflected in the burn ointment on his red face and hands. "Ooh-*wee*! I don't know where to start." One of the black soldiers glances at the tanker.

"I guess colored soldiers got to eat," Jim says in a lower tone. "They should have their own mess, sure. But things are upside down now."

The black soldier carries his mess kit to the wash station — one galvanized steel trash can of soapy water, another of hot rinse water. He doesn't look at Jim or the tanker as he walks away.

"See what happens when you mister our niggers?" the tanker says to Jim. "Now we supposed to share our wash water with those monkeys." The other two black GIs fold their mess kits and get up and leave.

The tanker gets up, steadies himself, then limps over to the wash station and urinates in the rinse water. "Hey!" Jim says, a little louder than he meant to. "How am I gonna clean my mess kit now?"

"Clean it outside with snow. Been snowing all night."

"That's not sanitary."

"Sanitary more than dinge water," the tanker says, pointing down at Jim. "Goddamned Army make us a peck a trouble we gonna have, putting them—" he gestures at where the black soldiers had been—"back in their place after the wah."

"Army drafts colored boys, brings them all this way, you're gonna put them back in their place after the war? What kind of chickenshit is that?" Jim says. He's talking to himself. The tanker is too far down the hall to hear, and Jim's eggs are cold. He eats them anyways.

INTRODUCING STELLA POLK
Huntington, West Virginia
July 20, 1938

"I forgot the colored hospital is stales only," Jim says to Norma as he walks into the kitchen. "Had to go back to the bakery. Ran late to my children's tap class."

It's been a year since he returned to Huntington from the Von Prince European & Oriental Circus. He has a delivery route for his Uncle Adolf's bread company. He also has a one-man dance academy that holds classes in the late afternoon and evenings, and on Saturdays.

"If you'd review your route the night before," Norma says, "you wouldn't—"

"I was still in my Sunshine Bakery costume when I pulled up to the studio." Jim doesn't like to be seen in that uniform. "There's a real doll and her mother waiting by the door." It had been Stella Polk and her mother Edna. Jim had taken in Stella's trim figure, straight back, ballerina calves, and the black leotards under her blue cotton dress. Cute kid. Looked about sixteen. Ginger Rogers' height, about five foot and a half. The dancing pumps hanging from her left hand had been an unneeded clue. Edna was mid-forties, Jim guessed. No, mid-thirties and worked hard. Five feet tall on her tippy toes. Looked tough as a pine knot.

"Women aren't dolls, Jimmy."

"Sure, Sis. The girl looks like Judy Garland in that movie. What was it? Mickey Rooney plays a jockey. The mother, Edna, asks me, 'Is this a dance school or a bakery?' Stella, that's the girl's name, is already blushing."

Norma picks up a kitchen towel, pulls a plate out of the oven and sets it in front of Jim. "Thankee, Sis," he says. "Thought I smelled cabbage."

"It's Wednesday." Blutwurst and cabbage has been the Tanzers' Wednesday night meal since before either of them could remember.

"They're with Billy Bryant's Showboat. It's at Riverfront Park."

"That calliope," Norma says, "'Oh Susanna' and 'Camptown Races' from 4 p.m. to showtime every day. Sounds like they're docked across the street. I'll be glad when they go up river. Here." She slides two slices of buttered black bread on her brother's plate, pours coffee in his cup, and sits down at the table across from him.

"They can't. The tug engine died. They're stuck in Huntington until it's fixed. Last show was yesterday. Edna asked me if I needed teaching help, said Stella's been dancing since she was five, has seven seasons on the Showboat."

"You have one children's tap class and one beginner's ballroom. You don't need help."

"I can teach better with a partner." He shovels a forkful of sausage and cabbage into his mouth, makes a sandwich out of the buttered bread, takes a large bite. "And I'll put together a Baby Astaires act," he says. "Jim and Stella, America's Dancing Darlings."

"Please don't talk with your mouth full. You're too old to be a baby anything. And you can't sing."

"George Burns doesn't really sing, just carries a tune."

Norma sighs. Another Jimmy Tanzer pie-in-the-sky special. "I read the book you ordered, *The Business of Dance Instruction*," she says. "No one's doing the country club dance lesson circuit around here. If you want to quit your bread route, you have to be wholehearted about your dance business."

He takes two gulps of coffee. "We can do radio too, Dumb Dora patter. I've got some jokes already worked out. When we to take it to New York, we'll—"

"New York?! What happens to the Tanzer Academy of Dance?"

"I'll sell it."

"I see," she says, knowing it's worth about a buck and a half. "How old is Stella?"

"She'll be eighteen in November."

"She's seventeen, Jimmy!"

"She wants to get off the river and lead a normal life," Jim says, cutting into his second sausage.

"And going to New York with a West Virginia nightclub act will be living a normal life, I guess. That's the last of the sausage. Do you want more cabbage?"

"Yes, please. New York is a fine place to live, Sis."

"You have a good set-up here to build your dance studio. The Depression has cleaned out the competition. There's only Frankle and you left in Huntington, and he's in trouble."

"Cleaned out people's wallets too, Sis. People can't pay for lessons. The demand isn't there."

Norma pours him more coffee. "Did you read the book I gave you? *How to Win Friends and Influence People?*"

"I will, Sis."

"Positive thinking. You don't need to run off. If you don't want to build a dancing school business, you can build your delivery route. Put soda pop, chips and candy on your truck, double your profit from the same stops. Let Uncle Adolf know the bakery gets a share and he'll support it."

"We're gonna make it in show business, Sis. It won't be easy, but talent and determination will get us there."

"The girl, maybe. But what about you?"

"That's uncalled for."

"Sorry. But I don't think Mutti has it in mind for you to run away to New York with a seventeen-year-old girl, leaving Vicky in Huntington."

Running away from his girlfriend is part of what Jim has in mind, although he's only vaguely aware of that. Vicky Snodgrass has waited out Jim's Civilian Conservation Corps and Circus escapades and expects a proposal of marriage. Lavinia is asking when he's going to make one.

"Edna will accompany Stella, of course. Did Mutti make strudel?"

"I'll cut it. She's pinned her hopes on you marrying Vicky."

"I'm not right for that girl," Jim says. He recalls how much Vicky's hands sweat and how her father scowls at him. "Mutti will come around."

"It'll take a while. You'd better stay in New York at least a year. Stormy weather ahead for Poppa. Mutti will take it out on him."

"We'll need a year before we're ready for Hollywood."

"Wake up, Jimmy, for heaven's sake. If you're going to work up an act with this girl, start a production company here. Book other entertainers while you're booking the Dancing Babies or whatever you're going to call your act. Put together a full show and sell the whole package to nightclubs."

"That sounds like—"

"Combine that with the dancing school. You could work out your act *and* make enough money to quit the bread route. You'd be a sap to sell the school."

" I deny the allegation and I deny the allegator."

"Your Amos 'n' Andy impression is terrible, Jimmy."

"Vat's zis my children are talking?" Lavinia says as she walks into the kitchen. They don't tell her.

11.

BASTOGNE, BELGIUM, DECEMBER 21, 1944

> The first act after intermission is a difficult position to fill, because the act must not let down the carefully built-up tension of interest and yet it must not be stronger than the acts that are to follow.
>
> — WRITING FOR VAUDEVILLE BY BRETT PAGE,
> THE HOME CORRESPONDENCE SCHOOL,
> SPRINGFIELD, MASS, 1915

"AIRISH THIS MORNING," Jim says. He and seventy other Team SNAFU soldiers are in some sort of order on the parade ground in front of Heintz Barracks. Their light comes from the partially covered headlights of the six trucks idling twenty yards away.

"If that means 'cold' in West Virginia, Showbiz, it's fucking cold, all right," Private Osceola Jones says. "And my arm is killing me."

"You should be on light duty."

"No light duty in Bastogne, if you can stand upright. Hasn't been six hours since I got back here. Where'd you go while I was getting patched up?" Jones stamps his feet on the flattened circle of snow around his boots.

"I got back early," Jim says. "Escorted prisoners."

"How'd you get that soft job?"

"I took a prisoner myself, kid from Milwaukee."

"Deserter?"

"*Volksgrenadier*. Whole family moved back to Germany before the war. The *Volksdeutsche* thing." Lavinia had maintained an interest in that idea until 1939.

"What a lulu. But he's gonna get sent back to the States courtesy of Uncle Sam, and we ain't."

"Wonder where he'll end up," Jim says.

"Maybe in those internment camps out west," Jones says. "Anywhere in the States is better than here." He takes off his helmet and pulls his wool cap farther down over his ears. "This cold could kill a man, was he to lay on the ground wounded."

"When were you drafted, Jones?"

"Couldn't be drafted. The Seminole nation is still at war with the United States. Technically speaking."

"You're pulling my leg."

"No. It's a nailed-down deferment."

"So why did you enlist?"

"I had a misunderstanding with the tribal police. The elders thought a change of scene would do me good. This is a change, alright, but it's not doing me any good." Jones puts his helmet back on and looks down at Jim's feet. "I need a pair of those shoepacs, Showbiz. These things—" he points at his own boots—"haven't got dried out for three days."

"You change your socks?"

"Not sure I could get my boots back on if I took 'em off."

"You'll get trench foot."

"And a ticket out of here."

"You could lose your feet."

"I'll order new feet from the Sears catalog when I get home. No rationing after the war."

"Just don't buy two left feet. Hey!" Jim is as delighted with that remark as he can be, given that he's waiting in the cold and dark to be sent into combat, towel around his neck for a muffler.

"That was funny, Showbiz. They don't hurt so bad. I'll give them one more day."

"Here." Jim takes his pair of dry socks out of his field jacket pocket.

"That's big." Jones takes them and smiles. "Thanks, Showbiz. Real square of you." He turns towards a switchboard operator who's absorbed with trying to put a clip in his rifle. "You mean to aim that thing at my head?"

"Oops," the man says, looking up. "This thing…" His voice trails off as he points the barrel towards the ground.

"Keep your thumb well clear of the bolt, buddy," Jones says. "You don't want to mash it."

Jim flexes his own right thumb and looks around. "New faces this morning. Missing some who went out with us yesterday."

"Even replacements need replacements now, things so bad."

Jim points to a young officer and says, "Didn't spot *him* yesterday. Where's *our* lieutenant?"

"Last I saw him, he was on a stretcher," Jones says. "Dangerous rank."

"I know," Jim says, remembering what Allie told him and wondering *what happened to that kid?*

"Saw some green lieutenants at the Hurtgen Forest," Jones continues. "You can't lead if you don't stay alive. Course, the ones that survived, what they learned, they're the officers we want."

"Sure," Jim says, rewrapping the towel around his neck.

"So, where do you think your entertainment buddies have skedaddled to, Showbiz? Paris? London? You're going to have to put on a show here all by yourself."

"Can't do it solo."

"LISTEN UP!" It's the sergeant. Parade ground commands like *atten-shun* or *for-ard harch* are rare in a forward zone. Combatmen won't put up with chickenshit. "We're moving out in ten minutes." He points to the trucks. "Gonna get colder today. You don't have an overcoat—" he points to a waist-high olive drab pile on the ground—"take one a those. Oh yeah, any a you speak German?"

The truck headlights reveal a black-edged hole in the overcoat on the top of the pile. Jim raises his hand.

"You soft duty *bastard*," Jones says, and smiles at Jim.

⋀

"I don't speak Yiddish, or whatever that was," Wolfgang Dietl, Captain, 2nd Company, 26th Panzer Division, says to Jim in High German. The hair above the German's gaunt face is matted with dried blood.

"What's the problem, Private?" the American logistics captain says to Jim. This G-4 has been pressed into service today as a G-2, Intelligence. He has no German.

"He doesn't understand me," Jim says, looking up towards the captain. "Maybe he speaks a regional dialect."

"Keep trying," the captain says. In his ignorance, he hasn't asked for the German officer's paybook, and so is unaware that Dietl's Berlin home address indicates that Jim's poor German is the problem, not some dialect.

Jim tries again. Dietl holds his hands out in the universal signal of non-comprehension, then winces and brings them to either side of his head.

Jim turns to the G-4. "I brought a prisoner in yesterday who spoke German like this man and has good English." He and Willi had a long talk on the walk back to Bastogne. The captain fails to note the slightly higher pitch in Jim's voice.

"You want a POW to question another POW?"

"He'll just translate, sir. He was born in America. My German is enough, if he tries anything."

"That's not going to…" The captain looks at his watch. His

first-ever intelligence report is due in two hours. You improvise when you have to in a forward zone. "Okay, Private, run and get him. We'll wait. Take your rifle." The American captain extends a pack of Camels towards Dietl. "Cigarette?"

"Ja, danke."

⁂

BY THE TIME they enter the interrogation room, Willie understands what Jim needs from him. He has discarded the civilian clothes that were under his *Volksgrenadier* uniform. *PW* is whitewashed in large white letters on the front and back of his grey jacket and trouser legs. "Hauptmann," Willi says, giving Captain Dietl a crisp military salute.

Dietl returns the salute and winces again. The two men proceed to speak in dialect-free German. "Your uniform is in shocking condition, Private," Dietl says to Willi.

"Yes sir. I was dragged a long way by this large one." He nods towards Jim. "I was unconscious. A shell blast."

"Your helmet?"

"It was on my head. Saved my life, I'm sure, Captain."

"Where is it now?"

"Some Ami has it for a souvenir."

"It's bad enough they use machines to do their fighting for them," Hauptmann Dietl says. "They shouldn't steal our property to amuse themselves."

"No, sir."

"The Russians are barbarians, but at least they fight like men," Dietl says.

"Yes, sir."

"Do you have a concussion?" Dietl says, gently touching his own right temple. "Have you been seen by an American doctor?"

Jim wipes the palms of his hands on his trousers. He is concentrating on at least getting the sense of the exchange.

"No, Hauptmann. Yes, Hauptmann," Willi says. "We have been treated well so far."

"We will do the same for them after Bastogne is liberated."

"Of course, sir."

"It is obvious I am woozy, grenadier," Dietl says. "Also obvious is your accent."

"My family returned to the Fatherland when I was a child."

"I see. This one—" Dietl shifts his eyes towards Jim—"his German is comical at best. But if you are part of a deception—"

"I do not dishonor my uniform. If you prefer, I will refuse to translate—"

"Who is the Swedish Nightingale, *grenadier*?" Dietl asks, leaning towards Willi.

"Ilse Werner, sir. A stylish woman."

"When do children polish their shoes and leave them outside their doors?"

"St, Nicolas' Day." The German captain says nothing. "Eve, of course. *Krampusnacht*, December 5th."

Dietl blinks several times and says, "Very good, *grenadier*. Report now to me your name, unit, where you trained, and where you were stationed prior to Watch on the Rhine."

Willi answers quickly and in detail.

The American officer holds up a hand. "Enough. Start with name, rank, and unit," he tells Willi.

"All right, *grenadier*," Hauptmann Dietl says, "let's get this over with. I have an astonishing headache."

Willi turns to the American officer and lies. "This officer is a Transylvanian Saxon. Barely German. I worked three summers at a German resort in the mountains there," he adds, to close the sale, "and understand the dialect."

"Good," the American captain says, turning to Jim. "Follow as best you can, Private. Hit him if he tries any tricks."

The only trick Willi has in mind is to get back to Milwaukee in one piece.

▲

"Mind if I join you?" the reporter asks, approaching Jim's table in the mess.

"No, sir," Jim replies, standing up. He has just finished eating.

The reporter extends his hand. "Bernie Levin, *New York Times*. Bunny." He wears a navy wool jacket with "War Correspondent U.S." stitched in gold letters above the right breast pocket.

"Jim Tanzer. Entertainment Specialist, Morale Corps Battalion 6817."

The reporter points his fork at his mess kit. "I see it's going to be pancakes with every meal. Guess we're tight on rations. They *are* pretty good, though."

"Donut flour," Jim says. "Requisitioned from the Red Cross dump after they evacuated." Jim and two other SNAFU soldiers carried the hundred-weight sacks. He takes a pull of coffee from his canteen. Still hot. Nice.

"Fortunes of war," the reporter says, putting the lid on his mess kit and pulling out his notebook. "Been over here a while, Private Tanzer?"

"I came over with *Hip Hooray* in October. The show."

"I saw it at Camp Shanks. Jimmy James Orchestra, Mickey Rooney." He knows better than to ask, *were you in the show?* "Were you drafted into Morale Corps?"

"We toured England," Jim says. "The show was disbanded and we were sent to France. We put together soldier shows in Paris and in the Repo Depots, the replacement camps."

"I saw *GI Gay Paree* at Theatre Marigny."

"I choreographed two of the numbers," Jim says. "Remember 'Barn Dance?'"

"Hilarious."

"'Can We Can-Can?'"

"GIs dressed as showgirls. Great number," the reporter says. "Nobody does cross-dress like the Army." They both smile.

"I borrowed that idea from *This Is the Army*," Jim says.

"Irving Berlin. Originality is undetected plagiarism, somebody said. Shakespeare borrowed half of *Hamlet* from Thomas Kyd. What did you do after *Hip Hooray* broke up?"

"I got assigned to Jeep shows as the front moved east. I was working with Mickey Rooney and an accordion player from Texas, Wes Novak."

"I saw a Jeep show up near Aachen. Vaudeville rises from the grave. A couple of guys and Red Buttons. He's a Catskills comedian." A loud clatter of plates comes from the kitchen. The reporter notices Jim flinch at the noise, and the abbreviated start to slide under the table.

"I know him," Jim says. "My wife and I were on social staff at Stiers one summer. We had a dance act, Tanzer and Sterling."

"You're a long way from the Borscht Belt. Are you doing shows in Bastogne?"

"Bastogne is within German artillery range."

"Don't I know it." The reporter extends a pack of Camels. "Smoke?"

"Can I take a couple for later? Thanks. The brass doesn't want soldiers congregating. I'm Team SNAFU. We've been moved around. I've done translating for interrogations."

The reporter lights his cigarette, clicks his Ronson shut, takes a long drag, blows smoke to the side. "You have German?"

"My mother was born in Germany."

"I know a *lot* of people in New York whose mothers were born in Germany. The only German words they know are *gesundheit* and *sauerkraut*."

Jim pictures Lavinia's cabbage. "She's pretty firm in her ways."

"Sure. I have a foreign-born mother, born in Minsk in 1875. …So, what's it like for an entertainer GI to be at the front, carrying a rifle?" The reporter knows a feature story when it falls in his lap. Song-and-dance man turned rifle-and-bayonet soldier, Christmas-in-battling-Bastogne angle at no extra charge.

If only you were Mickey Rooney, the reporter thinks. *That would be front page.* "Where are you from, Jim?" he adds, while Jim is still considering the first question.

"Huntington. West Virginia."

"Been there. I covered one of Billy Sunday's last tent revivals in Huntington. Long time ago."

"I saw it. He scared the fool out of me."

"Quite a showman. How's the war going for you?"

"It's confusing, Mr. Levin."

"Bunny."

"I don't know what's happening. None of us do. Thought the war would be over by Christmas and now this. Why are we here?" They both blink as an artillery round lands in the far distance.

"Bastogne, you mean?" The reporter takes a long pull on his cigarette.

"Yeah, I don't understand it. Why make a stand here?"

"You want the unabridged version?"

"We'd all like to know. They don't tell us anything."

"You've seen it. The Ardennes is rolling hills and steep valleys, small farms, dense forest. Harsh winters, heavy snow, blinding fog. Julius Caesar called it difficult terrain for large-scale movement of people and equipment. Only difference now is paved roads. Seven of them go through Bastogne. It's the hub."

"What does that mean for us?" Jim asks.

"Whatever Hitler's mad plan is, it requires speed. Getting ahead of us and disrupting any defense in depth. Encore of their performance against the French in 1940. *Spring* of 1940. A lot tougher in December. And since the Allies have complete air superiority, the Germans have to get where they're supposed to get, Antwerp I've heard, before the skies clear. A Ninth Air Force controller arrived yesterday. Here to call down fire and brimstone on the Germans, first clear day we get."

"Okay," Jim says.

"Panzers can't go through the woods. Logging roads are easy to mine and ambush. 28th Division learned that the hard way in the Hurtgen Forest. German tanks are too heavy for fields, unless the ground freezes three feet deep. They need roads. They need Bastogne." He stubs out his cigarette on the sole of his shoe.

"How are we supposed to stop them?"

The reporter leans in and lowers his voice. "Sure, we've been caught with our pants down. Ike and Brad gambled they could hold the Ardennes this winter with two infantry divisions spread thin as salami in a five-cent sandwich. They thought the enemy was too beaten-up, thought they'd stay bottled up in Germany while the Allies shortened supply lines. Wait for spring to make the big attack on the German heartland, the Ruhr. Why not? It'd be crazy for the Germans to counterattack west, what with the Reds grinding towards Berlin from the east."

"Didn't they already know Hitler was crazy?"

"Good one, Jim. At least Bastogne is an ideal piece of ground to defend. It's a gigantic fort—the woods and the hamlets are the walls."

"We were in front of Noville yesterday."

"Tell me what you saw."

"I heard a lot more than I saw."

"That's war," the reporter says.

"Who all is here with us? In Bastogne?" Jim tilts his canteen up, gets the last of his coffee.

"Have mine," the reporter says, pushing his mug across the table. "The 101st Airborne division is here, fifteen, maybe twenty thousand soldiers."

"They're tough."

"You know what Tolstoy wrote in *War & Peace*? About the flower of the Russian Army?"

"My sister has that book."

"As the war goes on, the weaker troops and officers melt away, killed, captured, re-assigned. What's left is the best. They have resilience, cohesion, leadership, and tactical skill. They make their own morale. That's the 101st Airborne."

Jim puts his last pancake in his field jacket pocket. *Nice detail*, the reporter thinks, making a note before continuing. "An airborne division has four battalions. That's four sides of a box around Bastogne. I'm not allowed to write that."

"Who else is here?"

"All the 101st field artillery plus most of the 333rd Artillery Battalion — negro gunners — plus a Combat Command from the 10th Armored Division and the 705th anti-tank battalion."

"I think I saw them moving up the road yesterday."

"Sure. And a mobile reserve of 28th Infantry and other orphans. That's you, Team SNAFU."

"How many Germans you think are coming?"

"Probably four times our force, with four times as many tanks."

They're silent as Jim carefully pours the reporter's coffee into his canteen cup. He spills a little when another artillery round lands in the distance, wipes it up with his sleeve. "Thanks. How can we fight that?"

"Your commander was commander of the 101st Artillery. McAuliffe. For him, Bastogne's the center of the face of a clock. He's put his guns in the middle, has a 360-degree field of fire. Now the German armor has a devil's choice. Has to mass to be effective. If they do, they're vulnerable to McAuliffe's guns."

"We'll hold out?"

"It'll be rough, but that's my bet. Unless we run out of shells."

"We have enough?"

"I guess McAuliffe knows. Okay, Jim, I've given you my story. Now you tell me yours. What made you decide to join the Army?"

▲

"Whether you're part of a bazooka team or you find one on the ground—a lotta weapons on the ground during combat—you need to know how to use it." The burly sergeant speaks to Jim and the cooks, bandsmen, mechanics, clerks, infantry, and other SNAFU soldiers assembled in the snow-covered pasture. It's overcast and bitter cold at sixteen hundred hours; full dark is an hour away.

"Pay attention and we won't be out here long. A properly handled bazooka will disable a tank, blow up a half-track, destroy a machine gun nest and, best of all, take out an .88. All this goodness from a hundred yards away." He looks at the men. "Now, you charge a gun, you may get a medal—if an officer happens to see it—but it'll be mailed to your family because you'll be too dead to wear it. Accurate bazooka fire is a better option. Who here qualified on bazooka in basic?"

Private Anthony Sorrento, 427th Bakery Company, steps forward. Only Private Sorrento.

"Planes overhead," Jim says. "You hear?"

"Nah. It's supply trucks," Private Osceola Jones says. "Lots of them. Pulling out of Bastogne. Scuttlebutt is we're about to be cut off."

Jim exits the barracks and walks towards the sound. He turns a corner and sees a line of trucks and ambulances, wheels hidden by exhaust, winking red brake lights stretching far into the darkness ahead. He approaches one and knocks on the window of the cab. The driver rolls it down. "Private Tanzer!"

"Pettigrew?" Jim says, his breath steaming in the cold. "What the Sam Hill are you doing here?"

"Brought the 101st up from Rheims day before yesterday," Pettigrew says. "I'm back with my truck outfit. Jeep shows are scrubbed since the German attack." He glances down at the half-open window, pulls the collar of his overcoat tighter around his neck. "We're bugging out."

"To where?"

"They don't tell us anything except 'follow the guy in front of you,'" Pettigrew says. "Blackout lights, no escort, just the rifles we have." He pats the stock of the carbine lying across his lap. "I'm supposed to be some kind of colored Edward G. Robinson, drive and shoot at the same time." He pauses. "The Sam Hill are *you* doing in Bastogne?"

Jim puts a gloved hand on the window. "Things didn't go so swell after you guys left me in Hosingen." His offended tone is accompanied by a wry smile.

"You got a beef?"

"Not really. That broken leg had to be evacuated."

"Been rough on you?"

"I haven't worked out a solo act."

"You want to try and ride out of here with me? See if the MPs allow a passenger?"

That's exactly what Jim wanted when he first saw the column. He walks around the front of Pettigrew's truck and gets in the passenger side. The truck in front of them starts forward. As they move out, Jim's thoughts turn to Osceola Jones, the sergeant, the reporter. He hopes they won't be hurt bad or killed. The column stops. Jim puts his hand on Pettigrew's right arm. "Wait. Those bastards aren't gonna let me through."

"You don't want to try?"

"Nah. They'll see my shoulder flash, know I'm Team SNAFU," Jim says.

"You're an entertainment soldier."

"Been helping interrogate prisoners, even doing some soldiering. Let me out." Jim gasps. He can barely believe he said that.

The column starts to move. As the driver behind them flashes his lights, Jim produces a packet of letters out of his jacket pocket. "Mail these for me when you get somewhere that's not all haywire."

⋀

An MP steps into the basement room where a dozen other SNAFUs are sleeping on the floor. "Looking for Private Tanzer!" he shouts, then waits. This is the fifth room he's been to.

"Yes?"

"I have orders to bring you to Colonel Kinnard."

"What does he want with me?"

"Hell if I know, Private. Let's go."

⋀

"Private Tanzer, your big moment has come," Colonel Kinnard says. "General McAuliffe wants a Christmas show for our wounded and the civilians in the cellars. Three performances. The aid station at the Sarma store and the Notre Dame cellar. The riding hall at the barracks has the most American wounded. You will start there."

"Yes, sir," Jim says, producing the map. "Can you get this to General Middleton?"

Kinnard looks over the map and hands it back to Jim. "Keep your map, Private. You got it this far. It's the best souvenir of the war." He smiles. "Until some paratrooper brings back Hitler's balls."

"When do you think I'll be able to get back, Sir, to my Jeep show unit?"

"Here's what I *know*, Private Tanzer," the colonel answers in a not-unfriendly tone. "Your unit is Team SNAFU, attached to the 101st Airborne Division."

"Yessir."

"Soldier, things are fouled up. That's war. And your *old* unit, well, Uncle Sam has probably replaced you with two younger, better-equipped entertainers. Will replace them with four more, the war lasts long enough."

"Yessir." *That's what I was worried about,* Jim does not say.

"There's a theatre on the Rue du Vieux Moulin. You'll find costumes and other gear there. A place to do your auditions."

"Yessir."

On the way back to the barracks, Jim hears many engines. The truck column has come back to Bastogne? No, no. It's the low-pitched drone of aircraft overhead. That awful whistling begins. It's German aircraft overhead. He breaks into a run.

AUDITION
NEW YORK
JULY 12, 1939

"GOOD MORNING, TANZER and Polk. Vat you got for me?" Sam Gold says in Yiddish-inflected Brooklynese. The proprietor of the Gold Talent Agency pauses to blow a stream of grey-blue cigar smoke over his left shoulder. He is hoping for a knife-throwing act. "Please don't tell me Baby Astaires. I got half a gross." He points to a pile of photographs on his desk.

"We do mixed doubles, Mr. Gold," Jim ad-libs, "like Burns and Allen."

"*Bist meshugeh?* Are you kidding?" Gold picks up some headshots, then drops them back on the pile. "I got a dozen mixed doubles I don't mention."

"We do swing and jazz, ballroom, foxtrot—collegiate, waltz, rumba, samba," Jim says. Stella Polk looks down at her feet, hoping Mr. Gold doesn't ask to see their samba. "Fast rhythmic, Lindy Hop, Balboa, Jive, Carolina Shag."

"Here's my problem. I got rhythmic steppers. Experienced ones. Half of them are dancing behind a counter at Voolworth's or vaiting tables. Can you sing, Mr. Polk? Butler's hires singing vaiters. I don't book vaiters. Or doormen, either." Gold smiles at young and pretty Stella Polk. She smiles back.

"We tap," Jims says. "Soft shoe. We—"

"The Silver Slipper, Kenneth's, and The Little Club all closed this summer. *Vus zug ikh yetst?* What can I say?"

"Buck dancing, clogging."

"Not in my office, please, vith the clogging. Maybe The Old Duck Club. I don't book Vaudeville reviews. That's dead." He re-lights his cigar. "You got something for me that all these—" he sweeps a hand over the photographs—"don't got?"

Jim clears his throat. "She sings. I do eccentric."

"Vat kind of sings?"

"Torch, rhythm and blues. Think of Martha Tilton."

"Good."

"I dance eccentric," Jim says.

"Now, you two," Gold says, "move the chairs and show me your best steps." They dance for about thirty seconds. "Miss Tanzer very nice. You are too tall for ballroom, Mr. Polk. Show me your eccentric."

"I haven't exactly worked that up as an act."

"Show vat you got."

Jim does the steps he's cribbed from Ray Bolger's *Wizard of Oz* scarecrow. Gold opens a desk drawer and pulls out a business card. "Get lessons." Tall and funny looking, Gold thinks. Good for eccentric.

"I emcee, tell jokes, do impressions," Jim says. Stella looks down at her feet again.

"Jokes," Gold says. "I'm interested. A good comic is vorth a hundred baritones. Make me laugh."

Jim tells a travelling salesman joke, a political commentary joke, and a joke about women drivers.

"Vat else you got comic?"

Jim hesitates. "I have a Li'l Abner impression." This is news to Stella.

"Abner from the funny pages? Give me your Abner."

"*Natcherly!*" Jim says and proceeds with a close imitation of his father discussing baseball.

"That's good, Mr. Polk. It's a bit, not an act, but it's good. Vat else?"

"I do Amos 'n' Andy."

"My Aunt Tildi in Lodz does Amos 'N' Andy," Gold says. "Leedle Abner is fresh. Verk on that one. Add some hillbilly steps, it could be an act."

"I will, Mr. Gold," Jim says. "Thank you."

Turning to Stella, Gold says, "Miss, did you bring music? Good. Sing for me—no piano today. I'll make allowances." Stella sings two verses from "You're a Sweetheart." "More Helen Forrest than Martha Tilton," Gold says, "but nice." She's cute. She's got talent. He likes her.

"Thank you, Mr. Gold."

"The Palace Salon for hairstyle, Miss Tanzer," he says. "You von't look like you're going to the high school dinner dance. You'll need a better dress for auditions. Ask Sarah on your vay out."

"I will."

"Enough for now. Eccentric dance and Leedle Abner, Mr. Polk. Get your hair and dress, Miss Tanzer, and come back."

"Thank you, Mr. Gold," Stella says. She and Jim are on their feet, waiting for goodbye and good luck.

Sam Gold looks at Stella while polishing his eyeglasses with the fat end of his tie. "I could book you both at Stiers."

"A nightclub?" Jim says.

"A resort. In the Catskills. The Borscht Belt. Two hours by train from Grand Central. Shangri-La for New York Jews. Fresh air. Mountain scenery. The resorts need replacements by mid-summer. You vould be social staff. You von't make much money, but free rent. Mort will have you eat with the guests: three *geshmack* meals a day. It's Lindy's with trees. A chance to develop your act in front of an audience. Just until Labor Day, but that's six veeks of verk. Some guest might see you and know somebody. It happens." He turns towards the door. "Sarah, get me Mort Stier." Then to Jim, "Call Sarah tomorrow."

"I will, Mr. Gold, thank you," Jim says.

Sarah speaks to Stella on the way out. "It's Loehmann's in the Bronx for dresses. Ten percent off for the entertainment trade. Don't mention Sam Gold until after they give you a price."

12.

BASTOGNE, BELGIUM, DECEMBER 22, 1944

Medium Field First Aid Dressing
Dyed Sterilized Dressing
Stock Number 2-393
Red color indicates back of dressing. Put other side to the wound.

Janesville Cotton Mills, Janesville, Wisconsin
Contract Number N14Q1-55692A

"It's too dark to read," Private Oceola Jones says to Jim. "What's *this*?" His voice rises as they bounce through a deep pothole. They're in the back of a deuce and a half with ten other SNAFU soldiers. The back side of night is fighting a rear-guard action against the approaching grey light of dawn.

"Casting call," Jim says. "Soldier show. Christmas Day. For our wounded and the civilians in the basements."

"It's too dark to read. Tell me what it says."

"'Morale Corps presents Bastogne Follies Christmas Soldiers Show. December 25th only. Calling for singers, dancers, musicians, impressionists, comedians, jugglers, magicians, stage hands. There's one in every squad! Cast and crew members excused from duty Christmas Day. Open auditions, December

24, 1400 to 1600 at the Théâtre Municipal de Bastogne, 17 Rue du Vieux Moulin, Bastogne. Civilians welcome. *Les civils sont les bienvenus.*"

"Christmas day off duty? I *needa* be in your show."

"What's your act?"

"Just like now," Jones says. "I act like I'm not scared and miserable. Got any smokes? I've got two Hershey bars."

"I spent my Camels. I can trade you four Fleetwoods."

"Sure. I'm gonna smoke 'em, not keep 'em. But four Fleetwoods are worth only one chocolate bar."

"You got toilet paper?" Jim asks. The bouncing truck is loosening his bowels.

Jones reaches under the white bedsheet poncho covering his overcoat, pulls out a wad of leaflets and hands them to Jim.

"What is this?"

"*Six Questions for the American Soldier*. German brainwashing. Safe conduct for us to surrender."

"You don't want to keep them for souvenirs?" Jim says.

"More a these than snowflakes around Bastogne. Not worth for anything but ass-wiping."

▲

"We advance on foot from here," the sergeant says. The truck has pulled off the road and stopped. "Combat zone. Keep yourselves six foot apart. No smoking, no talking after we get moving. Out now, take care a your bidness, and fall in."

Within sixty seconds Jim is squatting in the woods, trousers at his ankles, rifle leaning against a tree. He looks up from *Six Questions for the American Soldier* and sees a German on one knee, twenty yards away, aiming a rifle at him. "Don't shoot! *Nicht!*" Jim yells and falls onto his back on the forest floor. He feels a dull thud in his right shoulder, like he's been kicked. His mind reels. Reach for his rifle?

Surrender? Play dead? He doesn't move. Nor does the German.

"Tanzer, what are you yelling about?" The sergeant walks towards Jim. "Is it Fritz here?" Jim looks closer and sees a two-inch crest of snow on the German's helmet. The man's face is marbled green and white. A hand-lettered sign hanging from his neck says *Come and get your man, Adolf*.

"Musta been killed by an air blast," the sergeant says. "Lookit the broken branches on the ground."

"My shoulder."

"You're on a tree root." The sergeant turns towards the dead German. "Hate to break up this tableau, but somebody's gonna get scared and start shooting." The sergeant lifts the rifle out of the frozen soldier's hands and says to Jim, "Finish up and drag this poor bastard to the side of the road. Graves Registration will pick him up one a these days."

▲

"I heard about colored gunners, but now I believe it," Jones says to Jim. They've been halted just beyond Senonchamps. "Seen a picture in *Yank*, but I thought it was a publicity shot, like the Marine in a foxhole at Peleliu holding that Coca-Cola in one hand, rifle in the other, smiling like he's at a fucking barbeque."

"This war is mixing things up," Jim says.

The SNAFU unit has advanced to a large snow-covered field of undulating rises and dips. Jim sees stubby guns in firing pits, muzzles covered with tent halves and raincoats. Fresh brown earth is piled next to the pits. The crew on each gun are stacking shells and wooden boxes of powder charges.

"Need a SNAFU to hump a radio," the sergeant says, walking back towards the formation. When there are no volunteers, he points to Jim. "Tanzer."

"See you later, Jimmy," Jones says.

"Needham Johnson. Needy," the black corporal says. He and Jim are walking west in knee-deep snow, away from the guns. The blocky radio gives Jim the opportunity to bend over as far as he thinks is decent. "Forward observer, 969th Field Artillery Battalion, now. Hope that doesn't have a hood," he adds, pointing to the white sheet Jim's wearing.

"Camouflage. Against the snow. I'm Tanzer, Jim Tanzer."

"Just want to make sure I'm not paired up with a Klansman." Needy looks at Jim's shoulder flash. "What are you?"

"I'm not sure. I *was* a 4-4-2, Entertainment Specialist. Morale Corps."

"Well let me tell you, Private, the negro soldier is not properly entertained in this man's Army."

Jim tilts his head. He's never considered that. "I need to get back to my unit" is all he can think to answer.

"No rush," Johnson says. "Bastogne's surrounded. They didn't tell you that? Nothing getting in or out. …Don't look so worried, Private. Things'll get better when the weather clears."

"When's that going to be?"

"Nobody's telling the 969th anything but wind speed."

"I have orders to produce a soldier's show," Jim says, reaching under his overcoat, pulling a flyer out of the hip pocket of his field jacket and handing it Johnson. "Here in Bastogne."

Johnson looks it over and shakes his head back and forth. "All of Bastogne is in range of Kraut artillery. Even if some of us *could* come off the line for a few hours, the brass will never let us gather to watch a show."

"It's for the wounded in the aid stations. They're already gathered."

"Oh. Sure. Good idea. Boost their morale."

"You sing or dance or anything?"

"I'm staying with my guns." Johnson points over his shoulder. "But I'll keep your flyer for a souvenir."

They walk on in silence for a few minutes, crunching through the thin layer of ice on top of the snow. Jim thinks about the types of performers he's going to need for the show, and Johnson thinks about muzzle velocity and wind speed.

"I see you have an entertainment problem, Private," Johnson finally says, after he's satisfied with his calculations. "So do I."

"What?"

"My problem is, if I survive all *this* drama—" Johnson spreads his arms and turns a full circle—"this jumpin' frontline life here, how can I be satisfied teaching school? And not with just my job back home, but my life."

"Your life?"

"How can I be an American negro after the war? It's damn tiresome." He looks at Jim to make sure he's not wasting his words. "I've spent the last five months throwing thunderbolts at mortal men. It's biblical, Private Tanzer. I'm Elijah in fatigues. Surprised my head still fits in my helmet."

I can use that in Spamlet, Jim thinks. *Not sure how, but it's good.* "What do you mean?"

"The 969th is three batteries of four guns each. Howitzers, 155-millimeter. Ninety-pound shell. Three rounds per gun per minute when we get going. Shoot the sting off a bee eight miles away, every bee for a thousand acres. We just got proximity fuses that explode shells fifteen feet above the ground, kill soldiers in their foxholes. Downright intoxicating."

They walk on. Johnson stops to look west through his field glasses. "What is it, Private?" he says, still looking west.

"I thought I heard something up ahead."

"That was a tree branch cracking. Snow's heavy."

A new worry springs up in Jim's mind. "Are we in sniper range?"

"You'll know if we are. You're the first target, what with that radio antenna three feet up over your head. Keep your six from me, please." Two beats. "I'm kidding you, Private Tanzer," Needy says with a smile. "We probably *are* out of range."

Jim decides to risk standing up straight, pulling on the radio straps to relieve the burning muscles in his back. "What's going to happen?"

"We are or are not going to run out of shells," Johnson says, "while Hitler tries to draw to a royal flush. You SNAFU soldiers will backstop the parachute infantry, keep German commandos from getting through the seams and killing my gunners."

"What do you mean, seams?"

"The spaces between infantry company strong points. Somebody's got to plug them, buy time for defensive maneuver. That's anti-tank units and artillery."

"Buy time with what?"

"With whatever you got, Private Tanzer. Concentrated small arms fire. Rifles, machine guns, grenades, bazookas. Trickery, cussedness. You've been in combat. You know."

"Yeah, but I'm an entertainment soldier."

"Your SNAFU unit has mortar squads, right?"

"I don't know."

"I hope so. Time is everything, here, Private. The Germans have to kick down the door to Bastogne before the weather clears. Soon as the ceiling lifts—" Needy points up—"we'll get a supply drop, fighter bombers will be out and about, grasshoppers will spot for artillery three miles in front of the perimeter."

"Grasshoppers?"

"Piper L-something. Itty bitty plane. We get that supply drop, we'll put ten shells on every poor bastard Hitler's marched up to Bastogne." They walk on.

"Uh oh. *Here* we go." Corporal Johnson hands the field glasses to Jim. "See that smudge on the horizon?" He points west. "Diesel exhaust." He produces a map and a white cardboard chart. "That's not a circus parade. That's tanks."

"Should we go back and report?" Jim says.

Johnson points to the radio on Jim's back. "That's what you're for. Those tanks aren't coming here, Private. They mean to wall off the Glider Infantry at Flamierge. That's four miles west of us. *Then* they'll come for us."

Jim rocks back and forth on his feet as Johnson looks down at the cardboard chart. "Turn," Johnson says and slowly spins Jim around, then picks the handset up from the cradle on top of the radio. "Observer to Battery A. Over."

Thirty seconds pass. "Observer to Battery A. Over."

"This is Battery A. Observer identify. Over."

"Battery A, this is November Juliet. Over."

Thirty seconds pass. Jim continues to rock back and forth.

"Battery A, this is November Juliet. Over."

"Go ahead Julie. Over."

"Enemy armor." Johnson looks down at the chart. "Grid bravo foxtrot two seven. Target at romeo tango four one. Over."

"Repeat coordinates, Julie. Over."

"Grid bravo foxtrot two seven. Target at romeo tango four one. Over."

"Roger, Julie. Grid bravo foxtrot two seven. Target at romeo tango four one. Received. Out."

Johnson returns the handset to the top of the radio. "Those tanks are coming up the Roman Road. We aren't the first army to fight Germans here."

"How do you know?"

"Classical Studies. Ernst Borinski. Chased out of Germany for being a Jew. Professor at The Eagle Queen."

"Eagle Queen?"

"Tougaloo College."

"Negro college?"

"*My* negro college."

"I went to college for a year. Marshall."

"Okay, you know how to think analytically, Private. Now that you know German tanks will try to cut us off, are you thinking, 'I wonder if General McAuliffe is willing to sacrifice white soldier's lives—including my white life—to defend negro gunners?'"

"I wasn't think—"

"The answer is yes, yes he is. He's a white officer, sure, but he's a white *artillery* officer. He cherishes his guns and his children who man them, be they white or colored."

"You think we'll come under fire?"

"If I'm Colonel von Kraut, if I can I wall off the American gun position—that's us—I bring my tanks and .88s up to that tree line at the crest of the ridge to the south—" he points— "fire direct, then have my infantry advance behind walking mortar fire until they're in small arms range."

"*The-ay,*" Jim shivers in the cold. "Could get that close?"

"I want them that close. I'm still Colonel Von Kraut. I pin the American forward defenders down in their foxholes with machine gun fire, my infantry gets close enough to toss those door knocker grenades, then hand-to-hand combat. I count on half my men surviving long enough to kill or chase the gun crews, then I bring my tanks up to repel the counter-attack by you SNAFU soldiers."

"We're gonna counter-attack German tanks?"

"You have to. Then I pour men and armor through, stream into Bastogne before General McAuliffe can plug the hole in the American lines."

"Really?"

Johnson turns and puts an index finger up in the air. "But my problem—I'm still talking for Colonel Von Kraut—my problem is this battery's position is pre-sighted by the other American batteries spread around Bastogne. Batteries that have forward observers, men like us." Jim gasps when Johnson slaps him lightly on the shoulder. "You hurt?"

"I fell on a tree root."

"Sorry. Forward observers call in fire. American artillery's going to kill the other half of my infantry and a third of my tanks before they can close with this battery. So—now I'm *General* Von Kraut—to overcome the effect of McAuliffe's guns, I have to have two other actions just like this one, simultaneous, and take those kinds of losses."

"Why don't the Germans do that?"

"I don't think they brought that much dog to this fight."

"Do they have forward observers?"

"Probably looking at us right now."

Jim looks ahead. "Should we try to shoot them?"

"Let's leave well enough alone."

They walk on. The radio has become cold on Jim's back. Johnson points ahead and to the right. "We're going to move forward through that tree line, get over the rise so we can see fall of shot." Jim crouches as the freight train sound of artillery rumbles over the field. "Don't worry, Private," Johnson says. "Outgoing mail. There won't be much. We're down to 25 shells per gun."

Jim looks around. "We're safe here?"

"Good enough, for a forward observer. 'Safe' isn't the right word."

Jim bends at the waist. "We going to get return fire?"

"I judge the Krauts will keep moving. Their tank doctrine is speed."

"How long will we stay here by ourselves, you and me?"

"We—" Three tones come from the radio on Jim's back. "Hold on." The corporal turns Jim around again and picks up the receiver, talks back and forth with Battery A.

"Why are they calling me back?" Jim says after Johnson passes on the new orders.

"Hell if I know. Probably your platoon is moving out. The lieutenant's okay with me humping the radio for a while. When you get near the battery, make sure they know it's you." He points back across the snow-covered field. "If you hear incoming, dive in a shady patch. The ground is lower there."

Jim has made about three hundred yards back when the freight train flies over his right shoulder. The Germans *are* firing back. He knocks the breath out of himself diving on his rifle. He struggles for a breath as—CRACK!—the round lands in the woods a quarter of a mile stage left. He finally draws a breath. *This is a mistake*, he thinks. *This is all a big mistake.* He gets up and starts to run.

He reaches the battery and slows to a walk. As he looks for his sergeant, a nearby Howitzer fires. The pressure wave knocks Jim onto his sore shoulder. He scrambles up, covers his ears, and runs all the way through the battery, stopping at a line of large marmite food containers and a coffee urn, all perched on wooden ammo boxes.

A heavyset white sergeant wearing an apron beckons from a slit trench in front of the containers. Jim is in it a few seconds before—CRACK!—a round lands two hundred yards to the left of the battery. The whizzing shrapnel reminds Jim of the Hosingen water tower. CRACK! Another shell lands in the trees to their right. Pine needles and dirt rain down on the trench. Jim presses himself against the side.

"We've been hit!" the sergeant yells, pulling Jim up and pointing towards the coffee urn. A brown stain is spreading in the snow below it. The sergeant jumps out of the foxhole, runs to the chow line, wraps his arms around the coffee urn and waddles back. "Risked my damn life to get hot coffee to the men. Not gonna lose it now." Jim can barely hear him over the ringing in his ears. The sergeant leans the urn away from the gash and looks over. "You got a field dressing, Private?"

THE SHELLING STOPS after a horrible twenty minutes. Word is the German armor turned back down the Roman Road. One of the Howitzers is over on its side. A medic kneels beside a soldier crumpled on the ground above the firing pit.

Jim turns back and sees a captain and a lieutenant walking away from the battery. He can tell by the white bars painted on the back of their helmets. They walk further to the rear, the captain holding the right sleeve of the lieutenant's overcoat. The lieutenant's shoulders are shaking.

They stop and face each other. Steam comes from the captain's mouth. The lieutenant slumps. The captain puts a hand on each of the lieutenant's shoulders, and addresses him without forcefulness. He points back towards the battery. The lieutenant shakes his head no, wrings his hands. The captain reaches down and removes the lieutenant's sidearm from its holster, checks the safety, and tucks it into his web belt.

The captain looks back, sees GIs are watching, points the lieutenant behind a truck. The lieutenant glances back towards the battery, stumbles a bit.

"Green as grass, that one," the mess sergeant says. "Another ninety-day wonder. They're rushing them through OCS now, so many killed."

"He can't take it?" Jim says.

"Give him credit. He's not rolling up maps ten miles to the rear. He's here with us." The captain walks the lieutenant further back. "Well, he was," the mess sergeant says. "Better to send him back than have the men see him so shook up."

NEW YORK WORLD'S FAIR
OCTOBER 15, 1940

"LADIES AND GENTLEMEN, it's time for you to meet..." Jim speaks to the audience of sixty or so standing on a checkerboard floor, fifteen feet below the small balcony stage on which he stands with the headliner. "Elektro, the Westinghouse motoman."

This is the first show of the day in the Hall of Electrical Living at the New York World's Fair. Democracity, the slum and crime-free City of Tomorrow exhibit, is just across the Street of Wings. There are thirteen days left in the Fair's second and last season. The 1939 theme, "Building the World of Tomorrow," has been replaced in 1940 by "For Peace and Freedom." Today is Registration Day for America's first-ever peacetime draft.

The Norway and the Netherlands pavilions are gone, both nations conquered earlier in the year by Nazi Germany, who skipped the fair to focus on Czechoslovakia. France also fell, but their pavilion carries on in exile. The Soviet Union has given up on demonstrating that the world of tomorrow will be socialist. President Roosevelt and the League of Nations had condemned their attack on Finland. There was also the embarrassing sideshow of staff defections by way of the Flushing Line #7 train.

The fair is being upstaged by the spreading conflagration in Europe, starring Adolf Hitler as The Villain, and narrated live on the CBS Radio Network by Edgar R. Murrow's "This is London" reporting from the Battle of Britain.

Jim Tanzer points his rolled-up script towards a seven-foot-tall aluminum robot, oblong suitcase of a torso, stovepipe arms and legs, and Art Deco face fronting a fifty-five-pound head full of switchboard relays. An unsmiling, industrial version of the Tin Man. Westinghouse no longer exhibits robots with human faces, unlike 1931's Rastus, their negro robot. The national rate of unemployment has not been below 15% since 1930. Discussion of robots as job-destroying mechanical slaves would antagonize the new United Electrical, Radio and Machine Workers Union. The current publicity goal is to focus on industrial prowess. The company *does* sponsor *Amos 'n' Andy*, still America's most popular radio program. Neither Labor nor Capital is *regusted* by racial stereotyping.

Jim puts the Bakelite telephone handset up to his mouth. It's connected to a short-range radio transmitter mounted on his chest. By 1944, Westinghouse will have advanced this top-secret technology into proximity fuses for artillery shells.

"Elektro…come…here," Jim says, a little tentatively. He is a stand-in. Electro's regular straight man is stuck in traffic. Show notes call for Elektro's partner to be 5'2" or less, so that the robot looks gargantuan in comparison. The Westinghouse ad agency is mooting the idea of a buddy movie with Mickey Rooney. The robot has just ten inches on Jim Tanzer. It's not enough.

Responding to Jim's command, Elektro slowly bends his right leg in the middle, accompanying himself by a steady buzz which drowns out the faint honks from the nearby Grand Central Parkway. The right foot moves forward two feet. Elektro then pulls his rigid left leg even with the right, courtesy of rollers on the sole of his aluminum foot. The old kick and drag step. The effect is of an oversized aluminum butler with Parkinson's.

"And here he comes, ladies and gentlemen, walking up to greet you, under his own power…STOP!" Elektro hits his mark, a turntable in the stage floor. Like Minnie the circus elephant, Elektro only moves forward. Jim carefully turns the robot full front.

"He's almost human!" Elektro's production manager says from down in front of the electric dishwasher. A few in the audience nod in agreement with this absurdity.

"All right Elektro, how are you feeling today?" Jim asks. A freeze onstage always focuses the audience's attention. He cringes as the production manager hisses, "Slower!" Thinking Jim fears Elektro, several in the audience retreat a step. Jim tries again. "Elektro. How. Are. You. To. Day?" He's swell, and the two proceed with a classic, if sluggish, two-man act.

They make it to the finale. Jim taps a Lucky Strike on the rail that rings the balcony. "Say, Elektro, how about a smoke?" He wedges the cigarette into the corner of Elektro's aluminum lips. "You may now… Smoke. This. Cigarette."

"Light it, you *idiot!*" from below.

While he strikes a match, Jim covers his error with an ad lib. "No need to use your heat ray, Elektro. I'll give you a light." Several audience members put hands up in front of their faces. A woman holding an infant turns and walks briskly away. "You may now smoke this cigarette, Elektro."

"Jesus *Christ!*" from below.

"You. May. Now. Smoke. This. Cigarette. Elektro."

The crowd "oohs" as Elektro takes three puffs. Jim turns to the audience. "Elektro the Westinghouse moto man, folks. He's only two years old. Still learning. Say. Goodbye. Elektro."

13.

BASTOGNE, BELGIUM, DECEMBER 23, 1944

> I was initially opposed to Operation Torch, the joint British-American invasion of French North Africa. It was much later that I understood the political necessity. As the leader of a democracy, President Roosevelt had to make sure the electorate was entertained. The people wanted action. We had to start the show, even though we were not completely ready.
>
> — General George C. Marshall

"You're shaking so hard, Showbiz, looks like you're dancing," Osceola Jones says to Jim. "When you think about it, if a handful of infantry freeze to death, out here all night, is that any worse than sending us forward to be blown to bits by .88s? It *seems* worse, but I can't tell you why."

"Wa-wa, well, it takes longer," Jim says.

"Good one, Showbiz. Good one."

The SNAFU unit has been marched east a mile to another open field. There's nothing there but snow. Due to the risk of capture, the SNAFU soldiers won't be told until sunrise that this field is a designated drop zone, that they've been brought here to screen it from enemy patrols and to haul the cargo parachuted onto it.

The wind is whipping over the snow. Waves of foam break on Jim's knees as he stands up on feet he can barely feel. "My canteen is frozen," he says. "What time is it?"

"Zero two hundred hours. Say! Look at your rifle barrel, Showbiz. That's the moon." Jones looks up. "The sky's got clear!"

"You two," the sergeant has found their foxhole in the dark. "Patrol. Follow me."

"Hate a patrol, but I'll be glad to get moving," Jones says. "Never been so cold."

"On me," the sergeant says. "Krauts coulda infiltrated this far." They join two other SNAFU soldiers and move forward into the field.

"One thing about this patrol, Showbiz," Jones whispers loudly. "Makes that freezing fucking foxhole we just left seem downright homey."

"Clam up, Jones," the sergeant says. They move forward in silence.

⁂

"Good morning, men." A burly sergeant addresses the SNAFU soldiers at the edge of the field where they've been hunkering down since the night before. "This is a drop zone. We will establish a perimeter to the west of it. Pathfinders will be in first. Depending how many make it to the ground in one piece, we may help them set up their gear. I'll decide. You two—" the sergeant points to Jim and Osceola Jones—"take this bazooka."

The morning sky brightens to cornflower blue while they dig a new foxhole. Clear day, aching cold. No fog. Jones looks up. "You hear *that*, Showbiz?"

Jim pulls his wool cap up from over his ears. "What?"

"Engine drone. American planes. We may survive this war."

Jim follows Jones's index finger to six tiny birds in the sky. The drone gets steadily louder. "Skytrains. C-47s. Musta left England in the middle of the night. Gotta be pathfinders coming to set up the drop zone." Two P-47 fighter-bombers can be seen above the Skytrains. "Them cargo boys picked up two jugs for company. Thunderbolts."

Small black clouds begin to appear around the planes as they inch larger and louder. "Flak." Jones says. "Sounds like a string of Black Cats going off down the street."

Within a minute a grey rash has broken out in the crystalline sky. "Them two Jugs are peeling off for ground attack," Jones says. "Wouldn't want to be catching what they pitch. .50 cal and rockets. Look!" One C-47 drops a black squiggle, then another, then several more. Parachutes open, floating towards them. "The first stick of pathfinders. No bigger balls in the Army."

"I see tracers," Jim says.

"Them Krauts are shooting at our boys. Too far away, though."

In less than a minute, the lowest pathfinder drops an orange smoke grenade fifty yards in front of their position and lands a few seconds later. "The signal to the next stick," Jones says. "Dropping smoke, got his Thompson ready to fire. He's jumped a few times."

Eight other pathfinders land. Within a minute, they have rolled up their parachutes and bright orange smoke is billowing from the four corners of the drop zone.

Another C-47 squirts out more squiggles. "Look, here's the second stick," Jones says. The pathfinders already on the ground are setting up to signal the cargo planes following them, setting out directional beacons, raising radio antennas. "That one over there landed hard," Jim says, pointing ahead and to the right.

This pathfinder's face is plowing snow as his open chute pulls him along the ground. It catches on a stump. A medic runs towards him. Another pathfinder meets the medic at the prone man.

"The medic isn't doing anything. That man is dead."

"The pathfinder's still working on him," Jim says.

"Pulling off equipment."

After five more minutes of furious activity, the pathfinders are in business and signaling. "Hey, Showbiz, something in the woods over there!" Osceola Jones points over Jim's shoulder, a little to the left. Jim aims the bazooka. "Keep the tube still while I load the rocket," Jones says. Jim winces at a hard pat on his bruised shoulder. "Rocket ready," Jones says. "May be a German patrol, may be civilians. Don't fire until you know."

"I can't tell what…" Jim sees a flash of white at the tree line and pulls the trigger. Nothing. "The battery must be…" He lifts the tube and pulls the trigger again. *Whooo!* The rocket flies twenty yards over the tree line and disappears. The nearest pathfinder looks up from his radio. They hear a small *pa-koo* four beats later, when the rocket comes to earth.

"Jesus! You almost cooked me with the backblast, Showbiz."

"Sorry, I—"

A white and brown cow ambles out of the woods into the bright sunshine. She lowers her head to an exposed patch of grass. A calf joins her and begins to nurse.

"Goddammit!" The sergeant has run up. "That's not a mortar! Be sure of your target and fire direct, over the sights. You know that."

"Battery," Jim says. "The rocket didn't fire, then it did. Fire. I'm an entertainment—"

"You test the red light before the rocket was in the tube?"

"No, I was…I forgot."

"You two switch. Tanzer, you load. Stay alert. It's gonna be okay."

△

"Cargo planes?" Jim says.

"It's heavies at that altitude," Jones says. "God's wrath, headed for Germany."

Accompanied by an ominous drone, flights of twelve B-17 bombers pass slowly overhead for half an hour. White contrails stretch miles behind them, first narrow and then wide. The quiet after the heavies pass is displaced by a higher-pitched drone. The sound gets louder and the ground begins to vibrate. "So many Skytrains!" Osceola Jones shouts in Jim's ear.

Flack begins to dot the sky again. Jim sees a wing tumble up and away from a C-47. "That one's hit," he says, pointing. The plane keeps its position for a moment, then corkscrews away and down.

"Jesus. No smoke, no flames, no parachutes, no nothing," Jones says.

A few seconds later, a column of orange flame and black smoke rises into the horizon beyond the trees. They hear the explosion. "Carrying gasoline drums," Jones says. "Those flyboys, their worries are over."

The C-47s almost directly above are dropping red, yellow, green, and blue blossoms. Colored parachute canopies over crates and pods and bales. "You see the faces of the guys kicking the bundles out the bay door?" Jones says, then shouts up to the sky, "Merry Christmas!"

Jim can barely hear over the engine noise. "The colors," he says in wonderment.

"I remember," Jones says. "Red for ammo, blue for gasoline, green for rations, yellow for radios, white for yo-yos."

"Yo-yos?"

"That's a joke, Showbiz. White's for medical. Should I put in for a transfer to entertainment?"

A black pod under a blue chute lands forty yards to the left. A wooden crate under a yellow chute lands sixty yards to the right. An olive drab box under a red chute lands close behind them. Then Jim is covered by a shadow. "Duck!" Jones shouts, pulling Jim to the floor of the foxhole. The world goes dark, then there is a muffled thud. Jim feels no pain.

A gust of wind lifts the green parachute off and to the side of the foxhole before it settles back down, rippling on top of the snow. Ten feet away is a large wooden crate. *Merry Christmas from Corporal Mickey Rooney* is written in yellow paint on the side. *He's a corporal now?* Jim thinks. *I'm in up to my neck and Mickey hasn't fired a shot in anger, goddammit.*

"You two." The sergeant is back. "Give me the bazooka and start humping cargo."

The dead pathfinder is loaded last. Jim picks up his feet, another pathfinder his arms. The man is already stiff. Jim sees a thumbnail-size hole in the middle of a frozen black circle on the front of the dead man's jumper coat. "Shrapnel," the pathfinder says. "Pathfinder sticks are trained to function with up to 80 percent casualties. Butch was expendable. To the brass."

Jim looks down. The dead man's grey face needs a shave.

"Goddamned shame," the pathfinder says. "He was my buddy."

△

"Let me tell you before I tell the readers of the *New York Times*." The reporter and Jim are sitting on the floor outside the mess. "Von Lüttwitz offered a surrender. The German general."

"They're gonna surrender?"

"Not *their* surrender." The reporter chuckles as he tamps fresh tobacco into the bowl of his pipe. "What a soldier you've turned out to be. No, he offered McAuliffe the opportunity to surrender, seeing as Bastogne is surrounded. Said it's the humanitarian thing, what with so many civilians and wounded here. It was typed up. I've seen it." He lights the pipe and takes two big draws.

"Do...did we?"

"No. McAuliffe sent back a one-word answer: Nuts."

"Nuts? What does that mean?"

"*Stars and Stripes* is calling you guys the Battling Bastards of Bastogne. People back home can't wrap their minds around the scope of a world war, but they can understand a fight—you know, Lewis versus Schmeling. The defense of Bastogne has become an instant epic."

"It's not even finished," Jim says.

"No, it's not. And there'll be plenty more fighting ahead, after we get out of here. The only good news about that is the war's solving the Depression. Pulled eight million men out of the job market and into uniform. At the same time, Uncle Sam spends five billion dollars a month on war material from factories, farms, shipyards, steel mills and oil refineries. Stuff that gets used up."

"Blown up."

"For every combat man, there's nine soldiers behind them, and for those ten there are one hundred folks back home making what they need. Millions of new jobs, billions of dollars circulating in the economy. Plus a shared sense of purpose, patriotism. It's lifted people's morale."

BANG! They duck as the hallway shakes. A shower of paint chips and dust rains down. The ceiling light casts their shadows back and forth as it sways on its cord. A spider spilled from the ceiling retreats back up its silk.

NEW YORK CITY
October 16, 1940

"What'll it be, miss?" The tiny waiter, kippa on the top of his short grey hair, side towel stashed under his left arm, looks at Stella, registers how young and pretty she is.

"Hearts of lettuce and a fried egg sandwich on white. Please."

"Mister?"

"*Borsht. Pastrami oyf Kornbroyt,*" Jim says, looking at Stella and adding, "*bitte.*"

"*Borsht un pastrami oyf kornbroyt!*" the waiter says to Jim. "*Bis tu ein Yid?*"

"*Ikh bin ein goy.* I'm a gentile."

The waiter shakes his head, walks towards the kitchen. Where he comes from, men that size could be the golem.

Jim takes a sip of cold water. "You don't have to be Jewish to love borscht."

"No," Stella says. "Katz's is a little piece of Stiers on Second Avenue. Look, there's Sam Gold." She waves. "Hello, Mr. Gold."

Jim and Stella discuss family news, the Tanzer chickens, the increase in German bombing of London, Charles Lindbergh and the America First movement. Then *Gone with the Wind.*

"How's work?" Jim asks. Tanzer and Sterling Rhythmic Steppers are on hiatus due to lack of bookings. Stella is a production singer at WNBC radio. She also plays bit parts on *The Goldbergs*, *The Guiding Light* and *The Chesterfield Radio Theatre.*

"I soloed last Tuesday. Mitzi was out and Betty twisted her ankle roller skating in Central Park."

"How'd you do?"

"Pretty well. I trilled the flats on the up-chorus of 'Foolish Things,' but Mr. Scott told me afterwards that I did okay."

"You going to get promoted?"

"I'll never be anything but a background singer at NBC. Mitzi has talent. And besides, she's married to Mr. Scott. She's not going anywhere. How are things at the fair? I want to come watch you work on Saturday."

"I've got a week at the Borden's pavilion in the Food Zone. There's going to be a lot of dairy in the world of tomorrow."

Stella laughs. "It may be hard to keep kosher."

"Hey! Good one. I'm emceeing the two Rotolactor milking shows, ten and three. Big crowds. I'm in the greenhouse at the Electrified Farm the rest of the day. Nobody goes there. I mostly read the paper and write letters."

"They don't know what they're missing!"

"Let me just say, Stella Polk, the contribution that electrification has made to the comfort, leisure, and material advancement of the farmer in the past few decades is exemplified in the attractive farmhouse and the efficiently-operated group of farm buildings at the Electrified Farm."

"Already off book!" Stella says, laughing. "What will you do after the fair closes?"

"Singing waiter at Butler's, or non-union shows out of town," Jim says, shrugging. "I'll be Jimmy Jergens in New Jersey."

"Just the thing for a farmer's hands." Stella reaches across the table and closes her right hand around the base of Jim's thumb. "Soft, smooth, romantic hands." She colors up, lets go and laughs. Jim sits up straighter. He has something he needs to tell Stella.

"Norma says Frankle's Academy of Dance is closing down at the end of the year," he says. "Mrs. Frankle isn't up to it by herself. I can get a deal on rent." The deal is that the landlord forgets about what Jim still owes him. "Thinking about going back to Huntington after the New Year. I'll run my dance school again and book shows. I could book you when you come to visit Edna."

Three beats. Stella gets a funny look on her face. "I want to go with you."

Jim blinks twice, then says, "Say, we can pick up our act."

Stella could say the obvious, that Jim is too tall for ballroom. But she has something more important in mind. "I don't want to be your act partner. I want to be your wife partner. I want a family. Will you marry me, Jimmy?" She pulls his hand across the Formica table. Jim pulls back, but then relaxes his arm. He will.

14.

BASTOGNE, BELGIUM, DECEMBER 24, 1944

> The most valuable of all Morale Corps supplies is the pool of talent that is found in the unit itself. Every unit has its Bob Hope, its Lou Costello, its Barrymore.
>
> MORALE CORPS GUIDE, EUROPEAN THEATRE OF OPERATIONS, 1944

"BE READY, PRIVATE Tanzer," Willi says to Jim, "in case we happen upon hungry *Volksgrenadiers*. They'll expect you to point your rifle at them, for the correctness of their surrender." Willi and Jim are in a Jeep, less than a mile behind the front line in the northwest of the Bastogne perimeter. Jim is driving slowly, given the no-man's-land feel of the terrain. He shivers from time to time, despite long woolen underwear, two pairs of wool trousers, two pairs of gloves, a sweater over his wool shirt, an overcoat over his field jacket, and the wool cap he's worn under his helmet the last five days. His bedsheet poncho flaps in the wind.

The supply drop yesterday was mostly gasoline, medical supplies and artillery shells. Rations are dwindling. Jim has been assigned a Jeep and a trailer, and detailed to inspect outlying farms for foodstuffs to be requisitioned. He has obtained permission to spring Willi from the prisoners' work detail, pulling bodies out of bombed buildings in town. The distracted intelligence officer agreed that Willi's command of German dialects will allow Jim to immediately question enemy soldiers looking for someone to surrender to.

"We can't take prisoners in the Jeep," Jim says. "They'll have to walk themselves to the prisoner pen."

"They'll do whatever you tell them," Willi says. "It's quiet today. I'll wager *Generalleutnant* von Lüttwitz is consolidating forces for a final attack tomorrow, on Christmas Day."

"I'm producing a soldier show on Christmas Day."

"I can do a solo act. Handstands, tumbling, juggling, things along the acrobat line."

"Good. I'll bring you to the audition when we're done with this fatigue." From his Prince Von Duke Circus days Jim knows what strong, small men can do.

Willi points to a gnarled tree. "There'll be apples under the snow. We can come back if we don't find any in the cellars. Applesauce for Christmas will be cheery. I'm sure your airplanes dropped some cinnamon into Bastogne."

That could be funny, Jim thinks. They drive on.

"Stop, please," Willi says, pointing. Jim sees a brown patch where the wind has blown the snow off the top of a mound.

"Is that a rug?"

"Horse," Willi says. "Part. The rest of it must have been scattered by a shell. May I have your entrenching tool, Private Tanzer?"

"We don't have time to bury a horse."

"This won't take long."

"Okay," Jim says, handing over his shovel.

Willi gives the mound a sharp blow. More snow flies off. It's a hind quarter.

"What do you want with that?"

"Russian brisket," Willi says. "To survive a war, you must be willing to eat anything." He puts his foot on the blade of the shovel and works it through the hip joint. "Six kilos," he says, picking up the thigh without effort and heaving it onto the trailer. He points towards a large pile of stones and blasted wood, visible through the snow. "Now on to inspect his master's house."

"There's no kitchen left there," Jim says.

"Anyone from the countryside knows there's a root cellar under that pile."

"You're good at foraging, Willi."

"That's to be in the *Wermacht* in 1944. Iron rations become short rations and short rations become no rations. Want to stop a German attack? Shoot sausages at it. *Wurstkanone*." He smiles.

They clear away the stones and other debris above where Willi thinks the cellar will be. "That metal ring, there's the trapdoor," he says, and heaves it open. A waft of air hits them, a faintly vegetal smell of earth and stone. There is a patch of snow-white hair stuck to the underside of the door. A beam of light picks out a small figure lying on the packed dirt floor. "*Liebe Grossmutter*," Willi says from halfway down the ladder. "Little grandmother. Coming up when the shell hit."

Little grandmother's snow-white hair is pulled back so tightly, she appears to be smiling. It contrasts sharply with her maroon face, neck and hands. Her blue skirt, grey sweater, and pale-yellow apron are in place, as though she had smoothed them down after the explosion hurled her to the cellar floor. There are no shoes on her feet, however.

"Let's look somewhere else," Jim says to Willi. *Everything down there's been next to a dead person*, he thinks.

"There's plenty here she doesn't need now," Willi says, pointing towards potatoes and glass jars scattered on the dirt floor.

"I don't know, Willi."

"Orders. We must have it. But first it is proper we take care of *Grossmutter*. We will be brief."

There's a watering trough on its side in front of the tumbled-down barn. "The wood is roughhewn, but nicely joined," Willi says. "It will do. May I?" Willie points to Jim's bayonet, fixed to his belt by the scabbard. Jim gives it to him automatically, then wonders why. *Nah, he wouldn't*, Jim thinks, *we're buddies.*

Willie chips the trough free of ice and *thank-you*'s the bayonet back, handle first. He squats next to the trough, jerks it to his shoulders and then above his head, walking with it easily. Putting the trough down in the cellar, he crosses himself. He picks up the old woman as if she were a doll. Jim notices how big his hands are.

Willi lays the body in the trough. "May I have your canteen?" He pours water on a lower corner of the old woman's apron and wipes a black crust of blood off her upper lip. He steps back next to Jim, puts his hands together and says, "Let light perpetual shine upon her."

"Amen."

"Her family will find her before the spring thaw, if they are still alive," Willi says. "And bury her at the church. Or perhaps city authorities, or your burial soldiers."

"Graves Registration," Jim says, pointing towards a shelf. "Purple pumpkins?"

"Beets. Large. Delicious roasted. They make a soup of them in Russia."

"Good with sour cream," Jim says, recalling the breakfast borsch at Stiers.

Willie blinks. "You amaze me. Never mind. We must take them and the potatoes. And the preserves, of course." There are about four dozen unbroken glass jars of peas, carrots, green beans and tomatoes, root cellar cold, but not frozen.

After they gather the jars, Willi points Jim's flashlight down at the cleared space. "See where the floor is a little darker?" he says. "That's to explore."

"We need to get going," Jim says.

Half a foot down, Willi uncovers a burlap sack containing a homemade American flag and a handful of gold francs. He unrolls the flag. It's sewn-together strips of red, white and blue cloth. The forty-eight stars are done in carefully folded yellow cloth. *Que Dieu bénisse l'Amérique* is stitched in gold thread on the lowest white bar.

"Well done, Belgian woman," Willi says. He clicks his heels and holds the flag out to Jim. "Presented to America in the person of a tall soldier, James Tanzer, who came all the way from West Virginia, United States of America, to set us all free from the devil Hitler. And keep us free from Stalin, God willing." Jim takes the flag. "We will put back the money, Private Tanzer, by your leave. I think this family has given enough."

"Put this in the sack, too." Jim has filled out a requisition form for the food and the flag and gives it to Willie. "They'll need it."

"Honoring the paperwork! Proof of your German blood."

Willi puts the form in the sack, re-buries it, levels the dirt, and stamps the floor around it.

△

ROUNDING THE CORNER onto the Rue du Vieux Moulin at fourteen hundred hours, Jim and Willi see a handful of people and a mule standing in front of a huge pile of bricks and wood, roof tiles, theatre seats, and burned pieces of red velvet. Hit during last night's bombing, the Théâtre Municipal de Bastogne has pitched its guts halfway across the road. The waiting assembly includes soldiers and four civilians: a teenage girl with an uncanny resemblance to Judy Garland, a woman who reminds Jim of Edna Polk, likely the girl's mother, and an old man with a puppet on his hand. The mule is with a man wearing wooden farmer's clogs. A pint-size US Army sergeant levitates in front of the group, a ventriloquist's dummy sitting on the forearm of a soldier.

The blast has blown open the door of the abandoned café across the street. The soldiers and civilians follow Jim inside, excepting the farmer and the mule. It's cold inside, but there's no wind. The little wooden sergeant raises his head and addresses Jim in a high-pitched voice. "Are you going to get things rolling, Private, or am I going to have to put my boot up your keister? I'm Sergeant Woodrow Hardschaft. I'm here to shape up this outfit!" The lips of the ventriloquist are clearly moving, steam hovering in front of his face. *Well*, Jim thinks, *it's supposed to be an amateur show.*

"I'm glad I wasn't in that theater!" the dummy says. "I'd be a pile of splinters!"

Jim has seen dozens of ventriloquists, knows this chestnut. "You *are* a pile of splinters." He bends at the waist and salutes the dummy. "What's the name of the soldier with you?"

"We don't salute sergeants in this man's Army!" the dummy says, and on the third try gets his little wooden hand pointing up at the ventriloquist. "His name is Henry King. I'm a sergeant and he's a king. Ain't that a beaut!"

Jim waits for the ventriloquist to speak, but the soldier just stares at the back of the dummy's little helmet. "Well, Sergeant Woodrow, your uniform is in fine shape," Jim says. It really is. "How do you keep it so clean?"

"I run my squad by radio."

"I'm sure your men don't like that."

"So what if I'm not poplar?"

"You're not poplar?" Jim says.

"No. I'm an all-pine soldier. HA!" Hardschaft's head pops up and swivels 360 degrees. Willi laughs out loud.

"That was a terrible joke," Jim says with a smile. This is better than he expected.

"You *look* terrible, Private," the dummy says to Jim. "Unshaven, no tie, muddy boots."

"We're in a combat zone," Jim says. He knows his next line. "You should apologize for criticizing how I look."

"Okay. I'm sorry you look terrible."

The ventriloquist is still looking down. "Okay, soldier," Jim says to the dummy, "three shows tomorrow. Rehearsal at oh eight hundred hours, Heintz Barracks, building two, basement. I'm gonna call you Sergeant Splinters. We'll have a mixed audience for the civilian performance." *If King was a decent ventriloquist,* Jim thinks, *maybe the dummy emcees the whole show. No.*

Jim turns to the teenage girl. "What is your act, miss? *Une chanson* for *le* show?"

"I have English of school, *monsieur,*" the girl says with a shiver. "I sing."

The mother adds, in French, "*Un autre* Edith Piaf!"

"Please go ahead," Jim says. "We'll make allowances for no piano." He smiles.

The girl begins to sing "Somewhere Over the Rainbow." Sounds just like Judy Garland, if Judy Garland were a soprano. And had blue lips. Excellent.

"Can you dance?" Jim says. "*Dancez-vous?*" The teenage girl nods and does a chassé and a pirouette. Far from professional, but charming. "You'll be great," he says. "I'll have you sing, dance. You'll play Mary in the manger scene. Rehearsal tomorrow at eight hours in the morning, the Heintz Barracks, building two. I'll tell the sentry to expect you." He gestures at the farmer outside with the mule, says to the girl, "Translate, *s'il vous* please."

"I've never seen a handsome mule, but this one is truly ugly," Willi says to Jim. "Half an ear shot or bitten off. Skin condition to boot. Smells terrible, even in this cold."

"His name is Bonhomme the Dancing Mule," the girl says. "He can do many things."

We ought to call him Barnhomme, Jim thinks. *Hey!* "Okay, ask to see his act," he says.

She asks. The farmer clicks his tongue. Bonhomme rises on his hind legs, turns a circle, and drops back down. The farmer crosses his arms and turns his back. Bonhomme brays loudly and gooses him from behind with its head. The farmer jumps a little. *The mule is funny*, Jim thinks, *but the farmer needs to really sell it*. Bonhomme raises back up, puts his front legs on the farmer's shoulders and busses him on the head.

"Besame mucho," Jim says. "How did you train this mule?"

The farmer talks for a long time. "Abandoned here by a French circus," the girl says. "Too sick to work. The farmer nursed him back to health. Used him on the farm and eventually to entertain his friends. Taught him to march like a fascist."

What? Jim thinks, then turns to the mule. "*Marchez bonhomme, s'il vous plaît.*"

The farmer smiles, covers his upper lip with a forefinger, gives Bonhomme a Nazi salute and says, "*Armee allemande bonhomme—le mulet SS!*" The mule begins to walk, kicking out his front legs in a goose step. *Got my headliner*, Jim thinks.

The farmer speaks to the girl, and she turns to Jim. "The mule requires two packs of cigarettes. Lucky Strike or Camel. He smokes, if you want that in your show." Jim thinks of Elektro. *Nah.* The farmer speaks again. "He won't take Fleetwoods," the girl adds.

"Okay," Jim says. "I'll have them at rehearsal." Cheap for a big act, he thinks. He looks over at a soldier holding a trombone, leaning on the bar, smoking a cigarette. "Band?"

"28th Division."

"How did you end up in Bastogne?"

"I was in Wiltz. Saturday parade on the 16th never happened. By the 18th we were pulled into the line to cover the headquarters' retreat."

"You saved your trombone?"

"It kept me out of combat until last week. Caught a piece of shrapnel for me. Good luck charm."

"Where did you work before the Army?"

"AFM, Local 47. Los Angeles. I've got the Hollywood hundred-ten repertoire and jazz." He takes a final puff on his cigarette, field-strips the butt and sprinkles it on the floor. "I thought the war would be over before I got sent overseas; and even if it wasn't, thought I'd be miles behind the lines. That was Wiltz. Until Monday."

"What did you do in the fight?" Jim asks.

"Machine gunners' mate. It was that or bazooka loader. I wasn't keen on shooting it out with a German tank."

You said it, brother, Jim thinks. "What happened?"

"The horn section held off a Kraut company long enough for the gasoline to get driven west. Helped that the Panzers were road-bound and the engineers had laid mines."

Jim recalls laying mines in front of Longvily and shakes his head slightly. "Any ideas for the show?"

"Did some studio work for MGM. Do you know 'Der Frank-Führer's Mustard March' from that cartoon, *Dexter Dog and the Nutzis*? Spike Jones covered it in '42."

Jim knows the song. He thinks about the parade of cartoon Nazis and Bonhomme the mule. He smiles. "Funny."

Trombone plays the first bar of the Horst Wessel song. "You know," he says. "*They're nutzi,*" he blows a raspberry, "*plain nutzi,*" raspberry, "*in der FrankFührer's case.*"

"Hey!" Jim says. The big idea has landed. "We'll use that number for the entrance. The mule leads, cast sings in behind. The trombone brings up the rear." *Glue a Hitler mustache on that mule,* he thinks. *Hey! If Stella was here to see what I can do.* "Okay, Trombone, see you at rehearsal tomorrow. Who's next?"

"I'm an Irish tenor."

Dago tenor, maybe, Jim thinks. "Okay," he says. The short, olive-complected soldier looks like he'd be right at home coming up the Peabody Mine #8 elevator at the end of a ten-hour shift, if that miner happened to be wearing an OD field jacket stuffed with newspaper, and had jammed his helmet on top of a pink dish towel wrapped around his head. But every show can use an Irish tenor. He's in.

Jim thinks he recognizes the next soldier from bazooka training. It's Private Sorrento of the 427th Regiment bakery company. "You dirty rat," Sorrento says. He sounds like a washer woman from Chicago imitating a drunk imitating Jimmy Cagney. Saturday-night-beers-at-the-PX caliber, at best.

"What else you got?" Jim asks.

There's a decent Franklin Roosevelt: "The only thing we have to *fee-ya* is *fee-ya* itself." Then a poor Mae West: "I used to be Snow White, but I drifted." Then Edward G. Robinson, recognizable as such only by, "Tough guy, eh?" Finally, the inevitable Amos 'n' Andy: "Put your John *Hambock* on this line… Let's *Simonize* our watches… I'se *regusted*… Check and double check."

"You're in, Sorrento. Work on those. See you at rehearsal tomorrow. Okay, soldier," Jim says to a blonde GI who looks about fifteen. "What have you got for us?" The boy holds up two mess kit spoons. "You must be from the South," Jim says. *What holler?* he thinks.

"Norris, TVA Dam, Tennessee. Uh-huh, yessir."

"Okay, Kid Spoons, fire when ready."

The boy begins the drumline of a marching cadence:

CLACK-CLACK, *clicka-clack, clicka-clak, clicka-clak*
CLACK-CLACK, *clicka-clack, clicka-clak, clicka-clak*
CLACK-CLACK, *clicka-clack, clicka-clak, clicka-clak*
A-clack clack CLACK, *A-clack clak* CLACK, *A-clack clack* CLACK

"Gladiators Entrance," Jim says, thinking of the Prince Von Duke Circus. "That'll work."

Kid Spoons nods, clacks out a five-note bridge, and begins to sing:

I'm a so-jer, in the army of the Lord
Just a so-jer in the army of the Lord
Got my war clothes on in the army of the Lord
If I die, let me die in the army of the Lord

Jim puts up a hand. "Great. You're in. Now we have the Baptists covered. We'll use your drum line as a lead-in to the FrankFührer opener. And you'll be the Little Drummer Boy in the manger scene. We rehearse tomorrow at Heintz Barracks, number two, at oh eight hundred hours, shows all day after that." He looks at Willie. "I'll sing 'Bei Mir Bist Du Schoen' and bang, we've covered the three fighting faiths."

"It's banned in Germany as non-Aryan," Willi says. "You *must* sing it."

"Here is *Kasperle*," the girl says, gesturing to the old man.

"Come again?" Jim says.

"Polichinelle…Punch…Punch and Judy," Willi says. "The puppet."

The puppet wears a faded red jester's motley and a sugarloaf hat with a tassel. His hooked nose almost meets his jutting chin. Unknown injuries have left him a hunchback. The old man slowly turns the puppet's face towards his own. When their eyes meet, the old man raises his eyebrows and smiles. "*Je suis Polichinelle. J'ai survécu à un autre combat avec le bourreau*," he says. "*Le maître meurt, mais les marionnettes ne le font jamais.*"

"I am Punch. I have survived another fight with the hangman," the girl says. "The master may die, but the puppet never will." Out of the corner of his eye, Jim sees Sergeant Splinters turn his head 180 degrees and look his ventriloquist in the eyes. *The kid can ad lib*, Jim thinks.

Punch begins to ask about his wife and child, then goes into a bit about *le crocodile* and *le constable*. Jim thinks *the puppet can do a two-man act with Splinters*. "Tell him Punch is in the show," he says to the girl. "Tell him when and where for rehearsal." He turns to Willi. "I'll put you right before the manger scene. You'll stay onstage and perform for baby Jesus. It's holy. The mule will play this one straight."

A soldier in jump boots walks into the café with Jim's flyer in his left hand. Even in fading light, Jim can see the fierce pub sign of a shoulder flash, "AIRBORNE" stitched in bright yellow above a screaming eagle head. The paratrooper looks like central casting's idea of an actor to play Joe from Corporal Bill Mauldin's "Willie and Joe" cartoons: broad but slumping shoulders, dark circles under the eyes, gaunt cheeks, four days' worth of beard, cigarette perched at a forty-five-degree angle on his lower lip. A twenty-five-year-old man who looks fifty. His faded uniform is sagging, streaked with dirt and dotted with stains. He's wearing an olive drab Army blanket underneath his jump jacket. Rips at the knees of his trousers must have been sutured by a medic. His boots are caked with mud. A combatman.

"Thanks for coming," Jim says.

"Sure, but we don't salute in the 101st." He points to Willi. "SS?"

"*Volksgrenadier*," Jim says.

"Congratulations, Fritz." Paratrooper reaches out, grasps Willi's hand and shakes it. "I got to get crippled or killed before I'm outta the war." His speech rises and falls with his shallow breathing.

"I'm not used to seeing a paratrooper without his rifle," Jim says with a smile. "Even your mess cooks carry carbines."

Glancing at Jim's shoulder, Paratrooper says, "What are you, soldier?"

"Morale Corps. Not movies, though. MOS 4-4-2, Entertainment Specialist. Jeep shows. Soldier shows. Like this one."

Jim's flyer vibrates noticeably in the paratrooper's hand. "This made it up to the line," he says, holding it up. "Captain Summers picked my name out of a hat for two hots in the main mess, sleep inside a night. And this."

"That's a piece of luck," Jim says.

"It was a setup by Doc Vernon, our medic. I've been... I've been too long on the line. Got flaky the last couple of days."

"It's tough up there," Jim says. "I was—"

"It's not just being scared. Been scared since Normandy. Everybody up front is scared, everybody that's not bughouse. It's that we got pulled out of R&R a month too soon and trucked here, in this weather. Don't have enough ammo, enough clothes, enough replacements. And we've been in the fight—" he looks at Willi—"every day until today."

"I'll get you fixed up in the barracks tonight," Jim says.

"I'm a rag man now. Need time off the line, hot chow and sleep, soft duty, get some heart back. If this doesn't do the trick, I'm headed for the Blue 88 furlough."

Jim has heard of it. A combat fatigue casualty gets dinner, a shower, clean clothes, twenty-four hours' worth of sodium amytal, breakfast, and a ride back to the front line. "You're in a Morale Corps work party tomorrow," Jim says. "Rehearsal and three shows. Knit up the raveled sleeve of care."

"Sleeve of care?"

"Line from a play. Okay, Corporal, show me your act."

"Don't have an act. Can't play music, don't sing, don't dance. Grew up on a ranch thirty miles outside of Spotted Horse, Wyoming. Work and school, eat and sleep. No hobbies. Couple hours of Saturday radio run off the car battery, and for President Roosevelt."

"No act at all?"

"I know how to play dead."

"Okay. You'll be stage manager and a wise man in the manger tableau. Tomorrow at oh eight hundred hours at Heintz Barracks, number two, basement."

After everyone has left, Jim says to Willi, "We've got our talent. I'll go write the show. You go back to the prisoner pen."

"At gunpoint, please," Willi says. "For form's sake. But keep the safety on."

While Jim and Willi drive in the cold and dark, German ground crews at *Fliegerhorst Mönchengladbach* load fifty-kilo high explosive and incendiary bombs into Heinkel He 111s. The *Luftwaffe*'s midnight show in Bastogne will kill or wound scores of soldiers and civilians, and destroy many homes and public buildings. The latter will include the field hospital in the converted Sarma department store. Few of the wounded soldiers inside will escape the fire.

NEW YORK CITY
November 4, 1940

"Salmon mayonnaise for the lady." Jim knocks the lady's plate against the lady's water glass. Her cigarette smoke is in his eyes and he's anxious to get to his place before the first number. She raises her eyebrows. "And tenderloin of beef, medium rare, for you, sir."

Sir is a stout man in his forties. He tucks his napkin into his shirt collar. "I ordered celery and green olives for my wife. And consommé."

"Golly, sir, I brought them." Jim looks over at an untouched plate of celery and green olives at the next table. He takes a step, reaches an arm over, and nods slightly to the two men there, retrieving the plate and putting it in front of the lady. "My mistake. I'll bring the con—"

"Appetizers come *before* the entrees at most restaurants. Never heard of a deaf singing waiter." Three martinis onboard, the man is trying to impress his wife with wit. He does not.

Jim has trouble with the "waiter" part of being a singing

waiter. "It's timing, Tanzer," the headwaiter has told him, tapping his watch. "The chorus starts at ten after and twenty 'til. Get your orders out before then or your tables get cold food. Karl will stab you if he has to make your plates a second time." Chef Karl is a Tartar, waves his cook's knife and screams at the waiters. By ten p.m. he is drunk and Leonard the elderly sous chef is exhausted.

The band leader had decreed Jim's bass voice suitable for choir only, and won't change his opinion unless heavily tipped. Still, being a waiter at Butler's is a chance to sing for pay — fourteen cents an hour plus tips that run upwards of five dollars on a good night, more if the gangster who owns the place brings his friends in for a few laughs. Jim only gets Monday and Tuesday nights, and won't get better shifts unless a waiter with more seniority leaves. They never do. There's a Depression on.

15.

BASTOGNE, BELGIUM, DECEMBER 25, 1944

> When it comes to the final or dress rehearsal, the Morale Corps Officer should certainly attend. It is at this rehearsal that he will pass on all material and performances so that there is nothing censorable or of a nature that would bring discredit to the organization or cause embarrassment to the commanding officer.
>
> — Morale Corps Guide, European Theatre of Operations, 1944

"Merry Christmas, men. We had a visit from German bombers last night, but Santa Claus has brought another clear day."

"Yes, sir," the orderly says, jumping to attention and saluting.

"What are you working on, Private?"

Jim looks up and sees the gold star on the front of the helmet. The general waits. Jim stands and salutes. General McAuliffe returns it and says, "At ease, men."

"Yes, sir." Jim's voice trills a bit. "The bill for today's soldier's show. Orders from Colonel Kinnard."

"Yes, I know," the general says, tapping ashes out of his pipe. "We can't do what we want for our wounded, but that will be something."

"Yes, sir."

"What's your name, Private?"

"Tanzer, sir. Jim Tanzer."

"Morale Corps."

"Yes, sir. 4-4-2, Entertainment Specialist, Battalion 6817."

"How did an entertainment specialist end up in Bastogne?"

"Bringing a captured map to General Middleton, sir. From Hosingen. 110th Regiment, Company K. Captain Quinn. By the time I got here, it was old news."

"You carried out your mission, Private. The Army can't ask for more than that." The general begins to load his pipe.

"Yes, sir. I'm happy to be done with it, get back to my unit."

"The 28th Division got hit hard. You've seen some things in the last few days. What was their morale like?"

"Every time I've been around them, they were fighting, sir."

"That's what I thought." McAuliffe gestures with his pipe towards the typewriter. "What's on the bill, Private Tanzer?"

"I have a mix of soldiers and locals. All amateurs, sir, except for a mule." Jim pulls the paper out of the typewriter. "Here, sir."

```
            The Follies Bastogne, 1944

    1. Der FrankFührer's Mustard March, featuring
    Bonhomme the Mule
    2. Françoise Gencive, Bastogne's own girl warbler
    3. Private Henry King and Sergeant Splinters
    4. The Thunderer, Private Johnny "Kid Spoons"
    Norris, and Private Antonio "Trombone" Torres
    5. William Hoch, Balance and Juggling
    6. The All-American Tenor, Private Luca DeMasko
    7. Private Anthony Sorrento, Master of a
    Thousand Voices
    8. Puppet Theatre with Punch and Splinters
    9. Away In a Manger
```

"Sergeant Splinters?"

"A dummy, sir. Private King wants to be a ventriloquist."

"This William Hoch. Is he a journalist?" McAuliffe asks, bringing his pipe to his mouth.

"A POW, sir. American. Family moved to Germany in 1934. Not SS. *Volksgrenadier*. Drafted."

"You know the Geneva Convention forbids abusing prisoners of war."

"I won't put him on after the animal act."

The general smiles. "Starting off with the Mustard March?"

"Yes sir."

"I'd like to see your show, Private. But I think I'm going to be too busy today. You know you and your GI performers will be called away if the Germans mount a large attack?"

"The locals can carry the show. More singing, more puppets."

"You plan for contingencies. You'll be at SHAEF if personnel finds out about you."

"Thank you, sir."

General McAuliffe hands back the paper. "Good work, Private Tanzer. The men need a laugh. Don't let that Sergeant Splinters beef too hard about me." He smiles. "I'm doing the best I can until General Taylor gets back."

"He's terrible." Jim sees McAuliffe raise his eyebrows. "The ventriloquist, I mean."

"Of course. Very good, Private Tanzer. As you were." General McAuliffe turns to the orderly. "Private Martinez, tell Colonel Roberts and Colonel Kinnard I'm ready, if you please. ... Oh, Private Tanzer?"

"Yes, General McAuliffe?"

"Break a leg."

It's zero nine in the morning when the players walk to the riding arena. Dawn on Christmas Day. They will play the Seminary Chapel instead of the Sarma store aid station. The pall from last night's bombing hangs over Bastogne—wood smoke, cordite, burned dust, oil, singed fabric. Jim recalls London. Willi recalls Frankfurt.

A real rehearsal isn't possible. Jim talks them through the order of the acts, breaks down the "Der FrankFührer's Mustard March" and the "Away in a Manger" tableau. The mule arrives pulling a cart containing a puppet stage. The master of a thousand voices is a no-show. The puppeteer is dressed in a dark green double-breasted great coat over light blue trousers, topped with a dark green top hat. The 1914 uniform of a Belgian *Carabinier*. Rifleman. "*A combattu les méchants bâtards allemands*," the puppeteer says, and spits on the ground a little too close to Willi.

"He fought the wicked Germans in the Great War," the girl singer says. Her stage costume is a blue and white gingham pinafore, white ankle socks and black Mary Janes. Her hair is in two braids, tied with blue ribbons. She wears a blue wool cape.

The mule has a toothbrush mustache in the center of its upper lip. The farmer is wearing Sunday clothes. Beneath his coat, Willi wears a sleeveless undershirt on which he has drawn stars and ringed planets. He has *Wehrmacht* boxer shorts over long johns.

The enlisted performers are in uniform. The ventriloquist's dummy now wears a flashy general officers' service uniform, including khaki jodhpurs, riding boots, a white sidearm carved out of a bar of soap, and a gleaming little helmet with three gold stars on the front. He looks up at Jim and says, "When my head freezes, I talk like Win-thunn Chut-chill."

Christ, Jim thinks, *you're bad enough without the speech impediment*.

They pass a SNAFU unit forming up, trucks idling nearby. The dummy yells, "Pull up your socks and grab your cocks!" The soldiers smile and one gives a thumbs-up. Jim makes a mental note to speak to the ventriloquist about blue jokes. There will be women and children at the Notre Dame show.

The cast arrives at the riding arena. Ten yards from the door are several dozen corpses stacked like cordwood, partially covered by a frozen canvas tarp. "Hobnail boots. German," the Airborne GI says. Willi looks away.

Jim and the airborne soldier take the puppet stage, a jury-rigged spotlight, a Jeep battery, and a microphone into the cold and dim arena. It's filled with GIs lying on cots, or just blankets on the dirt and sawdust floor. "Downright gassy in here," Jim says. It's a fog of blood, ammonia, excrement, and the funk of six hundred men who haven't bathed in a long time.

"This could be a tough house," Trombone says. "Half the audience is flat on their backs. Reminds me of the one a.m. show at the Rio."

"At least they won't notice how bad Bonhomme smells," the airborne soldier says, breathing through his mouth.

A medic approaches Jim. "Major Swoboda told us you'd be coming. We made space in front for you." They had carried out the men who died overnight.

After set-up is complete, Jim draws a couple of deep breaths, hangs a smile on his big face, and steps in behind the mic. The airborne soldier hits him with the spotlight. The low buzz in the room falls away. "Ladies and gentlemen!" he calls out. "Soldiers of all ages! For your entertainment this morning—" a beat—"Morale Corps Battalion 6817 proudly presents—" a beat—"The Follies Bastogne 1944, a Christmas soldier show *extraordinaire*."

There's some muted clapping. Smiles break out in the audience as Trombone and Kid Spoons play the opening bars of *the March of the FrankFührer* from offstage. The men who can, sit up, or raise themselves on their elbows at least. Jim leans into the microphone and sings:

*Der FrankFührer says Krauts
are der master race
They're nutzi (blapp), plain nutzi
(blapp) in der FrankFührer's case
Krauts will heil der Hot Dog,
that's their wurst disgrace
They're nutzi (blapp), plain nutzi
(blapp) in der FrankFührer's case*

The spotlight hits the mule goose-stepping in on cue. *What a pro*, Jim thinks. The farmer follows, burlesquing a Nazi salute with his wrist bent downward. The other performers are trying to breathe through their mouths and sing and march all at once. It's mostly young men throughout the room. The girl singer is shiny, but no one can take their eyes off the mule.

Kid Spoons and Trombone come in last, and the performers march in place in front of the puppet stage. After the third verse, they turn and march out again. The music stops and the mule farts loudly. It goes over. "He's been eating the scenery," Jim ad libs into the mic. "Hey!" Sensing something special, he calls "one more time!" and the cast repeats the march and then retreats offstage. The mule takes a break, has a smoke.

"My orders are to give you a special Christmas present, let you know the brass in Paris hasn't forgotten you," Jim tells the audience. There's a faint chorus of boos. "Now, now, boys. I'm told General Patton and his Third Army will be here later today to bring you some other gifts."

Jim jumps when a shouted "I'm already here, goddammit" comes from behind him. The spot picks out Splinters, sitting on the puppet stage, legs dangling down. The ventriloquist is behind him, covered by a blanket.

Jim gathers his wits, "Good morning, Sergeant Splinters."

"Salute the rank, dogface! You know goddamned well I'm General George Armstrong Patton! Ol' Blood and Guts. My guts, your blood." The audience's level of engagement goes up three notches.

"Splinters!" Jim hisses at the ventriloquist. "You can't—"

"I'll shoot you for a coward, Private!" The dummy puts his right hand on his sidearm. "This is war!" Laughter bodies up in the arena. "The Third Army will arrive in Bastogne yesterday. That ought to keep morale high while you jumping beans wait to be rescued." The line sinks in, there are some boos from the audience, then someone shouts, "AIRBORNE DON'T NEED NO RESCUE!" followed by cheers.

Splinters is killing it, Jim thinks. *Let him rip. That's what Mickey would do.*

"I hear Ike has put First Army under Montgomery," Splinters says, waiting two beats for more boos. "That Limey bastard—" Jim winces—"is too much of an old woman to help me pinch off this Kraut bulge. Ask my boss, good ol' Omar Bradley." Splinters begins to sing, to the tune of "Button Up Your Overcoat:"

> *Button up your Sherman Tank*
> *'Cause the Krauts are mad.*
> *Take good care of yourself*
> *You belong to Brad!*

Jim holds up his hand. "That's enough singing, Splinters."

"Hey boys," the dummy says, undeterred, "Montgomery and Bradley are on the Eiffel Tower, admiring the view. Monty says, 'I say, Brad, anything I can do to put a smile on your face?' Bradley says, 'You could jump.'" More laughter and clapping. Splinters starts singing again:

> *Never mind the black beret*
> *Monty's just a fad*
> *Take good care of yourself,*
> *You belong to Brad!*

Jim can feel the audience leaning in. "Fook Montgomery" wafts up from the back of the arena, an Irish lilt right out of Hell's Kitchen. "We's wants our general back."

Two more verses and Jim considers yanking the dummy's head off, but goes with, "Now, now, General, that's not the way we talk about our allies."

"The hell with Monty. I'm gonna beat the Krauts by myself," Splinters says. "Gonna be wounds and glory. Your wounds, my glory. That's the best way to boost *my* morale."

"Morale is important," Jim says, trying to redirect the bit. "General Marshall said—"

"The next best way is French women," Splinters says. More clapping and whistling. "They're wild about me. 'Cause I'm all wood and three feet long." The audience draws a breath, then laughs. "I also don't mind waxing a WAC." The dummy puts both hands on his hips and thrusts them out. "BANG BANG!"

The Patton bit has gone *way* too far. "That's enough, Splinters. I can't—"

"But since there are no WACs in Bastogne!" the dummy shouts over him, "and every USO dame is a hundred miles west of here and still running, I'm gonna clean my own gear!" The dummy reaches a hand down and rubs his crotch.

The raucous laughter and loud whistles prevent Jim from throwing Splinters offstage. He glances at the audience for signs of MPs, but the spotlight fills his eyes. The best he can do is a loud "Only a dummy would talk like that."

"I'll tell the jokes here, Private," Splinters says. "Insubordinate me again, you'll be policing cigarette butts from here to Normandy."

I'm fucked, Jim thinks, *six ways from Sunday*.

"I told Ike," Splinters continues, "I'll turn Third Army on a goddamned dime, cut through the Krauts like a hot knife through butter. We'll be there by Christmas Eve. And here I fucking am, in goddamned Bastogne on Christmas Eve."

Jim isn't going to feed Splinters any more lines, but "That was yesterday!" comes from the audience.

"NOT IN PEARL HARBOR!" The dummy gets another big laugh.

Enough is enough. "Where's the rest of Third Army?" Jim asks, then signals Trombone.

"Never mind, you son of a bitch, that's a military secret. I'll pull your Airborne chestnuts out of the fire myself. Now form up and get—"

Trombone begins to play. Jim takes three steps back, turns and yanks the dummy out of the ventriloquist's hands, carries it offstage. "Goddamned Splinters thinks he's Mickey fucking Rooney," Jim hisses to Trombone while the show is holding for applause. "Wants to take over a show."

"He's drunk as a skunk," Trombone says. "The boys loved it."

"He'll be lucky not to be up on charges. I'll be lucky not to be up on—"

"*Some-verr...*" the girl begins to sing. Jim has forgotten to introduce her. She sings "Over the Rainbow" and two beautiful French songs. The audience is transfixed. A few bring their blankets up to their eyes. She acknowledges the applause and steps out of the spotlight.

Private Trombone starts up "The Thunderer." Private Spoons clacks in on the second bar. Willi takes over the spotlight and the airborne soldier steps in front of the players, does a manual of arms with Jim's M1 rifle. Tinny drumming comes up from the audience, a GI banging on an empty C-ration can.

Willi does a dumb act: starts off juggling K-ration cans, two hands, one hand. Full summersaults in place follow, then a handstand. He walks on his hands into the audience, offers a cigarette to one soldier, then lights it for him.

"Next, we have an Irish tenor. He's from—"

"This is no ordinary time." Heads turn towards the back of the arena. For an astonished second, Jim thinks that Eleanor

Roosevelt is visiting the wounded. Then he remembers the Master of a Thousand Voices. Must've been hit last night.

"All these wounded boys, all this mess, all this waste," Private Sorrento continues in pitch-perfect Mrs. Roosevelt. "This is Eleanor Roosevelt, presented by Sweetheart Soap, one of America's oldest and best-liked toilet soaps. Goodbye and good luck to you." Wild applause.

The tenor sings. "I should have known 'Danny Boy' would be depressing in a room full of wounded," Jim says to Private Trombone.

The puppet theatre intrigues the audience, Punch yelling in French at a mute Splinters — the ventriloquist has passed out — and slapping him with the stick. Jim returns to the microphone afterwards. "Soldiers, doctors, nurses, everyone. We end with the good news of our Savior's birth. Please join us in singing 'Away in a Manger.'"

Everyone in the aid station sings, who can. The girl singer makes a fine Mary. Splinters is in swaddling clothes. Large for a newborn savior, but he's got the part, Punch being too red and too small. The mule looks better with the sheet over his back. He's playing it straight. Kid Spoons is a fine Little Drummer Boy.

"Baby Jesus better keep his goddamned mouth shut," Jim says to Trombone.

"He will," Trombone replies, jerking a thumb over his shoulder. "His voice is passed out."

The tenor steps up and sings: *I'm a so-jer, in the army of the Lord.* The audience is on it by "army."

The sing-round ends with a spontaneous "*Gory, gory, what a helluva way to die*" from the airborne soldiers in audience, ending with, "*And he ain't gonna jump no more!*"

"'Blood Upon the Risers,'" the Paratrooper says to Jim. "Our song."

Jim nods, turns to Private Trombone. "Time to take this

show to Notre Dame. Wish I could take Bonhomme back to New York after the war. He and Mickey Rooney could ad-lib a new routine every night at The Palace."

"I'd pay to see that," Trombone says.

"They'd both chew the scenery at the same time!" Jim says with a laugh. *Hey!* he thinks. *Remember that line.*

"Listen to the applause," Jim says to Willi. "They're calling for more. We'll do the encore. Trumpet, Spoons, on me."

▲

JIM CHANGES UP the second show. It's mostly civilians in the Notre Dame basement—schoolgirls, old people, nuns, no more than a hundred wounded GIs. There's a lot of coughing. Smoke from fires still burning in the market square has infiltrated the basement.

Jim left the ventriloquist and Splinters at the riding hall. Willi stands in with Punch, deals with the puppet's screaming and hitting. The children chime in often. *Join the Army and learn something you didn't know,* Jim thinks, *like how to shoot a bazooka or where the word "slapstick" comes from.*

Jim pulls the Irish tenor back a little on "Army of the Lord," and the Airborne GI uses a crutch for the rifle drill, to be gentler with children, bored and scared as they are. Starved for entertainment, crowded together in that cellar for days, they laugh at anything within a mile of funny. Like the wounded soldiers.

It's just another day at the office for the mule. Bastogne's own girl singer sings nursery rhymes, makes the children comfortable. The Irish tenor gets frosty when Jim cuts "Danny Boy." No one likes to see their stage time cut, even if the stage is a crumbling, smoky basement.

Instead of the cigarette trick, Willi pulls Chicklets out of airy nothing. The children are delighted. *Never mind the mule,* Jim thinks. *What if I could get Willi back to the States?*

After the Notre Dame show, the players are on their way to the Seminary Chapel. An MP pulls up in a Jeep. He doesn't get out, just points at the soldiers and yells, "Forming up at Heintz Barracks. Get in." The Germans are making their last big push in the southeast around Eschdorf. By the time Jim gets there, they've fallen back.

The last show is done by the mule, Willi, the girl singer, and Punch. Willi marches himself back to the POW pen afterward, shouting "Geneva convention!" and keeping his hands up in the air. The ventriloquist and Splinters are arrested for drunkenness. There being no rear-echelon sons of bitches in Bastogne to man a stockade for GIs, they are put in with the German prisoners. The ventriloquist keeps his usual silence, but Splinters sings along on "Stille Nacht."

Christmas in war.

NEW HAVEN, CONNECTICUT
November 23, 1940

"New Haven?" Jim says, out of breath, to the driver in a grey uniform standing by the open Greyhound bus door. "Had trouble finding your slip."

He is Jimmy Jergens today, on a non-union job from a booking agent he doesn't know. "Yale, Class of 1909, reunion dinner and show. New Haven. Venue is a place called Mory's," the agent had said. "Big football game that day. It's your show to emcee. You'll have a student singing group, the Whiffenpoofs. They'll be first. Your comedian is Lenny Cohen. I got you a good Connecticut band, Jerry Spivak's Minutemen. They know the drill. No couples dancing; won't be no women in the audience. They'll meet you at Mory's at three, walk through the show. You can do your dance routine if you want practice. Work that out with Jerry. I'm sending a girl chorus, they're on last. They know their business. Leave them alone." It sounded a little hodge-podge to Jim, but he hasn't worked for two weeks, and it's fifty dollars cash plus expenses. He'll figure it out.

The bus driver looks at Jim with a raised eyebrow. "Your girls are already here. They know their way around Port Authority." The driver smiles, enters the bus and turns to the passengers: "10:20 to New Haven. All aboard."

The first thing that hits Jim is the smell of alcohol and perfume. Even through the cigarette smoke, he can see that some of the women are a little old and a little heavy for dancers. Half of them are asleep. They're wearing a lot of make-up for 10:20 in the morning. The oldest and heaviest of the women is sitting right behind the driver. Unlike the rest of her, her jet-black hair is perfectly arranged. "You must be Mr. Jergens," she says. "I'm Tilley Todd, the goils' chaperone." She pulls on Jim's hand. "Sit yaself next to me, handsome, and tell me all about your show tonight."

They're the worst chorus line Jim has ever seen, even counting the waitstaff at Stiers. Only two or three in the group have any professional dance experience. The Mory's manager shakes his head when he sees them, demands an extra ten dollars from Jim for security.

Lenny Cohen remembers Jim from Stiers. "You know what kind of show you're producing, right?" the comedian says. He's been around longer than Jim.

"The band is solid," Jim says. "You're a pro, Lenny. The students will sing Yale songs. I guess the girls play their chorus number for laughs."

Cohen smiles and pats him on the back. "Okay, Jim. It's your show. I'll do my ten minutes. I'm adding a new bit about women drivers. Give me the two spot. I'll get a cab, catch the train back."

"Let the goils be, handsome," Tilley Todd says when Jim asks for a walk-through of their number. "They know what their show is. You and Shoylee here—" she points to a plump redhead—"can have a dance on me when the woik is done."

The Yale Class of 1909 show up around 9 p.m., half in the bag, shouting greetings, slapping backs, puffing on cigars. "Bill, you sorry bastard, you haven't changed a bit, if we don't count grey hair, double chins and your missing dick, HA, HA, HA!" They drink their sidecars, their old fashioneds, their martinis, their champagne, and their punch in trophy cups. They tuck into toast and cheese, Caesar salads, beefsteaks, apple pie and ice cream. They have a monstrous good time singing the old college songs, tossing rolls at each other, and hallooing at Rochester, a colored waiter they recognize from their undergraduate days.

The Whiffenpoofs and Lenny Cohen are crackerjack. The Class of '09 is barely interested. There are calls of *"bring out the girls"* and *"put the dames on."* Jim scrubs his routine, moves up the chorus.

The girls don't get a chance to be awful. As soon as they line up on the stage, men from the audience get up from their tables, take them by the hand and leave the room. One 09'er carries Shirley the redhead out over his shoulder. The girls are all smiles. Even Tilley Todd leaves with an audience member. With half the audience gone, the other half gets up and staggers out. The band begins to pack up.

Each girl gives Jim two dollars as they get on the bus Sunday morning. Shirley adds a peck on the cheek. The booking agent calls on Monday to tell Jim the show was a smash, that he has another emcee job for him for next Saturday. A Chevrolet dealer's convention in Newark. "I'm booked all weekend," Jim says, untruthfully. He feels lucky he's not in a New Haven jail for violating the Mann Act.

16.

BASTOGNE, BELGIUM, DECEMBER 26, 1944

> Unburied dead should be removed as rapidly as possible and buried. This removal should be done in a most considerate manner and with the least confusion in order to sustain the morale of the troops. Bodies should be covered, especially if they are mangled or in an unpresentable condition, when carried or transported to the cemetery or other place of interment. Routes should avoid contact with troops as much as possible, and places of interment should be screened from roads if the situation permits. The removal should be accomplished with a reverent attitude toward the dead, and any tendency toward improper handling of bodies should be corrected immediately.
>
> FIELD MANUAL 10-63, GRAVES
REGISTRATION, DECEMBER 1944

"DATELINE DECEMBER 25, 1944, Bastogne, Belgium," the captain reads to Jim. "This long-time reporter and lifelong New Yorker has seen many, many good performances, and a very few great ones. Billy Sunday preaching to doughboys headed to

France in New York 1917. Caruso's final bow at The Metropolitan Opera House in 1920. The last of the Red-Hot Mamas, Sophie Tucker, at The Palace in '22. Opening night for Paul Robeson in *Showboat* in '25. Charlie Chaplin in *City Lights* in '31. Laurence Olivier's *Hamlet* in battle-scarred London just this year. Immortal performances, all. Then there is what I saw yesterday in Bastogne."

The captain stops reading, fixes Jim with an icy stare, then continues.

"Christmas morning in a makeshift hospital in an undisclosed location near the center of Bastogne. Bastogne, which is taking a pounding from German night bombers as I type out these words. Bastogne, where American grit and cussidness is throwing the wrench into Hitler's war machine."

The captain begins to read faster.

"About six hundred wounded men are holding out here, just as surely as their buddies are on the front lines, where they were before they were so grievously wounded. Surgeons just arrived by glider—heroes too—are doing what they can with what they have, not everything they need."

The captain stops and lights a cigarette. He doesn't offer one to Jim. "Not what the American public wants to hear," the captain says, and continues to read.

"Christmas morning in Bastogne. No oranges, no tree, no turkey. Just another grim day of fighting while Patton's Third Army drives north through ice and snow and the German Seventh Army. Then a trombone starts an oompah two-step. A chorus begins to sing the Spike Jones hit, 'Der FrankFührer's Mustard March'. A spotlight hits a tiny stage. We see a large puppet in the outfit of a certain well-known general, tapping his knee in time with the music."

The captain looks up at Jim. "You were ordered to put on a soldier show, Private Tanzer, not exhibit insubordination towards a general officer." He continues to read.

"The spotlight hits the door. A mule enters. A marching mule. Not just marching but goose-stepping. A goose-stepping mule sporting a Hitler mustache. Astonishing. A small parade follows him in. There is Dorothy from *The Wizard of Oz*, then an acrobat walking on his hands, followed by a GI banging out a stirring cadence on spoons, a trombone soldier, then another GI, a Morale Corps soldier—he's responsible for this tour de force."

The captain looks at Jim again, purses his lips, then continues to read. "Every man who can stand or sit up is watching and describing the scene to those who can't. The parade moves past the puppet, snaps off salutes, and marches back out. The mule turns around in the doorway and gives a loud Bronx cheer for Hitler—straight from the gut. Spotlight off. Simply the best entrance this reporter has ever seen. The room is in stunned silence for several seconds while the wounded soldiers consider whether they are wildly entertained or simply hallucinating. Then cheers and applause, then an encore."

"I'm going to skip ahead, Tanzer," the captain says. "Next came a tribute to General Patton fit to warm the heart of any citizen soldier. Freedom of speech; it's one of the Four Freedoms our boys are fighting for."

The captain scowls at Jim. "The story doesn't go into what that General Patton puppet said, so I'll tell you, Private. 'I'm George Armstrong Fucking Patton. I've got a three-foot wooden dick that never beats retreat.' Is that free speech, Private Tanzer? Is that what we're fighting for?" The captain waits, while Jim thinks, *yes, brass ass, yes it fucking is.*

"Splinters was ad-libbing, Captain," Jim finally says. "He has combat fatigue."

The captain returns a salute from a soldier standing in the doorway. "What is it, sergeant?"

"Sir. Major Becker requests I bring Private Tanzer. When you're finished with your interview. Interrogation of a prisoner."

"Alright, Tanzer, dismissed." As Jim starts to stand up, the captain adds, "Your C.O. will let you know about your court martial." All three men know this is an empty threat. Unlike killing and dying, military courtesy is not enforced in combat zones. "No more shows, no more dummies. That's an order."

▲

THAT THRUMMING SOUND. Jim looks up. The blue sky is dotted with C-47s. Hundreds of colored parachutes are floating down. A wooden crate under a red parachute canopy lands fifty yards ahead on the road. The driver slows and maneuvers the Jeep around it. "Ammo," the MP in the front passenger seat says, "probably shells. Don't stop unless you see a pink parachute."

"Pink?" Jim asks.

"Nurses."

Not bad for a miserable prick, Jim thinks.

They pull around a corner and drive another mile on a logging trail. Jim wonders about land mines, keeps his hands in his lap. They come upon a German soldier tied to a tree by telephone wire. He's in his grey shirt, no coat, stocking feet. His nose is badly bent, blood frozen around his purple lips. He looks up at Jim and the others quickly, then looks back down at his feet.

"Where's your top?" the MP says, meaning sergeant, to the two paratroopers manning a machine gun in front of the nearby foxhole. A steaming helmet full of water on a Coleman stove is on the ground next to the machine gun. One of the paratroopers is wearing a checkered quilt like a cape, his boots wrapped in brown padding. The other's field jacket is stuffed with the padding.

"Johnny and Pat here took care a his buddies," shouts a short and squat sergeant, arriving at an unhurried pace, steam coming out of his mouth. He can barely be heard over the engine drone of the C-47s overhead. He points a Schmeisser submachine gun up the trail at half a dozen grey corpses sprawled across the snow in impossible poses. "Caught the whole patrol crossing the trail at first light."

"Neat piece of work," the MP says.

"Ya got that right," the sergeant says. "Musta thought they was behind their own lines. Sounded like a drawer full of spoons, came across the trail all bunched up. *Volksgrenadiers.* Boys and grandpas." The drone of the C-47s begins to fade. "No officer, no Luger. Did find a field medical kit we're gonna keep. And all that too." He points to a stack of German rifles, leather ammo pouches, stick grenades, and a *panzerfaust.* "We're on our last box of belts."

Jim gestures towards the *panzerfaust.* "Better than a bazooka."

"This kid—" the sergeant points towards the tied-up German—"was tail-end Charlie. Ran right into a tree, knocked himself cold. We just walked over and picked him up."

"Why did you tie him to a tree?" the MP says.

"To shoot him. He was wearing part of an American uniform."

"What part?"

"An overcoat and shoepacs." The sergeant points to one of the paratroopers. "Which Pat is wearing now. Makes that Kraut a spy. But he's not SS. Hell, he's probably not eighteen. Sarge told us to save him for the G-2 and a proper firing squad."

"You didn't pretend you were going to shoot him, did you?" the MP says.

"Why would we?" the sergeant smiles. "That would be against what that's against."

Jim and the MP walk over to the teenage German. "What is your name?" Jim says in German.

"I don't speak Yiddish, sir," the boy replies in German, his voice breaking. He takes a long sniff.

Jim turns to the MP. "He speaks the *Plattdeutsch* dialect, low German. I don't understand it well enough."

"We're bringing him back anyways," the MP says. "Untie the kid and let's go."

The driver isn't in his seat when they return to the Jeep. He's bending down among the German corpses, pulling at a helmet. After struggling to undo a frozen chin strap, he steps back and kicks the dead German's face, jarring the helmet loose. He trots back to the Jeep with it under his arm.

"Is that how you want to be treated?" the MP says. "Jesus."

"I won't care how I'm treated if I'm dead," the driver answers.

"You mean *when* you're dead," the MP says.

The driver holds the helmet up at eye level and then turns it over. Jim stifles the urge to say *Alas Poor Yorick*.

"That's not gonna be worth anything in Bastogne," the MP says. "Only combatmen here. Kraut helmets on the ground like apples in November. Show that around, they'll make you for a garrison soldier. *And* it's holed."

The driver wiggles his index finger through the bullet hole in the front of the helmet. "Bag it," he says and tosses the helmet back over his head.

The young German in the front seat leans down slowly, rubs his tears onto his thigh.

⋀

"What is this dialect, again?" the G-2 says to Jim. They're listening to Willi and the POW talk in the room next door.

"*Plattsdeutch*," Jim says. "Willi, he's reliable. Like I said, born in Milwaukee, wants to return there after the war. And happy to be out of the fighting."

"Okay, Tanzer," the G-2 says. "The German boy is only a private; this won't take long. No one tells enlisted men anything, right?" He smiles at Jim. "But maybe he's seen things."

"The Amis say that you are a spy," Willi says to the boy in High German. "According to the Convention of Geneva they can execute you forthwith. Here is a piece of paper and a pencil. If you want to write your family, do it now; write their address at the top, the Red Cross will deliver it."

The boy begins to sob. Willi offers him a cigarette. A Fleetwood. "No thank you," the boy says in German. "It will make me nauseous. I tried a cigar at the pledge night celebration in Münsingen. I threw up."

There is a sandwich on a plate on the table, white bread with thick slices of cheese and Spam, and a glass of milk. The German boy glances at the food from time to time.

"I see we were both 26th Volksgrenadiers Division," Willi says. "I hail from Regiment 89."

"Regiment 78. I was conscripted last August. Six weeks training. We fought the Ivans at Krosno and at Debrecen."

"You have seen terrible things."

"So many. We were transferred west in mid-November to prepare for Watch on the Rhine."

"Do you have any English?" Willi says.

"*I surrender. Don't shoot. Mickey Mouse. Lucky Strikes. Doublemint. Sitting Bull. Billy Kid. Joe Lewis. FDR.*" The boy looks around, and in a low tone adds: "*Fuhkitler.*"

"Were you spying?"

"No. I found the rubberized boots yesterday on a dead Ami."

"What kind of Ami?"

"He was a sergeant, a technical. He looked like Herr Meuller, my schoolmaster. I felt sorry for him. And his family." The boy doesn't say that he panicked and shot the American when he was trying to surrender.

Willi is aware that something is being left unsaid. "You took his boots."

"Only because my own boots were soaked. I stepped into a stream yesterday, and my feet were becoming frozen. Our captain does not allow trench feet—you march until you can only crawl. Then you are left to crawl back to an aid station."

"This lot can hang you for impersonating an American GI."

"I knew the risk of being captured in the boots, but losing my toes was a certainty. We hear about comrades who have the East Medal from service in Russia but no toes or fingers."

"The Order of the Frozen Flesh," Willie says.

"Yes. The coat came from an American supply dump. We found crates of them. No one was wearing it. Other comrades took American clothing. We have been outside for two weeks; it's been so cold."

"What were you fellows doing patrolling behind American lines?"

"Reconnaissance. And capturing the American rations. There were so many airplanes, so many parachutes, so much cargo. We saw boxes land near our lines yesterday afternoon and we decided to go after one in the night, to see if we could get something to eat. We got lost."

"You still want to fight the Amis?"

"How can we? Their airplanes stretch from one end of the horizon to the other. We stop a tank and two more sprout up in its place. Germany is caught between American machines and Russian hordes. We were told after we broke through the American front lines it would be only Jews and bankers between us and Antwerp, that we'd be back in Paris by Christmas. They didn't mention artillery shells that burst in the air just over our heads. Or being hunted by Jabos."

"The American fighter-bombers," Willi says, nodding, remembering the frightful strafing, the awful smell of napalm.

"Jabos drove some men insane. They tried to surrender to them. But it was when we saw all that cargo dropping out of the sky, this is when we knew the war is lost."

"It was lost when Hitler declared war on America."

"One of the older men in my unit said God has set His face against Germany."

"How did he know that?"

"He said only God could make the American Capitalists clasp hands with the Russian Bolsheviks. Hitler is Pharoah and we are the Egyptians." The boy sobs.

"This war is so big and we are so small," Willi says. "The main thing is to survive."

"I am just a soldier. I swear by the Lord I am no spy."

"There is plenty of mixing of uniforms on both sides, that is true. It is so cold, and there are so many dead on the ground. But if you can tell them what they want to know about your unit, they will let you off the spy charge and ship you to a camp in England. You will survive the war, get back home to help your parents with next year's harvest."

"My father is a doctor professor."

Willy sighs. "Do you have anything for the Amis?"

The boy proceeds to confess to visiting a brothel where Jewish women were held as sex slaves for German soldiers. He begins to cry again. "Now I am no better than the lowest fellow," he says. "We were in battle the next day. That took my mind off my sin. But I recall it now." He looks up at Willi. "Have you done this thing, Comrade?"

"I too am ashamed," Willi says, although he's never had sex with a woman.

"If I die now, how can I face God? I need to do penance."

"That's all of us, Comrade. All of us. Tell me about the movements of Regiment 78. Then you can eat this sandwich."

⌃

"At ease," the sergeant says, more out of habit than need, to Jim and the other SNAFU soldiers not already up on the line today. Falling snow is melting past the towel around Jim's neck. He's done with the morning's interrogation detail. Willi is back in the prisoner pen.

The sergeant turns and points to a slender, middle-aged man standing in front of a 4 x 6 truck with a two-wheel trailer attached. "That is Captain Michael. Came in by glider yesterday." He lets that sink in. "Back row, you're attached to the captain today. Report in. You're dismissed."

The sergeant addresses the remaining SNAFU soldiers. "Ammo up and get in the trucks." He waits a few seconds and points at the slowest moving men. "You four: bazooka teams. Get your tubes and rockets."

My luck is holding out, Jim thinks, touching the can of peaches in his pocket as he walks with the others towards the captain.

"Good morning, men." The captain smiles at his new squad. Jim notices his hair is completely gray. "My first glider trip and hopefully my last. As you heard, I'm Captain Michael." He smiles again. "603rd Quartermaster Graves Registration Company." He ignores the audible groans. "Attached to Third Army."

"Undertaker," the soldier next to Jim says, too loud. He's drunk. Tanks of the 4th Armored Division broke through to Bastogne last night and there was celebrating.

"I'm addressing the squad, Private," Captain Michael says. "The 603rd will arrive in Bastogne tomorrow."

The drone of incoming C-47s begins to be audible, covering the noise of the soldiers stamping their feet in the cold. Jim wipes his dripping nose on his overcoat sleeve.

"But right now, *this* squad is going after parachute infantry lying where they fell defending the northwest perimeter. Place called Champs. The regiment advanced before those men could be brought in."

The drunk soldier bends over and yawns.

The captain holds his hand out, palm up. "If they get hidden under this snowfall, their people will get a missing in action telegram, hope they're POWs, suffer for months, be fresh grieved in the spring. Better they know now. That's today's mission. Since you haven't been trained for this duty, I'm going read to you from the Graves Registration Field Manual. Listen carefully."

Captain Micheal skips over procedures for bodies consumed by fire, torn apart and scattered by explosive action. He'll cover that if they come across the remains of airmen or tankers. He finishes with, "Photographing of any graves outside the continental limits of the United States is absolutely prohibited. Any questions? No? Into the truck and let's go!"

The benches fill up before Jim can climb in. *At least it's not combat*, he tells himself. Captain Michael sees him sitting on the truck bed, tells him to ride up in in the cab. Lucky break. As they drive, the captain inquires about the driver's particulars, then Jim's. Because he's used to approachable officers in Morale Corps, Jim asks the captain why he chose Graves Registration.

"Funny you ask, Private. My parents owned a small mortuary business in Germantown, Iowa. One of the reasons I volunteered in 1917 was to get away from all that."

"I felt the same way about my dancing school, sir."

"I served with the Big Red One," Captain Michael continues. "The 1st Infantry. I saw what happened to our boys who were killed in the Meuse-Argonne. Lost, misidentified, thrown in mass graves. Some families waited years to learn what happened to their sons. I saw what a mortician could do. Decided I'd get my license. I was hot to get married, and it was a steady job."

"Yes, sir."

"I asked for a direct commission in 1942 because I thought it was my duty. I had a skill the Army needed."

"Same with me, Captain."

"Course, the Army in a war, different kettle of fish for a mortician." He holds up an index finger. "First, there's the scale. I've got 118 men in my company. There are over fifty Graves Registration companies in the ETO alone."

"Five thousand men," Jim says, surprised.

"For over two million American soldiers in the ETO. With airmen, close to three million. One graves man for every six hundred soldiers."

"I guess you stay—*whoa!*" The truck hits a pothole.

"Second." The captain holds up two fingers. "The dead are different here than at home. They're almost all young men, just boys many of them. They should be in college, or coming into their own on the family farm, or in their trade. Marrying their sweetheart. Starting a family. Ushers at church."

"Going to dances," Jim says.

"Dances, yes. So many dead here, it's an assembly line. No open caskets in the ETO. I'm not trying to match skin tones, fix hair just right, help a grieving widow pick out a coffin or a hymn, tie a tie on the deceased."

"I hadn't thought about that." Jim wishes they could talk of something else, but Captain Michael has momentum.

"The Army moved so fast last summer. Left so many on the ground for us. And it was warm… In winter, this cold, you have more time. Unless it snows."

"How do your men handle it?" Jim says.

"They drink, some of them."

"Sure."

"By the way, a soldier in a combat zone shouldn't carry what you wouldn't want your wife to see, were you killed. Pictures, letters from girlfriends can slip through personal effects processing. Cruel on top of cruel."

"Sure," Jim says, thinking he'll toss out the new letter to Kitty Carlson he's been working on. No mail pickup in Bastogne, anyways.

"We stop here," Captain Michael says to the driver. They're about fifty feet beyond an Army ambulance that's crashed into a tree. The field up ahead is dotted with evidence of yesterday's battle, deep foxholes and all sorts of German and American equipment on the ground: clips, rifles, helmets, bandages, clothing, even letters. Several bodies lie twisted into the snow like cigarette butts.

The captain walks to the back of the truck. "Bring in rifles, grenades, sidearms, web belts, clips, overcoats, duck boots. Do *not* touch watches, rings, or other personal items. Do not go in their pockets—" a beat—"for cigarettes. If the man is frozen to the ground, bring me one of their dog tags and mark where he lies with one of these." He holds up a long bright orange garden stake. "I'll draw a map. Call me over if the dog tags are missing or blown into the wound. Any questions?"

"What if we see Germans?" a soldier says.

"They'll be dead. I'll put them on the map. Prisoners will bring them in tomorrow."

"Booby-trapped bodies?" another says.

"The Germans wouldn't have had time, this fight," he says. "Unless they came back after dark, but that's unlikely." He pauses, then adds, "If you see a Luger on the ground, *that's* a booby trap. Leave it alone. That's an order. You two men." He points at Jim and the drunk soldier. "Go back and recover the men in the ambulance. And any intact supplies."

"Yes sir," Jim says.

"The rest of you, start in that field." The captain points ahead. "The truck will come up after we bring in the men from that ambulance."

As he and Jim approach the ambulance, the drunk soldier points. "Bullet holes in two lines, front to back. Strafed. And they're telling us the *Luftwaffe* is finished. What a bunch a crap." Jim can smell the alcohol on his breath.

The front fender is in a perfect V shape around the tree trunk. Two dead paratroopers are on the floor in the back. "They tried to get out," the drunk soldier says. "But look, the driver caught a slug in the back of his head, crashed."

They start with the driver. Slight, maybe 125 pounds. Frozen in sitting position, head stuck to the steering wheel. The fine hairs where a mustache might someday have grown are white with frost. "One, two, three, *pull!*" Jim says. As they wrench him out and onto the ground, something flies onto the snow near Jim. It's a thin brass medallion, about an inch square, in the shape of a haystack.

"What is it?" the drunk soldier says.

"It's a medal," Jim says. "Says 'I am a Catholic. In case of accident notify a priest.'"

"Well, this wasn't an accident," the drunk soldier says. "Krauts shot him on purpose. You keeping it?"

"Captain's orders are no personal items. I'm putting it in his pocket."

"I can sell that. Lemme have it."

"His family's going to want it." Jim says, putting the medal in the boy's jacket pocket. *You drunk idiot*, he thinks.

The drunk soldier reaches towards the pocket. "He don't need nothing now." Jim blocks his hand. "Spoiling for a fight, ain't ya?" the drunk soldier snarls. "Why, I oughta—"

"The captain's looking over this way."

"Okay, okay. Get this stiff moving. Take care a you later."

They carry the boy to the trailer, their hands under his back and his knees. "Can't keep a good hold," the drunk soldier says. "Speed it up, I…*fuck!*" He drops his side of the body. The young driver is looking up. Jim bends down to close both eyelids at the same time, like in the movies, but they're frozen open. *What am I doing here?* Jim thinks.

"What kind of shit fatigue we gonna do all day?" the drunk soldier says, reddening in the face. He grabs the back of the driver's collar, drags him to the trailer, bends down, picks the body up chest high, takes two steps and heaves it like a medicine ball. There is a crack as the soldier's head hits the side of the trailer. "Don't do that," Jim says, walking towards the truck.

"That's how it's—" The drunk soldier freezes. Captain

Michael has a Colt .45 three inches in front of his forehead. Jim stops and puts his hands in front of his chest, palms out, in case the captain plans to shoot him next.

"That was misconduct, Private!" the captain says through gritted teeth. The other SNAFUs are now watching from up ahead. "You will pull that American soldier out of the trailer, carefully, put him back in the ambulance, then start over and bring him in with the respect he's due."

"I will, sir," the drunk soldier says, eyes wide. "Yessir."

"Left his home, his parents, his friends," the captain continues, eyes blazing. "Left his goddamned high school from the looks of him, and came all this way to save the goddamned free world. Has a mother, a mother waiting for her son to return, to start her life again." The captain takes a breath. "Whose heart will never heal after she gets her telegram. And she doesn't even know yet!" Jim wonders how Stella would feel.

"Yessir," the drunk soldier says. "I was just—"

"TAKE CARE OF HIM!" The captain lowers the pistol and turns to Jim. "Private Tanzer, see that this man does his duty." He points to the rifle slung on Jim's back. "Shoot him if he doesn't. That's an order." The captain clicks on the safety and holsters the pistol.

"Yes, sir!" the drunk soldier says, saluting the captain, who doesn't return it but instead says, "This is a combat zone," and walks away. Jim and the drunk soldier chair-carry the unlucky driver back to the ambulance, then back to the trailer. They lay him on his side so he won't roll around.

They go back and pull the two paratroopers out of the ambulance. These men were lying flat when they were killed. They're easier to carry. "Look at this one," the drunk soldier says, pointing to the gauze-wrapped knee of the dead GI. "Million-dollar wound got him on this ambulance. Then his luck changed. His number was up, no other way to see it."

For the three soldiers now on the trailer, the process of

officially killing them has begun. Within forty-eight hours, combining field work with a careful review of daily casualty reports, Captain Micheal will submit an estimate of three to five hundred unrecovered dead in the eastern Ardennes, not including civilians or Germans. He will request additional resources.

NEW YORK CITY
December 16, 1944

Stella, your audition was a success. Sam sends you this proof of the Leon & Eddie's New Year's Eve ad. He says get a new dress, pretty. By now you know what that means...tight! Let him know if you need an advance. Sam says be nice to Eddie, this is a big break. He can give you regular work at L&E, and place you in other clubs he has an interest in. But wear your wedding ring for good luck, and be sure to introduce yourself to his wife!—Sarah G.

Spend New Year's Eve at the World-Famous Leon & Eddie's, 33 W 52nd
Eddie Davis, Your Host and Strip Street's King of Comedy
Pops & Louie, Tap Tornadoes
Noel Toy, Exotic Fan Dancer
Stella Sterling, Chanteuse
Jackie Smith, Eccentric Dancer and Ventriloquist
And more acts!
Ten Dollars per Person, including Supper, Entertainment, Dancing, and "Breakfast in the Kitchen"
For Reservations Call Paul
TRafalger 9-2603 Ext. 350

17.

GOTHA, GERMANY, APRIL 12, 1945

```
WESTERN UNION
APRIL12, 1945 =
T28 32 GOVT=WUX WASHINGTON DC 16 1013A
MRS STELLA TANZER=
32 RAILROAD ST HUNTINGTON WEST VIRGINIA

THE SECRETARY OF WAR DESIRES ME TO EXPRESS
HIS DEEP REGRET THAT YOUR HUSBAND PRIVATE
JAMES TANZER HAS BEEN KILLED IN ACTION IN
THE ARDENNES. WHEN FURHTER DETAILS OR OTHER
INFORMATION ARE RECEIVED YOU WILL BE PROMPTLY
NOTIFIED. NO REMAINS CAN BE TRANSPORTED TO
UNITEDSTATES UNTIL AFTER TERMINATION OF
HOSTILITIES WHEN QUARTERMASTER GENERAL
WASHINGTON DC WILL IF POSSIBLE, UPON WRITTEN
REQUEST OF NEXT OF KIN BRING REMAINS TO
UNITEDSTATES FOR FINAL INTERMENT=
    =ULIO THE ADJUTANT GENERAL
```

JIM POINTS TO an Army chaplain standing over the dead men sprawled on the ground just inside the camp gate. "Is that a prayer?" He's asking Sam Plotkin, Camera Operator, Special Films Unit, 165th Signal Photographic Company. The two are in front of the recently liberated Ohrdruf Work Camp.

"That's the Mourner's Kaddish," Plotkin says. "Prayer for the dead."

"He's a Catholic chaplain."

"You throw everything you got at a place like this. What the hell is Morale Corps doing here?"

Jim outlines the journey. How he got to Bastogne. Being part of Team SNAFU, disbanded shortly after the siege was lifted. That he spent January, 1945, giving tours of Bastogne for support units moving east. That after the Battle of the Bulge ended late that month, he was three weeks in the hospital getting his shoulder fixed. It had fractured when he fell on that tree root near the 969th Field Artillery Battalion. He explains his subsequent assignment to light duty at Morale Corps forward headquarters in Luxembourg City, and that he has been attached to an Intelligence and Reconnaissance platoon since the first of April.

Jim doesn't explain that a few days after leaving Hosingen, Mickey Rooney was flown more than halfway around the world to entertain Pacific fleet and 20th Air Force personnel currently pounding Japan from the Mariannas. Jim doesn't yet know that Wes Novak—unbelievable luck—has been attached to the Jimmy James Orchestra in residency at the Red Cross Rainbow Corner Club in Paris.

"Now I'm directing tours of *this* place," Jim continues. "Patton ordered every GI in the area to see it. I'm also taking press through."

Plotkin gestures towards the dozen or so corpses just behind the gate. "You left all the dead where you found them?"

"That was orders. For the tours and for you guys to shoot. Evidence."

"It's true that no one will believe it without pictures." Plotkin winds his Bell & Howell Filmo and points it at the *Arbeit macht frei* sign over the gate. "Work will set you free! Stevens will want that shot," he says.

"Stevens?"

"George Stevens."

"George Stevens the Hollywood director?"

"Lieutenant Colonel George Stevens, the Hollywood director. *Swing Time, Gunga Din, Woman of the Year.* Now *D-Day, Liberation of Paris.* He'll be here in a few minutes. Tour the location, pick out shots. You take us through."

"People won't want to see this—" Jim sweeps an arm out—"before the feature film."

"They're just lucky they won't have to smell it. How long did it take you to get used to this?" Plotkin asks, stepping aside for a truck to enter the camp.

"I'm not retching anymore," Jim admits, "but I do skip breakfast. It's been cool at night, or we couldn't have stood it. As it is, they post guards so that crows and dogs—there are lot of stray dogs—won't disturb the scenes."

"Rats?"

"The prisoners ate them all before we got here."

"I've shot some terrible things in this war," Plotkin says, thinking of the gangly soldier staggering out of the surf and falling on Omaha Beach. "But this—" he gestures at the dead men—"takes the cake."

"It's worse than you think. There are *piles* of corpses inside. In the back of the camp there's a grill made from railroad tracks. Half-burned people still on it."

"They tell you that Ike and Brad are touring the camp today?" Plotkin says.

"I'm escorting the tour. I've got a prisoner to take them around."

"I'm sure Patton will show up. You know, cameras."

"I'd like to see him for myself," Jim says, then thinks of Sergeant Splinters and almost smiles. "I've been through the camp enough times, I'm starting to recognize some of the dead men. At first, you just see a pile. You think, what an awful sight, not, this was a person, he had a family, a job, hobbies, a life."

"Sunny day," the cameraman said, craning his neck around the grounds. "I'll be shooting in full light. Individuals can be made out. What else do I want to get?"

"We're making townspeople from Gotha tour the camp. MPs are bringing them through in small groups."

"Stevens will definitely want that."

"The first group that came through was led by the mayor and his wife. MPs made him wear his red Nazi sash. I saw the column half a mile away. Some of them tried to turn around when the smell hit them, but the snowdrops didn't let them."

"I want that shot," Plotkin says.

"These people," Jim says, "most of them just stare at the ground in front of their feet. I taught the MPs to say don't look away. *Schau nicht weg.* Today they're making the townspeople dig graves for the dead prisoners."

"German civilians digging graves for murdered prisoners," Plotkin says. "Stevens will want that shot. Maybe the mayor, with that sash on?"

"He hung himself," Jim says. "Couldn't face a world without Hitler, I guess."

"Is he still hanging somewhere? That would be a great final shot."

"I hope he is. You're only going to get women and old men digging the graves. No young German men left in Gotha."

"I did get boys hanging from trees, outside the town. Signs around their necks."

"The SS. They lynch soldiers for desertion," Jim says. "For morale purposes."

"What do the signs say?"

"*Ich Bin Feiglintg.* Means 'I'm a coward.'"

"*Oy gevalt.*"

A small observation plane begins to circle overhead. "Filming," Plotkin says. Jim nods. Plotkin fusses with his camera. They don't speak for a while, then Plotkin asks, "Intelligence and Recon, you said? How does an I&R platoon rate its own morale soldier?"

"We do shows in front of German towns," Jim answers. "Surrender shows. Patton's idea, I heard. Did one in front of Gotha and then discovered this place."

"Surrender shows?"

"To minimize casualties. Triple S script."

"Triple S?"

"*Wir schissen, ihr scheisst, ihr kapituliert.*"

"How's that?"

"We shoot, you shit, you surrender. The platoon stops half a mile in front of a town—"

"Out of sniper range."

"That's important, 'cause I'm sitting in the front seat of a talking Jeep."

"Talking Jeep?"

"Rigged up with a loudspeaker on the hood. After we get their attention with a small charge HE round on the church steeple, I make an announcement in German."

"What do you say?"

"I have a script. It translates to, 'Citizens of Krauthausen—' that was the town we did before Gotha—'Citizens of Krauthausen, displaced persons, and German soldiers: Greetings. We are General Patton's American Third Army. We are here to take you out of the war, one way or another. Proceed everyone to the town square. Pile all your weapons there, including knives. We will not detain civilians or unarmed *Volkssturm* over sixty. Soldiers will be treated humanely as American prisoners of war.' That last part is important. They don't want to be captured by Russians."

"Where'd you learn to speak German?"

"My mother was born in Michendorf."

"Mine was born in Daugavpils, Latvia," says Plotkin. "Before Hitler, the worst place in Europe for Jews. *Di alte heym.*"

"The old country."

"You speak Yiddish too?"

"My wife and I worked in the Catskills before the war. I heard *di alte heym* every day."

"What else did you say?

"*Mazel tov.*"

"To the Germans, I mean. Over the loudspeaker."

"'We will destroy any building where we find a weapon or a person. If there is a person who can't be moved, you will hang a white cloth out the window.' I would end my *spiel*—"

"You *do* have Yiddish."

"*Bissel.* I would close with, 'If we receive any fire, we will pull back and American heavy bombers will destroy Krauthausen and the surrounding farms.'"

"SS to be hung on the spot, I hope," Plotkin says. "*Shdim nisht zelner.*"

"I don't know that one."

"Devil soldiers. The bit about heavy bombers is good. Every German must know about Dresden by now." Plotkin refers to the recent incineration of the historic city and many of its residents by Allied bombs.

"Usually the mayor comes out first," Jim continues. "White flag. One town, Waldkappel, I think it was, a bomber stream came over as I was finishing my soliloquy. A thousand B-17s. The engine drone, the vapor trails, the ground starting to shake—"

"*Di roysh fun Got*…the wrath of God."

"The mayor ran towards us, one hand up in the air, pulling up his pants with the other. Hey!" Tanzer and Plotkin both shake their heads.

"I'm gonna tell Stevens about that scene. Maybe he'll want it recreated."

"It was some show," Jim says. *Mickey would have loved it*, he thinks.

"Speaking of shows," Plotkin says, "pretty little farms around here. Passed an old farmer on the hill just before we got here. Wearing a funny hat. Walking behind a horse and plough. Like he's in some Nazi version of Colonial Williamsburg."

"I pass that farmer every morning," Jim says. "He doesn't even look up."

"If he can go years ignoring a murder camp next door, I guess he can ignore an infantry column for a couple of minutes. Triumph of the will."

"I'd like to shoot him," Jim says. "Don't know why exactly, maybe because he won't acknowledge."

"Unless we shoot *all* the Germans, they're going to need something to eat next winter."

"They can have my Spam."

"Never tried it, Jim. *Treyf*. But I'll tell you, I've had all the shit on a shingle I can stand. Nothing but steak and chicken for me, after the war."

"Hey!" *That's going in Spamlet*, Jim thinks.

"That old farmer is scared stiff," Plotkin says. "Or a Nazi. Probably both. Farming kept him out of the fight, kept him alive. But never mind that bastard, finish about your surrender show."

"A Jewish chaplain joined us just before we moved up to Gotha."

"A rabbi."

"Said he had relatives there. He knew he wouldn't find them—we never find any Jews—but he wanted to see the house where they'd lived. We were waiting for a heavy weapons company to come up before we started the surrender show. Gotha was too big for just a platoon and a towed gun."

"And a towed rabbi," Plotkin says. "Smoke?" He extends a pack of Lucky Strikes towards Jim.

"Mind if I take one for later? Thanks. And then across a field comes a fellow in a pink and grey striped—it was a prison uniform. Heading towards us, waving a metal bowl."

Plotkin shakes a Fleetwood out of the pack, lights it—"Saving my Luckies to buy liquor—" and takes a long drag. "A bowl?"

"Rations bowl. No food without it, if there were to be any, that is. He's calling out, it's Yiddish. The rabbi is translating on the fly: 'American liberators.'"

Plotkin raises his eyebrows, looks Jim in the eyes. "*Amerikaner bafreyter.*"

"American angels."

"*Amerikaner mlakhim,*" Plotkin says.

"Righteous Americans."

"*Tsdikim...*" Plotkin's voice breaks, then recovers. "*Amerikaner.*"

"God's strong right hand."

"*Der rekhter hant fun Got.*"

"Help me, help us."

"*Helf mikh. Helf aunz.*"

"Water."

"*Vaser.*"

"As he gets closer," Jim says, "well, he's just skin and bones, filthy. We step back. No one wants this guy to fall on them. Our medic moves towards him. So does the chaplain—the rabbi. He's pulling a shawl out of his field jacket."

"*Tallit.* For prayer."

"'*Rebbe!*' the fellow shouts, more of a sob really, pitches forward on his face, in a dead faint."

"This could be re-enacted for filming," Plotkin says.

"The medic rolls him on his back. The guy is covered with sores, smells like..." Jim takes a long breath through his nose. "So rank. You can see a star on his shirt, a red triangle pointing down laid over a yellow triangle pointing up. There's a black

R and a long number stamped below it. Below that there's a black circle, white border."

"Yellow's the Star of David. He's a Jew." Plotkin says. "Don't know what the rest means. Leave it to fucking Germans to over-organize a murder camp."

"The rabbi covers him with the tail-out."

"*Tallit.*"

"The prisoner comes to," Jim continues. "The medic gives him a sip of water. The rabbi takes a small bottle out of the pocket, pours a little in his canteen cup and gives it to the prisoner."

"Wine," Plotkin says.

"The prisoner drinks it, coughs. They do this three times."

"*Baruch Atah Adonai, Eloheinu Melech HaOlam, Borei P'ri HaGafen,*" Plotkin says.

"That sounds right," Jim says.

"Blessed are You, Lord our God, King of the Universe, who creates the fruit of the vine."

"The rabbi looks up and says, 'The Seder is not usually celebrated at zero nine hundred hours on a Tuesday, but he may die before he can say *Yitzcorn.*'"

"*Yizkor,* Jim. Prayer. On the eighth day of Passover."

"The rabbi says, 'Go, for God sends you. Go and God will be with you.' Then something about *Irrusalem.*"

"'Next year in Jerusalem.' Go on," Plotkin says. "Gotta figure out how we're gonna get *this* on film."

Jim raises his right wrist. "The medic holds up the prisoner's forearm so the captain can see the tattoo. A number, six or seven digits, started with a one. The same number printed on his shirt."

"Matching numbers," Plotkin says. "*Fucking* devils."

"The medic says typhus. Typhus and malnutrition and dysentery, he says, and who knows what else. The rest of us move back another step or two. The captain tells the chaplain to ask the prisoner who is he, where the prison is, how he escaped and what German forces he saw along the way. The man says he's a political prisoner. Held in a labor camp on the other side of Gotha." Jim gestures broadly. "This awful place. He called it Ohrdruf. 'Bring him to the Jeep,' the captain says, then turns to the platoon and says, 'Don't worry, you got your typhus injection during basic.'"

Plotkin grasps his upper right arm. "We got so many injections in basic, how we supposed to remember typhus?"

"By this time the heavy weapons company is pulling up behind us. You could see a couple of old men in overcoats with a white flag on a cane just starting out from Gotha towards us. They dropped the canes and scrambled back down the road after the HE round. Way over their heads, but civilians don't judge that very well."

"Neither do Signal Corps cameramen," Plotkin says, and laughs.

"You ever hear an .88, Sam?"

"Too many."

"The prisoner smiled and cried, looked around like he couldn't believe it, kept repeating *Amerikaner mlakhim.* Chaplain got a name out of him. Nicolae Rosner. Elementary school teacher. Had been in a bigger camp, but was moved to Ohrdruf a week ago. Death march, he said."

"Devils," Plotkin says.

"Rosner said Ohrdruf is a work camp connected to that bigger camp. Said American fighters strafed his work detail yesterday, and that he escaped in the confusion. Said the guards were starting to leave the camp to the kapos."

"Kapos?"

"That's what they call the prisoner trustees. Deputy guards."

Once again, Jim sees Nicolae Rosner in the back of the Jeep, wrapped in a GI blanket, holding a canteen and biting into a fistful of K-4 biscuits. "As we got closer to the camp, you couldn't notice how bad Rosner smelled. We had to put our handkerchiefs or spare socks over our noses."

"It's worse now, I bet," Plotkin says.

"Sure is." Jim now points to the fence that surrounds the camp. "Bark still on the fenceposts. This looks like something we would've built in the Civilian Conservation Corps. But with barbed wire and a guard tower in each corner. At first, I thought it was logs laying around inside the camp."

"Bodies."

"So many." Jim points with his left hand to a body just inside the gate. "See the armband? He was a kapo. Left it too late to make his getaway. He was still twitching when I got here."

"Musta thought he could surrender to you guys," Plotkin says.

"He forgot the prisoners were men, not cattle. They killed him." Jim points to the dead men the Catholic chaplain was praying over. "Those prisoners were shot where they stood earlier that day. Must have been forming up, but the guards shot them rather than march them away."

"SS devils. What about the prisoners who were still alive?"

"Rosner's yelling '*americani*' as loud as he can. About a hundred prisoners filter out into the yard. Walking skeletons. Limping, really. Shaved heads, bruises, open sores, no shoes, black teeth, no teeth, some leaning on other prisoners, too weak to walk on their own. Not one could've weighed a hundred pounds."

"What did they do?"

"Seemed like they thought they were dreaming. Some fell to their knees, some were crying. Some walked right up to us, shook hands or hugged us." Jim touches his cheek where it was kissed a dozen times. "They pointed towards their barracks, long tumbledown shacks, began walking towards them. Rosner asked the rabbi to follow them. We did. For every prisoner limping around outside, there were three lying on dirty straw inside the barracks. They were sick, dying, most of them, if they weren't already dead. The rabbi said to them, 'Ich bin a Rebe Amerikaner.'"

"I am an American rabbi," Plotkin says.

"You could hear whispers in Yiddish, Polish I think, other languages. Like Pentecost. The prisoners began to wail; some that could, they reached out and kissed his hands."

"Biblical," Plotkin said. "We need to do that scene for the camera."

"Those men have been taken to a hospital. Or died."

"The other prisoners are all still here? We can stage it with them."

"Most of them. Getting medical attention and rations. And clothes we're taking from the Germans in Gotha. Like I said, the dead are left where we found them."

A deuce-and-a-half pulls up to the gate and several 4th Armored Division soldiers jump off the back and move into the camp. An older man steps down more carefully. Jim looks, then looks again. "Hello, Mr. Levin!"

The reporter walks over, handkerchief pressed to his nose. "What the hell?" he says. "It's Private Jim Tanzer of Huntington, West Virginia! You made it out of Bastogne in one piece. I'll have to show you my review of your Christmas Day soldier show."

"It was read to me," Jim says. He gestures towards Plotkin. "Bunny Levin, this is Sam Plotkin, Signal Corps, Special Films Unit. Sam, this is Bunny Levin, *New York Times* warco."

After exchanging details about New York delicatessens, synagogues, and public schools with Plotkin, Levin says, "I'm here to cover Ike's tour of the camp. At thirteen hundred hours, right?"

"Right," Jim says. "I'm detailed to escort that tour." He gestures at Plotkin. "Sam is shooting it for George Stevens. The director."

Levin doesn't bother to say that he knows George Stevens. His expression darkens as he looks over at the dead prisoners on the ground. "I went through on my own yesterday," he says, failing to mention he then worked most of the night on a column he knows the Opinion section editor will never run.

"It's hard to believe," Jim says.

"Goddamn *Herrenvolk*, blood and soil mythology *bullshit!*" Levin says. He opens his arms towards the rest of the camp, then puts the handkerchief in his pocket. "Just outside Gotha, the *picturesque* German town of Gotha, here on the *ground* is murder on an industrial scale, the product of mass-produced racist nationalist insanity. Unspeakable madness." He pauses and fixes Jim with a stare.

"Terrible," is all Jim can think to say.

"More than terrible, Private Tanzer. Hieronymus Bosch wouldn't have put Ohrdruf in painted Hell." Levins' face is reddening.

"Harry Mouse *who?*" Plotkin says.

"How do you justify beating, starving, slaughtering innocent human beings?" A vein is popping out on Levin's forehead. "Stacking their bodies like logs? How do you learn to see human beings as livestock, as vermin? How do you mine the darkest depths of human nature not for an hour, not for a day, but for *years*." His gaze settles on the bodies near the gate.

Jim says, "I heard there are other camps that—"

Levin won't be stopped. "Sow the wind, reap the whirlwind. At this slaughterhouse, *labor camp* they call it, the harvest has overwhelmed the German lust for orderliness." He turns and points to various landmarks as he speaks. "The crooked fences, buildings just this side of condemnation, the rutted roads, the slip-shod piles of the dead, the half-cremated corpses at that man-made Pompeii." Plotkin remembers his job, raises his camera and begins shooting.

Levin doesn't care. "Ohrdruf will show the American taxpayer, will show the soldiers, the airmen, the sailors what kind of evil we're fighting. Ohrdruf will show the world, will show Lindbergh, that self-righteous prick, Father Coughlin, that wicked anti-Semite, Hearst, Nye—the whole lot of them." Levin is in a deep lather.

"Let those bastards explain why this wasn't our business. *This is what all those wounded and killed American soldiers are for*, what all the machines are for, all the oil and gas, bombs and bullets, blood and brains we poured into this fight. And now we know why. To destroy German *schrecklichkeit*, the inhuman frightfulness, the fanaticism. How did the nation of Goethe and Beethoven, Schiller and Kant, descend to savagery?" Levin slams his fist into his palm. Plotkin blinks; Jim edges half a step back.

"Surely they have offended God. Has He not in His anger raised up mighty armies? Has not God caused American factories to pour forth armaments like clouds of locusts? Has not God united the Capitalist democracies of Britain and America with the Soviet Communists to drive their beloved Fuhrer, to drive Satan, back into Hell? It is a crusade, and it is God's will that it be finished, no matter the cost." Levin is done, looking at Plotkin, then Jim, then taking deep breaths.

"From your lips to God's ears," Plotkin says. Jim nods, wondering if any of this can be worked in *Spamlet*. Probably not. It's too awful.

⋀

Colonel Stevens arrives at twelve hundred hours to do the location scout, orders Jim to lead, confirms Plotkin has loaded his camera with 16mm color film. This slaughterhouse is too much for black and white.

They start with the office location. Stevens wants the windows closed, so the camera catches the Germans' reactions to the smell as they go through. "Hang that bastard back on the wall," he says to Plotkin, pointing to a portrait of Hitler on the floor. Stevens wants the sheet taken off the window, wants more light, so the audience can see dead *people*, not just a pile of skin and bones. "Give me a two-shot here," he says to Plotkin, pointing at a boy and an old man lying next to each other on top of the pile, faces clown-white with powdered lime. The director steps outside and retches.

"Two-shot?" Jim asks.

"Close-up of the two faces," Plotkin says. "That boy and the old man. Old man? Hell, he was probably twenty-five before the SS got their claws on him."

I was putting on shows at Stiers when I was twenty-five, Jim thinks.

Plotkin and Tanzer finish fixing the office set and catch up to Stevens. "This isn't right," Plotkin says. "We're keeping the dead men in degrading positions until the general's tour. They need to be washed and buried."

"It's terrible, Private," Stevens agrees, "but these men are still in the fight. You know, the fight over public opinion about the war. No one will see the Ohrdruf movie and say we should've stayed home."

Someone needs to tell that to Stella, Jim thinks.

At the end of the scout, Stevens says to Plotkin, "It's too much. We'll focus on three locations: the murdered prisoners by the gate, the pile of bodies covered with lime in the office, and this." He points to the giant grill with the half-burned bodies.

Back at the gate, Tanzer and Plotkin see MPs walking a column of civilians up the road from Gotha, followed by trucks carrying pine coffins. The men in the column are resting different-sized shovels on their shoulders like rifles. Plotkin gets the shot. "That fresh cut wood smells like incense in this *farsharben* place," he says as the trucks pull up to the camp. "God forsaken."

At fifteen hundred hours, Ike and Brad pull up thirty feet from where Jim and Plotkin are waiting. Patton arrives in his own Jeep, three gold stars on the front bumper. No mistaking them for German generals. George Patton, commander of the U.S. Third Army, half a million GIs rolling over what's left of the *Wermacht*, is dressed like the Army version of a ringmaster. Custom-tailored field jacket tucked into riding pants; jump boots; holstered Colt revolver, ivory grip.

"That's Patton," Jim says. *Splinters*, he thinks.

For the first time since 1942, Old Blood and Guts is not the center of attention. And the smell of Ohrdruf has put an upside-down smile and a gray tint on his hard-ass mug.

"It's rough, the first time it hits you." Plotkin says.

"You can't get it out of your clothes," Jim says.

General Bradley wears a standard issue olive green raincoat, wrinkled. "Omar the Warmaker," Plotkin says. "He looks like a small-town bank examiner wearing a helmet."

But Ike, Ike looks the part. Service cap, short combat jacket, five stars on the shoulders. He's the boss. The American Jehovah. Boiling mad, eyes narrowed, fists on his hips. "Beggars description," Eisenhower says to Bradley and Patton. "Starvation, torture, bestiality. Not a shred of decency."

"Too bad you aren't shooting with sound," Jim says to Plotkin, *sotto voce*.

"Yeah. Hey, look at that," Plotkin says. "Old Blood and Guts is stepping behind that truck."

"You gonna shoot Patton barfing?"

"That has to stay offstage."

As the group moves forward, the prisoner Rosner explains via Ike's translator, "Here men were beaten, sometimes to death...here men were shot...here men were hung by piano wire...here we assembled at 2 a.m. for work detail."

Ike turns to the reporter and says, "We're told the American soldier doesn't know what he's fighting *for*." He shakes his head a little and says in a tone of disgust, "Now at least he'll know what he's fighting *against*."

Members of the tour drop away as it goes on. Rear-echelon PR officers aren't used to dead people asking to be seen, demanding to be smelled.

⌃

On his way out of the camp in the early evening—still plenty of daylight—Jim approaches a middle-aged German man digging a grave. Chubby fellow, suit and tie, Homburg hat. Cherry red in the face and panting, the man has dug about three feet down. Not seeing Jim, he throws his shovel on the ground and shakes his head.

"*Was ist das!*" Jim shouts. The man turns and freezes. Jim picks up the shovel and swings it like a baseball bat.

The man ducks; the blade knocks the hat off his head. The German puts his hands in the air and screams, "*Ich bin kein Nazi!*"

Jim throws the shovel at the man's feet, puts his fist through the Homburg, then shouts "You're all Nazis! *Arbeit macht frei*, you rotten son of a bitch. *Zurück an die Arbeit!* Get back to work!"

"Hell of a performance, Tanzer," Plotkin says, winding his camera as he approaches Jim from behind. "You hear the news? Roosevelt's dead. MacArthur's gonna be President."

⌃

It's been two weeks since the unspeakable telegram landed on the Railroad Street house in Huntington. A gold star flag is in the window. The shades are pulled down. Stella has been contacted by the War Department about Jim's $10,000 death benefit. He never changed his beneficiary. A pre-printed condolence card from General Marshall arrived yesterday: "*His memory will live in the grateful heart of our nation.*" Stella and Betty Jo arrive in Huntington tomorrow. Jim's memorial service is scheduled for Saturday afternoon at St. Paul's Lutheran Church.

Norma is at the kitchen sink peeling potatoes when the phone rings. This is strictly to have something to do with her hands. The refrigerator is full of casseroles brought over by friends and neighbors. Cakes, pies, and biscuits cover the kitchen table. The phone rings. She hears Lavinia's "*halloo?*" then hears her mother howl like a kicked dog. Norma rushes to the living room. Lavinia is on the floor in a faint, telephone handset in her hand. After sitting on the floor and putting her mother's head in her lap, Norma takes the handset. "Hello?"

"It's Jimmy." The voice crackles with static. It could be her brother. But he's dead. "Is Mutti okay?" the voice continues. "I heard a scream. Hey, are you there?"

"We are here," Norma says, and draws a large breath. "This is a *cruel* joke on a Gold Star mother," she shouts. "Shame on you!" She slams the receiver onto the cradle. Remaining cross-legged on the floor, she reaches for a sofa pillow, puts it under her mother's head, blinks out an angry tear and thinks, *who would do such a thing?* And, *are the smelling salts still under the bathroom sink?* Finally, she thinks, *Mutti?*

The phone rings. She picks up the receiver.

"Hello? Sis?"

"What?"

"It's me. I'm at 12th Army in Frankfurt."

"*What!*"

"Signal Corps set up a link to the States for General Bradley. Mickey got us ten minutes. Wes is breathing down my neck. Sis? Are you there?"

NEW YORK CITY
March 12, 1945

THE WORK IS fronting the Ricky Ellis Band at the 500 Club in Greenwich Village. Contract. Regular schedule, no travel, two weeks' paid vacation in August. A chance to make good money, a chance to be seen by the big clubs, a chance to get Betty Jo and herself settled in New York. A break. Stella really wants it.

She sings a couple of numbers. No piano. The club owner

says, "Come sit on the couch, Miss Sterling. Let's talk." He gets out from behind his desk and takes off his jacket. She can smell the booze on his breath, see the excitement in his pants. "I like you," he says. "We'll get along swell."

For a couple of seconds, she can't believe it. Sam Gold doesn't send girls to casting couch auditions. "You're something else, I'll tell you that," the club owner says, sitting down on the leather couch and pulling off his tie.

She knows what he expects. But it's a plum gig. Will he settle for a hand job? No. "I don't do personal performances," she tells him. "I'm married. To a soldier."

She's out on the street in under three minutes.

18.

SPA WILDUNGEN, GERMANY, MAY 17, 1945

> Ranged in the order of their value, an audience will laugh loudest at these episodes:
> (1) When a man sticks one finger into another man's eye.
> (2) When a man sticks two fingers into another man's eyes.
> (3) When a man chokes another man and shakes his head from side to side.
> (4) When a man kicks another man.
> (5) When a man steps on another man's foot.
> …so long as the object of the attack—the other man—is not really hurt.
>
> Writing for Vaudeville by Brett Page,
The Home Correspondence School,
Springfield, Mass, 1915

Standing next to the kitchen door, Jim, Wes, and Mickey can see the back of the heads of the luncheon guests. They're in the ballroom of the Bad Wildungen Hotel at Spa Wildungen, aka Gau Hesse-Nassau in soon-to-be-banned Third Reich parlance. Until a few months prior, Spa Wildungen was *the* place for upper-class Nazis in central Germany to take the waters.

Now it's the headquarters of Omar Bradley's 12th U.S. Army Group, 1.3 million citizen-soldiers.

Back from the Pacific, Mickey has re-assembled his Jeep show squad for this command performance. Bradley, the "soldier's general," is feting the uncountable Soviet Army in the person of Marshal Conrad Koniev and his general staff. Even Stalin considers Koniev to be ruthless. The marshal has arrived here by way of Duklja Pass, Budapest, Berlin, and several smaller bloodbaths. He and his generals are hard men, survivors of Stalin's purges in the late 1930s and four years of Eastern Front savagery inflicted by and on the Germans.

Twenty general officers are distributed around five tables, three for the Americans and two for their Soviet guests. A flying accident has left Glenn Miller and his trombone somewhere at the bottom of the English Channel. Miller's 51-piece Army Air Force Orchestra is led by *his* replacement, Tex Beneke. They are seated at the back of the stage in clean and pressed suntans. The enlisted version of the greatest big band that ever performed. A statement of American soft power to back up the hard power on display in occupied Germany now, and moving ever closer to the Japanese home islands.

The Russian-language versions of the program for today's luncheon are somewhere in the Braunschweig Ordnance Depot. After the national anthems are played and the general officers sit back down, an American captain reads out the English-language program in Russian. This isn't strictly necessary, since Marshal Koniev has brought his own translator.

"Greetings to our Soviet Allies," the captain reads. "Welcome to this luncheon given by Omar N. Bradley, Commanding General of the 12th U.S. Army Group, in honor of Marshall Conrad Koniev, Commanding General of the 1st Ukrainian Army Group. The menu: Cold consommé, Florida pompano, Carolina roast chicken, buttered peas, creamed cauliflower, potato chips, greens salad, apple pie with Wisconsin cheddar cheese"—Jim recalls seeing Willi loaded onto a truck with other POWs in Bastogne—"Virginia cornbread, and coffee."

Jim has already been fed. Mickey insisted on eating with the stewards in the back of the kitchen, regaling them with jokes and stories. Neither Jim nor Wes had ever eaten at the same table with colored men, but they know to go along with Mickey when he ad libs.

"General Bradley," the captain continues, "has invited Jascha Heifetz, Mickey Rooney, The Glenn Miller Army Air Force Orchestra, the Kayne Trio, and the G.I. Jive dancers to perform for you today."

"Heifetz lives a couple of blocks from me in Beverly Hills," Mickey says to Jim and Wes. "He doesn't go to parties."

The captain names the officers of the 1st Ukrainian Army Group attending, then those of the 12th U.S. Army Group. "We might as well be in Waterbury," Jim says, "so much brass here." Then, "Waterbury, Connecticut. The Brass City."

"Let us know when you plan to use that one," Mickey says, tugging his earlobe and smiling, "so Wes and I can be ready to laugh."

On the back of the program is a cartoon map of the 12th Army's progress from early June, 1944, D-Day, in Normandy, to late April, 1945, in Torgau, where they linked up with the Red Army.

"Brad's all-American menu has a message for his guests," a quartermaster captain, thrilled to be standing next to the Hollywood star, says to Mickey. "With Germany up for grabs, he's reminding these Reds of the reach of the United States. The country that delivered them tens of thousands of trucks, Jeeps, guns, and other cargo to fight their war is also capable of bringing fish from Florida, Carolina chicken, and Wisconsin cheese to the middle of occupied Germany. Just for lunch."

"It's some show," Mickey says.

This isn't the first all-American meal for these Soviets in this war. They've eaten plenty of Spam over the last four years, thanks to Lend Lease and a million Iowa pigs who gave their porcine lives to nourish the Red Army and raise farm prices in the bargain.

Bradley and Koniev both come from humble backgrounds. Koniev's family were peasant farmers, while Bradley was a boilermaker on the Wabash Railroad before he made West Point. Neither commander generates publicity like Patton. That's okay with Brad, crucial for Koniev's survival.

The stewards place a bottle of Four Roses Kentucky bourbon and a pony glass at each officer's place. "That booze is from Brad's personal allotment, untouched since Casablanca," the quartermaster says to Mickey. "I'll get one for you."

"Okay," Mickey says, and turns to Wes and Jim. "Has to be the first time the Glenn Miller Band plays the Soviet anthem. Plenty of work for the horn section. Too bad Glenn isn't here to see it."

⟨⟩

GENERAL BRADLEY FORMALLY welcomes his guests. Marshal Koniev formally responds. The meal is served. Lieutenant General Dmitri Grishenko turns to Koniev and says, in Russian, "They are not the soldiers the Germans are. Their commanders are soft-hearted, and the bastards are stealing German gold and scientists from under our noses."

We would steal all that and the hay from the barns, Koniev thinks. He would make that joke if the Chief Political Commissar of the 1st Ukrainian Army Group—the slippery *politrik* Yuri Ivanov—was not within earshot. "But we must respect a nation that can move ten million men across two vast oceans," Koniev continues. "And so much cargo." He much prefers his Jeep to the ZIS staff car he felt obliged to arrive in today.

"Where is the bread?" Grishenko says. "Is this a meal or a snack?"

Koniev points to his plate. "This corn from the Virginia is bread to them."

"They serve a peasant loaf to the Commanding General of the 1st Ukrainian Army Group?"

"I've eaten plenty of Rzhevsky bread in my time, comrade. Virginia bread is not an insult."

"And they have their black servants pour the Kentucky vodka? Do they not care to act like hosts?"

"America is a new nation. It's all immigrants," Koniev says. "A machine nation, as Germany and Japan have discovered. Not yet civilized. A contradictory people. They call Prohibition, they outlaw wine and spirits. Then they don't. Puritans and Hollywood, Jim Crow and negro congressmen. Cowboys and Indians."

"They haven't even put on their dress uniforms," Grishenko says. "They are too casual."

"I make that to be an affectation. They want us to think everything comes easy to them."

"They do not have political officers. That has to affect morale."

"Undoubtedly," Koniev says. *They don't know how lucky they are*, he thinks.

"The so-called openness of the Americans is deception," Grishenko says. He is both making conversation with his boss and performing for the political commissar.

Grishenko's posturing has become tiresome for Koniev, makes him all the more ready to knock back a few. "Make a toast, Comrade," he says. "If it pleases you." This is not a request. Whether or not it pleases Grishenko is of no matter.

⚑

JIM TURNS TO Mickey. "*Yank* says they'll declare war on Japan now, the Reds."

"I hope," Mickey says. "Japs hold out too long, we're gonna

be wrestling on the deck of an aircraft carrier. I got to get home. Got movies to make. Before MGM replaces me."

"With those kamikaze maniacs buzzing around?" Wes says. "No thanks. The Krauts are horrible, but at least they aren't crazy."

"What I saw at Ohrdruf, I don't know about that," Jim says.

"And you're a Kraut yourself, Tanzer!" Wes says. "You've got two left feet, but I wouldn't go as far as 'horrible.'"

Jim smiles. "Thanks for nothing, buffalo chip."

"That's Heifetz tuning up," Mickey says. "Let's see what kind of a lead-in he gives us."

"Watch the Soviets now," the quartermaster captain says. "Brad's poking them in the eye with Heifetz."

"How's that?" Mickey says.

"The Reds love classical music. Heifetz is a genius. To see him in person is a once-in-a-lifetime opportunity. But he's a turncoat to the Kremlin. For leaving Lithuania and becoming an American citizen. He was already a virtuoso when his family emigrated after the pogrom of 1915."

"Sounds like his old man called the right play," Mickey says.

"All they missed was World War One," the captain says, "the Russian Revolution, the famine of '22, Russian occupation, then German occupation. Leaving out being killed by antisemites in Vilna, or by the Germans in one of the murder camps."

"So for these Ivans," Mickey says, "he's a bum."

"For the Kremlin he's a bum. Brad's guests have to play it cool here today. They don't give much away, but watch their eyes while he plays."

"Patton would feel right at home with the Soviet generals, costume-wise," Jim says.

"He'll want stripes on his trousers after he sees Koniev's outfit," Wes says.

"You could put a roll and butter on those shoulder boards," Mickey says.

"Their hats are the size of birthday cakes," Jim says.

"The sashes," Wes says.

"They each have about twenty pounds of medals on their chests," Mickey says.

"It's meant to make them look like Cossacks," Jim says.

"Zazzy," Wes says. The three have a rhythm going.

"Too bad Patton and Montgomery weren't invited," Mickey says. "It'd be swell to watch those two prima donnas try to wrestle each other for the spotlight."

"Sure," Jim says. *I'd like to see anyone wrestle it away from you, Mickey,* he thinks.

Then Heifetz's accompanist plays the opening notes of "Hora Staccato," a lively dance-like Eastern European melody requiring exceptional technique. Heifetz plays it and plays with it. Applause. Then another piece. The effortless fast scales, arpeggios, double stops, string crossings. The superb phrasing, dynamics, articulation. The emotional depth.

"If I played a violin, I'd break it across my knee about now," Mickey says.

"What was that piece?" Jim asks.

"Strauss's Violin Sonata in E-flat Major," Mickey answers.

"*German* music?" Jim says.

"Heifetz plays what he wants to play," Mickey says. "By the way, he's killing it, and we're the deuce."

"I've got tears in my eyes," Wes says. "That violin is singing."

"Never mind the waterworks," Mickey says. "The pressing question is how I'm gonna follow Jascha Heifetz with wrestling hokum. I'll come off like a sap-head."

"We'll be a change of pace," Jim says. "Comedy."

"Might as well be your marching mule act, Jimmy," Mickey says. "We've got to change things up."

"This is 'Flight of the Bumblebee,' Rimsky-Korsakov," the quartermaster captain says. "A tribute to Russia. Look, a smile and a nod from Koniev, and now all the Reds are smiling. They never smile."

Mickey gestures at Koniev, who is blowing his nose. "I might as well get on stage and do that for three minutes."

"Cornbread, potato chips and a *Meisterkonzert*," the captain says. "Brad's licking these Reds. That was a ragtime arrangement, Joplin, and now 'Yankee Doodle.' American music from an American immigrant. Perfect. Look at General Simpson singing along."

⩓

The Wrestling Burlesque is a marathon piece of stage business Mickey Rooney stole from his film *Boys Town*. They've been doing it since *Hip Hooray* rehearsals at Camp Sibert. They could do it in their sleep and blindfolded by now, but for Mickey changing on the fly based on audience reaction, or when he's bored and wants to watch Wes and Jim scramble.

Done it drunk, done it in nurse uniforms, done it in blackface, done it fourteen times in one day, done it roused from their fart sacks and asleep on their feet, soaking wet, in barns, in tents, in hospital wards, in open fields, on sidewalks, on steel decks. They've done it for troops who will never fire a shot in anger, for combatmen who won't survive the following day, for soldiers who can't write their own name, for officers with PhDs. They've done it in under a minute (incoming artillery) and they've stretched it to twenty (only one show that night). They've done it laughing so hard they fell down (the audience loved it). They've always done it well enough to make the crowd, from two GIs and a stray dog to a thousand 9th Army airmen, smile, laugh, hoot, holler, and forget their troubles for a while. It's not Shakespeare, but all the soldiers are starved for entertainment, starved for home, and the combatmen are starved for anything harmless and funny.

Because fighting has stopped in the ETO, but logistics haven't, the trio has new and better everything. Mickey and

Wes have wrestling singlets. Jim has a referee's white short-sleeve shirt, a black bow tie, white trousers, and size 13 white *Kriegsmarine* low quarter dress shoes. They have stage lights, courtesy of the Signal Corps. They have a prop guy who also does sound effects. They even have a painted backdrop, one side of a wrestling ring and crowd faces. What they don't have is a way to follow Jascha Heifetz on the bill.

"Let's blow," Mickey says.

"It's a command performance," Jim says. "We're under orders." This is strictly for form.

Mickey never skips out on an audience.

"Can we let the band go before us?" Wes says.

"Music back-to-back? After that genius?" Mickey says.

"And they aren't ready," Jim says.

"Well boys," Mickey says, "we aren't being asked to storm the beach at Iwo Jima." The applause for Heifetz has faded to appreciative murmurs. "Let's go and get it over with."

"Hey!" Jim says. "What if you wing your Puck monologue?" Jim and Wes have heard Mickey parody his *Midsummer Night's* lines on long Jeep rides. "It's high tone, cools the house, makes a bridge to the wrestling burlesque. You can put your field jacket on over your wrestling tights."

Mickey's eyes dart about, light up. "Puck. Yeah, I can see it, Jimmy. After this war, we're going to Hollywood, I'm making *you* a producer. Now, buy me time to work it out." Mickey turns away, beginning to smile.

Jim waits two minutes, then walks on stage as the room is starting to stir. "Marshall Koniev, and your distinguished officers of the First Ukrainian Armies," Jim says. "For your entertainment." Three beats for translation. "General Bradley and his 12th US Army Group takes great pleasure in presenting—" two beats—"a man who needs no introduction—" two beats—"the pride of the 6817th Morale Corps battalion—" two beats—"icon of the silver screen—" two beats. Sweat begins to trickle down Jim's back. Two stewards circle, refilling coffee cups. That helps. Three more beats as the translator stumbles over silver screen. "Oscar winner—" two beats—"creator of Andy Hardy—" two beats—"star of last year's smash hit, *National Velvet*—" two beats—"one of Hollywood's most talented and beloved performers—" two beats—"America's number one box office movie star." Two beats.

Jim draws a deep breath. "When duty called, Mickey Rooney raised his hand," he continues. "'I'll serve my country,' he said." Three beats. General Bradley turns towards the back of the room. "'I'll fight for freedom,' Mickey Rooney said." Three beats. "He's made us laugh, he's made us cry, he's entertained us." Three beats.

The room is slipping away. The quartermaster captain is examining his program with the aid of a Zippo lighter. "The most famous corporal since Napoleon," Jim says. There's a ripple of laughter; the room isn't all the way gone. "Here tonight to reprise his award-winning performance as Puck in the Warner Brothers production of William Shakespeare's *Midsummer Night's Dream*." Three beats. *C'mon, Mickey*, Jim thinks. "Where he carried Jimmy Cagney and Dick Powell." Three beats. The room is restless again. General Bradley motions for his aide.

"I first met this all-American soldier at…" A slight groan rises from the audience, but not loud enough that Jim cannot hear a whispered "ready" from stage right. "Allies in the fight for freedom, please put your hands together and welcome a true American patriot. The one and only—" Jim extends an arm stage right—"Mickey Rooney!"

Jim backs away, stage left. Only the microphone is in the spotlight. After ten seconds, there is a ripple of nervous chuckling. At thirty seconds, the American generals are shifting forward in their seat, looking around. Two of the Russian officers clasp their hands in front of their chests but they don't smile. At sixty seconds, Beneke takes three steps towards his band; they're going to have to go.

Mickey appears in the spotlight. In a tablecloth toga. His service tie is around his forehead. The expression on his face is otherworldly. The Americans lean in, as does Koniev, then the rest of the Russian generals. A Signal Corps photographer moves to kneel in front of Bradley and Koniev's table to get his shot—*Stars & Stripes*, *Yank*, even the AP will run this iconic photo of Corporal Mickey Rooney. Rooney looks over stage left and begins:

> *Thou speak'st aright; I am that*
> *merry wanderer of the night.*
> *Hey diddle diddle, Heifetz plays the fiddle*
> *But I will jest to Oberon and make him smile.*

Mickey steps down and pulls the Russian interpreter towards the stage with him. Koniev nods approval. In between each line, Mickey dances, gestures, mugs, floats the interpreter time to express the words and feeling in Russian. Mickey revivifies the dry bones of performances past, pulls this act out of airy nothing. The interpreter gets the hang of it, smiles, makes up what he cannot understand.

> *My fairy lord, come ye now,*
> *Froggy went a-courting, milked a cow.*
> *But soft, what light through*
> *yonder window breaks,*
> *'Splain dat to me, you rakes.*
> *It is the east at night, Japan is burning bright.*
> *Remember Pearl Harbor! Fight the fight.*
> *Against the envy of less happier lands,*
> *Wake Tokyo with thy knocking!*

The steps, the timing, the energy, the elastic face. Mickey Rooney. He continues with Aurora's harbinger and other remembered or invented lines. From the wings, violin cradled in his right arm, bow in left hand, Heifetz smiles. For once, he's not impossible to follow.

"What hempen homespuns have forming up been?" Mickey says, gesturing at the generals:

> So near the cradle of the fairy queen?
> Up and down, up and down,
> I will lead them up and down 'til Birnam Wood
> do come to Dunsinane.
> We're not in Kansas anymore, 'tis plain.
> I go, I go; look how I go,
> Swifter than slings and arrows
> from the Tartar's bow.
> Soft you, fair Europe, I have
> seen your greatness flicker,
> What fools these mortars be, I snicker.
> A crew of patches, rude technicals, that
> work for bread upon Athenian stalls,
> Will put on a show, intended for the
> great VE day, when Germany falls.

He holds for light applause, sparked by Jim and Wes from the back.

> If we shadows have offended, think
> who's on first, and all is mended,
> You have but slumber'd here, while
> these visions did appear.
> The stuff that dreams are made of,
> Here's looking at you kid, here's rising above.

Mickey looks up, then towards Bradley.

General, do not reprehend: if you'se
regusted, we will mend:
We that outlive the fight, come
home safe and right,
Will stand a tip-toe when this war is named.
The devil Hitler our boys have tamed.
We'll sing a song, to make amends ere long;
Else the Puck a liar call; So, good
night unto you all.
Give me your hands, if we be friends.
And Robin shall restore amends.

There is hesitant, then full applause. The room doesn't know what just happened, but they know it was rare. Turning to the Soviets, Mickey says, "One thread from everyone in the world made a noose for Hitler. Thank you, *Spasibo*, very much." Spotlight off.

It comes back on a minute later. "Ladies," Jim says. "And gentlemen. The 12th United States Army Group, property of General Omar Bradley, is proud to present the main event of the evening." Three beats for the translator. "A wrestling match, for the catchweight championship of liberated Europe. In this corner." Tanzer unfolds his long right arm palm up to an empty stage right.

Near the end of the skit, the ballroom shakes with the engine roar and propeller beat of a dozen planes buzzing the hotel; ordered up by Brad, but not on the program. The wrestlers stop and look up. Mickey pretends to faint in Jim's arms. The Russians aren't familiar with the P-47; they watch the American officers closely. As the thunder fades, Koniev's translator says something in Bradley's ear. Brad stands up and says, "Marshal Koniev hopes he didn't survive all those battles only to be killed watching low farce." Laughter. The Glenn Miller Band breaks into the first few bars of "American Patrol." Then the match resumes.

It goes over; it goes over big. Marshall Koniev slaps the table three times and stands up. Three times a toast is made; three times the whiskey is drunk. Bradley, who has never had three drinks in one go in his life, puts the kibosh on toast number four as it forms up at his table.

"Is this a Children's Day party," Grishenko says to Marshal Koniev, "or a celebration of the Allies' glorious victory after four years of total war?"

The spotlights open on Glenn Miller's Army Air Force Band. "American Patrol," "Tuxedo Junction," and "Moonlight Serenade." Tight as a drum. Next is Seattle's answer to the Andrew Sisters, the Kayne Trio, Marta, Jean, and Joan Kuzmenko. "Don't Sit Under the Apple Tree" and "Chattanooga Choo Choo."

"Those girls look good in suntans," Wes says to Jim, referring to the Kaynes' stage costumes, replicas of Army khaki.

"Tight suntans," Jim says, taking in Marta Kuzmenko's perfect ass.

The sisters step away and the band starts "In the Mood." Four couples, young GIs and WACs, bounce onto the stage and perform an amateur jitterbug demonstration. "Good enough," Wes says.

"They're ahead of the beat," Jim says, although the bouncy song and the eight young bodies in constant motion covers this up to the audience. "Hey! There goes Mickey."

Rooney has jumped onstage during the bridge and tapped the shoulder of one of the dancing soldiers, who gives way with a smile. Mickey then leads the WAC in a wild but precise jitterbug. At the end Mickey takes a bow, points to his partner who is bright red and breathing hard, and steps over to the band's drum set.

"Here we go," Wes says.

The drummer nods and steps aside. Mickey sits down, plays the opening drum line in "Sing, Sing, Sing." The brass comes in. The Soviet generals are stone-faced, under attack. The music is fresh and vigorous, an expression of boundless energy, modernity, loud proof of the benefits of freedom and democracy.

"The Russians must regret they have no colored." Wes says to Jim. "No colored, no jazz."

The American generals clap vigorously when Mickey steps away. Heifetz walks back onstage with a smile on his face, and nods to band leader Beneke. Heifetz begins to play. His accompanist smiles and follows. It's "Dance of the Soldiers," the lively, patriotic Russian military song written in 1938 by Boris Alexandrov. There is an involuntary swelling of Red Army chests, a welcome recognition that Heifetz is paying tribute to the victors—through death uncountable and grief unfathomable—of the Great Patriotic War. Paying tribute to the ineffable Russian soul. That Heifetz feels what they feel, how different they are from their American allies.

The first phrase is adagio. Heifetz is arranging the song on the fly. On the fourth phrase, the band tip-toes in, offering the violinist a bigger canvas. Mickey lays his drumsticks quietly on the snare and backs off the stage.

Koniev beckons his aide de camp, holding a hand over his head and rotating it twice with his index finger extended. "'Kazachiy Tanets,'" he says.

"The Cossacks' Dance," the American translator says to General Bradley.

The young Russian soldier salutes, pushes his service cap down on his head and walks towards the side of the stage. He pauses at the bottom of the stairs, catches the tempo, bounds up the steps and onto the stage, starts the dance. Arms extend to his side, legs cross over each other, boot heels are slapped. He leaps and bows. Heifetz pulls the tempo faster. Straight as an arrow from the waist up, the young soldier executes the *Otpad* squat-and-kick steps. Marshal Koniev is leaning towards the stage and nodding.

"Look at that," Mickey says, eyes going back and forth

between Heifetz and the dancing soldier. He inhales the performance like smoke from a cigarette.

After the dance is complete, Mickey shakes the young Russian's hand and hugs him, does a few neat *prisyadka* steps himself, then turns and bows to Heifetz. "Maestro," he says.

"Maestro," Heifetz replies.

This exchange cannot be heard over the clapping.

HUNTINGTON HERALD DISPATCH

April 27, 1945
Miracle on Railroad Street

Huntington—April 26, 1945. As many of our readers know, the telegram every serviceman's family dreads arrived at Bill and Lavinia Tanzer's house at 14 Railroad Street on April 12th. It brought the awful news that their boy Jim, son of Huntington, dancer and producer extraordinaire, was among the American soldiers buried in Luxembourg. Imagine the family's grief. Imagine how hard it was to pass the news along to Jim's wife in New York, the singer Stella Sterling.

Then imagine their shock and disbelief, then joy, when Jim called home from Germany yesterday! They told the *Herald-Dispatch* there had been a mix-up. Jim was alive. That's all they knew.

While some of our older Huntingtonians may recall confusion or long delays on notification of the families of the fallen during the Great War, this is the first occurrence of this kind of terrible mistake we know of in this war. It is with the greatest pleasure that the *Herald-Dispatch* issues a formal retraction of our April 13 obituary of James Tanzer of Huntington. Great to have you back for a return engagement, Jimmy!

19.

BERLIN, GERMANY, LATE JULY, 1945

> If it should be necessary to fight the Russians, the sooner we do it the better.
>
> —DIARY OF GENERAL GEORGE C. PATTON

"THOUGHT I'D HAVE the sink to myself, this early." This from a burly soldier, stripped to the waist, towel over his shoulder, who has entered the kitchen of the Berlin house where Jim is billeted. "What has you shaving at zero dark thirty, corporal?" The soldier leans against the stove.

"Meeting a train," Jim says, glancing at the soldier. "I'm about done. No hot water, though." Jim looks again quickly to confirm that he's seen the man before, taking in the thick purple scar from wrist to elbow on the man's right arm.

"At least we got a sink," the man says. "Don't have to shave out of our helmets."

"You're infantry," Jim says, dragging his razor across his cheek.

"Was. You?"

"Morale Corps. I'm a—"

There's a screech of brakes outside, then the loud thumps of tires mounting the front steps. "Three women in one night!" comes up from below.

"You got a hand job from a whore, Smitty, then you necked a fairy. Number three was pissing in your pants. You're so loaded you can't tell the difference."

"*SHHH…let's not wake the rest of the boys.*" A hood slams shut with a bang. "*HA-HA-HA.*" The noise continues as the pair get through the front door and, after much talking and shushing, get into an apartment and go quiet.

"Out drinking all night," Jim says.

"Best of times for single GIs in Berlin," the burly soldier says. "Easy duty, Army feeds and houses them, pays in dollars, plenty of liquor in Berlin, plenty of German women just trying to survive. Shangri-La."

"And no chance of getting killed," Jim says, rinsing off his razor.

"Unless they drive into a tree," the soldier says, "or get shot by accident. Guns and Jeeps and whiskey. Eighteen-year-old replacements. Glad I'm getting out of here."

"Going home?" Jim steps away from the sink. "Here you go."

"Thanks. Going home."

"How many discharge points do you have?"

"Enough to get me out of the Army. Eighty-two. They offered a commission if I re-enlist and stay here, but I've got a wife. And a little girl I haven't met."

"Me too," Jim says. "Well, I've met my daughter. I'll be here a while yet. Forty-eight points. The goddamned Army hasn't credited me the combat points I'm due." The soldier's vivid scar keeps Jim from mentioning that the Army also hasn't awarded him the Purple Heart he has coming, and the five precious discharge points that go with it.

"That's some major chickenshit," the burly soldier says. "Older guys like you and me, we joined to do a job and go home, not run away to the circus."

"Right," Jim nods. "That's right."

"Course, adult life back home…a real job, bills, car repairs.

But that's swell with me. I've had enough goddamned excitement to last me the rest of my life."

It finally comes to Jim. "I was part of Team SNAFU at Bastogne," he says. "Did you do bazooka train—"

"I never thought I'd enjoy this so much." The burly soldier waves his toothbrush around with his left hand. "Lost my toothbrush at the start of the Bulge. Wasn't until VE Day it seemed worth finding a new one." He starts to brush.

"I've got five Army fillings from basic," Jim says.

"We deserve everything they can give us. What train station you going to?"

"There's only one now, Anhalter, what's left of it," Jim says. "The only way I can keep my gear from getting promoted is to be there when the train arrives. Thieves will take everything not nailed down, sell it on the black market the next day."

"Morale Corps. Your gear is movies?"

"Theatre kits. Stage, lights, scripts, costumes, makeup. For soldier shows. I'm a 4-4-2, entertainment GI."

"The hell were you doing in Bastogne?"

"I got stuck in a place called Hosingen on the sixteenth. When the shelling started I—"

"Nah, don't tell me. Let's talk about going home."

"Okay."

"I'm going on the train to Antwerp. Sail home from there. Should be home in time for my daughter's birthday."

△

"Swell parking job," the burly sergeant says when he and Jim exit the building and find a Jeep halfway up the stone steps. "Surprised the tires are still on it."

"Save us a walk to the motor pool," Jim says. He raises the front hood. "Figures. Smitty and his buddies were too drunk to drive to the motor pool, too sober to leave the distributor cap."

The burly soldier takes a distributor cap from his field jacket pocket and hands it to Jim. "I don't need this anymore."

Jim drives. On the second block, they pass a grey-faced man on crutches wearing the remnants of a *Wehrmacht* uniform, rank signifiers removed. "I've seen enough one-legged men to last me the rest of my life," the burly sergeant says.

Berlin looks like an immense Roman ruin waiting to be bleached by the sun. They pass a line of women handing buckets from the street up into the pile of rubble that was a building. "Say what you will about the Germans, they don't like a mess," the burly sergeant says.

"Didn't care so much about the mess they made of London," Jim says.

"I doubt any of those women were on the bombsights."

"Come winter, the cold, those *frauleins* won't be able to live in those buildings, not even basements."

"Gonna be a hard winter for Germany," the burly sergeant says.

"Not hard enough." Jim pauses, then adds, "I was at Ohrdruf."

"The hell was an entertainment GI doing at a murder camp? No, don't tell me. I'm going home."

They stop at a crosswalk. A young woman is on the corner. "*Gehen sie vor*," Jim says to her. "Go ahead." She stays where she is and holds her hand out, two fingers extended. "The Berlin price for a woman," Jim continues. "Two packs, Luckies or Camels. Four if you're spending Fleetwoods. *Nein, danke, Fräulein*," he calls to her.

"They have to live," the burly sergeant says.

"The rations we give them are pretty meager," Jim says. "And Berlin is isolated. The people can't go into the countryside and trade their shoes for potatoes like they do in other cities." He starts the Jeep through the intersection. No other motor vehicles in sight.

"I was walking in the Tiergarten yesterday," the burly sergeant says.

"British sector," Jim says.

"Saw an old man feeding a duck."

"That's a luxury in Berlin," Jim says

"I turn away, hear *ponk-quack*! Sounds like a mortar shooting a duck. I look over, the old man is swinging his cane down on a duck with both hands. *Ponk quack! Ponk quack!* Then *ponk!* and one last long *quaaaak*."

Great impression, Jim thinks. *Too bad he's leaving*.

"The old man picks that dead duck up by the neck and slides it into a pillow case, tucks it under his arm like a football and walks away."

"That's something." They stop at another intersection. "Warm this morning. You see any camps?"

"I smell it too," the burly sergeant says. "Bodies under the rubble. We were at Buchenwald. It…" He pulls a letter out of the left breast pocket of his field jacket. "But that's over. I'm going home now." He starts to read the letter. They drive on in silence.

△

"Some poor German sonsabitches made a last stand here." the burly sergeant says as they approach the Anhalter station. The only outer wall left standing, the front façade, is pocked with bullet marks. They drive straight into the massive concourse, then towards an arriving train.

"That's the train," Jim says. "Track number three."

The burly sergeant looks at Jim and says, "I'm not worried about what I've seen. Or what I've done. What I've *become*, that has me worried."

"We saved the world from murderous tyrants."

"That we did. Yes. That's something. This is my stop, brother. Thanks for the ride."

Jimmy:

Here is my second letter today! I just got this clip from the Herald Advertiser about Willi Hoch. You can see our house behind him in the photo.

The reporter got the main facts right, Willi being born in Milwaukee, how his family went to Germany, that he was drafted into the Volksgrenadiers even though he was born in America, then captured at Bastogne by the famous son of Huntington, Jim Tanzer.

I'm proud of you, brother. Of course, this is the first Mutti and Poppa hear about you being at Bastogne! They still aren't over the killed in action telegram.

The reporter got some things wrong. Willi was at the POW camp in Ashford, not Kingswood. He worked on the Shepard Farm, not the Camp Dawson farm. The story says he and several other model prisoners were put on a night crew at the furniture factory to make coffins for the upcoming invasion of Japan. It was just Willi and one other prisoner. And Willi was sent to the factory because of his English, not because he was a carpenter before the war. That was the other prisoner. They don't get paid, by the way. Willi told me this is against the Geneva Convention, but not to make an issue out of it.

You already know that Mutti and Poppa are sponsoring Willi to stay in America while his citizenship gets re-established. But you will be surprised to read that Willi is now boarding with us in your old room! He has stories about you! He has to report to Sheriff Billingham on Monday and Thursday. Everybody likes Willi.

Write and tell us what you think!

Love,

Sis

∧

The train has come and gone. No theatre kit. It's quiet on the platform. Jim is sitting in his Jeep, working on *Spamlet*. A squad of children materializes out of the rubble and advances towards him. Jim pats the sticks of Wrigley's Spearmint gum in his shirt pocket and moves his rifle off the passenger seat and into his lap.

The children walk towards the side of the Jeep, ready to close with him or retreat. They are red-eyed and dirty, scratching their scalps and sniffling. The littlest has clean lines down his cheeks from a fresh cry. He can't be more than six. The leader—looks about twelve to Jim—begins wiping the Jeep windshield with a grey rag. Pure stage business, no discernable effect on the glass. He looks at Jim and says *"Zigarette? Chokolatt? Vrigly's?"*

The other children pull out rags and begin to pantomime polishing various parts of the Jeep. The leader points to the littlest one and says, "Vee are so hunger, *Amerikanischer Soldat*." The other children stop and rub their eyes with their fists. It would be comical if they weren't so skinny.

"*Wo sind deine Eltern?*" Jim says. Where are your parents?

They shake their heads. "*Hat uns zurückgelassen,*" the leader says.

"They left you behind?"

"*Nicht Nazis.*"

Jim hands a five-pack of Wrigley's to the leader, who puts it in his pants pocket. Jim points at the other four and says "*Zum Teilen.* For sharing."

"*Für Brot.* Bread," the boy says, and pantomimes putting something in his mouth. He tears one stick in four pieces, gives a piece to each urchin. He folds the foil wrapper carefully, puts it back inside its green and red paper sleeve, and gives it to the littlest child.

The littlest child is encouraged to speak. "My father is a brave soldier in the mighty German army," he says to Jim in German. "He will come for us, give us bread and chocolate and shoes, and take us to our school."

Jim's German has improved. "If your army was so mighty," he says in German to the child, "why did Germany lose the war?"

"The Americans had more machines and more Jews," the child replies. The leader points to Jim's shoulder flash and says, "*Bist du ein pilot? Danker? Cook?*"

"*Ich bin ein Unterhaltungs-GI.* Entertainment GI," Jim says.

"We can help for a show," the leader says. "A children's choir." On the "*kinderchor*" cue, the urchins gather closer and sing a ragged verse from "Lili Marlene."

"That's not the right song for children," Jim says. "What else you—"

"*Achtung, es ist die Barbaren!*" the boy cries out, pointing over Jim's shoulder. Jim turns, sees that six Russian soldiers in brown cavalry uniforms have appeared at the far end of the platform. One is female. Their Sharovary jodhpurs remind him of General Patton. The children break and run across the track. Except the leader. He judges the distance, reaches out a grubby hand and says, "*Fur die verk?*"

Jim pulls a K-ration can of Spam, a pack of Luckies, and two chocolate bars from his jacket pockets and hands them to the boy.

"Lucky Strike, *Rooseveltwurst, und Schokolade,*" the boy says, turning to run. "Fuh-kitler! *Gott* bless *Amerika.*" He is out of sight in ten seconds. The Russians have moved away laterally, they are just sightseeing.

"There's your good deed for the day," comes from close behind. Jim jumps, lifts his rifle. "Easy now, Mac. I ain't no werewolf." It's the crooked soldier from Fouquet's in Paris. In fatigues now, but there's no mistaking the face and the Chicago accent. "Don't I know you from somewhere?" he says as he glances at Jim's shoulder flash. "Morale Corps. Did we do business?"

"I might have seen you in Paris," Jim says.

"Been a few places since then. Bunch of us got court-marshalled over a misunderstanding about some cigarettes we were guarding. They commuted my sentence, made me a rifleman, 5th Division. Replacement. Almost got killed twice crossing the Rhine, once after that. Plus, I had to start over on discharge points. I'll be the last guy outta here for sure."

"How many points do you have?" Jim asks.

"Not near enough. And you can't buy any. You know, that German boy sells them goods you gave him, buys two weeks' worth of bread for his squad. If he don't get robbed."

"Doesn't the Control Council take care of war orphans?"

"If they can catch them. Those kids don't trust anyone. And the Army has plenty to provide for already—Germans who live here, plus all them dips."

"Dips?"

"DPs. Displaced Persons. Pouring in."

"You on duty at Anhalter?" Jim says.

"My duty is to look out for myself. Trains bring replacements. Green GIs wid dollars and cigarettes. They want souvenirs." He reaches into his pocket and pulls out a handful of iron crosses. "Trade wid dem before they know what things are worth. Here, have one."

"No thanks," Jim says. "Got one."

"You here picking up some PX cargo?"

"Theatre kit."

"What for?"

"*Hamlet*."

"Omelet?"

"*Hamlet*. Shakespeare."

The crooked soldier points to Jim's rank insignia. "Morale Corps is making T-5s out of college men?" Jim's a corporal now.

"I didn't finish—" Jim stops and straightens his tie. Two MPs wearing yellow armbands are approaching from directly behind the crooked soldier.

The crooked soldier turns around, turns back, steps on a tire and jumps in the back of the Jeep. "Yellow helmet band," he says. "8th Army cops. I'm wid you, remember." He smiles at the approaching MPs, says, "We don't want to get mixed up wid them guys," to Jim out of the side of his mouth.

"I'm not mixed up with anything," Jim says.

The crooked soldier reaches over the seat and picks up Jim's clipboard and points at a form. "Is that a 27-65?" He pulls a pencil out of his pocket, puts it behind his ear, and pretends to be reading the requisition form. Stage business. He puts down the clipboard and turns towards the two MPs as they walk up to the Jeep. He extends an unopened pack of Camels in his right hand. "How 'bout a smoke, men?"

One of the MPs looks about seventeen, defers to his older partner, the tough cookie. The older man waves away the proffered cigarettes and says to Jim, "We don't salute non-coms in this Army, corporal. Show us papers for this Jeep."

"These are for *my* Jeep," Jim says, handing over the form. "It's at the motor pool. I found this one parked on the stairs of my billet, thought I'd secure it, pick up supplies and then turn it in." The crooked GI nods in agreement. "I'm Morale Corps," Jim says. "Entertainment soldier."

"Turn it in this morning, corporal." The MP takes Jim's name, unit and service number, then turns to the crooked soldier. "You're not Morale. What are you doing in a stolen jeep?"

"I was on my way to the *Friedrichstrasse* mess this morning." The crooked GI points to Jim. "This T-5 pulls up and orders me to help him at the train station." Jim looks down at his feet.

The MP glances at Jim, then holds up a hand. "That's enough

of your malarkey. Seen you hanging around here, cheating soldiers. Show me your tags." He writes down the information, then looks at Jim. "Don't let this chiseler drag you into something you don't want to be caught up in, so near to going home." The MP turns back to the crooked soldier. "I don't want to see your face within a mile of this station again."

"Roger that, Sergeant."

The two MPs walk back the way they came. "Sergeant Chickenshit, I mean," the crooked soldier says in a low voice, watching them. "Thinks we're always on Army time."

"Need you to get out." Jim starts the Jeep. "I've got to get this back to the motor pool."

"Lemme ask you something," the crooked soldier says. "What are you gonna do after you get home, after you take care of your wife, you know what I mean?"

"I gotta get going."

"Sure. But what do you wanna do after the war?"

Jim will give him an answer then pull him out of the Jeep if necessary. "I may go to Hollywood. I may go home and start a booking agency. I got a daughter to think about."

"Either way, Corporal Morale, you're gonna need a stake. Call me Rumpelstiltskin, because in return for giving me a ride back to the motor pool, I'm gonna tell you how to spin wristwatches and occupation marks into gold you can send home."

"I don't want—"

The crooked GI holds up a hand in the universal *stop* position. "Never mind about Lugers. The best souvenir you can bring back from this war is money—enough money so's you don't have to follow orders in civilian life, so's you can buy a new suit, a refrigerator, a new car. Take care of your family. Go to Hollywood. Start your business."

"How?"

"Simple. You buy wristwatches at the PX, sell them to the Reds. They shell out heavy dough for watches."

"Why?"

"Ivan gets paid in occupation marks. They're worthless back in Russia. And Ivan can't convert them to rubles or dollars. But a wristwatch, back home he can trade a wristwatch for a cow."

"What am I going to do with occupation marks?"

"Convert them to dollars. American soldiers are allowed. Then you buy money orders to send home. You trust your wife, right?"

"Sounds too good to be true."

"Not just true, it's legal. For now, anyways."

"Huh." Jim wonders what Stella would think if he had some heavy dough when he got home. If not her, would Kitty Carlson go for him? *Nah*.

"Another thing. Ask Ivan if he has a broken one. Summa dem hayseeds don't even know to wind a watch. Here." The crooked GI pulls up the sleeve of his field jacket to reveal two watches on his wrist. "This is an aviator's chronometer, typical German craftmanship, complicated. Cost you $500 in the States." He points to a Timex Mickey Mouse watch. "Russians will give you twice as much for this one."

"Really?"

"You can start today. Give me your Timex and twenty bucks for Mickey."

"Okay. But if you're conning me, I'll—"

"'*Nah-rooch-nee-ah chah-sy*' means 'wristwatch' in Russian. *Nah-rooch-nee-ah chah-sy*. Or just hold up your wrist. If they offer you a drink, raise the bottle and put your lips to it, but don't drink anything. Could be vodka, could be aftershave. But you need to make the gesture."

"*Nah-rooch-nee-ah chah-sy*," Jim repeats. "*Nah-rooch-nee-ah chah-sy*."

JIM LEAVES THE Jeep and the crooked GI at the motor pool. He walks down Kohlestrasse. The first block is entirely ruins, sidewalks covered in rubble. Jim recognizes Russian words coming from behind the wall of a wrecked building. Glancing at the watch on his wrist, Jim walks up the slope of loose bricks until he sees six Russian soldiers standing in a circle. The one closest to Jim drops down to a cross-legged sitting position, falls backwards and begins to piss himself.

Through the opening in the circle, Jim sees—*hell's this?*—two legs, pale against the rubble, grey socks and worn-out Mary Janes on the feet. He sees the dark pubic mound, the breasts. The woman's dress and shift are pulled over her head, covering her face and pinning her arms.

A red-faced soldier is on his knees in front of the prone woman, unbuttoning his tan uniform trousers. He stops to take a swig from a bottle in his right hand and sprays the liquid on the woman's thighs, yells "*Natzist!*" She lies still, but for the rising and falling of her chest.

Jim looks up, sees a standing soldier pointing a German machine pistol at the woman's belly. Jim is back in the kill zone. Controlling a rush of fear and adrenaline, he puts his hands in the air and pivots towards some cover he noticed on the way up, a square pile of bricks. A place where he can unsling his rifle.

"*Amerikanskiy soldat!*" Jim stops and turns back. The machine pistol soldier is pointing the weapon at Jim with one hand, beckoning with the other. The pistol moves back and forth as the man sways in place.

Jim raises his hands in the air. *Christ!* he thinks. *Survived the Bulge so I can be killed in Berlin by a drunk Russian. This is going to be hard on my family.*

The soldier smiles, says, "*Nah-rooch-nee-ah chah-sy!*" and points at Jim's right arm.

"Wha'?" Jim says. Then it hits him. He points to his right wrist and calls out, "Mickey Mouse!" The other soldiers straighten up, then move towards him, accompanied by a wave of body odor and alcohol fumes. The one who was kneeling holds his pants up as he walks.

Jim lowers his arms, pulls up his right sleeve, and rolls his right forearm back and forth. He's really selling it. "Mickey Mouse," he repeats. The Russians follow him as he turns and steps slowly down towards the street.

As the wristwatch is handed around, Jim can see the woman behind them pull her dress down and scramble to her feet. One Russian turns towards her, then turns back and pulls a wad of occupation marks out of the hip pocket of his soldier's blouse. The woman retreats out of sight.

Jim comes away with six thousand Russian occupation marks and a Hamilton Tonneaus, crocodile band, that needs winding.

▲

"Tanzer, sir. Orders to report to you," Jim says, saluting.

"Corporal Tanzer, at ease," the captain says, putting down some papers he was reading. "You know about the DP camp in Zehlendorf?"

"I've heard the name, sir."

"Murder camp survivors. Mostly Jews. Men, women, some children. Displaced persons. They don't want to go home."

"I've heard about that, sir."

"These camps are all over Germany. Zehlendorf is just one. It's out of control. The DPs spent the first month of liberation eating and fucking, anyone would. They have no work while the Relief and Rehabilitation people sort out where they'll go. Palestine, Canada, America. They refuse to go back to Poland or Lithuania or wherever the hell the Nazis combed them out of."

"The Nazis are gone." Jim says.

"The local devils are still there, and now the Russians. All displaced persons here are under our protection, housed and fed on our cuff. They pretty much do as they please. Some of the DPs steal, work the black market. Some are violent, go out to rampage, come back to the camp at night to eat and sleep. The Germans are scared stiff of them." The captain walks around his desk, leans against it and crosses his legs.

"Yes, sir."

"Think of Zehlendorf as a hotel for traumatized human beings. Everything was taken from these people: family, friends, freedom, dignity, health. Their property, professions and trades. No telling what they had to do to stay alive."

"I was at Ohrdruf."

"Jesus. And there are more career criminals among the DPs than you'd expect."

"Why is that, sir?"

"Criminals have more experience with all-versus-all. That's Europe since 1939. Zehlendorf needs to put on a show. You're Morale and your card says you speak German."

"Sir, I—"

"And that's similar to Yiddish."

"Yiddish is—"

"Put 'em to work. WPA for survivors. Zehlendorf has teachers and cantors and tradesmen. There are actors, writers to adapt your script to Yiddish, musicians. Tailors to sew costumes, beauticians to do hair and makeup, carpenters and painters to make sets. Do *not* be efficient. Keep the most DPs you can as busy as you can for as long as you can. Change your mind several times."

"Yes, sir."

"We put up casting call signs at the camp three days ago." The captain begins to walk back to his desk chair, then turns around. "George Stevens—you know, the director?"

"I met him at Ohrdruf."

"I saw *Murder Mills*. Awful. A lot of sympathy back home

for the DPs. Colonel Stevens was going to make a movie at Zehlendorf. You know, smiling people doing calisthenics, gardening, children in school, women cooking. And putting on a musical. Some kind of Hebrew *Cheaper by the Dozen* set in an ex-*Wehrmacht* bootcamp."

"Yes, sir."

"Ike ordered Stevens to Potsdam to film Truman slapping Churchill and Stalin on the back. Casting call for that musical at Zehlendorf is tonight."

"What show am I doing?" Jim is hoping for *Brother Rat*, which he produced with 8th Army soldiers in June.

"Here." The captain hands Jim a script off his desk.

"*Die Dreigroschenoper? Threepenny Opera?*"

"It's the only German musical we have that's not by a Nazi. Bert Brecht. Screenwriter now, United Artists. You see the movie *Hangmen Also Die?*"

"Heard about it, sir."

"Brecht wrote it. The other one I have…" The captain picks up another script from his desk, "*Soldier's Hamlet*. I object to the Army crapping up Shakespeare."

"Yes, sir."

"Use DPs to translate to Yiddish and copy the script out by hand. Pay them if you have to. There's plenty of Kraut stationary at the Camp. Use the side without the swastikas."

"I guess they won't have to translate the score."

"Funny. Your troupe will do at least three performances at the camp, maybe tour the other DP camps after, we'll see how it looks. Private Kunkle?" An orderly steps up with an envelope and a receipt. "Sign it," the captain says, handing Jim a pen. "This is five hundred marks to buy what you need. Keep a record."

"I will, sir."

"Dismissed, Corporal Tanzer," the captain says, and drops *Soldier's Hamlet* in the trash can.

"Ordered to request a ride with your party to Zehlendorf, Colonel Marcus," Jim says to the colonel in the back of the Jeep. There's a lieutenant in the front seat, next to the driver.

"Expecting you, Corporal," the colonel says. "Do you plan to salute Lieutenant Bauer?"

"Yes, sir," Jim says, and snaps off a perfect highball to the lieutenant, who's getting up.

"Keep your seat, Lieutenant," the colonel says. "The corporal can sit back here with me."

Jim eyes the front of the shiny Jeep. "They aren't welding wire catchers on the new ones," the colonel says. "I doubt wires are stretched neck-high along the road anymore, but you'll have to take your chances, Corporal, same as me. But it's hard to find a Nazi in Germany now, let alone a Nazi partisan."

"Suggest we tie our shoes, sir," Jim says, "when we drive by trees close to both sides of the road."

The colonel laughs, then says, "You know how to keep your head down. You must have done shows near the front line."

"Many, sir."

"Private Canfield here," the colonel says, gesturing towards the driver, "graduated high school in May, got to Germany yesterday. Doesn't have memories." Private Canfield pulls the Jeep onto the road.

"I was told you're Morale Corps, Corporal Tanzer," the colonel says.

"Yes sir. 4-4-2. Entertainment soldier."

"That's an important job. Where you from, corporal?"

"West Virginia. Huntington. You, sir?" Jim can already tell Colonel Marcus is from lower Manhattan. He sounds like Sam Gold.

"I'm from New York."

"My wife and I lived on Delancey Street before the war."

"You married a *yidishe meydl?*" the colonel asks.

"She's a *goyishe froy.*"

"*Du veyst etlekhe yidish?*" He leans forward towards the lieutenant in the front seat. "I asked the corporal if he learned Yiddish on Delancey Street."

"A little. And from the Catskills."

"Small world. I worked a summer at Grossinger's, waiter, before I left City College for West Point. Will you go back to the Catskills when you get home? Or college on the GI bill?"

"I'm married. I have a daughter, Colonel. I'm probably going to apply for a GI loan to start a business. Booking, production. Maybe in Hollywood."

"How many points do you have?"

"Forty-eight. Morale Corps doesn't get any discharge points for combat. And I never got my Purple Heart." Jim points to the scar on his forehead. "So far. I'm gonna write my congressman."

"You won't be home until 1946, unless you get seriously hurt. All the action's in the Pacific now."

"I'll probably go there," Jim says. *Hope not*, he thinks.

They drive on in silence. They pass a burned-out panzer on the road. "Through and through," Jim says. "Had to be an M-79 A-P round." Colonel Marcus looks Jim up and down.

They slow to pass a group of women pushing a wooden cart piled with household items and an old man. One of hundreds the Jeep passes that are moving towards Berlin like ants towards a colony.

"The nonfraternization policy is ridiculous," Colonel Marcus says. "GIs don't want to be someone's tool for vengeance on pretty girls. No matter their sins."

"I'm married, sir," Jim says.

They pull up to the Zehlendorf gate.

Zayn oder nit zayn, dos iz di froog:
Vos iz nobler in der ziel tsu farbn
Di shlechts un shpots fun di
glitshen fun der groyser glik,
Oyder oyfshprengen mit a horde krigsgezelshaft
Un zi tsu ashlepn?

THAT YIDDISH HAS *a familiar cadence,* Jim thinks.

"Prince Hamlet's famous soliloquy," the old man standing in front of him says in English. "I vas with the Vilna Troupe in 1912. I played the Prince in the Moscow premier of *Hamlit*, the Yiddish version of the Prince of Denmark's tragedy. Vee toured Europe and zen America until the great var broke out. Now age has me for Polonius more suited."

"What is your name, sir?" Jim says.

"My name is Aryeh Potok. I'm happy to say it a thousand time a day. The Germans thought they took it from me when they gave me this." He pulls up his sleeve to show his tattoo. "A man is not a number."

"You will be in the chorus, Mr. Potok," Jim says. "We'll do a first read-through in this room tomorrow at oh ten hundred hours. Ten in the morning."

Next is a dwarf juggling colored balls and K-ration cans. "I'll bring you out in front of the curtain before the overture," Jim says through Potok's translation. "While the audience is finding their seats."

The dwarf says to Potok in Polish, "Before the war, I performed in *Pagliacci* at Grand Theatre in Warsaw. Now I'm a dumb act. It's come to this."

"He says he'll get things off to a good start," Potok says to Jim, who understands what was meant.

The next displaced person is a young male violinist. He lived and fought in the Naliboki Forest from 1942 to 1944. He's going to Palestine. Jim puts him in the orchestra.

"She vorked music halls in Lodz," Potok says, gesturing to a handsome middle-aged woman sitting across from Jim. The woman puts her palms on Jim's thighs and executes a handstand, placing her muscular buttocks four inches in front of his face. She dismounts, leaves a hand on Jim's knee, asks if Jim can sponsor her to go to America. He casts her as Polly Peacham.

The rest speak in English, German, or are translated by Potok. One says, "I was a professor of Medieval German literature at Leipzig until I was fired after the BBG."

"The what?"

"The *Berufsbeamtengesetz*, the law removing Jews in Germany from the Civil Service. Including teaching." He'll paint scenery.

"I was a student," says another. "Separated from my brother at Majdanek. Can you help me find him?" The ex-student will play Filch.

"I am a tailor. My wife died at Ravensbrück. Cholera." Costumes.

"I was a lawyer. My wife and daughter disappeared at Treblinka. I was sent to Stutthof. I have posted their names with the Tracing Bureau. Could you help me with the American authorities?" Tiger Brown.

"I'm a cantor. We say a Kaddish each morning for Patton's boys who died to liberate us. Work didn't make us free. It was the American Third Army." Cast as the Ballad Singer.

"Thank you. Next."

Berlin, Germany
August 20, 1945
DA Form 458

CHARGE SHEET			
NAME OF ACCUSED: James D. Tanzer	SERIAL NUMBER/ RANK: 15179485 Corporal	DATE: August 20, 1945	UNIT/LOCATION: 6817 Morale Corps Battalion Berlin, Germany
CHARGE: Violation of the 95th Article of War: Larceny and Wrongful ~~Approbation~~ Appropriation		RESTRAINT OF ACCUSED/DATE(S) IMPOSED: Mannheim Confinement Facility, August 11, 1945.	

SPECIFICATION:

In that Corporal Tanzer, did, on or about July 25, 1945, at Berlin, Germany, willfully without proper authorization, wrongfully remove military stores, to wit, a U.S. Army Jeep, serial number 20227236 property of the United States Army, valued at $1,070.

SUMMARY OF OFFENSE:

The aforementioned Jeep was reported missing from the motor pool on the morning of July 25, 1945. That same day, Pvt. James B. Tanzer was noted by MP Sgt. Alek L. Janovec, at ~~Barnhole~~ Bahnhof Station to be in possession of the vehicle without proper authorization or orders. He was ordered to turn it in ~~immedaitly Immediatley~~ right away. The aforementioned Jeep was never returned to the motor pool. At the time of his arrest, Corporal Tanzer was found to be in possession of 3,000 marks.

WITNESSES:

Sgt. Alek L. Janovec

Cpl. Charles R. Noyes

Pvt. Anthony Esposito

REFERRED FOR TRIAL TO THE General COURT MARTIAL CONVENED AT Berlin, Germany

20.

NEW YORK, NEW YORK, MARCH 8, 1946

To All Debarkees:

Welcome home and welcome to Camp Kilmer! The Post Commander and his staff assure you that everything will be done for your comfort and pleasure during your short stay here for processing and separation, your final stop on the journey back to civilian life.

You've been through a lot—why spoil it by looking and acting like anything but what you are—a good soldier. Don't be a "Sad Sack." Off post and on departure you are required to wear a tie.

Now that you're back, you'll have to stop and think about your manners, stop and think about military courtesy. You get a swell feeling when you toss a snappy "highball" to an officer and he tosses one right back at you.

Sure, we want to take souvenirs home to the family and kids. But play it safe; have your souvenirs and trophies inspected at time of processing. If possible, we'll remove the charge and return the shells to you. Do not throw ammunition into the rubbish. Several serious accidents have occurred at the post incinerator because of this.

CAMP KILMER POST

"Welcome to the 20th Century Limited," a red-headed soldier says, after Jim puts his barracks bag up on the luggage rack and sits down next to him. The soldier offers his left hand for a shake. "You still in the Army?"

"I got separated at Camp Kilmer," Jim says. "I'll buy some civvies when I get where I'm going, burn these duds."

"I'm Pat Quigley."

"Jim Tanzer."

The soldier eyes Jim's shoulder flash. "Quartermaster Corps?"

"Morale Corps. 4-4-2. Entertainment soldier. Was. I did Jeep shows, produced soldier shows."

"Guess you don't have too many awful memories."

Jim touches the can of peaches in his uniform pocket. "I was at the Bulge."

Quigley sits up. "Combatman *and* entertainment soldier. Now that's something. I see you weren't killed." He smiles. "You must not have gotten a bad wound, you just now getting home."

"Morale Corps aren't allowed to get wounded. Or get discharge points for combat."

"Army chickenshit, Jim. Sorry to hear it."

"Thanks, Pat."

Quigley pulls out a photograph. "Speaking of morale, getting home to my wife is gonna solve my morale problem." He points to the infant in the photo. "Gonna meet my son. That little prince is worth twelve discharge points."

"Sure," Jim says, looking down at his feet. Betty Jo earned him the same twelve points, but he wasn't on his way to see her, not just yet.

"You stopping in Chicago, Jim?"

"Long enough to catch the Super Chief. Headed for Los Angeles."

"Don't sound like you're from there."

"No. Going to Hollywood. Mickey Rooney's going to get me a screen test. I did shows with him in the ETO."

General Bradley's luncheon for General Koniev was the last time Jim performed with Mickey and Wes. After the *Threepenny Opera* tour and a week in the Mannheim stockade, Jim produced soldier shows at various installations in occupied Germany. Wes fractured his leg in a traffic accident in Paris and was sent back to the States. Mickey finished his last year in the Army doing big shows, including the *OK-USA* revue, and hosting his own program on Armed Forces Radio network.

Quigley glances at Jim's ears. "Screen test, huh?".

"And I wrote a play that Mickey thinks we'll get turned into a screenplay. It's an exposé of the Army called *Spamlet*."

"I was going to write an exposé of the Army myself."

"I'll join the 52-20 club," Jim says, "until I catch on out there."

"$20 a week unemployment for a year for veterans, not bad. I just read a column." Quigley holds up a newspaper. "Guy says we'll be right back in the Depression by Christmas, prices so high, all these soldiers back looking for work. I'm gonna wait that out in college, thank you GI Bill. But I'll take the twenty a week until I get registered, so my wife can quit her job."

"Mickey's gonna set me up," Jim says. *I think*, he doesn't say. He's starting to wonder about heading to California without a firm plan.

"What's Mickey Rooney gonna do, now that he's back in Hollywood?" the soldier asks.

"Another Andy Hardy movie." Jim keeps tabs on Mickey in *Variety*.

"You think he's too old to play a teenager?" the soldier asks.

"Sure. But Hedda Hopper says that the elevator shoes don't exist that will make him a leading man," Jim says. "Hey! But he started his own production company before the war. He'll give himself any part he wants."

Mickey returned to Hollywood two days ago, and was learning how far in debt he was due to financial improprieties at his production company and racing stables.

"I saw him in Rochefort," Quigley says. "Second day with my unit."

They only ever remember Mickey, Jim thinks. "First Infantry Division," he says, pointing to Quigley's shoulder flash.

"Was. I'm separated too. My parents want to see me in uniform one last time."

"You volunteer?"

"Drafted. Ended up in Second Engineer's Battalion, Second Division. Arrived in Belgium in December, just in time for the Bulge. We were at the northern shoulder. It was some show. You know."

"I was in Luxembourg when it started. Ended up in Bastogne."

"Folks at home won't understand what it was like. Can't. This is the last time I'm going to talk about it."

"You said it. How'd you end up in 1st Division?"

"I got hit at Pilsen." Quigly stops and draws a breath. "On May 5th. Can you believe it?"

"The day before the Germans quit? That's shit luck," Jim says. "Czech and double Czech."

Quigley laughs. "No wonder they made you an entertainment soldier. By the time I got out of the hospital, Second Division was back in the States, training for the invasion of Japan. Lucky wound, I thought. Then I got shipped out to First Division, Sixteenth Engineers. We were digging up mines and repairing bridges. They figured I could do *that* with nine fingers."

"Sure."

"They were right. I made it to sixty-five points last month and here I am. How come it took you so long to get back?"

"Twenty-four months service, eighteen overseas. And I have a daughter. Like I said, no wound or combat points for Morale Corps soldiers."

"Goddamned Army."

"I'll say. You know what's worse? The Army decided I was KIA. Buried me in Luxembourg. My family thought I was dead.

I called home two days before my memorial service. You can imagine what that whole thing did to my parents."

"And your wife. She thought she was a widow."

"My wife, sure." Jim has heard plenty from Norma *about* Stella but nothing *from* Stella since New York. He decides not to go into that.

"What the hell happened?" Quigley asks.

"Day one of the Bulge, I was in Hosingen, the first company strongpoint to be attacked." Jim has great economy with these words, having told this story several hundred times. "We were surrounded by noon. XO ordered me to give my tags to Levy, a Jewish soldier. Nice kid. From Newark. A cantor. Fine singing voice. Captain Quinn thought the SS would murder Levy if he was taken prisoner. He ordered Levy and me to run a captured map to regiment. I think it was mostly to get Levy to the rear. But Levy was called back. I went by myself."

"How did you get killed?"

"I heard Levy got hit in Hosingen on the third day. Body covered by snow, not recovered until spring thaw. He had a bazooka by him, and a wrecked German tank fifty yards away. Brave man. Anyways, my tags were still on him. The Army thought Levy was me. I didn't get paid for a month."

"That's fucking something," Quigley says. "Shit, I'm gonna have to watch my language now I'm going home."

"We all are. The hold-outs at Hosingen got killed or captured by the Germans. The whole company was reported MIA, including Levy. His family thought he was a prisoner of war, didn't find out he was dead until April."

"Man, that's hard."

"I got a Silver Star, posthumous. Had to give it back."

"Silver Star doesn't do much for his family."

"No. My insurance check arrived the day after my family, my wife, found out I was alive. The Army came and took it back.

Don't know but she might've preferred me staying KIA, get the money. Our marriage hit the skids when I went overseas."

"Doubt any woman wants her daughter to lose a father. And there's alimony if you divorce. There's child support."

"I guess." Jim has not considered alimony or child support.

"And I thought *I* had a war story to tell my grandchildren." The train lurches forward as cars are added to the back.

"Oh, there's more," Jim gives a grim laugh. "I got court-martialed in Berlin last summer."

"For what?"

"A crooked GI stole a Jeep, pinned it on me. MPs beat on my door at five in the morning, arrested me. Took all my money for evidence."

"Miserable pricks, those fucking snowdrops," Quigley says. "Shit, there I go again."

"I spent a week in lock-up at Mannheim. Charged with larceny and wrongful appropriation."

"Holy moley," the soldier says. "But you beat it?"

"My lawyer found the motor pool guy I turned the Jeep in to. This crooked GI, he was with me that day, stole a requisition form, checked another Jeep out in my name. I was cleared but my occupation marks never got returned to me."

"That right there's a story Hollywood will like. So, your wife and little girl there already?"

"Not yet. After I get established, I'm going to find work there for my wife." He hasn't mentioned this idea to anyone. "She's a singer."

"It might be hard for you. The veterans from Hollywood will be back looking for their old jobs. And there's no more war work."

"Don't know," Jim says. *Dammit*, he thinks.

"I guess some of those fellas are dead now," Quigley says. "Or too hurt to work. Sure, they'll need new men."

The two soldiers go quiet. Quigley pulls out a magazine.

Jim thinks about Stella and Betty Jo, the rest of his family. And Willi Hoch there in Huntington, also. And he's heading to California? The train lurches forward a few feet, and a conductor cries, "Twentieth Century. All aboard!"

"You okay?" Quigley says. Jim has jumped up and is pulling his barracks bag off the overhead rack.

"Gotta get off this train, go home first. See my little girl," Jim says as he shoulders his bag. *See can I keep a wife*, he does not say. "Good luck, Pat." Jim is already moving down the aisle.

"Have a good life, Jim!" Quigley shouts. "You're a crazy bastard," he says after Jim has made it to the platform. "But you're entertaining as hell." He stretches out onto the empty seat and closes his eyes.

OF INTEREST TO READERS OF *JEEP SHOW*

THOUGHTS AT THE End of the War is a previously unpublished column written by The Reporter, Bunny Levin, in February of 1946. He mentions Jim Tanzer, although not by name. To read it, go to *www.JeepShowBook.com/warco* or use this QR code

You will be asked to sign up for special offers (please do; no newsletter, no chickenshit!), but that is not required to read the essay or the other bonus content on the website. You can also comment there on *Jeep Show*, or ask me questions.

Thank you.

Robert B. O'Connor

ACKNOWLEDGMENTS

I AM GRATEFUL to my beloved wife, Doralina, for her unflagging support as I researched and wrote *Jeep Show*. Thanks also to my editors, Susan Leon and Jason Pettus. Peter Salisbury, Lanny Oakes, Jack O'Connor, and Richard Killblane, retired Department of Army Historian, read drafts and gave valuable advice.

Most of all, I want to thank the men and women who served our country in World War II, and all our veterans. We owe you more than my words can express.